Praise for Mrs. R

"What's more delicious than a nov⸠ ⸗, ⸠wists and turns that you don't know who's telling the truth until it's over—and even then you're not so sure? Lindsay Marcott's *Mrs. Rochester's Ghost* is just that book. A contemporary Gothic novel haunted by the ghosts of du Maurier and Henry James that is impossible to put down. Go for it."
—B. A. Shapiro, *New York Times* bestselling author of
The Collector's Apprentice

"Gothic and elegant, *Mrs. Rochester's Ghost* captivated me from the first page and kept me reading all night. Lindsay Marcott has created a seductive Big Sur landscape; peopled it with brilliant, complicated characters; and set in motion a thriller both terrifying and emotionally satisfying. I loved it."
—Luanne Rice, *New York Times* bestselling author of *Last Day*

"Smart, thrilling, and completely unexpected, Lindsay Marcott delivers the goods in the brilliant *Mrs. Rochester's Ghost*. Highly recommended for readers who like incandescent prose and deep deceptions."
—Gregg Olsen, #1 *Wall Street Journal* bestselling author of *If You Tell*

MRS.
ROCHESTER'S
GHOST

ALSO BY LINDSAY MARCOTT

The Producer's Daughter

MRS. ROCHESTER'S GHOST

A THRILLER

LINDSAY MARCOTT

THOMAS & MERCER

Published by Thomas & Mercer, Seattle

www.apub.com

Amazon, the Amazon logo, and Thomas & Mercer are trademarks of Amazon.com, Inc., or its affiliates.

ISBN-13: 9781542026383 (hardcover)
ISBN-10: 1542026385 (hardcover)

ISBN-13: 9781542026390 (paperback)
ISBN-10: 1542026393 (paperback)

Cover design by Laywan Kwan

Printed in the United States of America

First edition

To Peter Dorsett Graves,
whose imagination is boundless.

I have been faithful to thee, Cynara! in my fashion.
—Ernest Dowson, *Non Sum Qualis Eram Bonae*

ONE

In my mind, I can picture it clearly.

Thorn Bluffs. December 17. Their fourth wedding anniversary.

He's dressing for dinner, charcoal serge pants, a linen shirt the color of mist rise. Black sport coat, brushed and steamed by Annunciata an hour ago, hung within arm's reach on a padded hanger. Black silk socks laid out. Polished black loafers.

Should he wear a tie? Hasn't in years, except for the occasional mandatory event. A board meeting. The obligatory charity gala. His wedding, of course, somber butterfly clutching his throat. But tonight, no taking chances. An open collar might be something that could set her off.

He selects a tie. Silver-gray silk.

The reservation is for 5:30 p.m. at Sierra Mar. Unfashionably early, but she's at her most docile in the early evening after her second clozapine, and anyway, he couldn't give a damn about fashion. Everything arranged in advance. Corner table on the glassed-in terrace jutting out over the Pacific. The menu: pear and allium to start, black cod with caviar beurre blanc, chocolate ganache. No wine, of course. Cocktails made of lavender and lemonade.

She won't need to make choices. Nothing to decide.

And maybe they'll get through the dinner without incident.

He shrugs on the sport coat. Fastens his father's weighty chrome Breitling on his wrist. As he moves out of the dressing room, he hears the two German shepherds barking outside. They're agitated. They sense a threat.

An intruder?

He checks the property-cam monitor: the gates to the private road are securely shut. By boat from the cove? The violence of that lashing sea. No small craft could navigate it.

He steps out onto the terrace with its sweeping vista of ocean and bluffs. The storms of the last few days have subsided, and the sunset has illuminated the sky, the last clouds gold, pink, azure blue, but the sea is still turbulent, surging high against the bluffs. There's no boat in the cove or beyond it in open sea.

He shifts his gaze down to the beach.

Gives a start.

She's standing at the breaking point of the roiling waves. The tendrils of her long pale hair are streaming in the wind, and the handkerchief hem of her ice-blue dress flaps and flutters against her legs. She looks like an exotic sea anemone displaced from some placid tropical ocean.

She turns and looks up at the house. Does she see him?

He shouts her name, but the wind blows his voice back.

She turns back to the sea. Takes a step into the frothing surf. The water foams above her ankles, drenching the hem of the dress, weighing down the silky fabric.

And now he's running. Through the bedroom, down the floating staircase to the front hall. Bursts outside and keeps running. To the edge of the promontory, the gate in the stake fencing, the rickety flight of wooden stairs that scales the cliff. He takes the steps two, three at a time, collecting splinters in his bare feet, accompanied by an honor guard of the two bounding German shepherds.

As he steps onto the crescent of sand, he stumbles on a shoe. A silver high-heeled sandal, almost freakishly long and narrow: she has them handmade in Milan.

But he can't see her at all, not on the beach or in the water.

He screams her name again, then plunges blindly between rocks large and small into the swells. The currents are brutal: he's punched under by a powerful surge. His shirt and trousers drag him farther down. His arms scrape against stones; the icy force of the clashing waves overpowers him. The Breitling strap catches on a snag. Freeing it gives him forward momentum, enough to catch a towering swell and ride it back to flat rocks and, with his last strength, crawl back to sand.

He lies gasping. Snorting water up from his lungs. His eyes sting with salt and silt. The dogs nose and lap at him with concern.

And now Hector's face looms above him, impassive as always. He lets Hector help him to his feet.

He wipes his face with his hands. Looks for the silver sandal. Finds it, recruits the dogs to comb the sliver of beach for its mate. But it's been lost to the sea.

And so has she. She's gone. He's certain of it.

He can do nothing for her anymore.

Nothing except notify the police.

This, at least, is the way I imagine it happening.

But then again, I've always had a vivid imagination.

TWO

I should have seen it coming. *Carlotta*'s demise, I mean.

I should have had my eyes wide open long before it happened. Our ratings had been in free fall for the past two seasons. Our sponsors were evaporating like steam from cooling tea.

But *Carlotta Dark*, the small cable network show I wrote for, was no run-with-the-pack series. Edgy and erotic, with notes of black comedy. Addictively Gothic. It was set in the gloom of the nineteenth-century Adirondacks: We had vengeful ghosts luring newlyweds to gruesome suicides, vampires guzzling blood from cut crystal like so many dirty martinis. Young Carmelites who'd strip off their habits at the wink of a strapping gravedigger's eye.

How could it possibly be over?

I'd been with the show since it had begun six years before, starting as a lowly intern, then fighting my way up to writing staff. I was good at my job, and I loved it. Which might've seemed strange, since I don't look very Goth. My flyaway hair is light brown. My eyes a lucid shade of gray that tend to blab everything I'm feeling. And I rarely wear black. I think it washes me out.

But I'd always been attracted to the macabre. When I was little, I imagined a rather kindly skeleton named Mrs. Teeny Bones who lived under my bed and rattled her teeny bones whenever it thundered.

At Halloween, no princess tiaras for me. "I want to be a mummy," I insisted. And Mom, her theatrical heart tickled, gamely complied, bandaging me from neck to forehead with gauze she'd steeped in cold tea to make it look authentically rotten.

Maybe this penchant of mine came about because when I was three years old, my father blinked out of existence. I had no concept of death at that age, of course. All I knew was that one day I had a daddy with a lap to wriggle myself up onto and a mop of wiry copper hair to tug. And then I didn't.

Where's Daddy?

He had an accident, sweetheart.

But where did he go?

Go to sleep, sweetie. I'll leave on the night-light.

My father vanished. And after that, Mom died, too, in a way. She never remarried. Sent every suitor quickly packing and poured all her considerable passion into acting in community theater. Swapping real-life romance for the make-believe of the stage.

And so, yeah, I liked it when the dead didn't stay dead. When they came back, even as rattling bones or monsters in rotted rags or vampires slurping gore.

And, yeah, a show like *Carlotta Dark* was right up my alley.

And then that, too, blinked out of existence.

A blustery morning in October. The head writer, Wade O'Conner, called me into his office. Wade was both my boss and confidant—a handsome guy with the beginnings of a wattle from a habit of tugging the skin under his chin when he was worried. He was tugging on it like mad now.

"Bad news, Janie. You'd better sit down."

I felt my face pale. I couldn't take any more bad news. Not with the sick-sweet smell of Mom's memorial flowers still fresh in my nostrils. "What's happened?"

"We've been canceled. The end of next month."

"Canceled?" The word seemed meaningless. Nonsensical.

"Yep. They're replacing us with a wellness show. Six-minute cardio, berries that cure cancer. That kind of thing. Sorry to be the one to give you the news."

I stared at the photos of our show's stars above Wade's head. Perfect teeth. Profuse hair. It lent them a vague family resemblance. And we were like a family, weren't we? Cast and crew, one close-knit, never-to-be-parted family.

Lies!

I wanted to rip the grinning faces off the wall and smash them on Wade's desk, and I wanted to scream and kick and rage. But I didn't.

Instead I fell back on Mom's expression for all calamity, whether terminal illness or a misplaced recipe for caraway cookies.

"Shit, shit, shit," I said.

That was in October, and now it was the end of May, and I was perched cross-legged in the window seat of my Cobble Hill apartment, polishing off a bottle of Sancerre—opened God knew when because it was halfway to vinegar—my MacBook balanced precariously on my knees. I'd earmarked the afternoon for bills—a grim accumulation of them. It had been a wet, cold spring, one dreary day after another, and the dismal rain spattering the window drummed a suitable accompaniment.

I'd been out of work nearly eight months. I'd pulled every string, knocked on every door. But there'd been a wave of canceled series in the past year. A deluge of writers from bigger shows pounding on the same doors. "Just hang on till the fall," my agent told me. "It's dead in summer—things will pick up then."

But my severance had run out in March. My savings, never robust, were rapidly becoming a figment of my imagination. I'd been waking up at three in the morning, my thoughts revolving on a groove approaching panic. The rent on my apartment was exorbitant, even by Brooklyn standards. I'd scoured Craigslist and Airbnb for a cheaper place, blasted emails to everyone I knew. The only possibilities were hideous.

And in the meantime, the bills kept coming.

I took a fortifying swig of wine. Opened the first notice.

Tender Care Hospice Services. $2,647.19. *BALANCE OVERDUE.*

Shit. I'd forgotten about this one. Nine months since I'd scattered Mom's ashes from the Ocean City boardwalk (illicitly, before dawn) and I was still paying off what her insurance didn't cover. I'd wanted the best care for her. I didn't regret it. But now, suddenly, it all came rushing back to me: her dinette transmogrified into a hospital room; the curio cabinet crammed with vials and syringes; the bleeping monitors on the sideboard; and the *squeech, squeech* of thick-soled shoes on linoleum.

A searing bubble of loss, grief, guilt burst in my chest.

I leaped off the window seat and strode into the kitchen and poured the dregs of the Sancerre into my glass. I was drinking too much. I didn't care.

My cell jangled. I reached for it.

"So you are still alive." Otis Fairfax's sunny baritone. "How come you didn't answer my texts?"

"Sorry, I haven't checked messages today."

"Whoa. You sound like you're in a major funk."

"Yeah, well, maybe," I said. "It's been raining forever, and I feel like spring is never going to come. I mean real spring, with dogwood and daffodils and everything."

"Yeah, right. It's just the rain."

He knew me too well. Otis was the closest thing to family I had. Like sort of a kid brother—the kind who's forever wrecking cars and getting bounced out of jobs and then swears to God he's got it together this time, and if you don't actually believe him, you fervently want to. He'd moved to California two years ago to attend—and drop out of—a Sausalito culinary school. I hadn't heard from him in months.

"Where are you?" I said. "Still working at that tapas place?"

"God, no, I quit ages ago. The manager was a little Mussolini. I'm down in Big Sur now, working for a cousin of mine. An estate on the ocean, gorgeous, knockout views. It's called Thorn Bluffs, and I'm his private chef and kind of helping to run things."

"It sounds great."

"It is, and it's why I'm calling. I got that email you sent about needing a new place, and listen. There's a cottage here. It's really nice, and nobody's using it. You could have it, like, for free, for the summer, maybe even longer."

"Wait," I said. "You mean in California?"

"Yeah. I know it's a long way to come, but it's perfect for you, really. And you won't have to pay any rent." A cacophony of barking rose behind him. "Hold on a sec. Let me kick the dogs out of the kitchen." His voice added to the canine din: "Out, all of you! Outa here!" To me: "We've got five dogs right now, and naturally I'm the designated wrangler. So where was I?"

"A freebie cottage with ocean views. What's the catch?"

"Nothing. I mean, not a catch. Except Evan—that's my cousin— he's got a daughter coming back from school for the summer. She's thirteen and in that stage, you know? She was supposed to go to her grandmother's, but Grandma broke a hip. And her mom died a couple of years ago . . ."

I drew a breath. "How?"

"Oh, she worked for some NGO and was on a famine-relief trip to Africa and ate some dish she didn't know had peanuts in it. She was fatally allergic. Evan didn't even know he had a kid until then. It was a one-night thing, and the mom never got in touch."

"That poor little girl," I murmured.

"Yeah, crappy break for her. But I figured you could relate because of your mom, you know? Talk to her and all."

"Just talk to her?"

"Well, no, not just. She'll be going to summer school for some classes she flunked, but she doesn't focus well. She needs extra tutoring. You'd get paid, of course. In addition to the cottage. A good hourly. My cousin definitely isn't cheap."

"I've never tutored before," I said.

"It wouldn't be hard. French—you speak it, right? And, like, earth science, and that's easy—you can just go through the textbook."

"But why me? Why don't you get a professional tutor?"

"Evan hates having strangers around. I told him you're like family to me, and I'm family to him, so in a way we're all kind of related."

I felt light headed. The vinegary wine was going to my head. "So what does he do, this cousin of yours?"

"Second cousin once removed, actually. He's an entrepreneur. Finances start-ups, mostly in Silicon Valley." A little too casually, Otis added, "You might've heard of him. Evander Rochester?"

I placed the name with a shock. "The one who murdered his wife?"

"So you heard about that?"

"Well, yeah, Otis. It was all over the media just this last winter. His wife was a famous model. Beatrice McAdams, right?"

"Yeah, but he didn't murder her. Jesus! It was suicide. She drowned herself. She was schizophrenic or something. Everyone knew she was crazy—that's how she blew up her modeling career. She stabbed some *Vogue* photographer with a Chanel pin. Right between the eyes."

I gave a startled laugh. "Really?"

"Yeah, and worse things besides. Plus, Evan tried to save her, but he was too late. Her body got swept out to sea. The current is a killer here." He gave a kind of strained giggle. "Look, you won't be in any risk, if that's what you're afraid of. I mean, I wouldn't lure you here if you might get your throat cut in the middle of the night or anything."

"I don't know, O.," I said. "You don't always think things through."

"But I have thought this through. And I really, really want you to come. And you can help me with stuff here. I don't know how I'm going to cope otherwise. I'm swamped with things to do. And Evan's away most of the time, so it'll just be me here with Sophia and a couple of the help. I'm practically a prisoner."

I paused. "Why do I get the feeling there's something you're not telling me?"

"I'm telling you everything. Honest. And you'll love it here, I promise. We're close to Carmel-by-the-Sea. Lots of art galleries, you'll love that too." His phone bleeped. "It's him—I gotta go. I'll text you some pics." He hung up.

I finished off the Sancerre. Typical Otis. Suggesting I hop out to California like it was a jaunt to Montauk on the Hampton Jitney.

My text pinged. Two photos. The first a spectacular aquamarine cove encircled by sloping pastel-tinted bluffs. View from your cottage!

The second a blurred selfie, Otis in a white chef's apron, brandishing a slotted spoon. Me in the kitchen!!

I'd missed him. More than I'd realized. *Like family.*

Outside, the rain had tapered to a cheerless spritz, and the apartment was growing dim in the fading light. It was the first place I'd looked at when I'd had to immediately move out of cheater Jeremy's loft, and I'd grabbed it. Even if I could afford to stay here, I didn't want to—it was howling with bad memories.

Those places he'd mentioned—Big Sur, Carmel-by-the-Sea—they sounded romantic, all pounding sea cliffs and mission bells tolling in the distance.

And that poor young girl. Losing her mom so suddenly. I felt a tug toward her, even without knowing anything more about her.

Maybe I could be of some help to her. And help Otis hang on to a gig for a change. A new place. A new sense of purpose . . .

But what wasn't he telling me?

Something. I was sure of it.

BEATRICE

Braidy Lady is brushing my hair.

Gentle, she wants me to think she's going soft, but she yanks a snarl, and I snarl back, low in my throat, and she stops. I can sense her hand tightening on the handle of the brush. She'd like to hurt me more—I can feel that—but she doesn't dare.

I maybe took a bite at her once.

I can float a picture of it in my mind, her square brown hand, my sharp teeth sinking into it like a chicken thigh, and she hissed. Braidy Lady hissed like a brown snake and tried to put a witch spell on me, but now she's afraid, afraid of my clicking sharp white cat's teeth.

I don't know for sure. There's a fog twisting through my thoughts. But I like it when the fog is thick in my mind because it feels like swimming. Like being underwater but still being able to breathe.

I hear the door open, and I turn my head. He's there, standing in the doorway with his back to the shadows. He's all starey. Eyes black like coal.

He says something very loud to Braidy Lady. "Annunciata," he says. That's her name. It makes me think of the Virgin Mary.

You are the Virgin, Beatrice, Mary Magdalene's voice whispers to me.

Annunciata puts down the brush, and now they're talking together, my jailer and her. They speak in their secret witch language, the one they use when they plot against me.

I keep my smile pinned on my face as I take the brush. The handle is black like his eyes, and the bristles are made from the hairs of a wild boar. I tilt my head back and scrape the boar hairs down the long, long length of my hair, and I watch it turn silvery in the light.

He speaks to me now. "Today's the seventeenth, Beatrice," he is saying. "December seventeenth. It's our wedding anniversary, do you remember?"

I dig the boar hairs of the brush into my head. They feel like a thousand tiny daggers.

Yes, I remember. I walked down the aisle, and I wore white like the Virgin.

Did he think it was the first time I went down an aisle wearing white?

They paid me $2,000 an hour to walk down the catwalk aisles. I was the most famous girl, the most beautiful one. The virgin who wore the white dress, the bridal dress. The last dress before the finale.

"I thought we might go out to dinner tonight," my jailer is saying. "To celebrate our anniversary. Would you like that?"

I liked prowling the catwalk. Sometimes they put me in black lace and leather or sometimes spotted fur, like a leopard or a cheetah, or striped like a tiger, and I prowled up and down the aisle they called a catwalk, my hips swinging wide, my face a little fierce. My famous Beatrice McAdams walk. But at the end, I am always the bride, the virgin. The girl who wears the white dress.

Mary Magdalene whispers to me.

Don't forget the Russian girl, Beatrice. The very young one from St. Petersburg. The one they put in the white dress in Milan.

Yes, I remember. The new girl. Sixteen years old. The next Beatrice McAdams, they were saying. They couldn't see she was a sabertooth. So clever, she kept her claws hidden up inside the tips of her fingers and toes.

But I could see. In the procession, the finale in Milan, I watched her claws come out—sharp, horny claws breaking through her shoes, curling out from the tips of her fingers. I knew she was planning to pounce on me, to rip me apart, and I was afraid.

Quick, quick, I pounced first.

One flick of my hind foot and I took her down.

I heard her scream, and all around, people were making noises. But the girl was stealthy, she sheathed her claws so they couldn't see what she really was.

And then Fiona from the agency was on my phone. Like a crow and it scared me: *caw cracka caw, craw.*

Broke her nose, Fiona cawed. *Two teeth chipped. We'll be sued.*

Caw, caw. Crackety caw.

I put the phone down while she cawed, because I badly needed some snow white. I kept it in a shiny brown canister that used to contain tea. **CHAI DIARIES**, the tea canister said. **ORGANIC CLASSIC BREAKFAST**.

I sniffed up a little snow white from my canister so I could talk to Fiona.

My shoes were too small, I told her. *They were too tight for me to walk in. I stumbled. It wasn't my fault.*

It's the last time we'll cover for your shit, Beatrice. One more incident and we're cutting you loose. Do you understand?

"Are you listening to me, Beatrice?" My jailer's voice has sharp glass in it. It goes through me like a cut. "Have you been listening at all to what I'm saying?"

He still stares at me from the doorway with eyes all inky.

He thinks I don't know. About what he is planning to do.

So many words whispering in my mind, like prayers in church at Easter when all the pews are full and people stand in the aisles and there are lilies on the altar.

Lilies. I want to scream a little.

But I behave like a model prisoner. Words are floating through my mind, but I pick only the words he wants to hear.

"Of course I'm listening, darling," I say. "Happy anniversary."

THREE

I was lost.

I crept in my rented Nissan through fog thick as cotton wadding, fog that shimmered specter white in the headlights before dissolving into the witching-hour blackness beyond. My GPS had conked out twenty minutes ago, and I hadn't seen another car in almost as long. The Pacific Ocean pounded hundreds of feet below, and my pulse was pounding in synchronicity.

I must have overshot the turnoff to Thorn Bluffs. Easy to do on this twisty road, Otis had warned me.

Just over eleven hours ago, I'd left my apartment for the last time and boarded a Delta nonstop from JFK. Heavy turbulence over the Rockies, me on my third tiny bottle of cabernet. Then a sprint across the vast sprawl of LAX, only to find my Alaska Air connection delayed due to fog in Monterey. I tapped a guy in a green hoodie embossed with a giant clam. "Any idea how long it could be?"

"Fog's pretty intense this time of year. Could be twenty minutes, could be six hours."

Six hours! I had an impulse to turn and catch the next plane back to New York. But my apartment was now sublet to a Dutch photographer with pink hair. My bank account was nearly flatlined. Most of my friends were scattered to the winds.

I went instead to grab a Frappuccino.

Two Fraps, a turkey wrap, and a margarita later, my flight was called. Another rock and roll up to Monterey, a lengthy wait at the Alamo counter. And now it was almost midnight, and I was lost.

I crept around an almost invisible bend. A road sign materialized in the fog like ectoplasm. A rudimentary drawing of a pig with a brutish snout, a piglet in tow. The wild boar crossing! Otis had said it was a landmark.

Yes! I stabbed the air with a fist.

And now, there was the turnoff—a break in the thick underbrush marked by two round white boulders. I steered between the rocks onto a rutted lane and in several yards came to a high metal gate. Pressed the button on a black metal call box. An open sesame effect: the gates creaked apart.

I continued down a dark lane of worn-away asphalt flanked by towering black columns of redwoods. Thickets of ferns glistened like otherworldly plants between the trunks. Humpbacked shadows flickered in the foliage beyond. Every so often, goblin-like fingers groped the hood of my car.

A storybook road. It could lead to a gingerbread house. Or a beast drooling for blood inside a crumbling castle.

The road snaked and twisted upon itself, and just when I was sure some malevolent spell had taken me right back to where I'd started, the redwoods thinned to a clearing and the fog began to dissipate, revealing one of the most beautiful houses I'd ever seen.

Three stories made of redwood, glass, and steel. The top story with a deck that cantilevered toward the sea. The facade softly illuminated by ground lights nestled in natural landscaping.

I pulled into the drive. The front door flew open, and Otis burst out, wearing a monkish brown robe and pajama pants.

I gave a start as a beast face suddenly pressed against my window—black and hairy, with peering bright-black eyes.

"Pilot! Down, boy! Down!" Otis yanked the dog's collar, for that's what the beast was—a black, unclipped standard poodle. It broke away from him and cavorted off into the darkness. "Sorry, he's still a puppy. New here. Sophia just brought him home yesterday."

I staggered, travel-buzzed, from the car. He caught me up in a bear hug. "Shit, Janie, I'm so glad to see you—you can't even imagine!"

"Me too." So glad that tears welled in my eyes. "You haven't changed a bit!" He hadn't: his face was still like the Raisin Bran sun logo, round with spiky pale hair and crockery-blue eyes behind gold glasses.

"Neither have you. Except you're too skinny. This air will give you back your appetite. It's very bracing."

"Yeah, I noticed." I pulled my summer-weight sweater closer around me. "What a gorgeous house!"

"Isn't it? You know the architect Jasper Malloy?"

"Of course, great midcentury architect. He designed it?"

"Yeah, for himself, in 1962. And also died here twelve years later. There was a story it was haunted by him, so for a long time, nobody would touch it. It was a wreck when Evan bought it." Otis flipped up the Nissan's hatchback and swung out my suitcase. "Though probably the real reason was because Malloy's architecture had gone out of style. But now he's considered a genius and a visionary, and all his buildings are masterpieces. *Architectural Digest* is dying to do a spread on this, but Evan says no way. If they come around, he'll set the dogs on them."

"Is he here? Mr. Rochester?"

"Ev? Nah, away as usual. And Sophia's asleep. At least I think so. It's hard to tell—she keeps her music going twenty-four seven. But hey, you must be beat. Let me get you to your place." He popped the handle of my suitcase. "Leave the keys in the car. I'll get it moved in the morning."

I grabbed my carry-on and followed as he rolled my bag to a descending set of wooden stairs. The ocean now boomed like it was inches under our feet. The steps were slick with moss. I clung to the railing.

Any visions of luxury I'd had from the sight of the main house were dashed by the cabin at the bottom of the steps. Unpainted redwood surrounded by run-wild bushes. A peaked wooden roof. The remnants of a chimney. A sign faded to illegibility over the door. "What does that sign say?"

"Magritte Cottage. This used to be an artist colony in the 1940s. Ten cottages all named after painters. All burned down except this one."

He pushed the door open. A standing lamp illuminated one large room, simply furnished with rustic-looking pieces painted in faded primary colors. A bricked-over fireplace, the wall blackened around it. A very darkened gilt-framed mirror above it. A frayed braided rug over most of the planked floor. Opposite the fireplace, a pair of sliding glass doors slightly askew on their runners.

"It looks better in the daylight," Otis said anxiously.

"It's nice. Cozy." I dropped my carry-on and purse on the bed, a four-poster with a fuzzy plaid spread. "Reminds me of sleepaway camp. Except without the bunk beds."

"It's all original, except the glass doors. Malloy added those to give the ocean view. The furniture's from Evan's parents. They were archaeologists, mostly in South America."

"Retired?"

"If you call dead retired. Plane crash when Evan was at Stanford."

"Oh." My eyes seized on a rough arrangement of wildflowers in a glass on the bed table. "Pretty bouquet."

"Sophia picked them. She worried they'd already be wilted by the time you got here. Wildflowers don't last long."

"That was sweet of her."

"She can be. Sometimes." He ticked his spectacles higher on his nose. "So . . . there's a kitchenette through the folding doors. I left some stuff for breakfast in the fridge. The connectivity is okay, not great, worse with the cell. If it goes out entirely and you really need it,

19

you can go up to the house—it's heavy-boosted up there. Oh, and you can drink the tap water, by the way. It's from a well, and it's delicious."

I nodded, stifling a yawn.

"And you've got your own terrace. The view of the cove like I sent you."

I glanced at the glass doors. "No curtains?"

"I could tack some up, if you want. But there's nothing really out there."

I went over and peered out into the blackness. I could hear but not see the pounding water. "So that's where it happened? With Beatrice McAdams?"

"Where she drowned herself, yeah. Last December. Wearing a party dress. Crazy, huh?"

A cocktail dress and high heels. I remembered being captivated by that detail in the nonstop media coverage at the time.

Otis gave a little clap of his hands. "Hey, I'll let you crash. That bed's pretty comfy, I tested it out myself." He bounced a little on the balls of his slipper-clad feet, that way he'd always done. "I'm so truly glad you're here, Janie. You made the right decision. You'll see."

It didn't seem like the right decision. I managed a smile. "I really have missed you, O."

"Yeah, me too. Like crazy. And now we'll have each other's backs. Watching out for each other, just like we always did back when we worked at the Clown, right?"

"You bet."

We hugged again, and he left. I listened to his footsteps receding outside. A lonely sound.

I pulled out my phone. Just one bar, which quickly sputtered out like an extinguished candle.

There was an old black desk phone squatting on top of a dresser. I picked up the receiver. It was dead.

Who would I call at this time of night anyway?

I carted my carry-on bag with my toiletries into the primitive bathroom. The tap went on with a put-upon groan, then released alternating gushes of freezing and scalding water. I scrubbed my face free of travel grime. Brushed my teeth.

Trudged wearily back to the main room and began to unpack. There was a midget closet with peeling flowered wallpaper and a musty, old-maiden-aunt smell. A small bureau with drawers that stuck. I pried open the top drawer. It was crammed with fashion magazines: *Harper's Bazaar, Marie Claire*.

I opened one—a *Vanity Fair* from 2013—to a page marked with a turned-down corner. Full-page ad for Lancôme. The model was Beatrice McAdams at the height of her career. An exquisite silvery creature with hazy green eyes.

All the magazines in the drawer appeared to have folded-down corners. I flipped to a few more of the marked pages. Each featured photos of Beatrice in her heyday.

I tossed the magazines into a heap on the floor. Restocked the drawers with my undies, shorts, and tops.

I peeled off my travel-rumpled clothes. Pulled on a nightshirt. Filmy white linen newly bought for what I'd imagined would be balmy California nights. It floated sensuously to my knees.

I caught a glimpse of myself in the gilt mirror above the fireplace. A small pale girl in a thin white shift.

Not a beauty. Just pretty enough.

I felt a sudden overwhelming desire for a lover's touch.

The feeling startled me. I'd shut down that part of myself for almost a year. So why now, exhausted, in strange surroundings, so far from anything I thought of as home, did I feel nearly choked with desire? I leaned closer to the mirror's speckled glass, as if to search its dark depths for an answer.

Something moved in the reflection behind me.

I gave a violent start.

A figure, hovering just outside the glass doors. Hazy, white. Incorporeal.

My heart began to pound. "Mom?" The word escaped my lips involuntarily.

Whoever, whatever, it was receded into the dark.

I stood paralyzed a moment. Then, with determination, I turned and strode to the doors. Cupped my face on the glass and peered out.

Moonlight flitted in scrappy patterns between the branches of a tree limb swaying in the breeze. I gave a quick laugh. Just like me to conjure my mother's ghost out of a flutter of moonbeam.

I unbolted the door, jiggled it open on its uneven track, and stepped out into the brisk air.

The sea was a black expanse with white foamings of phosphorescence where the waves tossed. The faint outline of a cliff descended on the left, the silhouette of a cypress on its crest—like a mad woman with her hair blown sideways.

The surf now sounded like a war. Booming cannons. Clashing artillery.

And suddenly my skin prickled.

The kind of prickle that crawls up from the top of your spine and over your scalp when you're absolutely sure you're being watched.

I scuttered back inside. Heaved the glass door shut and locked the bolt. Then went to the front door. There was a keyhole, the skull-shaped kind for a large old-fashioned key.

I had no key. I felt a spurt of panic.

Stop it! I was spooking myself. My exhausted state. The disorienting effect of strange new surroundings.

I just needed to get some sleep.

I crawled into bed between fresh sheets and the plaid blanket. I thought again of that hazy shape in the mirror, and another fancy floated into my mind.

A mad woman in a cocktail dress.

Beatrice.

And then I drifted into unconsciousness.

FOUR

I woke up to the sight of startling beauty. Outside the doors, a misted blue sea stretched to the horizon, cradled by bluffs of ocher, violet, moss green. Pelicans skimmed the waterline. A hummingbird fizzed ruby and emerald at the glass, then flashed into thin air.

Nothing ghostly. No goblins.

I checked the time: 10:58 a.m.!

I propelled myself out of bed and into the scalding-freezing shower. Washed with a slice of pickled-looking green soap perched on the rim. Threw on the first clothes I pulled out—canary-yellow cotton shirt, white capris. In the kitchenette, I found a bag of freshly ground Jamaican beans. OJ. Homemade cranberry muffins. Otis had remembered I preferred honey to sugar.

I brewed coffee in a dinged-up Krups and took a steaming cup and a muffin out to the crumbling brick terrace. I ate sitting on the steps that led down into the property.

In the distance, an electric saw buzzed, and two men yelled back and forth in a splashing kind of language—a little like Spanish being spoken underwater. Dogs barked occasionally from below. A feeling of remarkable well-being crept over me.

My text tone sounded.

R u murdered yet?

I grinned. Wade O'Connor. He was teaching at UCLA while still hunting for a new writing gig.

I texted back: Not yet. Mr. R. not even here.

They put u in a spooky attic?
Nope. Rustic cottage with staggering view. I'm in paradise!!
Yeah? Don't eat no poison apples. Gruesome way to die. Mwahahaha.
I'll try my best not to.

The dogs below suddenly began barking frenetically. I stood up and went to the edge of the terrace, but even on tiptoe I couldn't see down to the beach.

I gazed out over the water. There were several large outcroppings toward the horizon, one of them particularly imposing. Very jagged—black and glistening. It looked to me like the ruined spire of a Gothic cathedral sunk beneath the water.

My eyes traveled to a lower promontory north of where I stood. I spotted something else that looked medieval. The top of a small tower, round with a crenellated top, poking above the trees. So what could that be? I wondered.

My text pinged again. Otis this time. U revived?

Yeah. Be right up.

I dumped my dishes in the minisink inside. Then I headed up the mossy little steps to the main compound. Otis was in the motor court unloading bags of produce from the back of his ancient Prius. "Hey," he greeted me. "Sleep okay?"

"Too well. I just got up. You're right, O., it's spectacular here."

"Told you."

"What's going on with all the dogs?"

"A dead tiger shark washed up on the cove. I've got to get it towed away before it rots and the smell gets up here." His arms full, he started to the house. "Hey, could you do me a big favor? Pick up Sophia later? She goes to a tennis clinic in the mornings, and it gets out at two o'clock."

"Sure, anything I can do to help." My rental Nissan was no longer in the drive. "Where's my car?"

"I had Hector—he's the gardener here—take it back to Alamo. We've got a car here you can use."

"I already paid for a month."

"I called, and Alamo's just going to charge you for one week."

I had an odd feeling of being trapped. "You should have asked me first, Otis."

"I thought you'd be happy. Not having to pay for the rental, right? And believe me, you're gonna like this one a lot better."

He headed to a side door of the house. We entered a large service porch where a woman with long white braids was attacking the floors with a Swiffer. She was tall and gaunt. I couldn't guess her age—fifty, sixty? Her nut-brown face looked carved from some obdurate tropical wood.

"Hola, Annunciata!" Otis yelled. "This is Jane. She is staying in the cottage."

I smiled. "Nice to meet you, Annunciata."

She returned a glare. Then resumed her punishment of the floor.

I trailed Otis into the kitchen—a stunner, all limestone and Euro stainless and another eye-popping view of the Pacific. "Annunciata's really deaf," he explained. "She's got hearing aids—top of the line, Evan paid—but she hardly ever uses them. He says she thinks they pick up spirit voices. I believe it."

"She didn't seem to like me much."

"It's impossible to tell. She's married to Hector—I told you, the gardener—and he's the same way. They worked for Evan's parents in Honduras, and I don't think either of them likes strangers. Maybe they're illegal. I never asked."

"Who else works here?"

"Just me and the Sandovals full time. There are others who come part time." He deposited the bags on a counter. "There used to be a lot more. A guy who was kind of a butler but called himself the estate manager. Two other full-time maids and a chef before me. And both Evan and Beatrice had personal assistants. The butler and the chef lived in the guesthouse behind the garage, but they all got sacked when the money got tight." Otis rummaged in a drawer, pulled out a remote. "Okay, this opens both the gates and garage. First button, gates—next three, garage doors. The third's got a blue Audi, that's the car you'll use."

I took the clicker. "Okay, thanks."

"The key fob should be on the seat. Tell your GPS 'Carmel Tennis Club.' You'll want to leave early. There's a lot of tourist traffic."

"Maybe I'll go in now. Unless you need me for anything else?"

"No, good idea, get the lay of the land. Oh, and you're having dinner with me and Sophia tonight. Since the lord and master is away."

"Great." I started to turn. "Oh, by the way, I need a key for my door."

"Didn't I leave you one? Like, by the bed?"

"No."

"I thought I did. I'll see if I can dig you up another. Wait, let me show you first where you'll be working with Sophia."

He led me to the center of the house, a floating staircase made of ash-colored wood. We descended to the lower level. "This floor is completely new," he said. "It's got a gym, a screening room. A couple more bedrooms. One for the Sandovals. They've got their own house on the other side of the highway, but sometimes one of them will stay over. Like if I'm away."

"So you weren't exactly a prisoner here?"

He gave me a puzzled look. Then threw open a pair of pocket doors. "This is the Ocean Room. Where you'll work."

A spacious room, more traditionally furnished than those upstairs. An undulating sea-green light flooded in from floor-to-ceiling windows on two sides.

"It's lovely," I said.

"It was Beatrice's favorite room. She spent a lot of time in here, lolling on that chaise." A tufted white chaise was positioned at a slight diagonal from one wall. "Evan never sets foot in here anymore."

"Won't he mind us working here?"

"Nah. He'll like that it keeps you out of his way."

Pretty cold, I thought. Even if he had murdered Beatrice.

Or particularly if he had.

I returned to the cottage. Swapped my flip-flops for sandals, grabbed my bag, and headed to the garage—a nine-car structure connected by a covered passage to the main house. I stabbed random buttons on the remote until the middle bay rumbled open.

"Wow," I breathed.

An Audi Coupe, sapphire blue with a white interior, crouched between a Land Cruiser and a Smart Car. In the Jersey burb I grew up in, car crazy came with the air, and here were eight mostly gorgeous ones, including a Tesla Model S at a recharging station. I stepped rapturously up to the Audi and slipped behind the wheel. Luxuriated in the buttery leather. A touch on the starter and the engine sprang to life with a sensuous purr.

The coast road where I'd felt so lost the night before was now a blast to drive. The ocean flashed in and out of sight, with occasional peeps of snowcapped mountains to the east. A tap on the pedal and I surged effortlessly into traffic on the main highway.

Twenty-two minutes to the turnoff to Carmel-by-the-Sea. Charming in a postcard kind of way. Whitewashed cobblestone alleyways. Tutti-frutti-colored geraniums dripped from windowsills. Pedestrians spilled from the sidewalks, snapping pictures, licking gelato. I lucked into a parking space and joined the stroll. Shelled out twenty-seven bucks for a Cobb salad at a sidewalk café.

Nothing seemed quite real. The geraniums. The gelato. A hazy sunshine added to the dreamlike atmosphere.

At a quarter to two, I got back in the Audi. The GPS steered me to the tennis club—a low building shaded by sycamores, the bark like Marine Corps camouflage. The parking area was jammed. I made a full circle before spotting a car pulling out—a high-end Range Rover, metallic blue. I cruised up beside it.

The driver, a woman, braked suddenly. *Odd*, I thought. I'd left more than enough room for her to maneuver.

She continued to back out, then swung forward and braked again directly beside me. Misted sunlight dazzled the window: I registered silver-blonde hair, finely etched features. Eyes hidden behind large and opaque dark glasses.

A tap on my opposite window made me jump. A fairly tall and tan girl flumped into the passenger seat.

"Hi," she said.

The Range Rover pulled sharply away. I stared briefly after it, then back to my passenger. "Oh, hi . . . Sophia? I'm Jane."

"Yeah, I know, Otis said." She twisted herself to wedge a racket and a neon-orange Patagonia duffle behind her seat.

"Thanks so much for the lovely flowers. It was so thoughtful of you."

"No problem." She wriggled a little. "So how come you get to drive her car?"

"Whose car?"

"Beatrice's. She used to seriously lose her shit if you even, like, looked at it."

Beatrice's car!

A sudden pinging made me jump again. "Seat belt," I said.

With the air of granting a particularly nonsensical favor, Sophia yanked the belt across her chest. Tugged her short-shorts from between the cleft of her buttocks, excavated a pack of Bubble Yum from the back pocket, and ripped it open. Crammed two pink slabs in her mouth. Chewed a moment. "I thought you'd look different," she said.

I began to pull out of the lot. "Really? How?"

"I don't know. Just different." Her voice sounded blurred. A moustache of sweat glistened above her bow-shaped upper lip.

She was certainly different than the waif I'd been picturing. A heart-shaped face bruised with magenta eye shadow, purple mascara, purplish-brown lip gloss. Earlobe-length red hair in want of shampoo. Orange tube top. Those short-shorts.

She blew a quivering bubble. Popped it. "Otis said you used to work for a TV show."

"Yeah, I did. A show called *Carlotta Dark*."

"Never heard of it."

"It was on the ALX network. It ran for six years, then got canceled."

"That sucks." She spat the gum back into the wrapper, crumpled gum and wrapper into a wad, and dropped it at her feet. Then let out a belch.

I caught the distinctive funk of regurgitated bourbon. "Have you been drinking?"

"No."

"There's no point in lying. I can smell it on your breath."

A shrug, one shouldered.

"Did you even go to tennis practice?"

"Yeah, I did."

"And?"

"We broke early 'cause the coach, Marianne, she's got, like, fibroids and gets these major cramps? So she had to go to the gynecologist. And I went to hang with Josh, the dude who runs the bar."

"He lets you drink?"

"I had, like, half a Manhattan. No big deal." A louder belch.

"It seems like a big deal," I said.

My attention suddenly shifted to the rearview mirror. A car was tailgating us. A metallic-blue SUV. Possibly a Range Rover.

I slowed to see if it would pass. It lessened its speed to remain behind me.

I had a wild thought: it was Beatrice McAdams chasing me.

Sophia suddenly let out a low gurgle, like the sound of oatmeal coming to a boil. I swerved to the shoulder and stopped. "Roll down your window. Breathe."

She whirred the window down and hung her head out, gulping in fresh air. Then she dragged her head back in and slumped crookedly against her seat.

"Okay?" I asked.

A feeble assent. I pulled back onto the highway, compulsively checking for a metallic-blue SUV behind me. It was gone.

Did I really think it was Beatrice? My old childhood yearning for the dead not to stay dead. *Ridiculous.*

I drove back as fast as I dared, swung carefully onto the Thorn Bluffs private road, taking the switchbacks as gently as possible. Pulled to a stop in front of the house. Helped Sophia out, half hoisting her by the shoulders. Guided her inside. "Where's your room?"

"Down the hall."

I supported her down the long hallway past the central stairs. She lurched for a doorknob and tottered inside, collapsing on her bed. I followed her in. An unholy mess: I waded through an archipelago of tangled panties, athletic socks, puddles of perfumed goo, tokidoki shopping bags, a spilled-out box of sport tampons. I noticed a gold Zippo lighter. A fish tank with no water.

I went into her equally slovenly bathroom. Found a glass that didn't look like it was actively cultivating a norovirus. Filled it from the tap and brought it to her. "Drink some water. Just a few sips. It will make you feel better."

She turned her face to the wall. "Are you going to tell my dad?"

"No," I said.

She turned back to me. Just enough to shoot me a slit-eyed glance. "But if you keep on doing this, I'm sure he's going to find out."

"How do you know? He's hardly ever *here*. You've never even *met* him."

"That's true. But here's what I do know. I know I used to be your age once. And that somewhere in this pigsty of a room there's a joint stashed away. Or a bottle of something. Or both. And I'll bet cigarettes too. And I also know that if you want to hide your drinking, bourbon's the worst way to go. Anyone can smell it on your breath a mile away. You're way better off with vodka."

Another slitted peep at me.

"I'll just leave the glass here. But trust me, you'll feel a whole lot better if you stay hydrated."

As I closed her door behind me, I heard a rustling. Then the clink of a glass being lifted off a surface.

I felt a little surge of triumph. Maybe I could be of help to her after all.

"Do you think I should go check on her again?"

"Nah." Otis set a tureen on the table: cioppino, chunky with fresh seafood and fragrant with anise and oregano. "I've found it's better to just let her sleep it off."

"So she's done this before?"

"Yeah, a couple of times. Annunciata likes her rum and once left a bottle around that Soph got into. And maybe another time after tennis.

But she really can be sweet sometimes. I was hoping that was the side you'd get first."

We were settled in an alcove on the sea-view side of the kitchen. Five dogs milled and begged at our feet. I finally had them all straight. The poodle, Pilot. Julius, an obese bulldog. A terrier mutt, Hermione, who'd lost a leg to a fox poacher's trap and was now fitted with a prosthetic contraption. Also a pair of black German shepherds—siblings, Minnie and Mickey—who still appeared to be sizing me up.

"By the way," I said, "why didn't you tell me it was Beatrice's car?"

"The Audi? So what? It's an amazing car, right? And it's just sitting out there."

"It feels kind of ghoulish for me to drive it."

"Don't think about it like that."

"It's going to be hard not to. Please, O., just ask me before making any more decisions for me, okay?"

"*Okay.* I will." He ladled out bowls of the cioppino.

I was suddenly very hungry. I quickly downed a couple of spoonfuls. "I didn't know Sophia had even ever known Beatrice."

"Yeah. Soph first came here about a month after her mom died. From what I know, it was Beatrice who wanted her shipped off to a boarding school."

"Your basic wicked stepmother?"

"Your basic off-her-rocker stepmother." He took a taste of the cioppino and grunted. "Too much oregano."

"Not for me. It's delicious." I wolfed a little more. "So what's that kind of medieval tower sticking up across the grounds from my cottage?"

"Oh, that. Jasper Malloy's old drafting studio. A mini version of his ancestors' back in Ireland. It's where he dropped dead, by the way. While working at his drafting table. His body wasn't found for weeks, and it was all decomposed and eaten by animals by the time it was."

I put my spoon down.

Otis grinned. "It's just used for storage now. Evan says no one's allowed to go in it. He doesn't have to worry. It gives me the creeps just to go near it."

"Malloy's ghost?"

"Somebody's ghost."

I paused for a moment. "Hey . . . Otis? Are you sure . . . I mean, positive, that your cousin is innocent?"

"Evan?"

"Yeah. Do you think it's possible he could have killed Beatrice?"

Otis evaded my eyes. "No. I mean, not in cold blood. But he can get pretty mad sometimes. I mean scary mad. So on the spur of the moment, if she drove him to it . . ." He shook his head. "But he didn't, okay? It's the media that stirred all that up. They wouldn't let it go. They drove him away from here for months."

"Really? Where did he go?"

"His house up in San Francisco. Gorgeous Victorian on Russian Hill. He didn't come back until almost May. And now he's had to rent it out because his money is so tight." Otis's tone suddenly hardened. "But look. Just drop all this, okay?"

I didn't think I could totally drop it. I took a different tack. "A weird thing happened at the tennis club today. Somebody seemed to recognize the Audi and began following me. A woman driving a metallic-blue Range Rover. Maybe some friend of Beatrice's?"

"She didn't have any friends. There's a brother. A real asshole. I think he drives a sports car."

"This was definitely a woman. Maybe somebody who works here?"

"There's only the Sandovals full time, but they've got a truck, and anyway, Annunciata doesn't drive. Lots of people come and go, but I wouldn't know. Car ID'ing isn't really my thing."

"She had pale-blonde hair. Silvery." I gave a little laugh. "I had this utterly crazy thought. I mean, it's pretty insane. But what if it actually was Beatrice?"

"Back from the dead? And driving a Range Rover at the tennis club?"

"I know. I'm probably just writing stories in my head. But it's kind of an intriguing mystery, isn't it? That whole thing about her."

"It's not, I told you," he said vehemently. "She was nuts. She committed suicide—end of story."

"Except it was only his word that she did. And you said her body was never found."

He put down his spoon. "Look, Janie. Don't get involved with Evan's affairs. Seriously. I'm not kidding about this."

Would I disappear as well? "Okay, I won't," I said.

We were silent a moment. But then we began to reminisce about our early days in New York. Laughing ourselves silly over memories of the East Village dive bar we'd both worked at. All tension disappeared. We washed down the cioppino with chilled Montrachet ("I get to drink the dregs of Evan's bottles," Otis said). For dessert, a fresh-made mascarpone fig tart.

He refused to let me help clean up. "Seriously. I like to do things exactly my way. But you could walk Pilot if you want to help. He's hyperactive, even for a poodle."

"He could use a good grooming," I said. "And Julius is wheezing. When was he last taken to the vet?"

"Never since I've been here. Why don't you take over the dogs? That would be a huge help to me."

"All of them?" I glanced dubiously at Minnie, who was eyeing me in a way that kind of dared me to make a sudden move. "The shepherds too?"

"You're one of the family now. They'll accept you." He glanced outside. "The fog's coming in—you better take a flashlight. There's some in the service porch. And one of the jackets—it gets chilly."

I called to Pilot, and he instantly scampered with me into the service porch. I selected a flashlight and grabbed a quilted jacket from a hook. It swamped me, but none of the others looked any smaller.

The fog streamed in white scarves and pennants, with a bright half moon playing hide-and-seek among them. I walked briskly down the asphalt drive, Pilot racing figure eights around me. We cut across switchbacks toward the highway. I kept to the gravel shoulder as the grade descended.

A pair of headlights glowered in the mist, then swept swiftly by.

The highway continued to dip. Pilot romped ahead and disappeared from my sight around a curve.

"Pilot!" I heard him barking but couldn't see him. I quickened my steps.

I found myself in the middle of a dense cloud. Fog gathered in the depression in the road.

"Pilot?" I yelled again. "Where are you?"

Excited yapping. But he was a ghost dog.

The roar of a motorcycle echoed from around the far side of the bend. Through the blanketing cloud, I caught a glimpse of the poodle trotting onto the road.

"Pilot, get back here!" I screamed.

The motorcycle's headlamp glowed dimly as it appeared on the near side of the bend. Pilot barked with sudden frenzy. The headlamp veered crazily. Pilot darted off the road into the underbrush. A sickening sound of tires skidding out of control on gravel. A shout.

With horror, I watched motorcycle and rider slam down onto the gravel shoulder.

I ran toward the rider. He was sprawled crookedly next to the bike, but his limbs, encased in black leather and jeans, were moving stiffly. Alive, at least. With a groan, he hoisted himself up onto his elbows.

"Are you okay?" I shined my flashlight on him.

He whipped his head. "What the hell are you?"

"Just a person," I said quickly.

He yanked his goggles down. "For Chrissake. I meant *who* are you? What are you doing here?"

"Taking a walk."

"What kind of lunatic goes out for a walk in this kind of fog?"

"Maybe the same kind of lunatic who drives way too fast in it."

"You call that fast? Christ." He gingerly gathered himself into a sitting position, then flexed his feet in the heavy boots experimentally. He took off his helmet and shook out a head of rough black curls. A week's tangle of rough salt-and-pepper beard nearly obscured a wide mouth. The prominent nose might be called stately on a more good-natured face. "What the hell was that creature in the middle of the road?"

"A dog."

"A dog?"

"A standard poodle. Unclipped."

"Fuck me." He put the helmet back on, then pulled a cell phone from his jacket and squinted at the screen. "Nothing," he muttered.

"The reception's kind of iffy around here. Do you want me to go get help? I can get back to my place in about twenty minutes."

"Twenty minutes." A snort. "Do you know how to ride a bike?"

"A bike?" I had a confused mental image of myself pumping an old Schwinn.

"A motorbike," he said.

I glanced at the toppled machine. A Harley Davidson, a behemoth of black and chrome. "I could give it a try. I drove a Vespa all through Umbria one summer."

"A Vespa. Christ God almighty." He flung out an arm. "Help me up, okay?"

I approached him tentatively. He was over six feet and powerfully built. About twice my weight, I guessed. "I'm not sure I can pull you."

"Yeah, you probably can't. Stoop down a little."

God, he's rude. I did, and he draped his arm around my shoulder, transferring his weight. My knees buckled a little but didn't give. He began to stand, crumpled slightly, then got his balance and pulled himself up straight.

I suddenly became aware of his intense physicality. The power of his arm and shoulder against my body, the taut spring of the muscles in his chest. As if he sensed what I was feeling, he shook off my support and stood on his own feet.

"At least you can put weight on your feet," I said. "That's a good sign."

"Are you a medical professional?"

"No."

"Then your opinion doesn't count for much at the moment."

Go to hell, was on the tip of my tongue. But the fog's chill was making me sniffle. It seemed absurd to attempt a stinging retort with a dripping nose. I swiped it surreptitiously with the sleeve of my jacket.

He walked, limping slightly, to the Harley. "This thing's supposed to take a corner. That's the main goddamned reason I bought it!" He gave the seat a savage kick. Then howled, "Son of a fucking bitch!" and hopped on his nonkicking boot and shook a fist as if in defiance of some bully of a god who particularly had it in for him.

I laughed.

He whirled on me. My laughter froze. The look of fury on his face sent a thrill of alarm through me. I edged backward; I felt at that moment he could murder me without compunction and leave my corpse to be devoured by coyotes and bobcats, like the body of Jasper Malloy in that tower.

But then, to my astonishment, he grinned. "You're right. I look like an ass."

Pilot suddenly came crashing out of the underbrush.

"Is that your mutt?"

"Yes. Though, actually, not mine. He's a recent addition at the place I'm staying."

He stared at me, a thought dawning. I forced myself to stare back: deep-set eyes, dark as ink. I was about to introduce myself, but he yanked the goggles back over his eyes and stooped to the handlebar of the bike. "Help me get this up. Grab the other bar. You pull and I'll push."

"It's too heavy."

"I'll do the heavy lifting. Just do what you can."

Obstinately, I didn't move.

"Please," he added. He made the word sound like an obscenity.

I took a grudging step forward and grabbed hold of the handlebar with both hands. I tugged it toward me as he lifted his side with a grunt. The bike slowly rose upright.

"Hold it steady," he said.

It felt like it weighed several tons—it took every ounce of my strength to keep my side up as he straddled the seat. He grasped both bars. Engaged the clutch, cursing in pain as he stomped on the pedal. He glanced at me briefly.

And then, sending up a heavy spray of gravel, the Harley roared off into the enveloping fog.

"You're welcome, Mr. Rochester!" I shouted into the deepening gloom.

BEATRICE

Thorn Bluffs, December 17
Midmorning

It's time for me to take the poison.

My jailer has come to my room again. He has the vial strangled in his fist.

"Ready for your meds, Beatrice?" He looks like a pirate now. Pirate black curls and black eyes and his black jeans have ragged bottoms.

The poison comes sometimes in green and sometimes in yellow, and sometimes it's the color of the dust in a grave. At the dungeon, it came in an injection machine to squirt down my throat. But it's always to keep me prisoner.

I start thinking about the dungeon. The Oaks, they called it. He took me there in his car with no motor, the one he made run on his thoughts alone. He told me I had done something very terrible, and he left me there all locked up.

Lilies. The voices all whisper together in my mind. *You killed the girl named Lilies.*

I hear my jailer's phone purring. He looks at it with a fierce frown. He begins to tap. Click, click, click, click.

I think some more about The Oaks.

Isn't this a nice room, Beat? he had said to me. *So cheerful, don't you think? Terrific view.*

He couldn't fool me. I could see it was a dungeon. There was no view. No windows. Only video screens with bars in front of them. Behind the bars, the screens showed pictures of dirty hills with trees that looked like dark-green umbrellas.

I could have changed the channel and looked at what was really behind the bars. The cement blocks of the dungeon.

But I was too stealthy. I didn't touch the channels. I kept them tuned to those hills and the umbrella trees.

The dungeon keeper was very fat. Pasty puddles of fat cheeks and big puffs of breasts and bottom. She could smell my fear when she came to me with her tube of poison. She called it a medicinal oral syringe. "Nothing to worry about, Beatrice." She squirted poison from it under my tongue.

But I could feel the poison seep through me, turning my blood dark green like the umbrella trees. And I grew fat and puffed up, too, just like the dungeon keeper, and I felt sleepy all the time.

And then my jailer had come back to the dungeon. And he had brought me back here, and now he keeps me his prisoner.

Until he can get rid of me for good.

He wants it to happen tonight, Mary Magdalene hisses at me. *You won't let him, Beatrice. You have the plan.*

"Sorry, Beat." My jailer's voice rises over Mary's. He stuffs his phone in his pocket. He shakes a poison pill from the vial into the palm of his hand. "All set?"

It's yellow today, the color of a corpse. The extrastrong kind. So I won't resist when he comes to get rid of me.

I am a model prisoner. I part my lips, and he places the corpse-colored pill on my tongue.

"Here's your soda." He gives me the chalice to sip, and I do.

I open my mouth to show him the poison pill is gone.

"Good." He smiles. "I've reserved at Sierra Mar for five thirty. You'll want to dress up. Otis has somebody coming to do your face and hair."

I dip my head. *Yes.*

"You'll look gorgeous, Beat. You always do. Oh, and hey, Sophia sent an anniversary card. She'll be home in a few days, you know." He shows his phone to me. "Balloons."

I see bubbles falling and falling inside the screen. They are purple and pink and green, like the poison when it bubbles inside me. I scream, "Take it away!"

When I scream, the pill slips down from behind my tongue and into my throat. I start to cough, and I choke.

He puts the chalice back in my hand. "Drink some more, Beat." I drink again, and the poison pill slides all the way down.

"Rest up now. I'll come back up later." And then he's gone.

The poison, Beatrice. Mary's voice is harsh. *You have to get it out. Now!*

I walk very quickly into my bathroom. I sink down on my knees in front of my bidet.

I put two fingers far, far down the back of my throat. It all comes up—the Dr. Brown and the yellow and green food from my breakfast and the pus and the mud from the poison that has already begun to work.

I pick out the yellow pill in all the pus and mud. My jailer is clever, he put traps in all the drains, and he tests the water seven times a day.

I swirl everything down the bidet except for the pill.

I go into my closet room. I open my shoe closet. I push a button, and all the shoes start going round and round. I stop them and select one.

A rosy pink pump with a glass high heel. It has a pointed toe.

I bury the corpse pill deep inside the toe. Where even my jailer will never find it.

FIVE

I made it back to the cottage feeling shaken and chilled. *Like a first-rate martini,* I thought. Except, no, the best martinis were stirred, and suddenly I began to crave one.

A shrill ring cut abruptly through the room. The old desk phone. The one that was dead.

I stared at it warily. It continued to ring insistently: whatever ghost was on the line was not taking no for an answer. I picked it up.

"He's back," said Otis.

"I thought this phone didn't work."

"The cord is frayed. Goes off and on. If it's on and you press star, it rings on an extension over here. Anyway, Evan's back. He had an accident—his Harley skidded on some loose gravel and went down."

"I know, I saw it happen. I didn't recognize him at first."

Otis wasn't listening. "He's lucky he didn't break his neck. He wants to see you. You don't have to get dressed up or anything. Just come over soon. He hates to be kept waiting." He hung up.

I pressed star to call him back. The phone was dead again.

What if Rochester was blaming me for the accident?

So what? What was the worst he could do? Certainly not murder me in full sight of Otis.

I pulled on dry clothes, ran a comb through my damp hair. Made sure my nose had stopped leaking. I headed up through the fog to the main house, letting myself in through the side service porch.

Otis was in the kitchen, peeling foil from the top of a bottle of Cristal. I caught a whiff of marijuana. "Hey, just in time. You can bring him this." He popped the cork. "He's in the Great Room. It's right after the stairs, the double doors. You'll hear music, just follow it."

I took the bottle. "What do I call him?"

"Evan, like most people do. He hates Evander."

I began down the hall. The mellow strains of Lauryn Hill, "Killing Me Softly," drifted to me. One of my favorite songs. I felt strangely resentful. Like he had no right to it.

I paused at the threshold of the Great Room. Pictured him inside, sitting by a smoldering hearth. Brooding about his injured ankle. Well, so be it. I squared my shoulders and strode briskly inside.

A room with high ceilings, the ocean-side wall made entirely of glass. Modern furniture and elegant flat-weave rugs. Abstract paintings glowing on white walls. There was indeed a large stone hearth at the far end, but Evander Rochester was not seated brooding in front of it. Rather, he was planted firmly on both feet beside a coffee table spread with a lavish buffet, and if he was brooding over anything, it was whether to choose a slab of baby back ribs or a slice of lacy cheese. The German shepherds crouched in a kind of heraldic posture on either side of his feet.

He turned at my entrance. "I cried for madder music and for stronger wine."

I glanced at him, startled. Was that a quote?

He made a "gimme" motion with his fingers. I handed him the Cristal.

"Want some?" He gestured with the bottle.

I hesitated. *Is he aware of our recent encounter?* "Sure. Thank you."

He topped off a large chalice-like goblet and handed it to me. I sipped. Fresh tasting and delicious, the bubbles tickling my nose.

He waved an expansive hand over the buffet. "Have a bite. Fairfax is a first-class cook."

"I know, but I've already eaten, thank you."

"Suit yourself." He went for a cold sparerib. The dogs began making mewling noises. He fed the rib to one of them (Mickey?), another to its sibling (Minnie?). Then he polished off one of his own and tossed the bone, not over his shoulder into the fireplace as I half expected, but back onto the platter. Then lowered himself into a semireclining position on one of two facing couches. "Well, don't just stand there. Sit."

I stiffened.

"Oh, for Chrissake! *Please*, have a seat. And could we *please* skip the niceties? I like to say what I want, and I expect everyone to do the same."

I doubted that. At least the second part. Still, it seemed absurd for me to be hovering above him. I sank into the nearest chair.

He fixed his eyes on me. An unrelenting black stare. "So you *are* real," he said.

So he does recognize me. "Did you actually think I wasn't?"

"I've got to admit I wasn't absolutely sure. The way you appeared out of the fog—you and your spirit animal. Like creatures out of some weird spell. Of course, I'd just been dropped on my head, so I wasn't thinking too clearly about anything."

"I seem pretty real to myself, if that's any help."

"Not much." He continued to stare.

"How is your ankle?" I ventured. "Not broken or . . . anything . . . ?"

"It hurts like a son of a bitch. So if you want another laugh at my expense, now would be the time."

I suppressed a laugh. "No, I'm good. But you might feel better if you get out of those boots."

He glanced at his feet as if they had obstinately and independently encased themselves in thick leather. He sat up, began tugging at the left boot, grimacing in pain.

"Here, let me help." I rose and started to him.

"Stay back!"

The dogs snarled.

Startled, I sat back down. Felt a pulse of anger. What did he think I was going to do?

He jimmied the boot off his left foot, then the other. Then he slouched back on the couch and stared at me just for a change.

I was finding it a little easier to stare back. He looked no more handsome than he had in the dark—if anything, the interior lighting emphasized the crag of his forehead and the scruffiness of his beard. He'd taken off the young-Brando biker jacket and was now in a white pocket tee with a slight rip at the shoulder, giving him a young-Brando-in-*Streetcar* appearance. I had the image of him throwing back his head and howling, "Stell-a!" Smothered another giggle.

He spoke. "So how do you like it here?"

"I like it very much. It's incredibly beautiful."

"The cabin okay? You weren't expecting anything fancy, were you?"

"No. I mean, I didn't know what to expect. But it's perfectly comfortable and charming."

"It's a shack," he said.

The conversation faltered again. Amy Winehouse now drenched the air: "Will You Still Love Me Tomorrow?" Low and a bit ominous, the bass drum like a heartbeat.

My eyes roamed the room for some memento of Beatrice. A photo, maybe. A copy of *Harper's Bazaar*. Anything to suggest she had ever existed. There was nothing.

"You're not from Tennessee, are you?" he said abruptly.

"No. Why would you think so?" It dawned on me. "Did Otis say I was?"

"He told me you grew up on the same block in Memphis."

I'll strangle him. "We didn't. We met in New York about eight years ago. At a club called the Clown Lounge. We were both bartending there."

"The Clown Lounge?" A spark of amused interest.

"A grunge place. Lots of drugs, fights sometimes. The owner was a mean drunk who regularly stole our tips. I don't know why Otis would tell you anything different."

"It's not hard to know that Fairfax is fond of embroidering the truth." He crossed his arms over his head, revealing a tattooed band around his left bicep. Words written in some strange alphabet. Sanskrit? "So tell me something about yourself that *is* true," he said.

My mind suddenly went blank. My life seemed devoid of incident, every day as vacant as the next.

"Where are you really from?" he prompted.

"Originally? Lowood, New Jersey."

"Rich commuter suburb?"

"God, no."

"Gritty working-class town?"

"Not particularly. I mean, it wouldn't rate a Springsteen song."

A fleeting smile. "Still have ties there? Lots of family?"

"No, no ties. No immediate family at all."

"Poor little orphan girl, huh?"

I felt a knife slice through me.

"We're all orphans here," he said brusquely. "One way or another."

What does he mean by that? I said quickly, "I might have an aunt still alive. My aunt Joanne."

"Might?"

"She ran off when I was three. Nobody ever wanted to talk about her. I don't really remember what she looked like, but for some reason, I think of her as looking like a giant frog."

"A frog?" Another gleam of interest.

We were interrupted by the sound of rattling dishware. Otis appeared carrying a laden tray. He set it on the coffee table: the remains of the fig tart, a carafe and espresso cups, a cigar box made of polished ebony. Rochester reached for the tart, excavated a fig, and popped it into his mouth. "Good."

"There's a drop of Chambord in the crust," Otis said. "Jane's already had two slices."

I shot him a death ray.

Rochester flipped the cigar box open. "Only one of the Churchills left?"

"It's lucky there's any. Those Russian guys you had here? They were sucking them down like candy."

"Why didn't you stop them?"

"Um . . . 'cause they had names like Vladimir and Sergey and were maybe packing guns?"

Rochester let out a laugh of pure delight. It had a remarkable effect on his face, softening the crag of his features and accentuating the intelligence of his eyes. I could suddenly see why a beautiful woman might fall in love with him.

Otis began piling the finished plates onto the tray. "Anything else you need?"

"No, we're good."

Otis glanced quickly at me, then hoisted the tray and walked briskly out.

Rochester poured two cups of espresso, pushed one across the table to me, then selected a richly colored cigar from the box. Rolled off the red-and-gold band and clipped the end. "Ever try a Cuban cigar?"

"Me? I've never smoked. At least not tobacco. Except a few Salem Lights at parties."

"Want to try one of these?" A mocking dare in his eyes.

"Sure. Why not?"

I took the cigar he extended and placed it between my teeth. It felt huge. Phallic. No Salem Light. He slid a lighter—a vintage gold Dunhill—across the table. I clicked it and held the flame to the end of the cigar and drew in a strong puff. My mouth filled with what tasted like scorched dirt. I began to automatically inhale, and harsh smoke bit my throat, causing me to choke.

I willed myself, *Do not inhale. Do not swallow.* My eyes wept with the effort not to cough. And then, miraculously, the urge receded, and in its place, a heady little buzz—though from tobacco or triumph, I couldn't tell. I blew out the smoke.

Rochester granted me a look of amused respect. Made that "gimme" finger motion again. I relinquished the cigar to him.

He took a drag. Then he clicked off the music with a remote. The thundering surf became prominent. "What's wrong with my daughter?" he asked.

I glanced at him cautiously.

"I stopped by her room when I came in. She looked like she'd just come off a five-day bender. You drove her home from her tennis lesson, so I'm asking: What's wrong with her?"

"That's something you need to talk to her about."

"I did, obviously. She said she had the stomach flu. Bullshit. She's got the constitution of a young horse." He scowled. "She's a mess. She dresses like a Tijuana hooker and has a mouth to match. That school she's at is costing me a fortune, and she's barely hanging on there. Christ! She's just turned thirteen. I know she drinks. Fairfax tries to hide it from me, but I'm not an idiot."

I chose my words carefully. "She's a very young girl who recently lost her mother. It's hardly surprising she's acting out."

"Is that what you call it? Acting out?"

"I can't really call it anything. I've spent less than an hour with her."

"You must have formed some opinion."

"None that I'd feel right about sharing."

"Look," he said. "I didn't expect to have her here right now. It's a difficult time for me, and I can't deal with some kid acting out."

"That *kid*," I said, barely controlling my voice, "is your daughter."

"What do I know about being a parent? I didn't even know she existed until a year ago."

I stared at him with unconcealed disgust.

"Okay," he conceded. "That was a shit thing to say. Don't get me wrong. I want to do right by her. But I'm in a critical position right now. I've had to downsize my office and staff, and I'll be spending a lot more time here. And, frankly, if I'd known I was going to be around so much, you would not have come."

I shot to my feet. "If you give me a day, I'll make arrangements to go somewhere else."

"Oh, for Chrissake! Sit down."

"I won't stay in a place where I'm not wanted."

He made a sound of deep exasperation. "Fairfax was right—Sophia needs tutoring, but more important, she needs someone to relate to. I asked her what she thought of you. She said you were okay."

I couldn't help a laugh. "That's extravagant praise coming from a thirteen-year-old."

He allowed a smile. "Just stay out of my hair, okay? And keep out of the grounds beyond the compound. It's too wild. I can't be responsible. That goes for the beach as well. Is that clear?"

"Stay out of your hair, and don't wander into the woods. I think I've got it."

"I can't allow visitors. And no posting about me or Sophia or any of us here. One photo on Instagram and you leave."

"I had no intention of doing that."

"Then we understand each other. Good." He stood up, and I did as well. He extended his hand. "Welcome to Thorn Bluffs, Jane."

He knew my name. I'd have bet good money he didn't.

I took the hand he offered, and it closed firmly around mine. His was so much larger, the palm warm and dry. Something shivered in me, almost like an electrical sensation.

A cell phone burred, and he released my hand. "Good night," he said and turned to take the call.

I left the room and went back to the kitchen. Otis hastily set down his joint. "How did it go?"

"Why the hell did you tell him we grew up together?" I said.

"Oh. Crap. I didn't think it would come up."

"It did. It was bound to sooner or later. God, Otis! What were you possibly thinking?"

"I guess maybe that it would make him feel better about getting you here. You know, like, if I knew you all my life. And then once you were here, I figured he'd hardly even notice you. But it's okay, right? He didn't kick you out or anything."

"Not yet. I won't be surprised if he does. And I don't think I should wait until he does. I think I should try to hunt up another place to go for the summer."

"No, I'll make it okay," he said frantically. "I'll tell him it's all my fault. You won't have to leave, I promise."

"I'm sorry, Otis, but I can't believe a single word you say anymore." And before I softened, which I knew I would at his stricken expression, I stormed out of the house.

In the cottage, I mentally replayed my interview in the Great Room with agitation. Strange man. Arrogant, rude. A tinderbox temper.

That he was capable of violence, I had little doubt.

Of murder?

Possibly. Or at least driving his wife to the desperate measure of suicide.

Her absence sure hadn't affected his appetite.

I thought of that spark I'd felt, that electric whatever, when Evan Rochester's hand had closed around mine. What the hell was that?

And then I began to feel jittery.

More than just jittery: it was like my body was trying to burst out of my skin. And then something even stranger began to happen—though not entirely strange for me. My eyes began to haze, and a tiny yellow star exploded in one eye, followed by other larger stars in both eyes, and then bands of neon-orange zigzags began streaming across my vision. A migraine.

Technically, not a real one. No excruciating headache. This was called a visual migraine. But still weird—hallucinatory and almost excruciatingly disorienting. The bursting stars in my eyes. The zigzagging patterns.

Mom used to get them too. She called them texts from an alien planet.

The aliens now seemed to be texting me a particularly urgent message:

Idiot. You. Idiot. Didn't you learn anything with Jeremy?

I flopped down on the bed and squeezed my eyes shut, but the zigs and zags and supernovas still played against my closed lids. I began to hallucinate an image of Jeremy Capshaw. The man I'd been in love with. Crazy, dizzy in love.

I could see him vividly: an artist, poetically thin in paint-stained jeans, at work on one of his soot-colored canvases I thought revealed something dark and thrilling in his soul.

Another star exploded, and now it was Holly Bergen's face that I imagined. Holly, my best friend. Hauntingly beautiful, thick mahogany hair, a lithe dancer's body. Kind to everyone and all animals. I pictured us sharing that slummy Williamsburg apartment. The elevator, like a bad dog, rarely coming when it was called. Cockroaches so brazen they should have been on the lease.

The freezing Valentine's Day when the ancient boiler had finally given up the ghost. I saw the two of us huddled in coats in front of the stove. Holly reading my palm.

Oh my God, babe! You've got the longest heart line ever. It means you're going to find love everlasting. I could hear her bright looping laugh as she showed me her own palm. *Not like me. My heart line's just this skimpy little nothing.*

The scenes fast-forwarded. I was living with Jeremy now in his Bushwick loft. Lying on the futon on the floor after a long bout of lovemaking. My phone was ringing. A stranger's voice, an admitting nurse at New Mercy Hospital in Lowood.

My frantic dash to the hospital. The overworked young surgeon with black bags under her eyes. The x-rays had shown a huge mass lurking, like the deadly spider it was, on a lobe of my mother's right lung.

Mom lifting terrified eyes to me. *I want to go home, sweetheart. And promise never to make me come back here.*

Never. I promise, Mom.

The migraine was now reaching a peak. The zigging bands cascading, one after another. I pressed my fists against my eyelids, but the bands kept coming, and they brought more scenes from the past.

I was now spending all my weekends in New Jersey tending to Mom. Jeremy so understanding and me loving him the more for it. And then the mild weekend in March when Mom had rallied a bit and I had caught a crack-of-dawn Sunday train into New York. I would slip back into the loft and surprise him before he was awake.

The aliens were texting: *Idiot. You. Idiot.*

And now I was unlocking the door to our loft. Confused by the sight of two people in the kitchen. One naked except for boxer shorts. The other in the purple-and-gold kimono I'd brought back from Kyoto. The boxer shorts pressing against the kimono's back, hands inside the kimono's open lapels. The kimono writhing like a lizard. And then a sudden scrambling of limbs.

Holly running after me. *We didn't mean it to happen, babe. We didn't want to tell you until, you know, your mom . . .*

Until what? I hissed. *She dropped dead?*

The sting of my hand slapping her face. Her startled cry of pain. And the sound of a laugh. Jeremy laughing.

The migraine was diminishing now. The bursting lights began dimming, then blinked out. The streaming bands of zigzags—those messages from Mars—were fading away.

I sat up. I still felt jittery and unsettled.

I'd suppressed thinking about this for almost a year. Somehow the encounter with Evan Rochester had stirred it all back up.

Poor little orphan girl.

I'd never told Mom what had happened with Jeremy, but my broken heart must have oozed something poisonous, because she sank rapidly after that. By June, she had withered beyond recognition. Her skin was the color of an old candle stub, the flesh almost completely melted away. Her nose, once so cute and snubby, became a tiny sharp bone, like a parakeet's beak.

One day at the end of September, I held a glass of tepid water to her lips and guided the straw. She took a sip. "Joanne," she had murmured.

"It's not Joanne, Mom," I said. "It's me, Jane."

She shook her head. "A letter came. Once. For Jane."

"A letter? From Aunt Jo, you mean?"

"Her handwriting. Her *r*'s always looked like *s*'s."

"What did it say?"

"I didn't open it. Ripped it up. Threw the pieces down the toilet."

"Why, Mom?"

Another shake of her head. She drifted off to sleep. By evening, her breathing became harsh, each breath further and further apart.

I held her wasted hand in mine. Squeezed it tight. I imagined I felt the ghost of a pressure back.

"Please don't leave me, Mom," I begged her. "Please, don't go away."

She had let out a single gentle breath, like a sleeping baby's sigh.

And then I had been left all alone in the world.

My jitters finally subsided. I gave myself a mental shake.

Yes, I had been left an orphan, but I was hardly a child. There was nothing to pity me for. I shouldn't have betrayed any such feeling to Evan Rochester.

He had physical attractions. I had to acknowledge that. He had, after all, married one of the most beautiful women in the world. But he didn't attract me. That shock of whatever when he took my hand—I was just starved for physical contact.

I thought again about the complete absence of Beatrice Rochester in the Great Room. Or in any other room, except that one—the Ocean Room. Her favorite. A single white chaise.

Why has that been kept there?

There were secrets on this estate; I was certain of it. Secrets in that room.

And maybe I could uncover some of them. Find out what had actually happened to Beatrice the day she disappeared, all dressed up for their fourth anniversary. An audacious idea. But it gave me a thrill to imagine it.

I was exhausted. I went to get my nightshirt from the hook on the closet door.

It wasn't there. And yet I definitely remembered hanging it on the hook that morning.

I glanced reflexively at the glass doors. Something flickered.

Moonbeams, branches.

Only that. Nothing more.

BEATRICE

Thorn Bluffs, December 17
Late morning

A voice floats into my head. "Beatrice, your masseuse is here. She's set-ting up in the Ocean Room."

This voice is not in my head. It's on the intercom.

It's the boy with the golden spectacles.

You don't have any time, Mary whispers. *You need to get the blade. To get the blood. The plan.*

"Shut up, shut up!" I want a massage. I'm shaky and jumpy and afraid to do the plan.

"Something is the matter, Mrs. Beatrice?" Annunciata is here, come to take me to the Ocean Room.

Did she hack my thoughts, or did I say the words out loud? I can't think. The fog is too thick in my mind. But now I find new words.

"Nothing is the matter," I say to Annunciata. "I'm ready for you."

She walks with me down all the stairs to the room with the spar-kling light. The masseuse is there with her little table folded out. She has hair the color of rust and a chin with square corners.

"Good morning, Mrs. Rochester. My name is Brenda. How are you today?" The light from the big windows sparkles on her like lemon sprinkles.

I put my fingers together, pointed upward. Praying hands.

She makes praying hands back to me. Then she fluffs a white towel and holds it up for me to hide behind. I don't need to hide. I untie my silk robe and let it slip silky to the floor. I walk naked and lie facedown on the massage table.

The towel settles over my bottom. Brenda offers a little bottle for me to sniff. "This lotion contains two essential oils. Coriander and bitter orange."

I inhale an edible scent. My mouth feels as dry as stale crackers.

"Are you good with this one, Mrs. Rochester?"

I find the words to say. "Yes, thank you."

My eyelids fall shut like shutters as cool lotion pools over my shoulders and then down the long dip of my back. Fingers, hands kneading deeply.

The towel rises, and I roll over onto my back and the towel descends, covering my nipples and my belly button and my vagina. More lotion, Brenda works my feet, my special long feet. I'm a cat, purring. She is kneading and stroking, springing sensations up from my high arches.

I hear a voice outside. The boy with the golden spectacles who cooks for us now. He's scolding one of the little dogs.

He's out of the kitchen, Beatrice, Mary Magdalene whispers in my mind: *Go there now!*

No. The sensations of the massage are too lovely.

Get a frigging move on it, you silly twat!

I sit up and brush off the towel, and I swing myself off the table. "That's all."

"But we're not finished yet. Don't you want to finish the session?" Brenda's voice is wobbly. She's afraid she won't be called again.

I pick up my robe and slide it on. I can feel the rusty waves of her worry rippling over me.

Hurry, Beatrice!

I go quick up the stairs. My heart beats fast. I stop just before the kitchen, listening hard, but there is nothing but the patter of a little dog and the sound of the dishwashing machine. I keep on going into the kitchen, and a dog wags up to me. Hermione. The one with the fake leg.

My jailer is crafty. He gave her the new leg. He wants everyone to think he's a very kind man.

I move past Hermione and pull at the long drawer that holds the knives. But it won't open, even when I pull harder. It's locked up tight. And so are all the drawers and the cabinets, all locked up.

Your jailer hides the sharp things now, Mary reminds me. *So you can't defend yourself.*

I feel a scream rise up. It gurgles in my throat. At the same time, I hear the dishwashing machine gurgle water down the drain. I walk quick to it and pull down the door, and steam blooms hot in my face.

There are footsteps coming into the pantry room from outside. Quick, quick, I grab at a silver gleam, a knife, and then I shut the dishwasher door and go to the refrigerator. I open it up.

"Hey, Beatrice. Want something to eat?"

It's the boy with the spectacles. Not a very young boy, not beautiful. Thorny, pointed hair, and his eyes are milky blue. "Want me to make you something? No trouble."

I reach for a nectarine. I bite it. It has gone a little soft, and the juice dribbles down my chin. I close the refrigerator door and turn around.

The boy's eyes behind the golden spectacles go all circles. His mouth forms a big pink O. He spins on the balls of his feet and scampers away like a scared puppy.

And now here is Braidy Lady. "Señora!" she cries out, and her eyes are also wide and staring.

My robe is hanging open. Is that it? I don't care. When I am back-stage changing outfits, I am often naked, changing from panties to a thong. *Hurry, Beatrice,* my dresser hisses. I change from a bustier to braless. I am naked, and so are the other girls, and the boys, too, and nobody cares at all.

Annunciata takes the ends of the belt and ties them tight around me.

The Jacuzzi, Beatrice, Mary whispers. *It makes the blood flow faster.*

"Please turn on the Jacuzzi," I say to Annunciata. "Very hot, please."

"I do, Mrs. Beatrice. Come upstairs with me."

I go with her, feeling the sharp point of the knife in my robe pocket prick against my thigh. She doesn't find it.

She doesn't know it's there.

SIX

Madder music and stronger wine.

They were the first words that came to me when I woke up the next morning. What Evan Rochester had said when I came into the Great Room. "I called for madder music, stronger wine." I washed, dressed. Consumed a muffin while standing in the kitchenette and took coffee to my computer. Typed the line in the search box.

A poem by a Pre-Raphaelite poet named Ernest Dowson about a man obsessed with his dead lover. He parties hard, trying to forget her, dances and drinks and flings roses with abandon. But when the partying is over and he's alone in the dead of night, he realizes that in his soul he still belongs only to his dead and gone love, Cynara.

I have been faithful to thee, Cynara! in my fashion.

Could that be Rochester? Was he still obsessed by the dead and gone Beatrice? Even—or perhaps especially—if he had caused her death?

But he kept no sentimental mementos.

The net connection remained pretty strong, so I googled *Evander Rochester.* Thousands of results. The first pages dominated by the events of last December 17. I clicked on an article from the *San Francisco Examiner.*

Rochester's statement. He'd been dressing to go out to dinner to celebrate their anniversary. Heard his dogs making a commotion and went out to the deck. Saw his wife on the cove about seventy feet below, wearing a sapphire-blue cocktail dress. Watched her begin wading into the dangerous surf. He raced down and dived in after her, but he was too late. He found one of her shoes—a high-heeled sandal—on the beach. All that was left.

I pictured it. The famous beauty in a cocktail gown walking purposefully to her death in a cold gray sea. Leaving one shoe, like Cinderella, behind.

I continued reading. A gardener on the estate (*Hector!*) cited as a witness. He had hurried down to the beach but got there only after Mrs. Rochester was gone.

A brother, Richard McAdams of Miami, Florida, had released a statement: "My sister was not suicidal. She had a bipolar condition, but it was controlled by medication. Her husband mentally and physically abused her, and I can and will produce evidence that this is true. He killed her for her money, to keep his financial speculations afloat. That will also be proved."

I searched for evidence of the proof in future articles. Either the police had kept it confidential, or the brother hadn't produced it.

There had been extensive land and sea searches for the body, but it was never found. Or anything else to definitely pin the murder on Rochester. Or even offer proof that it *was* a murder.

So maybe Otis was not covering up anything. His cousin was innocent.

And could be, in fact, still fixated on his wife.

The net failed, then strengthened. I googled *Beatrice McAdams*. Millions of hits. I clicked on her wiki bio on the first page.

Born Beatie June McAdams. Meth head mom. Unknown dad. Got shuttled in and out of various foster homes in the Florida Panhandle. Discovered at fourteen by a photographer at a middle school swim meet. (*A swimmer. Interesting.*) Modeled locally for a couple of years, then signed with Elite, changing her name to the more uppity-class "Beatrice." With her older brother, Richard, as guardian, moved to Manhattan and launched a hugely successful career. Over the next ten years, on and off the list of most highly paid models in the world (three times on the cover of *Sports Illustrated*, tying with Christie Brinkley but two fewer than Elle Macpherson).

I skipped down to the description of her increasingly erratic behavior. Kicked off a Virgin flight for spitting on an attendant. Chucked a bread plate at a waiter in a South Beach restaurant (eight stitches, lawsuit, settlement). Deliberately tripped another model, a young Russian girl, on a runway (chipped tooth, broken nose, lawsuit, settlement).

Dropped by Elite, dropped by two lesser agencies. Then dropped out of the scene.

I pulled up a YouTube video—Beatrice on the *Today Show*, giving Hoda tips on applying mascara. Her voice a half pitch higher than I'd imagined, a backwater twang sometimes sneaking in. Another YouTube video: Beatrice on a catwalk early in her career. Her distinctive walk—the Beatrice McAdams cheetah walk, it was called. Slightly predatory, always ready to pounce.

And, yes, she was exquisite—but there was already something a touch deranged about her. That walk. The forward jut of her head. A too-bright gleam in her eyes. I felt it was just this bit of crazy that gave her an edge over dozens of other gorgeous girls. It was impossible to take your eyes off her.

A knock at my door. "It's me," called Sophia.

I got up and opened the door. She stood slouched, her tennis duffle slung over her shoulder. Her face, pale beneath her tan, was scrubbed of the bruised-looking makeup. Her hair, freshly washed and not quite dry, looked like poured maple syrup. She could almost have been a different girl.

"Did you tell my dad?" she said.

"No, I told you I wouldn't. But he guessed anyway from the way you looked."

"So was he mad?"

I measured my words. "More like concerned. You can't blame him, can you?"

"Is he gonna send me away? I mean, like, right away?"

"No. Why would you think he would?"

She shrugged, joggling the duffle. "He doesn't want me here. He tried to pay St. Mag's to keep me there. My school, St. Margaret? But it shuts down in summer, so they couldn't." She peered over my shoulder. "Can I come in?"

I opened the door wider, and she loped into the room. Long limbed, athletic, like her father. Her eyes shot to the wildflowers she had picked, drooping now over the rim of the glass. "I knew they'd die," she said.

"They were still fresh when I got here. That's what counted."

She glanced around the room. "Don't you get scared all by yourself down here?"

"I did a little the first night. But in the morning it seemed ridiculous. I'm not really that far from the house."

"I'd be scared." She plunked herself down on the unmade bed.

I straddled my one chair. "I'm looking forward to our sessions," I said. "What level French are you at?"

"Second year. But I suck at it. Earth science is easy—I only got an incomplete because I didn't take the final. Algebra, I just never studied, so that's the only reason I flunked it."

"Algebra? Am I doing that with you as well?"

"Yeah, it's one of the makeup classes I'm taking."

Otis had found it convenient not to mention that. I'd have to brush up on it quickly. "I'm pretty fluent in French," I said. "I spent sophomore year of college at the University of Lyons, with a family there."

"So can you tell me how to say the word *skank*?"

"*Skank*? Like, as in *skanky*?'"

63

"Yeah. There's this girl at the tennis clinic—she's always making remarks about my dad and Beatrice. She doesn't care if it's true or not. And she pretends she's expert in French. So I want to call her a skank in French and see if she gets it."

"Okay, well . . . *putain* is a good word for it. Or you could say *salope*, but that really means 'bitch.' You could use them both. *Putain de salope*."

She tested the words. "*Putain de salope*. Okay, thanks." She placed her palms behind her, rocked back on them. "So what was your TV show about?"

"You can watch it on Netflix. It was kind of Gothic, if you like that."

"We had to read *Wuthering Heights* last year in English. That's a Gothic romance novel, isn't it?"

"The greatest, in my opinion. Did you like it?"

"Kind of. I skipped a lot because the writing was archaic." She shot me a glance to see if I knew the word. I remained deadpan. "Plus it was kind of gross in some parts. Like when the guy, what's his name . . . ?"

"Heathcliff?"

"Yeah. Like when he digs up Cathy's coffin so he can look at her after she's been dead for years? And then he breaks off part of her coffin, so that when he gets buried next to her, they can rot together. Gross, right?"

"I guess I'd call it horrific. But it's not the part most people remember. They respond to the great passion between Cathy and Heathcliff. How his love for her obsessed him even long after her death."

"Yeah, but . . . like, rotting? Wouldn't he be better to want their spirits to mix together instead of their guts?"

I grinned. "Okay, you're right. The rotting thing is gross."

She returned a small smile. "Can I ask you something?"

"Sure. Anything."

"Do you think my dad killed Beatrice?"

I glanced at her quickly.

"It's what everybody says, right?"

"I don't know. I'm new around here."

"Yeah, but it was all over the net and everything." She chewed her upper lip. "I don't think he did it. I think he's still madly in love with her and waiting for her to come back."

Like the lost and gone Cynara. I said, "What makes you think so?"

"He keeps all her things exactly the way they always were. Like, in her bedroom and her closets."

I couldn't help asking, "Beatrice had her own bedroom?"

"Yeah. All her clothes are still there. She used to have this girl named Kendra who brought her stuff to try on? But she'd scream at her, calling her a bitch and the *c* word because she said Kendra was bringing her fat sizes. So Kendra quit. And Beatrice started driving up to Silicon Valley, the fancy malls up there? She'd come back with all this designer stuff in teeny-tiny sizes. I can't wear it. Maybe you could."

The idea sent a chill through me. "I doubt it. She was a lot taller than me."

"She was five feet ten. An inch more than me. But she bought, like, size *minus* two. And now it all just sits there with the price tags still on. Plus all her jewelry too. I borrowed these." Sophia flipped a thick lock of hair behind one ear to reveal a dazzling diamond hoop.

"Oh my God, Sophia! Are you allowed to take them?"

"Nobody said I can't. And she didn't want them. There was this one night when I was first here? She was up on the deck outside her room and throwing all her jewelry off of it. Until my dad made her stop, and then Hector climbed down the cliffs and got some of it back. But there's still some left out there."

I pictured emeralds, rubies, diamonds glimmering like dewdrops amid the gray-green vines. "You need to put those earrings back. And you should ask your father before taking anything."

"I always put it back. And he's okay with it."

I wondered what else she might have borrowed. I flashed on my vanished nightshirt. "Sophia . . . by any chance, did you come by here last night? Wanting to talk or something?"

"No. Why? Did Otis say that?"

"No. I just had a feeling somebody had been here."

"Maybe it was me sleepwalking. My mom used to sometimes. She took pills before she went to Africa so she wouldn't get malaria, and they made her sleepwalk."

"She sounds like an amazing person. What was her name?"

"Bethany. It's my middle name too."

"Pretty name. Do you have photos of her?"

She pulled out her phone. Scrolled rapidly. Handed it to me.

A video of a woman not much older than me. Lovely round face, red hair a shade darker than Sophia's. She'd probably have preferred to be ten pounds slimmer. She was on a lakefront beach, wearing a polka dot one-piece, and she was trying to hide her thighs, crossing her arms over them, and she was shrieking but laughing, too, in that way all moms do: "You rat, stop! You promised—put that thing away! I'll get you for this!" and off camera Sophia was giggling helplessly.

I felt my heart break in two.

An elephant trumpeted. Her text tone. She snatched the phone back. "Otis. He's in the car. He gets perturbed if I'm even, like, two seconds late."

"Okay, go. I'll pick you up later."

"You don't have to. I'm going over to my friend Peyton's house for dinner, and then her brother's going to drive me home."

"What about our lesson?"

"Oh crap, yeah. I forgot. Tomorrow." She started to leave.

"Wait," I said emphatically. "After today, no more skipping sessions. No excuses. I mean it, Sophia."

"*Okay*, I won't," she said and shuffled out the door.

My text began pinging. Three emoji texts from Otis. Begging forgiveness for lying to Evan.

Weepy cat emoji.

Speak-no-evil monkey emoji.

Assortment of weepy cat, wailing baby, eye-rubbing teddy bear, hangman's noose, and (bribe offer?) chocolate chip cookie emojis.

I texted back: Ok forgive u. Don't pull anything like that again.

Won't. Swear to god.

He texted again. Don't forget about dogs. Crazy busy now but come later and will show u feeding and shit.

Ok.

I returned to my computer. Closed the window on Beatrice's bio. Looked up a local mobile groomer—Pampered Pooch—and scheduled them to come here at the end of the week. I researched a good vet on Yelp and made a series of appointments for all five dogs, beginning with the wheezing bulldog.

Then I began to prepare for tutoring. I ordered *Algebra for Dummies* and *Let's Review Earth Science* from Amazon and downloaded a thirty-minute lesson (twenty minutes to download with iffy Wi-Fi), "Beginner Algebra." A woman fluting equations in a reedy voice. I took copious notes. Then I browsed new Wi-Fi routers and ordered an inexpensive plug-in, which might at least give a little boost to my connection.

I lunched on the remains of my breakfast provisions. Jet lag began to creep up. *Yoga,* I thought. I googled *yoga Carmel-by-the-Sea.* Impressive variety. Every type from Bikram to something called aura healing. Much as my aura could have used a good tweaking, I decided on a Vinyasa class at three fifteen, walk-ins welcome. I wriggled into yoga clothes, stuffed a towel into my tote. Texted Otis I'd be right up to talk about the dogs. I headed up to the house.

All morning, I'd caught sounds of activity from the compound, and now the motor court was jam-packed. A FedEx truck was backing out. A green van disgorged men and women wearing orange shirts and bearing cardboard boxes. I passed a flatbed truck with the Harley Davidson mounted on it and nodded to a hairy guy securing it with chains.

Otis came out the side door, looking even more harried than usual. His Daft Punk T-shirt was wrinkled, and his gold-framed glasses sat askew. "What's going on?" I said.

"Ev's setting up his new HQ in the guesthouse. I'm manning the front gates. God forbid anybody gets in who's not supposed to." He led me inside to an enormous pantry, gave me a quick rundown on dog foods, then showed me their various water and food bowls in the connecting service porch.

A tall vase with several dozen tightly furled white tulips encased in green cellophane sat by the door. "Nice flowers," I said.

"Yeah, for Ev. Somebody spent a bundle. They should go to the office, but I can't leave here." He eyed me hopefully.

"I'll take them. I'm just heading out to a Vinyasa yoga class in Carmel. Where's the office?"

"The path going behind the garage. Follow the delivery guys." He picked up the vase and thrust it into my arms. "Huge help, thanks."

I balanced the heavy cylinder in my arms, cellophane tickling my nose, and went back to the motor court. I followed one of the orange shirts down a gravel path to a small house that echoed the glass-and-stone architecture of the main house.

Inside, more frenetic activity. Walls being knocked down to create one open space. Orange shirts everywhere, uncoiling thick snakes of cable, setting up various devices. The reek of fresh paint. Bam! went a hammer. A drill snarled. Somebody fiddled with music like some manic Spotify station switcher.

I looked quickly around. He wasn't there.

Am I relieved or disappointed? Relieved, of course. I had promised to keep out of his hair, and here I was already invading his office.

I headed to a relatively uncluttered desk, stepping over cables as adroitly as if I were back on the *Carlotta Dark* set, and put the vase between a power drill and an open carton of soba noodles.

"You. Jane!"

The voice came from on high. I looked up with a start.

He was balanced on the top rung of a ladder, fiddling with a track of LED lights. "Stay there."

My heart sank. I watched him climb down the ladder, still favoring his injured ankle. He'd trimmed the wild-man-of-the-mountain beard, and his black curls now cleared the frayed collar of a white Oxford shirt. It made him look ten years younger.

He unhooked a Bluetooth from behind his ear. Glanced at the vase. "Did you bring this?"

"Yes," I said. "But it's not from me. It was delivered to the house."

He plucked a square white envelope attached to the cellophane. Slid out the card. A smile briefly played on his lips. He tossed the card on the desk.

I caught a glimpse: a single elegantly looped initial, handwritten in green ink. The letter *L*.

"So what do you think?" he said.

I glanced quickly up. "About what?"

He waved a hand. "All this. Will it do me for an office?"

"I suppose so. How many people will be working here?"

"None. My people will stay up in Los Gatos."

"So . . . just you?"

"Just me." That stare. I'd forgotten how unnerving it was.

I would not be unnerved. I met his stare. "Your business is investing in start-ups, right? Apps and things?"

"And things."

"Anything particularly interesting right now?"

"I think so."

"An app? Or . . . another thing?"

A quick smile. "A very other thing. A biotech start-up. A company called Genovation Technologies. We're developing biobased software for the application of producing clean industrial technologies."

"In English, please?"

His smile broadened. "It's a kind of green technology. To make simple plants like algae produce chemicals to replace those made by more toxic processes. For example, certain chemicals in perfumes and cosmetics."

"So I'll be dabbing algae behind my ears?"

"Not quite. It's on a molecular level. You wouldn't know the difference. But perfume would be just the start. There are hundreds of potential applications. Paint. Clean fuel for cars, planes. There's no limit, actually." His face became increasingly animated. "It will be great for the environment. For the planet. It could be a real game changer."

The way he spoke, with such passion: I felt another shock of that electric spark, and I turned my eyes away. "It sounds like a pretty good business."

"I'm betting on it," he said. "If it isn't, this all goes up in smoke."

"This office?"

"A lot more than that. Practically everything I've got." But it was clear he did not expect to lose the bet. He was that sure of himself.

Mariah Carey's helium-high notes suddenly pierced the air. "How's the treble, Mr. R.?" a male voice yelled. Mr. R. shot a thumbs-up, and the volume lowered.

And suddenly, as if having materialized out of thin air, a man was hovering near us. A small man with a weathered face beneath a wide-brimmed straw hat.

The famous Hector. Annunciata's husband.

The one who had also gone down to the cove the afternoon Beatrice purportedly walked into the water. But had gotten there too late to witness what had actually happened.

Evan began speaking to him—that underwater-sounding language I'd heard on the property the day before. My name swam by. Hector glanced at me with neither hostility nor friendliness. More like indifference: *you may be here, or you may not be—it's all the same to me.*

He concluded whatever mysterious business he'd had with his employer. And vanished as instantaneously as he'd appeared.

"What language was that you were speaking?" I asked Evan.

"Miskito. With a lot of Spanglish thrown in, mostly for my benefit."

"Is that the writing on your tattoo?"

His eyes narrowed. "What?"

"The tattoo on your arm."

He glanced at his forearm with a frown. "No. This is nothing. Gibberish." He picked up his Bluetooth.

"Wait, one other thing," I said. "I've been driving the Audi. I had a rental car, but . . . well, it got returned to Alamo by mistake. I'll lease another car right away."

"Something wrong with the Audi?"

"God, no. It's a sensational car. It's just that . . . well, I didn't know it belonged to your wife."

"It's leased under my name. You're not grave robbing, if that's what you're thinking."

I flushed angrily.

"It needs to be driven. If nothing else to keep rats from making nests in the engine. Drive the damned thing." He rehooked the Bluetooth behind his ear and made his way back to the ladder.

I turned and marched to the door, torn between anger and confusion. There seemed something so cold about the way he'd spoken about the Audi. It was just a car, okay, but wouldn't a grieving spouse feel a little sentimental about it? And talking so flippantly about grave rob-bing . . .

He wasn't longing for his wife to come back, like the lost Cynara. He had already shrugged her off.

Except Sophia said he kept all her clothes and jewelry intact in her room. She thought he was still madly in love with her and was hoping—maybe even expecting—her to come back.

It was a puzzle. An intriguing as much as an infuriating one.

And I felt more determined than ever to find out what I could about what had really happened last December.

I got into the Audi, carefully closing the door, as if slamming it would desecrate Beatrice's memory. I started the engine—protecting it from rats' nests. As I backed out, I nearly clipped an old brown pickup truck parked haphazardly behind me, and I braked hard, causing some-thing to roll out from under the front seat.

A lipstick in a gold tube.

I uncapped it. A pale and shimmering shade of lavender.

One that would perfectly complement a beautiful woman with green eyes and silver-blonde hair. With a shiver, I tossed it into the glove compartment.

L is for lipstick, I thought.

So who was the *L* who'd spent a bundle on a vase of still tightly furled tulips?

It was a letter I decided I didn't like at all.

The Audi was sensational. I raced ten, fifteen miles per hour above the speed limit, passing slower cars with a whisper of a tap on the gas pedal. The landmarks on Highway 1 were already beginning to seem familiar. Mama and baby wild-pig crossing. Farm stand advertising a yucky combo: **GARLIC CHERRIES LIVE BAIT**. The Esalen Institute where you steeped in hot tubs naked with strangers. I sang along with Adele on the radio, belting out the lyrics.

As I crossed the vertiginous span of the Bixby Creek Bridge, a vehicle driving in the opposite direction pulled a U-turn and elbowed into my lane several cars behind. The driver was either drunk or insane. Horns blared.

The vehicle began swooping around the cars ahead of it. More furious horns. It swerved in directly behind me. *Idiot!* I glanced in the rearview mirror.

A Range Rover. Metallic blue.

I felt a tick of alarm. It came up closer on my tail. I glanced again in the mirror, glimpsed light-blonde hair, large dark glasses. I increased my speed to the exit to Carmel-by-the-Sea and merged onto Rio Road. The Range Rover turned as well and surged fast up behind me, almost ramming my bumper.

"Crazy bitch!" I muttered.

She stayed close on my tail as I continued on Rio Road. The Carmel Mission appeared on the left, and I veered hard onto the bordering road. I heard a thud and a scrape of metal behind me. I looked back: the Range Rover had clipped a concrete parking curb and jolted to a stop. *Good!*

I circumnavigated the Mission to Dolores Street and sped toward the center of town. But after several blocks, I pulled over. I shouldn't be running away.

The crazy thought flashed in my mind again: *Beatrice.*

And maybe she hadn't meant harm to me but was frantic to impart some vital information. Or to implore me to save *her* from harm.

Ridiculous. *Still*, I argued to myself, *I should find out for certain*. I turned around and drove back to the Mission.

The Range Rover was gone. And so was my chance to confront the driver.

My GPS was still calmly recalculating the best route to the Prana Yoga Studio. I followed its instructions to a neighborhood on the west side of Carmel, a yellow-shingled bungalow on a mostly residential street. I pulled into the packed-dirt parking area in front.

The Range Rover cruised up to the curb across the street.

I drew a breath. Waited a moment to see what would happen. Nothing. It simply sat there, engine idling.

What does she want?

I tentatively opened my door. Then, more resolutely, I got out and began to stride across the street.

The driver's door of the Range Rover cracked open. A tall, slender figure with pale-blonde hair climbed out. My pulse pounded. But it wasn't Beatrice McAdams Rochester.

It wasn't even a woman.

SEVEN

"Why are you driving my sister's car?" The blond man came closer to me, his fists slightly clenched, body spring-loaded.

"You're her brother!" I exclaimed.

The resemblance to Beatrice Rochester was startling. Same luxuriant silver-blond hair (his slightly receding in dagger shapes at the temples). Same perfect bone structure and willowy build. Like Beatrice, his skin was pale, almost translucent, his lips delicately etched.

"I'm Richard McAdams," he declared. "Answer my question. Who are you, and where did you get my sister's car?"

I was truly getting tired of uncivil men. "It was lent to me," I said coldly.

"Who lent it to you? Evan Rochester?"

"As a matter of fact, yes."

"Why?"

"Because I'm staying at Thorn Bluffs and I needed a car."

"Are you sleeping with him?"

I flushed with deep anger. "What?"

"You heard me. I want to know if you're sleeping with my sister's husband. It's a straightforward question. Yes or no?"

"It's none of your business."

"My sister was murdered at Thorn Bluffs. Everything that goes on there is my business."

The bluntness of his statement gave me a moment's pause. "That has nothing to do with me. And I don't know for sure that she was murdered."

He took a belligerent step closer. "My sister was bipolar, but her meds kept her stable. It was not a fucking suicide." He slid his dark glasses to the top of his head. His eyes were a more amber-tinged facsimile of his sister's. "What's your name?"

"Again, none of your business. And you could have got us both killed. You were driving like a maniac. You followed me once before, and if you ever do it again, I'll call the police."

His lips compressed so firmly they lost color. Then his eyes darted behind me, and his expression made a lightning change from menacing to benign. "Namaste, ladies," he called out.

I turned. Two women of late middle age, both toting rolled yoga mats, were heading into the studio. "Namaste," one called back pleasantly.

And now, with visible calculation, Richard McAdams tried another tack with me: his eyes softened; his mouth assumed a boyish smirk. "Look, I can see your point. My fault for overreacting. It was seeing her car yesterday at the club, another woman driving it. It was a tremendous shock to me. And I was actually just on my way to Thorn Bluffs when I saw you go by, and it was just as much a shock as yesterday." His eyes flicked briefly back across the street, this time to the Audi. "The car is one of a kind, you know. The paint was customized for Beatrice when she bought it. Sapphire blue, her favorite color."

"I thought it was leased," I said.

"No, bought and paid for by my sister. And again, I'm sorry if I got reckless. I lost my head." He was oozing with contrite charm now.

"I don't blame you one bit for being angry. Some maniac chasing you all over town, right? Tell you what. Why don't we start all over again?" He removed a leather card holder from inside his jacket and, with an almost sleight-of-hand motion, slipped out a card. "I'm Rick McAdams. How do you do?"

I glanced at the card: RICHARD MCADAMS ATTORNEY-AT-LAW. A mobile number. A Miami address. "What kind of law do you do?"

"Trusts and estates. Wills and the like."

"In Miami?"

"No, I've moved here. I'm not actually practicing at the moment." He waved off my attempt to return the card. "Please, keep it. And you are . . . ?"

"Jane," I said simply.

"Great to meet you, Jane. And again, let me apologize. My sister and I were extremely close, and her loss still seems very recent to me. The idea of another woman already taking her place . . ." A forlorn shake of his shoulders.

"I haven't taken her place," I conceded. "I'm not with Evan Rochester. I'm a friend of Otis Fairfax, who works for him. Otis arranged for me to use a cottage there for the summer."

"Oh, Otis. Sweet guy. So you're on vacation in Big Sur? Lovely."

"Not exactly a vacation."

He gave me a questioning look. I ignored it. "Listen, Jane, why don't you let me buy you a drink? To make amends. I know a place near here that makes the best mojito in town. Tinker's, I'll give you the cross streets." His charm had become effusive. "Did you know that in the town of Carmel proper there are no street numbers? We just use cross streets. It keeps us quaint."

He was used to women melting in his presence. And he was astonishingly handsome, a slender build enhanced by expensive clothes—well-cut seersucker jacket, white linen pants. But despite his beauty, there was something repulsive about him. Slithering. Like some bottom-feeding creature on the ocean floor.

"It's a little early for drinking," I said. "And I have a yoga class. I'm going to be late."

"Then after. I'll wait. We really need to talk, Jane. If you're staying at Thorn Bluffs, there are things you need to know." He lowered his tone. "Evan Rochester is a monster. He abused my sister. He beat her. He threatened her life, and then he took it. I'll explain it to you."

I hesitated. His tone intensified. "So what do you say? After yoga?"

I was suddenly no longer in a frame of mind for Vinyasa. I didn't trust him, but I was intensely curious to hear what he had to say. "Okay, let's go now. I'll follow you."

He led me about a mile to a restaurant in a small clapboard house tucked down a cobblestone alley. I circled several blocks to find a parking space. By the time I got to the restaurant, he was already at a table for two. He waved energetically with both hands over his head, as if I needed to locate him through a dense crowd, though the dining room was almost empty.

"Mojitos coming up," he said. "I took the liberty of ordering. Hard to find a parking spot? Tourist season. I hate it like poison."

A young waitress set frosty glasses in front of us. Rick's amber eyes twinkled up at her. "Thanks, love." She simpered a little in the bright beam of his charm.

He directed himself back to me. At this close distance, he looked less handsome. More shopworn. Like an overused marionette, head jerking slightly this way and that, as if pulled by invisible strings.

"So what are these things I need to know?" I said.

He plucked both mint sprig and lime slice from the rim of his glass. Took a deliberately long sip. Keeping me in suspense. "You should know who you're dealing with, Jane," he said. "For your own protection, if nothing else."

"You think I'm in some kind of danger?"

"Maybe yes, maybe no. But I *can* tell you that Evan Rochester is a sociopath. He's got absolutely no conscience. No regard for the feelings or needs of others. He can be charming if it suits him. But he'll do whatever it takes to get what he wants. And if it destroys somebody . . . he'll feel no remorse." Rick's face now loomed a little closer to mine. "My sister lived in terror of that man, Jane. He threw her down a steep flight of stairs. I saw the bruises, Jane. Her broken ribs. Her beat-up face."

I shuddered.

"Did you know, Jane, that he had her locked up in a mental institution?"

"I know she'd been hospitalized. It's no secret. You said yourself she was bipolar."

"Yes, but even after she was stabilized on meds, he kept her shut up in that place. God knows how long she'd have been there if I hadn't made some calls to get her out. Of course, now I regret doing it. I can't help thinking maybe . . ." His voice broke. "Maybe if I hadn't, she might still be alive." His eyes misted, turning them a shade more like his sister's. "When she came back, that monster kept her locked up. Drugged and isolated. Even from me. Like she was his prisoner. Shut off from the world."

I looked at him dubiously. "There were quite a few people working at Thorn Bluffs back then."

"All under his strict control. That couple, the Sandovals? They acted as her keepers." His head jerked one way, then the other. "She was terrified he was going to kill her, and finally he did."

"Why haven't you told this to the police?"

"I have, of course. But sociopaths like Rochester can lie more convincingly than most of us can tell the truth. He had easy explanations for everything. She was suicidal. She threw herself down the stairs. *She* was the one who got violent." He squeezed his eyes shut for a moment, overcome with emotion.

My throat felt suddenly tight. I took a long swallow of the mojito. "So you're accusing Evan Rochester of being a sociopath wife beater who went too far and finally killed her."

"Oh no, not like that. He's one cool customer. He planned the whole thing. Staged that first so-called suicide attempt as an alibi, so when he actually did murder her, he'd get away with it."

"And you have proof of that?"

"It's the only explanation that fits. It would guarantee him getting all the money. You see, Beatrice wanted to divorce him. Like I told you, she was terrified of him." He leaned ever closer, battered puppet's face looming just inches from mine. "You know about this biotech company he's invested in?"

"A little. He said it would be great for the environment."

"Also great for his wallet. He's a gambler by nature. He's won big, but other times he's lost just as big. This time he's bet it all. And he's on the edge of going bust." His face was now so close I could smell his lime-scented breath. I shrank back. "There was an earthquake about a year ago. It was five point three on the Richter scale. It ran right under this company's lab. Huge damage. The rollout of their process got pushed back another year. But in the meantime, Rochester had to keep paying on all his costs and loans. He was out of cash, so he borrowed against his assets. Thorn Bluffs. His house in San Francisco. Other properties."

"So?" I said.

"They were jointly owned by Beatrice. If she divorced him, he'd have had to buy out her half. The only way he could do that would be to sell off most of his stake in this company. Which he definitely did not want to do." Rick gave a bitter laugh. "You know how much he stands to make on this deal?"

"No idea."

"He's on the brink of getting enormous new funding. Once it comes through, this company will be valued at about six billion dollars. Rochester will personally pocket several hundred million."

A billion. Hundreds of millions. The numbers bobbled through my mind like parade balloons.

"So you tell me," Rick continued. "Bankrupt versus filthy rich . . . is that worth killing for?"

Part of me just wanted to get miles away from this man and the things he was saying. But a greater part of me was eager to know more. "Assuming any of this is true, how do you think he killed her?"

"My guess? He drugged her into unconsciousness. Carried her down to the water. Held her under until he was sure no breath was left in her body."

"Or he could be telling the truth. She drowned herself."

A dismissive snort. "My sister was a competitive swimmer. We grew up in Florida, she practically lived in the water. She was like a mermaid. She couldn't have drowned herself, even if she tried." His head jerked, puppet on a string. "No, Jane, there's only one way she could have drowned. If he did it. Though, of course, he might have killed her some other way. And then got rid of her body."

I let my eyes fix on a painting on the wall above his head. A pastel of an upholstered chair, a white blouse flung over one of its arms. As if a woman had meant to come right back for it but never had.

"Did you know, Jane . . . ?" Rick's voice dropped to an insidious murmur. "Are you aware of the fact he's already begun to get my sister declared legally dead?"

I glanced back at him. "Really?"

"He filed with the court several weeks ago."

Could that be true?

"But you could help me, Jane. Help me get justice for my poor sister." He was irresistibly seductive now. Or trying to be. "The police still hold him under suspicion. They're as sure as I am he's guilty. But the DA will never file charges unless the evidence is airtight. You could help me get something."

I shook my head violently. "No."

He placed a hand on mine. "You're very pretty, Jane, you know that? You could use that with him. He's always had an eye for pretty girls."

I slid my hand out from under his.

"If you were nice to him . . . he's got an enormous ego. Under the right circumstances, if you were being extremely nice to him, he couldn't resist bragging to you." His murmuring voice was seductive, almost caressing, and it made my skin crawl.

I rose to my feet. "I'm sorry for your loss. But there's nothing I can do for you."

His face suddenly drained of any charm. His lips stretched in a bloodless grin. "You know, Jane, that if you do come across anything relevant, it makes you a material witness. You can and will be subpoenaed. And if you conceal anything, you will be charged with felony obstruction of justice."

"Thanks for the warning. And for the drink." I began to turn away.

"Your friend is already skating on very thin ice," he said.

I stopped. "Just to be clear. I hardly know Evan Rochester."

"I'm not talking about him. I mean your real friend, Otis Fairfax."

I felt a tremor of apprehension. "What has he done?"

"He lied to the police. About where he was that night. He could go to jail. I'd hate to see that, Jane. And I'd really hate the same thing happening to you." Rick raised his glass in a mocking salute.

I walked as fast as I could back to the Audi. I popped the glove compartment. I pushed the lipstick tube to the side and searched for the car's registration. There were two thick manuals and another folded document—the lease agreement from Audi Monterey for an Audi S5. The leaseholder was Evander Edward Rochester.

Rick had lied about Beatrice buying it. Evan had told the truth.

Obviously, I could not believe everything—or anything—Rick McAdams said. Including the thing about Otis being in jeopardy with the police. That was a bluff. Otis hadn't even been at Thorn Bluffs yet when Beatrice disappeared.

Or was he there? I tried to remember what he'd said: *I left that tapas place ages ago.* With Otis, "ages" could mean weeks or decades.

I called him. *Pick up, pick up . . .*

"Sup?" I heard traffic. He was in his car, the elderly Prius.

"It was her brother!" I said. "The person I told you who was following me."

"Huh? Whose brother?"

"Beatrice's. Remember? I told you I thought a blue Range Rover with a woman driving was tailing me? It wasn't a woman. It was Beatrice's brother, Richard McAdams."

"Whoa, wait. How did you find out?"

"Because he followed me again just now, and I just came from having a drink with him."

"Whoa," Otis repeated.

"Are you in your car? Where are you going?"

"Up to SF for the night. But so what'd he say, McAdams?"

"He's positive Evan murdered his sister. He says Evan beat her and then claimed she threw herself down the stairs. And then he locked her up in a mental hospital against her will. To make it look like she was suicidal so he could get away with murdering her."

"It's crap. That guy will say anything to get Beatrice's share of the estate. And listen, don't tell Evan about this. He hates that guy, and it could cause him to do something."

"Like what?" I said.

"I don't even want to imagine. Just don't tell him."

I paused a moment. "Otis . . . did the police ever question you about any of what happened?"

"Me? Uh, yeah. Once. Two detectives, a lady and a man. They asked me what I knew and where I was and that was that."

My heart sank. "I thought you were still living up in Oakland."

"No, I was already at Thorn Bluffs. But not actually *there* when Beatrice drowned, so they had no right to be up my ass."

"You made me think you'd never met her."

"I never *said* that. I mean, it was *like* I didn't know her. She was almost always upstairs or in the Ocean Room, and Annunciata was in charge of her. Sometimes she'd wander around, but she was always stoned on meds, and Annunciata would get her back to her room."

Rick McAdams's words: *That couple, the Sandovals, acted as her keepers.* "So would you say she was mostly kept shut in and cut off from talking to anybody?"

"Uh . . . I don't know. She was bonkers—she wasn't capable of anything."

"And afterward—after she drowned—when Evan was living up in his San Francisco house, did you stay here without him?"

"No. I went up too. Great house. Wish he didn't have to rent it out."

I sighed. "So is there anything you didn't tell the detectives? I mean purposely kept back from them?"

A tick of hesitation. My heart sank further.

"No. I was at this restaurant in SoMa, Alioso, like I told them. But the place was mobbed, so I guess that's why nobody remembers seeing me there. And, well, maybe I didn't stay as long as I told them."

Shit, shit, shit. "Are you covering something up?"

"I'm *not*. There was this girl—she had some flat in the Mission—so I went there, but then couldn't remember her name or exactly where she lived, so I just didn't say anything about her. I swear to God that's what happened."

Who were these gods that Otis swore to? Not ones who were sticklers for veracity. "We'll talk about this when you get back."

"I've told you everything."

"Yeah, okay," I said. But I doubted it.

What else wasn't he telling me? About his part in that day? About Beatrice?

BEATRICE

I am in the Jacuzzi now. It froths hot at my nipples.

Hot to make blood flow faster. For when I use the blade.

I take a very deep breath. I fill up my lungs to the very last cell. And then I slip down off the bench and keep sliding down, until my head is underwater. The jets are beating on my body. The sunshine forms crazy patterns through the bubbles, and it makes me remember the sea cave, where my jailer took me.

It was on the island of Barbados.

Yes. I remember. I had been there on a photo shoot.

It was for *Sports Illustrated*, the swimsuit issue. But I was not going to be on the cover.

"Sorry, babykins." Fiona from the agency made cooing sounds. "This year you're just one of the pack. Diversity's what they're after right now. No blondies for the cover."

They put me in a white one-piece swimsuit with cutouts, like a jigsaw puzzle of snow with missing pieces. I posed on white sand. "Arch your back, darling. More. Now give me fierce, darling. Yeah, that's it. Snarl fierce, Beatrice. Beautiful, most beautiful girl in the world."

And then I was back at the hotel, outside under big swooping sails, where there was a firepit, and that's when he arrived. He showed up with his starey eyes, and the other girls were twitter, twitter. Like baby birds with their beaks hanging open.

Why were they all atwitter? He was not a handsome man. His body was handsome, yes. He was a cat like me. He moved with stealth—like he had a gun slung at his hips—but he did not have a beautiful face.

Very stealthily, I took a photo of his face, and I sent it to Ricky. He texted me back. A player in Silicon Valley. Wins big but also loses big. Too risky BJ.

But I couldn't stop looking at him. And when I saw him watching me, I went to him. They had sprayed my body golden brown all over, and my hair was silver and gold, and my eyes were the color of the sea. I could tell he wanted me, and I wanted him too.

And the next day he took me to the sea cave. "Barbados is famous for them, Beatrice." He said that to me. "They're fantastic. It's like you can walk underneath the sea. I know one the tourists can't get to—it's on a friend's private beach. Do you want to come with me?"

I went with him to the sea cave, and we climbed down deep inside, and it was very beautiful. The sunlight came from far away, and it was like being in church, the light all misted, and there were twisty columns that came up from the bottom and also hung down from the top. They looked like the statues of saints.

I wanted to see all the saints, so I kept going deeper and deeper into the cave, until I went down a passage and it became black as night. I was very frightened, all alone in the dark, and I screamed loud, and I heard him shout my name. And then I felt him close. "Take my hand, Beatrice. Hold on to me." He wrapped up my hand in his. And he led me out of the darkness and back into the chapel, with the faraway light and the saints hanging upside down.

You loved him then. The voice of the very young one called Beatie June now rises up in my mind. *You loved him when he rescued you.*

Yes. I remember. And then he took me back to my room at the hotel with the swooping sails. I opened the door and left it open for him to follow. The bed in the room had a shimmery white net around it to keep away mosquitos, even though there were none at such a fancy hotel. But when I lay down on the bed, the shimmery mosquito net fell all around me, like the bridal dress on the catwalk.

Men are all the same. They can't come inside me quick enough. I part my long golden legs and arch my long back, and they moan like the ocean as it surges in and out from the shore.

But this one was not the same. He was tender and kind. "You've had a scare." He'd kissed me soft on my forehead and left me alone.

He put you in the dungeon. Mary's voice is loud in my head. *Now he wants you gone for good. You heard the words on his phone last night.*

My lungs are starting to hurt, but I stay under in the Jacuzzi. The sunbeams are hula dancing over my head. I need to rise.

But I keep remembering more about the island of Barbados.

EIGHT

There was a silvering in the air by the time I returned to Thorn Bluffs. Only a few vehicles remained in the motor court. An electrician's van. The battered brown pickup truck.

An unwelcome surprise in my cottage. My bed that I'd left rumpled was now made up military tight. My breakfast dishes were no longer in the sink. Every surface gleamed. Annunciata had been here with her Swiffer. I pictured that fierce figure washing my coffee mug, squaring the corners of my sheets. *Thinking what?*

There was a churchy scent in the air. It was coming from a lit candle on my bed table. A votive with a Hispanic Madonna hovering on a cloud.

It seemed funereal. I blew it out.

And the fashion magazines I'd heaped beside the bed were gone. Just to be tidy? Or to keep me from examining them too closely?

I'd bought some provisions at a deli on a street charmingly named Casanova. Turkey and swiss club. Tubs of assorted salads. Apples, peaches. An Argentinian Malbec from a bargain bin. I stuffed it all in my minifridge, except for the Malbec. I unscrewed the top and reached for a glass.

Bad idea: only four thirty and I'd already put down half a stiff mojito.

I went instead to my laptop and began checking out the things Rick McAdams had told me. There had been an earthquake last summer, 5.3 on the Richter scale, near Livermore, California, and it had caused major damage to several tech sites, including Evan's biotech venture, Genovation Technologies. A *Bloomberg* article confirmed that Evan launched a funding round a few months later to raise $350 million.

"Worth killing for." Rick McAdams's insidious words.

I found an item dated April 26 of last year on a gossip site: "Supermodel Beatrice McAdams treated at the Monterey, California, ER after an accident at her glamorous Big Sur estate."

An accident. No suggestion of self-harm or foul play.

So how could I know for sure?

I pictured Evan Rochester in his new office space. I wondered if his ankle still hurt like a son of a bitch.

I thought of his hand enclosing mine. The electric thrill that had shot through me. A similar thrill as I watched him describe his game-changing new tech. His passion for it animating his features.

"Sociopath." Rick's slithery, seductive voice back in my mind.

A wave of jet lag swept over me. I suddenly felt as lost and all alone as I had the night I'd arrived. I curled up on my newly made bed and fell into a deep sleep.

I slept for several hours. When I woke up, I stepped out onto my terrace to further clear my head. It was still daylight, but misty now, the ocean and the bluffs in soft focus. I glanced over at that strange medieval tower—the architect Jasper Malloy's drafting studio. It looked romantic in the mist. Off-limits, Otis had warned me. No one allowed to go in it.

Why? What could it be hiding?

There was a washed-out service road behind the cottage that appeared to lead in the tower's direction. I could go for a run. Get to the tower and back while it was still light. I felt suddenly compelled to do it. I went back inside. Put on running shoes and pulled a fleece over my yoga top and then launched myself onto the road.

It veered in a wide loop toward the highway. I soon realized running was impossible; large sections of the asphalt were eroded to ankle-snapping patches of rubble. I could only walk briskly. It would take longer than I had expected.

After about twenty minutes, a brown pickup truck came rattling from the opposite direction. Hector Sandoval at the wheel. I put a hand up in greeting.

He drove by without acknowledging me at all.

Where is he coming from?

I pushed myself to go farther. Wondered if it was too far, if I should turn back. But in about fifteen minutes, the road looped back toward the sea, and to my relief, the tower appeared ahead.

I approached it curiously. It was sited on its own promontory, a smaller and lower one than the compound was built on, and it looked even more mysterious up close. A crenellated top, like a crude crown. Thin vertical windows. The redwood base and windowsills were rotten, causing the entire structure to tilt. It creaked and groaned in the freshening breeze.

The door—heavy, wooden—wasn't locked. It opened to reveal a circular space crammed with a jumble of old furniture and artifacts. I stepped cautiously inside.

Bars of light from the narrow windows wriggled like sea snakes across the jumbled stuff. An odor of rot and mold and dust. The tilting floor made me slightly seasick, like being on a boat that was starting to capsize. There was furniture like the South American pieces in my cottage, made of once brightly painted wood. Gilt crucifixes and statues of saints. Blackened paintings of conquistadors. Rising in the center of all this clutter, a rusty spiral staircase that stopped in midair.

A staircase to nowhere.

I picked my way to the back. A metal drafting table thick with dust was set against the far wall. *Where Jasper Malloy died, alone and forgotten.* I pictured his body slumped over it. Decayed. Gnawed on by wild animals. I shuddered.

There were a few mildewed architectural drawings pinned to the wall above the table. Each labeled *Thorn Bluffs*, with a date in 1962. Renderings of the not-yet-built compound.

The tower did one of its groaning things. Startled, I stepped backward and kicked something on the floor. A thick glass goblet—the same type Evan Rochester had poured champagne into the night before.

I picked it up. Reddish-brown dregs in the bowl that smelled faintly of cherry. Not champagne. Some sort of liqueur. Or a kirsch?

I set the goblet back on the floor, and as I did, I spotted something pushed far back beneath a large armoire. Something obviously hidden from casual sight. I scrunched down to look.

A rectangular object, about three feet by four feet in size, tightly wrapped in a white drop cloth. Probably just another blackened conquistador. Except no, it wasn't covered with a layer of dust. It hadn't been there very long.

I wriggled it out and propped it up against the armoire. Took off the drop cloth.

I gasped.

A framed portrait of a young woman painted in the style of Modigliani. Cropped dark hair, a pale oval face crooked slightly to one side. Exaggeratedly long neck. But the image had been grotesquely mutilated. Eyes gouged into gaping black holes. Mouth slashed to a shrieking rictus. Furious slashes on the bodice and all around the sides of the painting.

It seemed personal—like whoever had done this had wanted to do it to the real-life girl in the painting.

And suddenly, I just wanted to get the hell out of there.

I rewrapped the painting in the drop cloth and shoved it back underneath the armoire. Then I bolted outside and continued walking fast onto the far point of the promontory. I stood inhaling the cleansing ocean air. Letting it clean out the dust and rot from my nostrils. The sight of that hideously mutilated portrait from my eyes.

The tide was ebbing: the surf sounded more like a moan than a roar. I gazed down at the small cove below. A deep and ragged U shape sealed off on both ends by gargantuan boulders. The mist had begun to roll in, making the cove seem completely isolated. Desolate.

But then, suddenly, the sparkle of a firefly. It twirled briefly in the mist before blinking off. It triggered a memory.

I was four or five. Sitting with Mom on the back stoop, watching tiny lights flash in the weeping willow.

"They're called fireflies, sweetheart."

"So are they all going to burn up?"

"No, silly Billy. It's not real fire. It's a light they turn on to let the other fireflies know they're looking for love."

Why did she blink out her own light so soon? Give up on real-life love? I felt a bubble of grief rise from my chest: *Why did you give up on love, Mom? Settle for pretend romance on a stage?*

As if in response, the firefly glimmered again.

And something struck me: there were no fireflies on the Pacific coast. They didn't exist west of the Rockies. I was pretty sure of that.

And even if it were a firefly, the spark would be too tiny to see from up here.

I kept my eyes fixed on it. And now there seemed to be a figure in the sparkle. Whitish. Like the figure I'd imagined outside my sliding glass door, this time moving slowly in the tiny light.

My pulse quickened.

A heavy gust of fog obscured my view, and when it passed, the glimmer was gone, and there was nothing down there at all. Nothing except sand laced with gray foam and glistening rocks and the heaving sea beyond it.

Nothing could have disappeared so quickly.

Nothing except a ghost.

I laughed at myself. Still writing stories in my mind.

The fog was rising at a rapid rate, and the temperature had plummeted at least ten degrees. I was suddenly cold. I hugged my arms around me, headed off the promontory. As I did, I heard a cry. Faint, as if reverberating up from the shore, but distinct nevertheless.

Like the shriek of a tortured soul.

And now I pictured that mutilated portrait of the girl, her mouth slashed into that hideous scream. It sent a shudder through my already agitated brain. I broke into a run, back onto the service road, stumbling on the patchy asphalt until the tower was no longer in sight behind me; then, panting, I slowed my pace.

Everything was fast becoming obscured by smoky fog. The pines and shrubs were now just flat silhouettes. Cutouts pasted in an album. The old road kept disappearing beneath my feet.

I thought of children in fairy tales, Hansel and Gretel. Lost in dark woods. Prey to witches, wolves, mythical beasts. And as I thought this, the black shadow of just such a mythical beast slithered out of the fog ahead. It came at me, crouched low on all fours.

And right behind it, another mythical figure, crooked, striding furiously, encased in its own unearthly light.

BEATRICE

My lungs are bursting, but I stay under in the Jacuzzi. And I remember more about the island of Barbados.

I remember how I took my jailer to my room the next night after he saved me from the sea cave. I took him into my bed, and we stayed there all night. Except very late that night I took my phone and crept out to the end of the hall. I sat down on a carpet made of coconut hair. I called Ricky in Miami where he was going to night school to become a lawyer.

I whispered to him. "I like this one, Ricky."

"Then you better get him fast, Beatie. Before he finds out your prognosis. He'll want a prenup, but we'll make him give you a wedding gift. Blue-chip art. Van Gogh. Modigliani."

"I'm out of snow white, Ricky. I sent you money, didn't I?"

"Yeah, got it this morning. I overnighted a canister to you."

I went back to the bed under the white veil. I stayed the next day with my jailer, and then another, and we hardly ever left the bed, but I kept the snow white in the tea canister from Ricky snug in the bottom of my tote bag.

And then a message on my phone from Fiona. "Where the fuck are you, Beatrice? Don't know what you're frigging up to and don't care. Hair and makeup tests start tomorrow. If you don't show, you've pulled your last stunt, swear to God."

I told my jailer I was supposed to be in Paris. "I'm booked to walk for Valentino and Alexander McQueen. You made me forget."

"I can get you there. It won't be a problem."

He made a phone call. He told somebody to charter a jet.

He was very happy—he liked saving me. And I loved him very much.

And for my wedding present we went to Paris again. We went to an auction house, and he made a gesture, a very small gesture, with his hand when a painting by Amedeo Modigliani came up for sale.

The painting of the girl.

Maybe I'll stay here under the Jacuzzi forever.

NINE

A magical beast and a hobgoblin. I didn't feel particularly afraid. More like fascinated. I stood raptly, waiting as they approached.

The beast resolved itself into Minnie, the female German shepherd. And the hobgoblin became Evan Rochester, walking swiftly but still with that hint of a limp, a pair of LED lights fastened around his neck. Minnie ran close circles around my feet, barking, and a moment later, Mickey appeared and joined her in keeping me tightly herded.

Evan strode furiously up to me. "I told you to stay out of the grounds."

"I thought if I kept to the road it would be okay."

"The road? There's nothing left of it. Can you even see it right now?"

"A little."

"A little. Christ almighty! In another fifteen minutes, the fog will be twice as thick. Do you have a flashlight?"

"No."

"Do you even have your phone?"

I shook my head.

"Do you have any idea how close we are right now to the edge of the bluff?"

The mumble and moan of the ocean suddenly seemed right beside us. I pictured that vertiginous drop. The tide sweeping me away.

"You could have easily wandered over the edge. Christ almighty God."

I felt light headed. "I didn't realize."

"You didn't realize," he repeated. "What the hell are you even doing out here?"

"I was just out for a quick run. Or walk, actually. It was still light when I started. I went a little too far. And then . . ." I hesitated. I decided not to mention the tower; he was too angry right now. "Then I stopped to watch a ghost."

He gave a violent start. "What?"

"Just something I thought I saw down on the cove. The one below the tower."

He seized me by the shoulders. "What did you see?"

"Let go," I said. "You're hurting me."

He immediately released his grip. "Tell me exactly what you saw."

"Nothing much, really. I was looking down from that other promontory. I saw something sparkle. A few sparkles of light. And for just a second, it seemed like there was something down there."

"Like what?"

"Like a whitish kind of figure. Walking on the beach. And then a patch of fog came swirling in, and when it cleared, there was nothing there. I'm sure there never had been anything."

He stared at me. His expression unreadable.

"It was just my imagination," I continued quickly. "I like imagining things like ghosts. I used to write about it." I kept my eyes fixed on his face. "But there couldn't have been anything. It was impossible, wasn't it?"

He didn't reply for a moment. "It's natural to see sparkles of light on the water. Bioluminescence. It makes the surf glow. And the fog can play tricks with your sight. I've seen things that seemed so real . . .

so real that sometimes I've had to stop myself from reaching out and trying to grab it."

Beatrice? Was it her ghost he imagined seeing in the fog? Wishing—or fearful—that I had seen her too?

"There was something else," I said. I watched him carefully. "I heard a sound, a strange sort of cry. Almost like a child screaming. I can't really describe it. But it gave me chills."

He paused again. "An owl. A barn owl. Their calls can sound almost human. Eerie if you've never heard them before. Or a juvenile great horned owl."

I nodded.

The fog continued to thicken around us, isolating us in the pool of light from his LEDs. He stared past me, silent, lost in some dark mood, as if forgetting I was even there. The dogs milled restlessly, waiting for a further command.

I became aware once again of his intense physicality. His height. The breadth of his shoulders. The power of his musculature. The rage had faded from his face, and I no longer felt threatened. Just the opposite, I realized. I felt protected.

I moved a small step closer to him. "How did you know I was out here?"

"Hector. He saw you."

"Does he always report everything to you?"

"Pretty much, yeah."

"And Annunciata too?"

"If it's something I need to know."

"They sound very devoted."

"They are. Just as I am to them. I got them out of Honduras after their son and daughter-in-law were killed by the cartels. They sent Hector and Nunci a video of the execution."

My eyes widened with horror. "That's . . . I can't even imagine."

"Yeah."

For a moment, I couldn't breathe, consumed with the horror of it. "How did you get them out?"

"I flew them. I'm a pretty good pilot. My plane was big enough to take us all."

"Was it dangerous?"

"Somewhat. It was late at night. The weather wasn't ideal, particularly over the mountains. But I don't mind taking risks. It was a lot worse for them."

I pictured it, the bucking flight over dark mountains. The traumatized couple. It stirred something deep inside me.

The fog continued to thicken. He still made no move to return to the compound. "Listen," he said abruptly. "I need my daughter to get back into that school. I'll pay you a bonus if she gets off probation."

"That's not necessary," I said quickly. "I'm going to do everything I can to help her. And I can't guarantee she'll pass."

"I'll make it worth your while if she does. I know your situation. You need money."

I flushed. "Did Otis say that?"

"He didn't have to. I checked you out before you came."

I stared at him. "What do you mean? You snooped into my finances?"

"I hired people to, yeah."

My voice was shaking. "What did you find out?"

He smiled. "You really want to know?"

"I do, yes."

"All right. I found out you really are an orphan. Your father killed himself on a New Jersey highway when you were little. Your mother died last year, small-cell carcinoma. No siblings. I didn't know about Aunt Froggy."

I stared at him incredulously.

"For a couple of years, you lived with an artist in Brooklyn. Moved out suddenly, paid overmarket rent for a place in Brooklyn."

"You had no right!" I swiveled in a rage, began to walk away. But it was too dark, the fog too obscure. The ocean pounding so close.

He caught up with me, grinning. "I see I'm not the only one with a temper."

"You snooped into my personal life without my even knowing it. I feel . . . violated."

"Come on. Did you really expect me to have a stranger living on my property, getting close to my daughter, without checking first? And don't tell me about feeling violated. I've had every inch of my private life invaded for the past six months. Mine, my wife's, every detail about us dragged through the mud. And what they couldn't find out they made up. Can you honestly tell me you didn't look at any of that crap yourself?"

I was caught short. "Okay. I did, some. But last night, in the Great Room, when you asked if I was from Tennessee, you already knew the answer. Was it a test?"

"I suppose."

"And after I passed the test, why didn't you tell me the truth?"

"I should have. I've got a lot on my mind right now."

I felt a wash of conflicting emotions. Maybe I should have expected him to check on me. But digging into my personal life. My relationships.

And something occurred to me. What he'd said about my father. Killed himself. Not died in an accident.

There was the grumble of an approaching vehicle, and then twin halos, like marsh fairies, floated around a bend. "There they are," Evan said and stepped toward the halos.

Hector Sandoval's old pickup lurched up to us, stopping with a grind of gears and brakes. Annunciata beside him. Braids undone, abundant white hair streaming witchy down her back. Evan went to the window, conferred with Hector. Annunciata handed him something.

The truck rattled forward into the veil of fog and began to execute a painful K-turn. Evan turned back to me. "Nunci said you needed this."

He handed me a large iron key. "Keep your door locked at all times. Raccoons are ingenious at getting in. And skunks."

The key was heavy and cold in my hand. "She cleaned my cottage today. Annunciata. She doesn't have to do that. In fact, I'd rather she didn't."

"It's her job. She does every room on the compound. Except Sophia's. Nunci's afraid of snakes."

"Does Sophia have a snake?"

"A ball python in a tank. It has a habit of getting out."

The fearsome Annunciata afraid of pet snakes. It made her seem more human. "She left a candle burning. A votive with a Madonna on it. It's nice of her, but it seems like a fire hazard."

He smiled. "The Virgin of Guadalupe. To keep spirits at bay. Not much of a hazard."

The truck pulled back up beside us. Evan stepped to the back, unhooked the rear panel, and yanked it down. "Climb up. They'll take you back."

"What about you?"

"I'll walk with the dogs."

"I can walk with you."

"No." He said it not harshly.

I hoisted myself awkwardly, one knee first, onto the truck bed crowded with gardening tools, pots, sacks of soil and gravel. I perched on a stack of burlap bags. Drew my knees to my shivering chest.

"You're cold." He shrugged off his heavy denim jacket.

"No, I'm okay."

"The hell you are. You're turning blue."

He draped the jacket like a blanket over me, tucking it around my arms and waist. A surprisingly tender gesture. The warmth of his body heat seeped from the jacket into me.

He stepped back, waved to Hector, and the truck began jouncing away. Thoughts swirled in my mind like the fog that now encompassed everything. The sparkle on the cove, the hazy figure. The hideously mutilated portrait.

Rick McAdams's accusations and threats.

What was real; what were lies?

I drew the collar of the jacket to my nose. Inhaled leather and soap and sweat and cigar smoke.

I shivered again, but this time not from the cold.

TEN

The following day, I succeeded in making the yoga class I'd passed up to go have a drink with Rick McAdams. Vinyasa proved to be the kind of yoga that kept you in perpetual motion, one pose flowing into the next without pause. The seven others in the class were sinuous beings who twisted and pretzeled nonstop for fifty minutes without seeming to break a sweat. I, on the other hand, was sopping by the end of the session. I staggered to the changing room to towel off.

A woman dropped onto the bench beside me. "It gets easier, trust me."

I'd noticed her in the class. Fortyish. Lean. So flexible that her tomahawk of mink-colored hair brushed the mat in back-bending poses.

"I hope you're right," I said. "You're really good."

She shrugged. "I was born rubbery." She began to vigorously towel her shoulders and elaborately tattooed midriff. "You're Jane, right? The one living at Thorn Bluffs?"

"How did you know?"

"Rick McAdams. Bumped into him at a bar last night. He said you'd probably pop up here sooner or later."

I became wary. "Is he a friend of yours?"

"Not really. I just know him from around. Everybody does—he's that kind of guy." She eyed me with insinuation. "He certainly seems taken by you."

"Oh God, no," I protested. "I really don't think so."

"I believe it. You're adorable. I'm Ella Mahmed, by the way." She stood up and shimmied a green tunic over her head. Smoothed it deftly over her torso. "So are you relocating to this area?"

"No, I'm just here for the summer. I'm tutoring Evan Rochester's daughter."

"Yeah, Rick mentioned that."

How did he know? I hadn't mentioned it to him.

Ella Mahmed rummaged in an enormous African-print tote bag. Pulled out a flat-brimmed cap and smashed it far back on her blade of hair. "I've got something of a connection to Thorn Bluffs. My first ex-wife was the architect of record on the renovation of the house."

I glanced at her with greater interest. "It's gorgeous. Your ex is a terrific architect."

"She's good enough, but she actually just drew the plans. Rochester was clear what he wanted. Modern, open. The way Jasper Malloy designed his most famous houses. Funny, though, not Thorn Bluffs, which was for himself. It was like a rabbit warren, a lot of cubbies and secret passages and shit. I guess he went a little nuts at the end of his life. He croaked there, you know. In his drafting studio."

"I've heard that." I grimaced. "You must know the estate pretty well."

"Not really. Hallie and I got divorced soon after she started the project."

"Oh, sorry."

"Don't be. It was alimony from Hallie that paid for the ceramics gallery I now own. Mystic Clay, it's on Monte Verde. You should come by sometime."

"I'd love to. Though I won't be able to buy anything. Unless you sell *I Heart Carmel* mugs."

"Ha, no, definitely not. Art pieces. I sell to the rich. Tech moguls, rich Asian tourists. Once almost to Beatrice Rochester."

My interest shot up another notch. "Almost?"

"It's a good story. Maybe I'll tell you when you come to the gallery." She dived back into her tote, took out a phone. "Give me your info, and I'll send you mine. It's great to have you around. We really need some fresh blood in our little circle here."

We exchanged info. I left feeling buoyed by the idea that maybe I'd made a new friend. For the first time, I felt a real connection to Carmel.

My text sounded. I glanced at it.

Mojito time?

I gave a start. Rick McAdams. Still stalking me.

I texted back: How did u get my number?

Not hard. We need to talk more. Serious.

I glanced up and down the street, looking for the metallic-blue Range Rover. It was nowhere in sight. No. And stop stalking me. I'll call the police.

I have friends among police. Don't forget what I told u about your friend.

Threats. I blocked his number.

I went from yoga to the tennis club to pick up Sophia. I was early. I sat on the sidelines watching her play. She had grace and speed and a keenly competitive spirit that reminded me of her father.

I praised her skills on the ride back. "I loved watching you. You're a natural athlete."

She shrugged but looked pleased. "My mom always said I didn't get it from her. She was a klutz at sports. She said I got it all from my dad's side."

"Did she tell you a lot about him?"

"Nothing. She just said he was smart. And tall and I'd be tall too. And when I was old enough, she said I could find him myself if I wanted. She'd help me." She gave a sheepish little smile. "I used to pretend that I'd find him, and he'd be Roger Federer."

I felt a pang. She didn't get a beloved tennis star. She got a man who was usually too busy amassing a fortune to pay much attention to her. And who—oh, by the way—was suspected of murdering his wife.

She plugged herself into her phone and didn't speak again for the rest of the ride. I dropped her off in front of the house. "The Ocean Room, thirty minutes. I'll see you there."

I hurried back to my cottage to shower and change. Deliberated over what to wear. Nothing too schoolmarm but not like a kid, either. I finally chose a bright-red T-shirt and a black knee-length skirt. A bit of jazzy, a bit of sober. I jammed my laptop, a notebook, and a few pens into my tote and then headed up to the main house.

The silver Tesla was backing out of the garage. *The jacket, the warmth of his body seeping into me.* I pushed the memory away.

The car swooped quickly around and pulled up to me. Evan whirred down the window. "I decided you're right about the Audi. Use the Land Cruiser from now on. It's old but in good repair."

"Is this a punishment?" I said.

He looked at me, puzzled.

"For breaking the rules last night."

"Christ, no, I'm not that petty. I realized an Audi S5 is not a car for these back roads. And you'll be carting dogs around, or so I hear from Fairfax."

"Yeah," I said. "I've taken over dog-wrangling duties from him."

"Good. Don't let the shepherds intimidate you."

"They won't. In fact, I think Mickey has already started to warm to me. At least, he wags his tail when he sees me. Minnie, maybe not yet."

A smile played briefly on his lips. "I suspect she'll become very devoted to you quite soon."

I flushed in spite of myself.

He started to roll his window up. "Wait," I said. "There's something I want to ask you about."

"Yeah?"

"Last night. You said something about my father. That he'd killed himself on a highway. But it was an accident. The road was icy—his car skidded. Were you being sarcastic?"

"It was in the report. My investigators aren't in the business of sarcasm."

Could he have misread it? "I want to see that report."

"It's not possible. Anything else?"

I hesitated. "No."

He rolled up the window, and the Tesla glided silently away.

I continued walking down the slope that led behind the house to the level of the Ocean Room and entered it through the tall doors. Otis had set up a card table and two folding chairs on one of the rugs. The ocean light shivered pale green through the room.

I set my tote on the card table. One of the legs wobbled, caught on something under the rug. I pushed the table aside, then knelt down and rolled the rug a little way back.

There was a large stain on the bleached oak floor beneath it. Faintly reddish and shaped like an amoeba. Someone had scrubbed it but failed to get it out entirely.

Could it be blood? My pulse quickened.

I rolled the rug farther. The stain was extensive. If it was blood, it would have had to come from a pretty significant wound.

Maybe even a lethal wound.

There was a silver medallion placed in the middle of the stain. It was what had made the table leg wobble. I picked it up. Beaten silver, very tarnished, with a simple cross embossed on one side. Rudimentary symbols on the other—a crescent, a star, a heart pierced by an arrow.

A religious medal of some sort?

Sophia's footsteps echoed through the hallway outside, and I put the medal back on the floor and quickly rolled the rug over it. I pushed the table back to a place where none of the legs would be in contact with the medallion. Then I sat down and composed my face as she shuffled in.

Purple backpack hooked on one elbow. Phone in opposite fist. Earbud cords still dangling at her chest. Tinny rap notes emanating from her head. She sat down heavily.

"Earbuds," I said.

She plucked them out, tossed them on the table. "So how long do we have to go?"

"Until five o'clock. You know the deal."

A piglet squealed. She'd changed her text tone. She glanced at the screen. Giggled. Tapped.

"Phone down, please," I said.

"One second." Tap, tap, tap.

I snatched it from her. "I mean it, Sophia. Not until we're done."

Her brow furrowed. Her mouth set. I braced myself for a test of wills.

But then she let out a sigh, one that declared she was the most persecuted, the most *put-upon* person in the history of the entire world and slumped a little farther down in her chair.

"Okay," I said, "let's begin with French."

She excavated a textbook from the backpack. Slid it across the table. *Bien dit!: French, Level II.* "My class is at where the paper is."

I flipped open to a folded sheet of notebook paper inserted in the binding. "Future tense of irregular verbs?"

"Yeah."

I groped for a moment about where to begin. "Okay, give me a sentence using *être* in the future tense."

The piglet squealed. Her eyes darted to her phone. I muted it.

"A sentence?" I said.

She gave me a face. *"Jane sera une putain de salope."*

My temper flared. She was pissed about her phone. About her mom. About the entire world. I got it. But I wasn't going to put up with it.

"Okay, the tense is right," I said crisply. "But 'Jane will be a skanky bitch' isn't really a full sentence, is it?"

A shrug. One shouldered.

"It needs completing. For instance, you could say 'Jane will be a skanky bitch if she talks trash about me to André.'"

Eye roll. *"André?"*

"Or whoever."

"I don't know how to say 'talks trash.'"

"You know what?" I said. "I don't really either."

In spite of herself, she dropped her brat face and giggled. Her eyes darted around the room. "You know, Beatrice used to hang out down here a lot."

"Yeah, I know. Otis told me."

"There was this one time? I came in and she was looking out the window, like, way out at the water. At that big rock out there. And she was, like, talking to it."

I swiveled to look. That immense jagged outcropping that was like the spire of a sunken Gothic cathedral. "What was she saying?"

"I don't know. Her words were all jumbled. She called it Mary. Like the rock was *named* Mary. It creeped me out, so I just left."

She wanted to divert me from the lesson and was coming perilously close to succeeding. I was very tempted to ask her more. But it wouldn't be right. Not now, probably not ever. "*Plus d'anglais*," I said. "Let's run through some conjugations."

A slog through the verbs *être* and *avoir*. Then I had an inspiration— a lightning round, past tense to future tense. It was more like a game— it sparked her competitive spirit—and she got into it. I moved on to other verbs. Not just irregular ones but more colorful ones. *Chatouiller* (to tickle). *Dévêtir* (to undress).

I had her make up sentences about future torments to a hapless nerd named André. It made her giggle (*glousser*) and get goofily inventive.

So far, so good. We moved on to algebra. I'd downloaded a number of elementary problems, which I had her work through. She aced them. I'd have to cram harder to keep ahead of her.

By four thirty, she was beginning to sigh and scrunch her brow and glance longingly at the door. On the dot of five, she lunged for her phone.

"One more thing," I said. "I have an assignment for you."

"We're supposed to do all the work here."

"Who says? I want you to write an essay in French, all in the future tense. One page. Due in a week."

"About what?" she said.

"Anything you want."

"Like *what?*"

"Well . . . what would your future dream job be?"

She sucked her lip. "Fashion designer? My mom and I used to watch *Project Runway* together."

"Perfect. Write a page about how it will be when you become a famous fashion designer."

She grabbed her phone, textbook, backpack and fled.

I got up, stretched. This was definitely not going to be easy. But I felt oddly elated. She had made a little progress. It gave me a glow of satisfaction.

Otis came clattering downstairs and sidled warily into the room. "How did it go?"

"Okay. Really good, I think."

He mimed *whew*, hand swiping his forehead.

"Yeah, I feel that way too," I said. "She did try her best to distract me, though. By telling me things about Beatrice."

"Oh God. What?"

"She said Beatrice used to talk to that rock out in the cove. And that she called it Mary."

"Not surprised. The rock probably talked back to her. She heard voices, you know. It was part of her syndrome."

"Wasn't she on meds?"

"Yeah, but I guess they didn't always work. Sometimes she seemed pretty strongly demented."

I zipped up my tote. "Did you know there's a large stain on the floor underneath this rug?"

"How do you know what's under the rug?"

"Something was making the table wobble, so I rolled it back. There's a sort of reddish stain. And there's a religious medallion placed on top of it."

He gave a snort. "Annunciata puts those things everywhere. Don't ask me why."

"So what caused the stain?"

"Could've been anything. When Beatrice got herself into a state, she was prone to throwing stuff around. Once I made this chicken tikka masala for them, and maybe it was too spicy for her or something, so she dumped the entire plate on the floor. She ate her lunch down here a lot, so who knows what else she dumped?" He gave a little shake of his shoulders. "How about a drink? There's half a bottle upstairs of Pauillac de Latour with our name on it."

"Sounds fantastic."

"You earned it." He put his arm around me and gave me an exuberant squeeze. *My sort of kid brother,* I thought.

The closest thing I had to family.

Later. After the gorgeous wine and instructions from Otis about tending to the various dogs . . . and after my solitary deli dinner, catching up with messages and sending breezy keeping-in-touch notes to my contacts . . . I was again at my computer, trying to focus on an article about volcanoes for Sophia's earth science lesson. But my mind kept twisting elsewhere.

Beatrice mumbling to a jagged black rock out in the water. The mutilated portrait stashed in the crumbling tower. Rick McAdams's puppet head jerking to and fro, hissing accusations. "Monster. Can lie easier than most of us can tell the truth."

Was that true? And how could I possibly find out?

Something shrieked outside, and a chill ran down my back. The same shriek that had reverberated up from the eerie little cove. It sounded now like a child in mortal terror.

A barn owl, Evan had said. Or a juvenile great horned.

I listened hard for a while. It didn't come again.

I turned back to my computer. The Wi-Fi booster I'd ordered hadn't yet arrived, but the connection, though low, was serviceable. I pulled up a YouTube: "Western Barn Owl Screaming." A flat-faced owl perched on a branch at night. A screeching call. Chilling.

But not what I had heard.

I did another search. *Screech owl.* A spooky flutter of high short whoops.

Not even close.

I listened to other owls, barred and spotted and pygmy, and then the calls of hawks and gulls and pelicans and eagles. And four-footed animals, coyotes and porcupines and skunks and anything else I could think of that might be lurking in these woods—until the Wi-Fi flickered out.

I'd found nothing like that ghostly, chilling shriek.

A new thought came into my mind. Something was out there. Or someone.

Watching me. Waiting.

I got up and pushed my dresser in front of the glass doors. Extra protection from whatever it was.

And then I lit Annunciata's votive candle on my bed table.

Protection from spirits.

BEATRICE

Thorn Bluffs, December 17
Noon

Two hands grab me under my armpits and pull me from underneath the Jacuzzi bubbles.

Braidy Lady's face is red and fiery. "You don't come up, Mrs. Beatrice."

"I can hold my breath a long time," I tell her.

She says again, "You don't come up." She reaches for my silky robe next to the Jacuzzi.

She'll find the blade, Mary Magdalene screeches. *Don't let her do it!*

"Annunciata," I say, "please bring me a Dr. Brown. My mouth is very dry."

She glances back at my bedroom doors and then back at me. She doesn't know what to do.

"Now! I need it now, right now!" My voice goes high, higher, I can't stop it.

Her face glows fiery again. She walks very fast into the house.

I swing myself out of the Jacuzzi and put on my robe. The pointy knife pricks at my belly.

Get the blood, Beatrice. It has to be now. Do the plan today.

I think again of the island of Barbados. How I loved him there. I don't want to do the plan.

But now I can't think anymore, the fog swirls thick. I start walking, my famous Beatrice McAdams cheetah walk, up and down the deck.

I hear voices talking, but they are not in my mind. They come tangling up from the ground below. I go to the railing and look down.

I see the brown truck that belongs to the small man, the sorcerer Hector. Next to it is the big white Land Cruiser car with all the dents in it. My jailer is down there and also Hector. It's their voices I am hearing.

They are plotting together in their secret witch language.

I watch Hector go to the back of the brown truck. He slides out something all covered in white. He pulls open the cover.

My eyes open wide.

It's the girl. The one named Lilies.

And she is back in her picture frame. Back inside the picture that was painted by Amedeo Modigliani.

My jailer had taken me to the auction house in Paris, and he bid the highest for this picture for my wedding present. "Modigliani. Just like you wanted, Beat." And he hung it on the bedroom wall, and the girl looked down at me while I slept.

Yes, that's her in Hector's truck. Her eyes are oval shape, and she makes sour cherries with her mouth. I can see her little breasts under her square white blouse.

But I don't understand. I killed her.

You didn't kill her, Mary hisses. *I told you so. You heard her voice on his phone last night.*

The fog is in my mind.

I watch my jailer now pick up the girl. Gently, by the edges of her picture frame, like a precious jewel, like a ruby for the queen's crown. He carries her to the Land Cruiser.

Hector lifts up the back hatch. He slides something from out of the back.

It's a big flat wooden box. Hector and my jailer fit the girl in her picture frame tight into the box.

A laugh bubbles up inside me.

It's a coffin. She *is* dead.

I killed her with my manicure scissors, that day in the month of last April. Yes. I stabbed her eyes, and I cut up her mouth and her breasts. And then I wrote her name all around her: Lilies, Lilies, Lilies. And now my jailer is going to bury her, along with her picture frame. The same way he had buried the old dog, Delilah.

Hector bangs nails into the top of the box. Then he puts the coffin box inside an even bigger box made out of wood and slides it back into the Land Cruiser.

The boy with the golden spectacles comes outside, and he speaks to my jailer. I watch him climb into the front seat.

It's a trick, Beatrice, Mary tells me. *It's a plot to trick you. To make you think she's dead. But now you see that she isn't.*

I don't understand.

You heard her voice on his phone last night. You heard the words she said. You know what he is going to do.

I feel a scream come up from deep, deep inside me.

You have to do the plan today.

I take the blade from out of my robe pocket. I walk fast back toward the glass door of my room. Annunciata comes out with my Dr. Brown, but I don't want it, I shove past her, hiding my blade so she can't see it.

I go inside my bedroom and lock my door.

I take out the sharp little blade.

ELEVEN

I assumed that if I didn't cause any further nuisance, Evan would take as little notice of me as he would some animal—a deer or a woodchuck—nesting harmlessly on his property. But I was wrong.

Three days after he'd fetched me in a fury from the tower road, I was walking Pilot at dusk, as I now regularly did. At the first turn in the road, the shepherds, Minnie and Mickey, came racing hell bent from behind us. Pilot joyously greeted them, and all three went crashing into the underbrush. And then Evan came up, no longer limping, walking so quickly I expected him to pass me by. To my surprise, he slowed into step beside me.

He was sunk in a dark mood. Trudged heavily beside me in silence. But I was not in a gloom, and I refused to be dragged down.

After some minutes, I said lightly, "Could I ask you something?"

He gave me a dark look.

I persisted. "Why do you have gibberish tattooed on your arm?"

"Oh, that. It was supposed to be English."

"Supposed to be?"

A snort of disgust. "I was nineteen, in Cuernavaca. Wasted on mezcal. I wrote down what I wanted and then passed out. The damned *vato* couldn't read my writing."

I laughed. He threw me another dark look.

"What's it supposed to say?" I asked.

"'I want to be true to the morning.' D. H. Lawrence. At nineteen, I thought that meant something."

"But it does," I said. "Mornings are when everything is fresh and new and seems full of possibilities. I'm at my best in the morning."

"I'm a night person," he said abruptly.

I might have guessed.

We did some more silent trudging, until at last he broke the silence. "I have a question for you." His gloom seemed to have lifted a little. "About Aunt Froggy."

I glanced up at him. "My aunt Joanne?"

"Why do you think of her as a frog?"

"I'm not sure. She shows up in my dreams sometimes—she's a giant frog in a pink dress, with a croaky, frog-type voice. It scares me. The dreams are nightmares. I'd always thought she was dead. I found out from my mother she wasn't, just before my mother died."

"Did you ever try to find her?"

"A little bit. Online. But it's a common name. Joanne Meyers. There are thousands of them, so it seemed hopeless. And . . . well, maybe I was reluctant to. Because of the nightmares." I gave a quick laugh. "Stupid to be afraid of dreams."

"Not really. No one can be sane and have no fears at all."

I shot him a teasing look. "Then what are yours?"

"Do you really expect me to tell you?"

"Yeah, I do. I just told you one of mine."

"Okay. I'm afraid of the dark."

"Liar," I said. "You just said yourself you were a night person."

"Then you can pick which one you want to believe." He was teasing me now.

And after that, our conversation came effortlessly. Darting from one topic to the next the way I'd seen small black-and-white butterflies flit from flower to flower outside my cottage. I found myself telling him things—silly things—about myself. About the Clown Lounge, where I'd met Otis, and how Otis had shown me the ropes. How to make drinks with names like Sloppy Pussy and Adios Motherfucker. How to deal with the owner, the drunken Afghanistan vet, Dooley, who threw darts at anyone he didn't like. "Which was pretty much everyone," I said.

He laughed in that way that entirely transformed his face.

I found, disturbingly, that I liked making him laugh.

We walked for some time. The fog scattered silver on the foliage, and the shadows deepened to violet. It began to seem to me like we were the only two people left in the entire world, and that was exactly the way I wanted it to be, and perhaps he did too. And maybe when I stepped to avoid a gnarled root in my path, I stepped just a little wider than necessary so my arm brushed against his.

Then we were back in the compound, and he said, "Good night," and turned rather abruptly to his gorgeous house, whistling for the dogs to follow. And I went back alone to my rustic cottage. And thought again, *Well, that's that.*

But to my further surprise, he continued to pay me attention over the next weeks. Stopping me as I backed the Land Cruiser out of the garage or headed out of the main house. Asking solicitous questions: "The Cruiser running okay? Brakes still good? Do you have everything you need for your tutoring?"

Checking up on me, I presumed. Making sure I was doing right by his daughter. Following his rules.

But he began to linger a little longer. His questions became more personal. What music did I like? "Are you into jazz at all? How about hip-hop?" Did I travel a lot, or was I more of a homebody? "Did Fairfax show you my library? There are some first editions that you might find fun to look at. And feel free to borrow anything else."

He listened to my replies with a kind of absorption that made me feel—at least in that moment—that I was the most fascinating person he'd ever known.

I began to look forward to these encounters. Each time I walked Pilot, I'd listen for footsteps coming up behind me and would feel a twinge of disappointment when they didn't.

And finally they did. I was halfway down the drive when he strode quickly up with the shepherds. He looked at me with mock reproach. "You might have waited instead of making me run a marathon to catch up with you."

"If I knew you were coming, I might have," I said. "Though I do know one thing. You like to get your own way, even if it requires people to read your mind."

He gave a laugh of delight. "Am I that easy to figure out?"

"No," I said truthfully. "At least not to me."

"But I'm that unreasonable?"

"Sometimes, yeah."

"But you won't let me get away with it, will you?" he said. His face was shadowed by the redwoods' dark canopy, but something in his tone of voice, low and intimate, made my heart somersault.

We continued walking. But Rick McAdams's words whispered at me. *Manipulative. Charming when he needs to be.*

Was it true? Was he just manipulating me for whatever purpose?

More than ever, I felt a driving need to find something definitive. To find Beatrice. Or her remains. Or some definitive proof that would clear his name.

Or else prove he was the cold-blooded monster most people seemed to believe he was.

Before I got myself into something I could no longer control.

TWELVE

It was over three weeks now that I'd been at Thorn Bluffs. I'd just returned from a midday yoga class. Ella Mahmed had been there, and I was liking her more and more. She was smart, brassy, quick to laugh. We'd nailed down a day for me to visit her ceramics gallery.

I'd also become familiar with a group of other women in the class who called themselves the "Semi-regulars." They had names like the start of a children's counting rhyme—Connie, Terry, Honey, and Pam. They were all divorcées, except Pam, who was widowed. They favored chunky jewelry and Goddess leggings.

They all thought Evan Rochester was sexy as sin.

And they all had damning stories about him.

Connie: "He once pulled Beatrice out of a restaurant so violently he could have broken her wrist."

Honey: "She tried to run away one time. But he captured her before she could escape and kept her under strict lock and key afterward."

They'd heard the stories from friends. Or friends of friends. Gossip. Which of course couldn't be trusted. Though I was dying to hear the "good story" Ella had promised to tell me. I had the feeling that hers would be authentic.

I now slotted the Land Cruiser into its bay and climbed out. As I clicked the door closed, I heard a deafening roar: a black-and-yellow helicopter flying over the compound. I watched it descend like a gargantuan hornet to the helipad a short way inland. As I walked to my cottage, it rose straight back up and began to fly north, the crowns of the redwoods bowing in its heavy chop.

I recalled Otis telling me Evan used to commute by chopper on weekends from his house in San Francisco, but now he only chartered one for the most urgent meetings.

Who is he off to meet so urgently now?

The letter *L* flashed into my mind. The single initial written on the card attached to the vase of expensive still-in-bud tulips.

Nonsense.

The chopper dwindled to a speck in the distance. I continued to my cottage, unlocked the door with that heavy iron key. I had a sudden hollow feeling. A stillness hung heavily in the room, despite the eternal crash of surf outside.

A bit of my morning coffee remained in the Krups pot. I poured it into a saucepan and reheated it, making it palatable with an extra dollop of honey. My text sounded.

Wade O'Connor, who continued to check in regularly.

Find any body parts yet?

I gave a laugh. Replied: Not even a bone.

Why not? U been there long enuf to find whole skeleton.
Sorry, no trace of B. But sometimes think maybe she's found me.
Whoa. What??

I sat down at the table. Paused. Then texted: Hard to explain. Every so often get the feeling somebody watching me. Thru my glass doors.

123

Whoa!!! Mr. R. Peeping Tom?

No. Happened one nite he wasn't here. I paused again. Something else. Sometimes I hear strange shriek outside at night. Gives me chills.

My phone rang almost immediately.

"So what are you saying?" Wade demanded. "Somebody's spying on you, and you think it's Beatrice? Wandering around in the woods at night?"

"No. I mean, you know that sometimes I let my imagination run away. Especially when I'm here alone at night. It gets kind of easy to have ridiculous thoughts."

"But what's with this shriek?"

"It's hard to explain. It's like a child screaming in terror. Evan said it was an owl of some kind. But I've listened to a lot of owl calls online and didn't find anything like it. And then a couple of times I thought I've seen some kind of whitish shape. Kind of ghostly . . ."

"Whoa, wait. Now you're saying she's a ghost?"

"No. It's just that I've felt some kind of presence outside. The housekeeper here, Annunciata, I think she does too. She keeps a candle burning on my bed table. A votive candle. It's to keep away evil spirits."

"So it's an evil ghost?"

"No!" I said emphatically. "I'm sure it's nothing at all. Just my curiosity about what might have happened to Beatrice. Which you keep stirring up, if you recall."

Wade gave a grunt. "Keiko is not going to like this. She thinks you never should have left New York in the first place for such an iffy situation. I sort of agreed. And now I'm definitely thinking you should get the frick out."

The idea of leaving gave me a sudden panic. I said quickly, "Come on, Wade. You and I both love making up stories. There's no reason I need to leave. And I don't want to. I'm making progress with Sophia, I can't just abandon her now. And Otis depends on me too."

He made a ruminative sound. "Look. We're going to be out in Marin County next month. Keiko's roommate from Yale is getting married. We're bringing Benny, and we were thinking of driving up to the giant sequoias afterward. But maybe we could come down your way instead."

"Don't change your plans for me. Seriously, Wade. I'm fine."

"I sure as hell hope so," he said.

Fifteen minutes later, my phone rang again, this time Wade's wife, Keiko. She worked for a boutique bond company, she was no-nonsense in the warmest possible way, and I was as close to her as I was to Wade, as well as an unofficial godmother to their five-year-old son, Benny.

"Did Wade tell you I was losing my mind?" I said.

She laughed. "Not exactly. He said he's worried you might be getting carried away with your fantasies, or worse, you might actually have some weirdos around. I think it's a great idea for us to drive your way. We can take Benny to the Monterey aquarium—he'll adore that. We'll swing by your place first."

"I'm not supposed to have visitors here. I can meet up with you in Monterey."

"Now, you see? You're not allowed to have visitors—that's got me even more worried."

"It's really not that sinister. Evan just likes to protect his privacy."

"You call him Evan?"

"Well, yeah. What do you expect me to call him? Mister?"

She sighed. "I don't know, Janie. But I think you're a lot more vulnerable than you realize. After all that awful stuff you've been through in the past year. I'll feel better when I've actually laid eyes on you."

"And make sure I'm not murdered yet?"

"For starters," she said.

"I won't be," I told her. "I promise. And if you do come, I'll be thrilled. Tell Benny I miss him, and give him a big kiss for me, okay?"

"He says he's too old for kisses now. He's okay with hugs."

"Then tell him I'm sending a big old hug right at him."

I hung up. Finished my leftover coffee. Wade was right: I was spinning lunatic stories. Beatrice's ghost peeping in at me. Making shrieky ghost sounds. If there really had been any peeping, it was far more likely to be by somebody alive and kicking.

But who? Not Otis. God no. I couldn't imagine that.

Sophia sleepwalking?

Maybe.

Then I thought of my panic at the idea of leaving Thorn Bluffs. It was true what I'd told Wade. I didn't want to abandon Sophia or Otis. But I hadn't told him the entire truth.

That I couldn't stand the idea of leaving Evan Rochester.

That giant hornet carrying him away. The hollow feeling it had left me with.

Stupid. I needed to get a good grip on myself. I had a tutoring session shortly; I needed to look composed.

I hadn't picked up Sophia today—Otis had collected her after a dental appointment he'd had in Carmel. I headed out to the Ocean Room a little before four o'clock, passing through the breezeway that connected the garage to the main house. As I began down the slope to the lower level, I suddenly froze.

Annunciata was directly outside the Ocean Room doors. Bent over the shrubs, sprinkling a white powder on the roots. I'd had no contact with her since Otis had first introduced me. She had continued to clean my cottage but always in stealth. Somehow knowing when I wasn't there. It gave me the willies.

It was ridiculous to avoid her. I continued up to her and spoke loudly. "Hello, Annunciata."

She straightened. Her braids, tied with bright-blue yarn, swung against the sturdy girth of her waist. Other than the color of the yarn, her outfit was unchanging—men's dungarees, a loose khaki-colored shirt, rope-soled shoes.

She wiped powder from her fingers on the leg of her dungarees. Glared at me.

I persisted. "Thank you for cleaning my room. And for the candles." Had she heard me at all? Yes—she gave a curt nod.

I stood uncertainly a moment. My smile felt stretched ear to ear. I nodded back at her, then turned self-consciously and proceeded into the Ocean Room. I sensed her eyes still on me.

The room danced with a pale gold light that was almost fizzy. I put my things on the card table, and when I looked back out, Annunciata had moved away.

Drawn by the source of the lemonade light, I went over to the tall windows. The cove sparkling silver and blue looked inviting. As if wading out to take a swim—even in a cocktail dress—might not be such a terrible idea.

My eyes traveled to that jagged spire of a rock. It now looked made of polished glass. The ridges on it stood out in sharp relief.

It looked close enough to think maybe you could just wade right out to it.

I turned from the window and moved to a recessed bookshelf in the adjacent wall. It was sparsely filled. A black porcelain bowl. A green obelisk. A mounted geode, dull gray on the outside, dazzling pink crystal within.

The bottom shelf held a number of coffee-table-size art books. *That ruined painting hidden in the tower.* I squatted down and browsed the titles for one on Modigliani.

They were all on Renaissance art. Titles like *Masterpieces of the Renaissance. The Art of Florence. Italian Renaissance Sculpture.*

I pulled out a couple and sat down cross-legged on the floor. Opened the first. *The Early Renaissance in Italy.* On the flyleaf, a signature in black ink: *Beatrice McAdams Rochester.*

I felt a tingle. *Her book.*

One page had a corner turned down. I felt another tingle. Like the fashion magazines I'd found in the dresser of my cottage—each with folded corners marking photos of Beatrice in her prime.

I opened the art book to the marked page. A full-page color plate of a sculpture by Donatello: *The Penitent Magdalene*. It didn't resemble Beatrice in her prime or otherwise. It was carved almost crudely in wood—and it was not the young and beautiful Mary Magdalene. This was an ugly old hag. Emaciated, sunken eyed. Almost toothless.

But the hands were beautiful—long fingered, the raised fingertips almost, but not quite, touching. And they were heavily encircled in black ink.

Why? To make them look bound together? *Like a prisoner?*

I opened the other book. *The Art of Florence.* Again, a signature on the flyleaf: *Beatrice McAdams Rochester.* And again, a single page folded at the corner.

It opened to the same reproduction—*The Penitent Magdalene.* The hands of the statue again furiously encircled in black ink.

But this page also had a scratchy kind of black writing that filled all the margins. More like slashes than scratches. With a shock, I remembered the slashes around the edges of the Modigliani portrait in the tower.

So both this writing and those slashes must have been made by Beatrice. But what did a Modigliani from the 1920s have to do with a Renaissance sculpture? There was no resemblance at all between the works.

I examined the encircled hands of the Magdalene. Strong, ridged hands. Making a prayerful gesture. Fingers creating a steeple shape.

A church steeple.

An idea occurred to me. I sprang to my feet and looked out at the cove again—at that huge jagged outcropping. The one that reminded me of a ruined spire of a sunken cathedral.

I compared it to the hands of the statue in the book. My heart began to beat faster.

I could imagine that Beatrice in her madness might think there was a resemblance. The steeple shape. The ridges in the rock face like the veins in Mary Magdalene's hands.

Mary. Sophia had said Beatrice called the rock by that name.

I glanced over my shoulder at the white chaise. The one Otis said Beatrice had spent so much time lolling around on. The way it was placed in the room, slightly angled—it gave an unobstructed view of the cove. And of that jagged steeple-shaped rock.

I thought of that faint reddish stain hidden by the rug in the center of the room. Annunciata's tarnished silver medallion placed on top of it.

What had happened in this room?

Outside, Annunciata moved again into my sight. I put the art books back on the shelf and went to the card table. I opened my laptop and kept my eyes fixed on it.

"I wrote the thing." Sophia tore two pages out of a spiral notebook and handed them to me.

It was the French essay I'd assigned her at our first session over two and a half weeks ago. She'd given a litany of excuses. So much homework from her *real* classes. Overtime practice for an upcoming tournament. I had finally threatened to take her phone away. "You can't do that," she protested.

"I can and I will."

"I'll tell my father if you do."

"Be my guest. He'll back me up. I guarantee it."

I was pretty confident she wouldn't test it. She hadn't.

I looked at the essay. Longer than I had expected—two full pages, written in block lettering. I began to read.

"You're going to read it now?" A tone of dismay.

"You bet I am. I've waited long enough."

She fidgeted while I read it through. It was full of errors. Sloppy mistakes. Words used wrong. But it was also remarkably vivid and inventive.

In the future she will win *Project Runway* with an amazing dress (*une robe incroyable*) composed of fake monkey fur and recycled brown paper and a hem of candy kisses (*bonbons bisous*). She will make an ensemble for Lady Gaga to wear to the Grammys and also a hat with a nest of eggs. The eggs will open, and baby doves will fly into the audience. And Gaga will tell her to make every new ensemble for her and for all her friends.

I read the last line with a pang:

Et puis je serai riche et je sauverai beacoup d'animals. Et egalement j'adoppterai une douzaine enfants orphelines.

She will be rich, and she will rescue many animals. And, equally, she will adopt a dozen orphan children.

I looked up. "It's terrific, Sophia."

"You think?"

"Yeah, I really do. There are lots of mistakes. Your spelling is atrocious. You've *got* to start using accent marks. But you've really learned the future tense. And it's incredibly creative. I love that you want to adopt a lot of animals and kids." I wrote a large A on top.

A flush of pleasure lit her face. She was starved for this kind of praise, I realized. Particularly when she knew she deserved it.

"I've got an idea," I said. "For the earth science lesson, let's go to one of the beaches near here and gather up rocks. Then tomorrow we can identify them and classify them."

"Awesome!"

The outing was a success. We brought Pilot, and at the beach, he romped in and out of the surf, trailing long tresses of kelp. We filled bags and stuffed our pockets with black and green and speckled rocks and shards of mussel and clam shells until we couldn't carry any more. We hauled our booty back and spread the rocks on the promontory to dry. Otis came out to admire the display. He made venison chili, and we ate in the screening room watching *National Velvet*—my choice so Sophia could get to know Elizabeth Taylor, who my mother had adored (though Sophia liked Piebald the horse a lot more).

Afterward, I slipped back into the Ocean Room and collected the art books—seven all together—and carted them back to my cottage. I began looking through them all.

Each one had a corner turned to a reproduction of *The Penitent Magdalene*. But only the one book—*The Art of Florence*—had scratchy writing in the margins. I examined the writing again, searching for the word *Mary*. I could only pick out a few capital *S*s and *E*s. And what seemed to be a lot of capital *L*s.

Or maybe I just had the letter *L* on my mind.

L as in lipstick.

That single initial *L* written in green ink on a white card.

Maybe it had nothing to do with that reddish stain underneath the rug in the Ocean Room. Or the religious medal placed on top of it.

And yet I couldn't shake the feeling that it did.

BEATRICE

I am in my bedroom, and I am still holding the little blade, and I am breathing very hard.

But Mary's voice is soft. Gentling me to do the plan. *A shopping bag, Beatrice*, she whispers soft, soft. *Hurry, Beatrice, go get one.*

I put the blade back in my pocket. I walk into my closet room and open one of the many doors. There are lots of shopping bags on the floor. I choose one that says **NEIMAN MARCUS**. It's shiny and black. It has tissue paper inside it and a sweater all folded up and new. I dump out the sweater and also the tissue paper, and I bring the bag into my big white bathroom.

I place it on the floor next to my shower.

Outside in the hallway, Braidy Lady is knocking soft on the door. "Mrs. Beatrice? I have your Dr. Brown's."

Don't take it, Beatrice. She's put a witch spell on it.

The knocking stops. But I know Braidy Witch is out there. Weaving her spells.

Don't worry about her. Now is the time, Beatrice. Do it now!

I take the little knife out again from the pocket of my robe. I toss the robe onto the floor.

I step naked inside my shower.

I am suddenly screaming so hard inside me, I don't think I can hold it in much longer.

Keep it inside you. Remember the witch at the door.

I keep my scream inside. I raise my arm up high over my head. There is hair in my armpit and also on my legs and vagina because they won't let me have a razor anymore.

I place the sharp point of the knife in the hair that grows in the deepest part of my armpit.

I am screaming inside.

I stick the point in my armpit very hard. I feel the sharp sting.

It makes me feel good.

THIRTEEN

Evan did not return that night or the next. I asked Otis where he'd gone.

"LA. He's got a big-time investor on the hook. A venture capitalist, guy named Dillon Saroyan."

"When will he be back?" I kept my tone casual.

"He did not confide that information to me. He might not even know."

Good, I told myself. His presence had been starting to muddle my thinking.

I scoured Beatrice's books, page by page, searching for other marks she might have made, but there weren't any. The library in the main house held a collection of art books, and I searched those for Renaissance titles or any that might have belonged to Beatrice. These were mostly on mid-twentieth-century art and architecture, with several on Asian and African art.

None had Beatrice's signature on the flyleaf.

None was on Modigliani, either, though he was mentioned as an influence in a couple of the midcentury books.

I was strongly tempted to go back to the tower. Get a closer look at that grotesquely mutilated portrait. But I couldn't risk that road at night with its dangerous proximity to the edge of the bluffs. And during the day, one or the other of the Sandovals seemed always to be watching—like they had the shaman-like ability to be in several different places at once.

After four days of Evan's absence, I had stopped constantly listening for the chop of a returning helicopter. That afternoon, I headed into Carmel to make my long-promised visit to Ella's gallery. I arrived just before two o'clock. A one-story building awash in flamingo pink on Ocean Avenue. It contained a collection of small galleries, Ella's marked with a placard:

MYSTIC CLAY
BY APPOINTMENT ONLY

She swung the door open before I could even ring. "Saw you on the camera. I keep the door locked not because of burglars. To discourage the lookie-loos." She gave one of her brass-bell laughs and ushered me inside.

A stark white space lit by rows of dangling incandescent bulbs. The ceramics—vases, bowls, platters, a few fanciful cups and sugar bowls—were displayed on blond wood shelves behind glass. "All my stuff is contemporary," Ella said. "No Ming vases, no Wedgwood teapots. None of it is really functional. No practical use except to nourish the spirit."

"I could definitely use some spirit nourishing," I said. "I want to look at everything."

"And so you shall." She began steering me from piece to piece, regaling me with mini lectures on ash glazes and lead glazes, and colorants made of cobalt or copper, and the meaning of multiple firings.

Some of the pieces were thick and muddy. Some were delicate, as if spun from the filaments of spiderwebs.

One was like nothing I'd ever seen before. A yellow-glazed vase shaped like a Grecian urn and overlaid with a macabre collage.

Faded-out sepia photos of Victorian ladies. A woman's cartoon face with huge lurid lips. A leering, naked old man on a toilet. Vines with peculiar flowers writhed between the images, and banners with strange sayings floated by.

"Tell me about this one," I said.

"Interesting. It's the same one Beatrice Rochester picked out."

I glanced at her. "Is that the good story?"

"Yep." She removed the vase from the shelf and placed it on a long viewing table. "It's by Grayson Perry. He's British. A cross-dresser, very flamboyant. And brilliant. As you can see."

I peered closer, both captivated and repelled at the same time. "Are those cracks part of the technique?"

"No, they're part of the story. When we're done here, I'll make us tea in the office and tell you."

We moved on to the few remaining pieces, but my mind remained fixed on that peculiar vase. Finally, she led me into her office, a cubbyhole in back. She brewed clove tea in an Iranian samovar. Set out a plate of lacy cookies. "Rose water. I made them myself. Bet you never guessed I was so domestic."

"No, but somehow I'm not surprised." I bit into a crumbly wafer. "They're delicious." She poured out the tea into square cups. I said, "Okay, you've got me on the edge of my seat. What happened with the vase?"

She plunked herself into her chair. "Okay. Well. Mrs. Rochester—Beatrice—she showed up here about a year ago. No appointment, but I recognized her in the camera and buzzed her right in. She'd put on weight, but her face, still so beautiful."

I nodded. I could imagine.

"I started to give her my standard rap, but she made a beeline for the Grayson Perry. It seemed uncanny. Like it had called to her. And I mean literally called out to her."

I flashed on the rock in the cove. Beatrice talking to it. "She used to hear voices. So maybe it did call to her. In her mind."

"Yeah, I've heard she did, so maybe. Anyway, I took it out of the display and put it on the table, and she was, like, enraptured by it. She said, 'I'll take it.' Just like that. I told her the price. Seventy-two grand. I expected her to haggle. They all do, even the richest. Especially the richest." Her laugh pealed again. "But nope, she just waved her credit card. I was over the moon, of course. But when I ran it, it was refused."

"Maxed out?"

"A black Amex, no limits. It was canceled. Amex told me to cut it up. I told that to her, and she smiled at me in a way that gave me the shudders. And then she turns and starts walking out, and as she passes the table, she knocks off the vase."

"On purpose, you mean?"

"I couldn't be sure. It broke but, thank God, didn't shatter. She didn't stop, just sailed on out the door. I was flipping out. I paged the guard, and then I went outside. The guard was confronting her, and she was starting to get really agitated and yell and scream."

"What did you do?"

"I didn't know what to do. And then this brand-new Tesla comes cruising up, and Rochester gets out. He had obviously been close by, right?"

My attention was riveted. I nodded.

"And Beatrice looks at him with a kind of panic, and . . . well, he snaps his hand around her wrist. Like a handcuff, you know? Like she was his prisoner."

He kept her prisoner. What Rick McAdams had said. And the Semi-regulars had said something like it too.

"I told him she broke an expensive vase," Ella continued. "He said 'Send me the bill.' There was a look in his eyes that scared the shit out of me. But Beatrice had calmed down. Pretty quickly, in fact. He got her into the car and drove away."

"Did you send him the bill?"

"I sure did. For the entire price. He paid up immediately. I contacted him a few times to ask where to send it but never heard back. Finally, I had it restored, and, well . . . there it sits. If he wants it, he can have it. I won't even charge for the restoration."

"Did Beatrice ever come back here?"

"Nope. I never saw either of them again. But when I heard what happened . . . I felt bad. Like maybe I could have intervened somehow. That it would have made a difference."

"Probably not," I said softly.

"Yeah, probably not." She took a sip of tea. "But, hey, I don't mean to alarm you. I mean, like, scare you off his place. Though I guess you already know he did away with his wife."

I looked at her, startled. "Are you so sure he did?"

"You're not, huh?"

"My friend Otis who works for him is convinced it was suicide. And there are other possibilities."

"Like what?"

I paused. I didn't want to believe he was a monster. Or anything close to it. "Maybe she just ran off, for whatever reason. Or maybe she's still somewhere at Thorn Bluffs. Didn't you tell me there used to be secret passages in the house?"

"Yeah, according to my ex, Hallie."

"Maybe there still are. Hidden passageways. Or rooms."

"No, I saw the plans for the restoration. Not even a secret broom closet. It was a total gut, and the new place is all open plan and modern. But I get where you're going. Rochester didn't kill his wife—he's still got her shut up somewhere." She gave a snort. "It wouldn't surprise me if he had a dozen wives locked up somewhere."

"No," I said quickly. "I meant she could be hiding. Just a wild thought."

"It's a fun idea. But I doubt it. Hallie supervised the construction, she'd have known if there was any conceivable place to hide." Ella refilled our cups. "Do you want to see the plans?"

"Sure. Do you have them?"

"No, but Hallie probably does. I'll call her and get her to send you a scan. I've thrown a few referrals her way—she owes me."

"Great." Maybe they'd give some answers. Help me figure out what was reality and what was just my ever-active imagination.

The plans arrived via email from the architectural office of Hallie R. Bookman that evening. I scrutinized them carefully. They were exactly like Ella had described—all modern and clean lines. Exactly as the rooms I'd been in so far at Thorn Bluffs all appeared to be.

But I'd never been to the top floor where Evan and Beatrice had had separate bedroom suites. Things could be changed after construction, couldn't they? Rooms rebuilt. Walls moved.

I looked up at the sound of a distant rumble outside. It grew quickly to a deafening roar. The chopper returning to the helipad.

I felt a quick thrill. *How long will it be until I see him?*

I saved the plans to a file and clicked it shut.

The next evening, he was waiting for me in the motor court with Pilot and the two shepherds when I came up to fetch Pilot for his walk. "There you are," he said. As if I had obstinately kept him waiting.

"Yeah, here I am." My tone was breezy. But my heart was scudding.

Once again, we fell immediately into easy conversation, as if it hadn't been five days since we last were together but just five hours. I described Sophia's essay. Her future career as a fashion designer. Doves hatching on Lady Gaga's hat. "It was truly brilliant," I said.

"So she's making improvement?"

"She is, yeah."

"And she's stopped acting out?"

"Not entirely, no. I think she needs more attention. From you, I mean. You need to spend more time with her."

"Time is the one thing I'm short on right now. When all this is wrapped up, I'll have plenty of time for Sophia."

"By then she might not have any time for you," I said sharply.

He narrowed his eyes with irritation. Then gave a relenting grunt. "I'll have dinner with her tonight. How's that?"

"It's a start. A good start if you can keep from answering your phone before dessert."

"Christ," he muttered. The dogs had roamed too far out in the brush, and he whistled to herd them back in.

A question was forming in my mind. A risky question, but my curiosity was too intense not to try to get an answer to it.

I said, "Something has stained the wood flooring in the Ocean Room. I wondered what it was. A refinisher might be able to get it out."

Was it my imagination, or for one brief moment did something dark cross his face? Dark and terrible. But it vanished instantly, if it had been there at all, and he spoke easily. "My wife once threw an open bottle of wine at Raymond Thurkill, who used to be my estate manager. I plan to redo that room. It's too feminine for my taste. I'll have the floors refinished then."

Easy answers.

I said nothing further about it. But when I parted from Evan in the compound, Rick McAdams's warning flashed in my mind. *You don't really know who you're dealing with.*

And a week later, it became clear to me that I didn't.

FOURTEEN

"Where are those blasted girls?" Otis grumbled.

I was sitting beside him in the Explorer, the largest vehicle of the Thorn Bluffs fleet. "I just texted Sophia," I said. "They'll be right out."

It was the Fourth of July. Over a month of my precious three had now flown by. Evan was throwing a fireworks party for his employees, which we were attending, on a beach above Santa Cruz, about seventy miles up the coast.

Otis leaned on the horn. Minutes later, Sophia clambered into the back seat, followed by a girl from her tennis clinic, Peyton Dreyer. She'd recently become Sophia's best friend, and Sophia spent as many overnights at Peyton's as she could wheedle permission for. They now sported nearly identical outfits—jeans with sparkly heart and kitten patches and splashy cropped jackets. Their eyelids were greased with iridescent blue swoops that reminded me of hummingbird wings.

"What do you two have on your eyes?" Otis said.

Peyton issued a do-I-really-have-to-explain-this? sigh. "It's statement makeup. Because we're attending an event."

"It's a statement," Sophia echoed.

I swiveled. "I think you both look gorgeous."

Sophia beamed. Peyton took it as her due and munched on a strand of hair. She was a year older than Sophia, with a pretty, slightly pushed-in face, half screened by curtains of brown hair. She exuded an attitude of privilege. It made me uneasy to see Sophia copy her.

Otis cracked a can of soda. I caught a whiff of cherry. "What's that?" I asked.

"Dr. Brown's Black Cherry soda. Diet."

"It's gross," Sophia remarked. "There's boxes and boxes of it in the pantry."

Otis began to pull out of the compound, steering one-handed. "Beatrice drank it," he said. "It disguised the aftertaste of her meds."

"Did you ever bring a glass of it to the tower?" I asked him.

"You kidding? Told you I never go near that place."

"Somebody did. There was a glass with dregs of it."

"Jeez, Jane. Did you go in there? I told you nobody was allowed."

"I almost went in once," Sophia put in. "But there was a tarantula climbing up the door, and it freaked me out, so I didn't."

"You're making that up," Otis said. "We don't have tarantulas."

"There are totally tarantulas in central California." Peyton was something of a know-it-all. "Extremely large ones. They're hairy and have fangs, and the females devour the males after they mate. And sometimes if she doesn't want to mate with him, she kills him first. Before he can copulate with her. And *then* she devours him."

"That is so gross," Sophia said.

"No, it's not," Peyton said haughtily. "It's just natural."

"Let's have some music." Otis began streaming an emo-rock mix to vocal disgust from the back seat. They plugged into their phones and leaned their two heads together, swiping and tapping and giggling.

We meandered in heavy holiday traffic up the peninsula coast road. After about an hour and a half, we turned off the highway to a dusty parking area. We tramped down a packed-dirt path to a beach of pebbly brown sand, where a small crowd was already densely encamped on blankets and tarps. Kids raced between the tarps. EDM throbbed from towering speakers.

An intern—young, floppy haired, East Indian—corralled us. "I'm Khalim. I've been on the lookout for you guys. There's a space for you reserved down in front." He led us zigzag through the crowd. I glimpsed Evan, who had come down early in the morning to supervise the setup. He was surrounded by people, with others hovering for their turn.

We spread out our tarp on the reserved space. Otis scavenged, returned with a bounty—Cokes, Tecate, ballpark snacks. Sophia and Peyton grabbed Cokes and bags of Wavy Lay's. We began to get in full party swing.

"Hey, there's Malik!" Otis waved to a nearby couple with three gangly teenage boys. The dad saluted Otis. I recognized him—Malik Anderson, Evan's chief lawyer, whose sleek red Porsche coupe was a regular in the motor court. I had exchanged small talk with him from time to time—a charmer with freckled black skin, a buffed bald head, canny dark eyes. Always exquisitely dressed—even the windbreaker he had on now looked bespoke.

Peyton and Sophia began to rustle and preen and strum their hair, sidling glances at Malik's sons. The boys began to roughhouse, fully aware they were being checked out. The girls soon ditched Otis and me to join them. Then Otis sprang up. "I'll fetch us more eats."

I found myself alone. But not lonely. It was a beautiful evening. The sun was settling plumply on the ocean like a fat orange hen onto a dark nest. There'd be fireworks soon, and I loved fireworks. I felt exquisitely alive, as if I'd had a long illness and was finally coming back to health.

I caught a scrap of Evan's voice and saw him approach Malik's tarp. He dropped down beside Sophia and Peyton, began talking to them, and whatever he was saying made them preen again and giggle with delight. Sophia said something, and he laughed in that full-throated way that I loved. I felt a warmth pulse through me.

He caught my eye and smiled. He gave Sophia's shoulder an affectionate squeeze, then jumped up and came over to me. "What took you so long?" he said.

"We were just a little late. Sophia and Peyton wanted to look special."

"They succeeded." He reached for my bottle of Tecate, took a swig. Handed it back. "Sophia's coming into her looks. She could become a knockout."

"I'm sure of it."

"She's coming into her brains too. Or at least some of them. I can thank you for that."

I flushed happily. "She just needed a little more confidence. Maybe I've helped her get that."

"What do you think of the friend? She seems like a pretty self-possessed kid."

"I'm not sure what I think yet. She's got a lot of influence with Sophia. It might not be such a good thing."

"If it's her influence that's getting Sophia to wear clothes that cover her backside, that's not a bad thing." He slouched himself back onto his elbows. He was wearing the black denim jacket he'd tucked over me in the back of Hector's truck. I remembered the sensation of his body's warmth seeping through me. I looked away from him, made a pretense of surveying the crowd. "This is a fantastic party. It's very generous of you to do it."

He made a disparaging sound. "Nothing compared to what I used to do. But next year . . ." His voice became playful. "Next year I'll have three times the crowd. Four. I'll get whoever does the Macy's fireworks to do them for me. And a top DJ. Or else a live act. Who would you like to hear?"

Did he assume I'd be here a year from now?

"Anybody at all?" I said.

"Anybody. I'll book them."

"Okay, David Bowie, then. Or Prince. Or wait, Aretha. Definitely Aretha."

He stared at me, suddenly not playful. "There's a lot I can do. But I can't bring back the dead."

I flushed again, this time deeply. "I'm sorry, that was stupid. I shouldn't have . . ." My voice trailed off.

He grabbed my Tecate again and drained it. He looked suddenly very happy. "It's all happening for me, Jane," he said. "It's all finally coming together."

"With your deal, you mean?"

"Yeah, with Genovation. All the financing is clicking into place. It's been tough. Christ, really tough. I gave them everything they asked for, but they kept wanting more, more. I was damaged goods. I get it. All the damned rumors about me. But now it's all going to happen."

"So you won't lose Thorn Bluffs?" I said.

He smiled. "No, I won't. I came close, though. Very close to losing everything. The jackals were circling. They were just waiting to get to my corpse. But they're going to be disappointed. I'm going to recoup every nickel I've lost and a hell of a lot more."

I diverted my eyes. "That's good. I'm happy for you."

"Are you?" he said.

That he was about to become preposterously rich? I wasn't. Not in the least. I looked back at him. "Of course I am. You've worked hard and taken risks. I'm happy it's all paying off for you."

"And what if it had gone the other way? If I'd lost everything, my money, my property? Even my freedom?"

I felt suddenly like a cold shadow had passed through me. Like the shadow of a premonition. As if what he'd described—losing everything, even his freedom—these were things that were actually going to happen.

"Would you still stick by me if I went bust?" he pursued. "Or would you drop me cold and walk away?"

"That's a ridiculous question," I said. "What difference would it make to me if you lost your money?"

"Most of these people here, it would make all the difference. They'd be off in a shot."

"They're your employees, not your friends. Your real friends would stick by you."

He looked at me intensely. "You are my friend, aren't you?" His voice was low. "I think you are."

Just a friend? Was that how he thought of me? Except everything in his eyes, his expression, was telling me differently, that he was as drawn to me as I was to him. Could I be that wrong?

Not even the most proficient liar in the world, even a sociopath, could fake that kind of emotion. *Could they?*

He glanced up. Malik Anderson was approaching us. "Hey, Malik. Do you know Jane?"

"Of course I do, the Thorn Bluffs cottage dweller. We've met several times." Malik smiled at me with melting charm. "Enjoying the party?"

"I am, very much."

He said to Evan, "We need to talk a second. I just heard from Saroyan's people."

Evan leaped up. "Problem?"

"A few issues with the term sheets. Nothing major, but better to deal with them now. There's good cell reception in the setup tent." Malik gave me a rueful smile. "Sorry, Jane, I'll have to steal him away."

"I understand." I glanced at his family's tarp. "Where did the kids go?"

"To the grill station to grab some burgers."

I rose to my feet. "I think I'll go check on them."

"Tell them the show is going to start soon," Evan said. "It's almost dark." He turned with Malik toward a white flat-topped tent pitched near the water.

I began threading through the crowd, running into Otis carrying an overloaded cardboard tray. "Where are you going?" he said. "I was just bringing us dinner."

"The fireworks are about to start. I'm going to fetch the girls from the grill station."

"Good idea. There's a lot of weed around."

The music amped up. A Sousa march, all brassy patriotism. A far cry from the Queen of Soul. The crowd stirred in anticipation. I continued on to the grill station set up just past the footpath to the parking area. As I approached the path, a woman heading down from it waved at me. Someone I knew.

"Hi, excuse me!" As she came closer, I realized I didn't know her; she was a stranger who simply reminded me of someone else.

She was dressed more for a cocktail party than a brisk California beach. Sleeveless linen dress with a short skirt. High wedge sandals. The gauzy pale-pink scarf lassoing her neck was for fashion, not warmth. "Excuse me," she repeated. "Do you have any idea where I could find Evan Rochester?"

"I was just with him," I said. "He was heading to the setup tent."

"Where would that be? I'm in something of a hurry. I've got to get to another event in Cupertino."

That explained the cocktail gear. "Keep going toward the water. You'll see the top of a white pitched tent."

"Are you sure he's there?"

Her peremptory tone made me take an instant and pronounced dislike to her. "No, I'm not sure," I said curtly. "But even if he's not, he's pretty easy to spot. He's tall with dark curly hair . . ."

"I know exactly what he looks like."

There was now a proprietary note to her voice that made me dislike her even more. It didn't help that she was strikingly lovely. Long limbed. Slender. A cap of shiny dark hair accentuating an oval face and almond-shaped dark eyes. "Good," I said. "You'll have no trouble finding him."

Her face tilted a little. Appraising me. "You're not with his company, are you?"

"No."

"So who are you with? One of the VCs? Hagersly Brothers?"

"No," I said. "I'm just with myself."

She narrowed her eyes, seemingly torn between curiosity and suspicion. The rim of the sun blazed briefly, then blinked out below the horizon, and the breeze coming off the water freshened. She hunched her shoulders in a shiver. "It's freezing on this beach."

"It usually is at this time of day. It helps to dress for it."

That face tilted again. "Yes. Well, thanks for your help." She turned away, and as she did, a gust of wind sluiced under her scarf, causing it to flutter high up her long neck. I glimpsed a birthmark on the nape.

An ugly birthmark. Large. Reddish purple. Parabolic in shape and slightly puckered.

Or no, not a birthmark. More like a scar.

Maybe from a burn?

She was obviously eager to keep it hidden: she quickly yanked the scarf back over it and knotted the ends more securely, and only then did she continue on into the crowd.

I watched her thread her way through the sand with difficulty in those ridiculous heels. Someone shouted her name, and she turned. "Laura," it had sounded like. Or it might have been "Lana." It had been mostly swallowed by the surf.

But definitely a name that began with an *L*.

There was a loud sizzling.

A white snake writhed up into the sky and exploded into twin white chrysanthemums above the ocean's black horizon.

"Hey, Otis?" I was the designated driver on the way back. The girls, having gorged on junk food and flirting and illicit gulps of beer, were sound asleep in the back, and Otis was nodding out as well.

"Yeah?" he muttered.

"There was a woman who arrived late tonight. In her late twenties, very pretty, short dark hair. She looked dressed for a cocktail party."

"Didn't notice."

"Her name was something like Laura or Lana. And she's got a kind of a scar on the back of her neck."

He turned a puzzled face. "What are you talking about?"

"A girl who was looking for Evan. I thought maybe she was the one who had sent him the tulips."

"What tulips?"

"There was a vase of white tulips delivered when Evan was first setting up his office. A large bunch, not open yet. Do you remember?"

"Oh yeah. Were they tulips? I thought they were some kind of lilies."

Then he was asleep, snoring lightly.

BEATRICE

Lilies, lilies, lily, lilies.

The voices are all singing together in my head as I stick the blade into the deepest part of my armpit very hard.

The pain is sting sharp.

My blood begins to spurt out, and I let it spill onto the knife and cover the blade and the handle and then drip onto the shower floor.

And then I make a second cut. This time on the line of my pubic hair between my vagina and my thigh. The blood trickles down through all the hair grown downy soft on my leg.

I make one more cut. A very small slit at the top line of my pubic hair.

Sting sharp. It feels good.

It makes me feel like Beatie June.

Blood trickles down all over me now, and I rub the knife in it, screaming, screaming inside me. I put the bloody knife inside the Neiman Marcus shopping bag.

And then I pull out hairs from the top of my head. I yank out small bunches by the roots, and I wipe them in the blood coming out of the cuts, and I also put the hairs into the Neiman Marcus bag.

And now I slide down and sit on the floor of the shower. There's blood trickling all over me. I pull my legs up tight against me and squeeze my arm close to my body, so the cuts will stop spurting out blood.

And now I start to remember the first time I ever cut myself.

It was when I was twelve years old. I remember I was living at the foster home with the mama named Amity, but child services sent Ricky to a different home, and Mama Amity refused to give me his phone number.

But Ricky found out where I was. And early in the morning he threw dirt at my window, and I climbed out, and we hitchhiked to Fernandina Harbor. Ricky borrowed a speedboat from the marina. He was very clever—he could start any engine without a key. He drove it way out into the sea, and then he stopped and threw out the anchor.

He stabbed a shrimp head onto a hook and threw the hook into the water, and in a little while, the line bobbed up and down. Ricky pulled it up and an ugly-looking fish flopped around in the boat.

"Yo, BJ, it's a puffer. Watch this."

The puffer fish had a bumpy white belly. Ricky poked at it, and it puffed itself up into a big ball with a big blow-a-kiss mouth.

I laughed. I puckered up my lips, and I bent over to the puffer fish. Ricky grabbed at me. "What the fuck you doing?"

"I was going to kiss it. See if it turned into a prince."

"Jesus, Beatie June! Are you brain dead or what?"

"I was just joking, Ricky. I thought it would be funny."

He smashed the puffer fish dead against the side of the boat and slammed it back into the water. "They're deadly poisonous," he said.

Then he drove the speedboat superfast, and we started to bounce around in a scary way, and Ricky gave a whoop. "Riptide!"

The boat was chopping hard like we were going to go over, and I screamed, "Stop! I'm scared, I don't want to drown."

"You could swim this current, BJ. You won your last eleven heats in a row. You blew all those other bitches out of the water."

"I can't, Ricky. This is too strong."

"Sure you can. Here's what you do. They're narrow fuckers, riptides. You let it take you until you feel it start to lose pull. Then you break to the side and swim to shore. Easy for a hot-shit swimmer like you."

The boat was still chopping, and I was still screaming. "I can't swim it, Ricky, it's too strong."

He gave a crazy laugh. "There's only one way to find out."

And he pushed me off the boat into the riptide.

I remember it was cold and strong and tried to gobble me up. I was very frightened. And Ricky swung around with the speedboat, and he was laughing as he pulled me back up onto it.

I was all covered in mud and sand and seaweed. When I got back to the foster home, Mama Amity slapped my face hard with her slipper. She called up child services and reported Ricky to them. Then she locked me up in the aluminum shed out in the backyard. "Two hours this time, Beatie. You try running off again, I promise you it'll be a heck of a lot more."

It was very hot in the shed, and there were spiderwebs with spiders in them, and I was frightened. But this time I refused to holler out.

There were sharp things in the shed too. Tools with rusty blades. I picked out one that had a very thin sharp blade that wasn't too rusty, and that was the first time I made a cut. Between my leg and my pubic hair, because it was in a place Mama Amity wouldn't see and report me to the child services.

It had felt good. Sting sharp.

It made me not think about anything else.

The way it still does now.

But the blood is still trickling out from me, and maybe it won't stop. And I feel frightened again.

FIFTEEN

*I'm lying on a beach, gentle waves surging close, and I am naked, and Evan
is lying close beside me. He's naked too. And now I'm melting into him, and
a sweet, swooning sensation surges like the soft waves, engulfing my entire
body.*

*Except someone is watching us. I feel horror. But I can't make myself
look.*

*And now, suddenly, I'm back in my cottage. I'm in bed. But someone is
still watching me, someone right outside my glass doors.*

*I need to wake up, to open my eyes, but I'm paralyzed. I can't move
my eyelids . . .*

I woke up with a start, drenched in a sweat of terror.

I glanced at the glass doors. It was barely dawn, and the view was
blanked out by a gray quilt of fog. I waited for the horror of the dream
to dissipate, and it finally did.

But not the certainty that someone had been there.

Somebody real. Watching me sleep.

I climbed out of bed, put on my robe, sneakers without socks. Went
to the doors, wrestled one open. Yelled into the mist, "Who's out there?"

The breeze crackled like conversation through bushes and branches. A stuttering bird called from high in an unseen tree.

I stepped out. Listened intently. Something fluttered in a bush at the bottom of the steps. Something caught in brambles, barely visible through the mist. I hesitated, then went down to investigate.

It was a scrap of thin, dingy material. I tried to pull it out, but a thorn pricked my finger. "Ouch." A tiny spurt of blood appeared at the tip, and I sucked it.

I noticed something else. Underneath the bramblebush, there was a patch of old asphalt. And another slightly farther into the foliage. The remnants of a narrow path leading into the thick overgrowth— like a munchkin version of the worn-out asphalt road in front of the cottage.

I felt I was still half in a dream—one that compelled me, Dorothy-like, to follow this path. I carefully pushed aside thorn bushes and tall dew-drunk ferns and edged several steps farther in. Sharp swords of new-growth pine threatened to stab me. Rotted fronds and leaves squished beneath my feet. That distant bird gave its stuttering cry again.

I gave a start as an animal scuttered through the bushes.

I continued for several more yards, swiping a cloud of gnats from my eyes. I ducked under a low pine branch, and then my foot landed on something hard.

A corroded sheet of metal about four feet square thickly covered by pine needles and dead leaves. Maybe left over from the renovation? I scuffed some of the debris off with my sneaker. It was a hatch of some kind. A handle—a rusted iron ring—near the edge.

Am I actually in a dream?

I stooped down and grasped the ring. It felt cold and solid. Not dreamlike. I pulled: it took all my strength to lift it several inches. Beneath the hatch lid, I glimpsed the top of a staircase—a metal spiral staircase—encased in a metal shaft.

I gave the ring a stronger tug and managed to pry it open another inch. I could see that the shaft had caved in a few feet down. Most of the staircase was filled with dirt and stones.

A rustling in the foliage behind me. I gave another start and let go of the ring. The hatch fell shut with a loud clang.

Behind me, in the mist, I could almost imagine a hazy white figure amid all the streaming white. I took a step backward, and now my robe became entangled in brambles. I wildly yanked at it, got entangled more, then managed to yank myself free. I thrashed through the bushes back to the cottage steps and scurried up them and hurried inside.

I pulled the door shut behind me. And shoved the dresser in front of the doors.

I was trembling. I made coffee, mud-strong. Drank two cups. As my head cleared and I stopped trembling, it began again to seem like a dream. The strange hatch. The metal staircase spiraling down into dirt and rock—like the one in the tower that rose to midair. The dim white figure in the white mist. Only the stinging scratches on my face and on my arms, the spot of blood on my finger, assured me it had been real.

I recalled my feeling that somebody had been right outside the doors.

Watching me while I slept.

It couldn't have been Sophia sleepwalking. She had spent the night at Peyton's, and Peyton's older brother was bringing her home later.

The mysterious Sandovals? Could they have come a lot earlier than usual? I went out again, this time up to the motor court.

The Sandovals' brown pickup was not there.

On an impulse, I clicked open the garage. The Tesla was not at its docking station. *He didn't come back last night.*

That wasn't unusual. Evan sometimes stayed overnight at a hotel near his offices in Los Gatos. It would have made sense last night if he'd wrapped up late.

So he was definitely not peeping in at me while I was asleep.

That left Otis. He'd still be sleeping off all his drinking the night before. *Wouldn't he?*

No, I couldn't even consider the possibility of Otis.

As I headed back to the cottage, I began to think of the woman who had arrived late to the fireworks. That lovely face framed by the lustrous dark bob of hair. A face tilted arrogantly to one side as she summed me up.

Who had she reminded me of?

I recalled the sound of her name—a name that began with the letter *L*. Like the initial written on a card attached to a vase of flowers that were not tulips. They were tightly furled lilies.

I hurried into the cottage and went directly to my laptop and typed in a search: *Evan Rochester + Lily*. Page after page of hits. My heart sank.

But they all seemed to be about a game app called *Tiger Lily Ninjas* that Evan had invested in early in his career. It had been a gigantic hit in Japan. Nothing, at least in the first dozen pages, attached him to a woman of that name.

I substituted *Laura* and then *Lana* in the search box. No relevant results.

I was wrong, then. She was just a guest who happened to be in a big fat hurry and wanted to quickly greet her host. Except I couldn't believe it. That proprietary tone of voice: "I know exactly what he looks like."

I flashed on something Rick McAdams had said. Evan had already begun to have Beatrice declared dead.

Because he's involved with someone else?

Another missing piece of the puzzle. One I didn't want to think about. But which might be the most crucial piece of all.

Sophia stomped down to the Ocean Room midafternoon. "It's not fair I have to do this today. It's still totally a holiday."

"It's a Wednesday. Lots of people have to work today. We can't afford to skip any more sessions. You've only got six weeks left until your first exam."

"Six and a *half*. It's not *fair*." She plopped sullenly into her chair, exuding a strong waft of a flowery perfume.

"Why are you wearing perfume?" I said. "Are you covering something up?"

"No."

"You haven't been drinking? Or vaping?"

"*No.*"

"Does Peyton smoke?"

"No. Alcott—that's her brother—he smokes, but he's sixteen, so his dad lets him." She flipped a strand of hair behind her ear—one of Peyton's signature gestures—and a bracelet of blue stones slipped down her arm from her wrist.

"Is that bracelet from Beatrice's room?" I said.

"I told you, she didn't want her jewelry. And my dad doesn't care."

"You've asked him?"

"Yeah. Just so long as I don't bother him when he's on the phone. Which is literally *always* because I don't count at all."

"Of course you count, Sophia." I said it sharply. I was in a mood of my own and had no patience for hers.

"No, I don't. He's still wrapped up in Beatrice even though she was totally mental. She killed Delilah, you know."

I shot her a look. "Who's Delilah?"

"My favorite dog, Minnie and Mickey's mom, and Beatrice poisoned her. She hated her. She hated all the dogs, and she hated me too. And she probably would have poisoned *me* if I didn't go away to school."

"I doubt that very much." I reached into my tote and took out a FedEx packet. "Hey, I got you something. It came this morning." It was a hardcover copy of *The Little Prince* in French. I'd been looking forward to its arrival.

She ripped open the packet eagerly. Her mouth drooped. "A book."

"*Le Petit Prince*. I first read it when I was your age and about a dozen times afterward."

"We did it last year at St. Mag's."

I had the urge to smack her. "Okay, fine. Then you should be able to translate it quite easily. Begin, please."

She lifted the book's beautiful cover like it was oozing pus. Said the prince looked like a total dork and the rose was a snot. She mangled the first few pages of Saint-Exupéry's incandescent prose.

"Okay, stop." I yanked the book away from her. "If you're not even going to try, then it's pointless. Just leave."

"I can go?"

"Yeah, go."

She grabbed her things and bolted out.

But a couple of hours later, she appeared at my door. "I'm hungry. Otis texted he's caught in a traffic jam and he's gonna be really late." She peered inside. "Do you have anything here?"

I sensed a piercing loneliness from her. I mentally reviewed the contents of my fridge. Wilted kale. A pear. "I tell you what. Why don't we go up to your house and scrounge something up?"

In the kitchen, I surveyed the vast pantry. I wasn't much of a cook. When Mom was dying, I'd tried to coax her failing appetite with comfort foods from her childhood—kugel and potato knishes from *Joy of Cooking*; matzo ball soup from a recipe on the Manischewitz box; and when she could no longer get down solid foods, I made her egg creams with extra Hershey's. None of that would work right now. I hit on an earthy-looking brown bag of imported penne and had another idea. "My mom used to say, 'Always start with macaroni. And then you can throw in just about anything else, and it will always turn out good.' So start picking out ingredients."

I put a pot of water on to boil. We both began selecting ingredients and threw them into a large copper-bottomed saucepan. Otis's home-made broth. Chopped-up remains of a porterhouse. Sour cream. Greek olives. Our choices got sillier ("Stinky cheese, ew, gross!" "Chocolate chips? No way!"). Finally, we got something that smelled palatable. "What do we call it?" I said.

"*Le* gloop," Sophia suggested.

"*Le* gloop! *Parfait!*"

We put on music—shimmied and danced to Bey and Ariana while the dogs capered around our feet. Then both Minnie's and Mickey's ears rose straight up, and Pilot went bounding into the hall.

"Dad!" Sophia yanked the blue bracelet off her wrist and thrust it into my hand. "Don't let him know."

I stuffed it into my back pocket.

Evan appeared in a barking swirl of dogs. He went directly to the stove. Lifted the lid of the saucepan. "What's this?"

"It's *le* gloop," Sophia said. "Otis is stuck, so we made it for dinner. It's going to go on pasta. Do you want some?"

"Yeah. I'm starving. Bring it on."

We ate in the kitchen, white bowls on an ebony wood table. Sophia chattered. About Peyton's trophies for horseback riding and her brother Alcott who thought he was so hot because he was captain of lacrosse. Then she asked me, "So what was it like working on a TV show?" and I said, "Like being part of a big quarreling, backstabbing family. But one that could be really loyal and comforting when you really needed it."

Evan wolfed his portion and went back for seconds. He talked about eating fried rattlesnake in Honduras. "That is so disgusting," from Sophia.

"It was delicious. I might fry up your python the next time I get peckish."

"No way!" she shrieked, but her eyes were shining.

And then Otis arrived in a fluster. "Truck overturned on the Cabrillo, cantaloupes, zillions of them, rolling everywhere! What are you all eating? Gloop? What the hell is gloop? It smells peculiar." But he scooped a plate and joined us.

Sophia fed scraps to Pilot when she thought no one was looking, and Evan caught my eye in amused conspiracy. Otis fastidiously picked out a tomato seed from his food. And I thought: *We're like family. This is my family now.*

A wave crashed with sudden force on the bluff outside as if to mock me. *It's not for you. This too will be swept away.* A cold chill ran down my back.

And too soon Evan was seduced by his buzzing phone and got up. Sophia wandered to her room and Snapchat, and Otis began to clear. I got up as well.

Evan paused. He turned to me and traced a scratch on my face. "What is this?"

"Nothing," I said. "I ran into some brambles behind my cottage."

"What were you doing out in the brambles?"

Chasing another ghost. "I noticed a path. An old asphalt path in the bushes. I was curious."

"A fire path. They run all through the property. Don't tell me you tried to follow it."

"Just a few steps. Then I came across something strange. A metal hatch in the ground. It's covering a circular staircase that's all caved in."

He smiled. "It's an escape hatch. Jasper Malloy put it in when he built the original house. An escape route from his imaginary enemies. It caved in long before I bought the property."

"Where did it go to?"

"Down to the cove. Where there was no place to escape. Malloy was just a paranoid old drunk." He touched my scratched face again. "Don't

160

go back there. It's too dangerous. There are thorns that could gouge your eyes out." His phone sounded again. He gave me a final glance, put the phone to his ear, and continued out through the service porch door.

A pot banged loudly in the sink. Startled, I looked over at Otis.

"When did you two get so chummy?" he said.

"What do you mean? Shouldn't we be friendly?"

He began attacking the gloop pot with a Scotch-Brite. "He'll suck you in, you know, just like he does everybody. He'll lure you onto his side, and then he'll want you to do something."

"Something like what?"

He shrugged. "Whatever."

"What do you mean, O.? Did he make you do something you didn't want to do?"

"No." He bent deeper over the sink. "Forget it. It's nothing."

"He hasn't lured me into bed with him, if that's what you're getting at. He hasn't even tried."

An incredulous snort.

I sighed. Began to clear plates.

"Leave the dishes. I'll get it all."

I hovered uncertainly a moment. I'd never heard him sound so bitter. But he was bent low over the sink, not inviting any more questions.

I remembered the sapphire bracelet in my pocket. I headed out of the kitchen down the length of the house to Sophia's room. Tapped on the door. "It's me."

The door cracked open. Her nose poked out.

"You need to put this back." I held the bracelet out to her. "Immediately."

"I will. Tomorrow."

"No, now. You lied to me, Sophia. You said your dad told you he didn't care if you borrowed jewelry. Either put it back right now, or I'll have to give it to him."

"Okay, I'll do it." She sidled out, closing the door behind her, and headed with me to the staircase, dragging her heels. She stopped at the base of the stairs. "I don't like to go up there at night."

"Why not?"

"It's too freaky. It's like she's still up there. And sometimes in my room at night, I can hear something moving, and I know it's not my dad because it's when he's away."

I glanced up at the top floor. There actually was a kind of spooky light on the landing. "I'll come up with you."

"Can't you just take it? Please, *please*, Jane? I'm sorry I made fun of the Little Prince—I really do like him. And all you have to do is put it back on her makeup table, that's where I got it. Please—I promise I'll never take anything again, ever."

She really was frightened. "Okay," I relented. "You don't have to. I'll do it."

"Thank you," she breathed. "Her room's the door on the left. Dad's is the other one." She turned and raced back to her own room.

I headed quickly up the floating stairs. At the landing, the source of the eerie light became apparent. A glass clerestory ran the length beneath the ceiling, and the last golden glow of twilight was slanting in. There were two sets of wide pocket doors at opposite ends of the floor. I took a quick glance at Evan's on the right, then moved purposefully to Beatrice's. I slid open the doors and stepped in.

Ghostly. It was the word that sprang to my mind. White-painted walls and white furnishings. Ice floes of white rugs drifting on pale floors. The huge windows were curtained in gauzy white.

Everything spotless. Not a speck of dust anywhere. The bed looked freshly made, Annunciata's tight corners. I smoothed my hand over the white satin coverlet. Imagined Beatrice lying there. Dreaming her mad dreams.

On the white wall facing the bed, there was a rectangular discoloration where a picture must have hung for some time before being removed. It would have been the first thing Beatrice saw when she opened her eyes in the morning.

I flashed on the Modigliani in the tower. It was about the right size, at least as I remembered it.

If it had been hanging here, why had Beatrice destroyed it? Gouging out the eyes, those wild slashes across the mouth and breasts. *Like it was personal.*

I looked around for the makeup table, found it in a large adjoining dressing room—a glamorous white table with a three-sided mirror bordered with lightbulbs. On the mirrored top there was a Mason Pearson hairbrush made of boar's hair. Long blonde hairs still tangled in it. Beside it, a lipstick in a gold case. The same shimmering lavender as the lipstick in the Audi. *Could it be the same one?* I wondered.

If so, who put it back?

I recapped the case. Set the sapphire bracelet down beside it.

A square archway opened from the dressing room. I glimpsed an enormous closet lined with mirrored doors. I stepped into it: a Busby Berkeley image of myself reflected back at me in the many mirrors.

It occurred to me: there was no such enormous closet with so many doors in the plans Ella's ex-wife had sent me. This must have been added later. And if so, maybe I'd been right about hidden spaces. Maybe there was a secret room or passageway concealed behind one of these doors.

I opened one at random. Inside, a rotating rack crammed with dresses. Long, short, in between. The racks and dresses took up the entire space. I shut the door, opened another. Jackets and blouses just as jam-packed on another revolving rack. I turned to the opposite doors and selected one.

Shoes. Hundreds of pairs on tiered revolving racks. Stilettos and flats, boots and sandals. Each meticulously aligned with its mate. I gave one of the racks a slow spin, dazzled by the variety of stunning footwear. Then suddenly I stopped the rack. One pair of shoes was misaligned— the left was put in backward and crooked. I lifted it off the rack.

A rose-colored kidskin pump, with a high Lucite heel. Extremely long and narrow. I knew that Beatrice was reputed to have had very long feet, but this bordered on the freakish. I turned it over, looking for a size.

Something flew out of the pointed toe.

I rummaged through the thick pile of the carpet. A small pebble. Pale yellow, oval shaped. Encrusted with dried yellow mud. I brushed off some of the mud.

Not a pebble. It had markings. A number, just legible: *200*.

I had a sudden, violent memory of Mom. Her terrible last days. Wasted to a skeleton. She couldn't keep anything down, water, medications . . .

"What are you doing?"

I whirled at the sound of the voice behind me, dropping the pill back onto the carpet.

Evan stood in the archway. His eyes were cold, black. His face impenetrably dark. I opened my mouth but couldn't speak. My heart pounded.

He came up to me and took the shoe from my hand. Stared at it dispassionately, turning it one way, then the other. "My wife had unusual feet." His voice was flat. Emotionless. "They were a problem for her in runway shows. She was forced to jam them into the designers' sizes. By the end of a fashion week, her feet would be bruised purple and black. Bleeding. She'd be in agony. Her own shoes, like this one, she had custom made in Milan and Paris."

I still couldn't speak. Those eyes like black ice.

"What were you looking for?"

"Nothing," I managed. "I'm sorry. I shouldn't have intruded."

"No," he said. "You shouldn't have."

I walked quickly past him, back through the bedroom to the hall. I quickened my steps as I continued downstairs and out the front door. *Stupid, stupid.* I continued walking fast down the drive, my heart pounding, expecting to hear the German shepherds come bounding behind me, Evan's footsteps following, his face black. The black ice of his eyes.

Stupid, I thought again. *What had I expected to find?*

Hidden chambers. Beatrice, or her skeleton, secreted in it.

When would I stop writing stories?

Except I had found something. I turned and hurried back to my cottage. Unlocked the door, went directly to my laptop.

I began searching.

Clozapine 200

Pale-yellow oval.

Atypical antipsychotic medication.

Used to treat schizophrenia, schizoaffective disorders. Helps to decrease hallucinations, disturbed thinking, and heightened emotions. Suppresses suicidal impulses or the urge to hurt others. Restores the ability to function in the everyday world.

Possible side effects include:

Drowsiness.

Dry mouth or drooling.

Dizziness or sensation of spinning.

I stared at the symptoms. *Hallucinations. Suicidal impulses.* I took out my phone. Hesitated.

Otis's warning: "Don't pry into his affairs."

He needed to know. I tapped out his number. My heart pounding as it rang. Would he answer?

"Yeah?"

I steadied my voice. "There's something you should know. There was a pill hidden in the shoe—the one I was holding. Clozapine. When you startled me, I dropped it onto the carpet."

He was silent.

"Your wife might have hidden it there. She might have found a way not to swallow her meds. There could be more hidden in her other shoes."

"Okay," he said.

"So . . . okay. That's all."

I hung up.

BEATRICE

Thorn Bluffs, December 17
Early afternoon

I cut myself many times after that first time in Mama Amity's shed. It always made me forget about everything else. But then I didn't do it for a long time.

Until right now. And now I stay sitting on the floor of my shower, squeezing my thighs tight against each other and my arm against my side, but the blood keeps creeping out of me. Creeping and creeping. I watch it slither onto the white tiles and turn itself in a pinwheel as it sneaks toward the drain.

"Mrs. Beatrice?" Braidy Witch is back at my door. "It's time for your lunch." I hear the key turn in the lock.

"I need private time," I yell loud.

"Okay, Mrs. Beatrice." Annunciata knows that the poison they give me causes things to go wrong with my bowels. I need my private time.

Look, Beatrice. Mary whispers to me. *The blood is over.*

Yes, it's stopped, there's no more of it creeping out onto the white shower tiles. I turn on cool water and let it wash me clean and also wash away the red blood snake from the white floor.

My jailer tests the water for poison but not for blood.

The next part of the plan, Beatrice. The bra. The dress.

I turn off the water, and I walk naked and dripping wet into my closet room, bringing with me the Neiman Marcus shopping bag. I open up one of the closets that has my dresses. I press a button, and the dresses start to march around. It's like the grand finale when I'm walking in a show. I watch them march around and around, and then I press the button again and stop the grand finale. I choose a dress.

A dress by Christian Dior. It's made of blue silk chiffon, and there are flowers floating on it like lily pads.

Lilies. It was the name the girl gave herself when she came down from the picture frame.

I am a cat, I growl, I rip the Christian Dior dress with my teeth, and I take the pieces I've ripped off and rub them on the cut in my armpit. Blood oozes up again, and I put the bloodied pieces into the Neiman Marcus bag.

And then I go to the drawers where all my lingerie is folded up. I take out a bra. Ivory silk. 34B. It's the size I wear except when I have my period, and then I wear a 34C.

But I don't get my period anymore. The poison dried it all up.

I use the bloodied-up knife to stab and slice up the bra. I put pieces of that, too, into the bag.

And now I go back to my dress closet and tear the clingy wrapping off another dress. I roll up the rest of the bra and the Christian Dior dress in the wrapping and stuff that into the shopping bag as well. There will be nothing left for the witches to find.

Get his frigging hairs. Mary's voice is now like a foster mama. *Finish the frigging plan. Now, while there's still time.*

Ricky's voice comes up. *And get dressed! What are you, brain dead, Beatie June? Get your skinny butt in gear.*

SIXTEEN

I spent the rest of that night tormented by the memory of Evan in Beatrice's rooms. His frozen eyes. The blood-freeze cold in his voice.

If I'd ever harbored any idea he might be attracted to me, I could let go of it now. I had obliterated any chance of it. He'd want nothing more to do with me after such an outrageous invasion.

He might even kick me out. And maybe that would be for the best. Stop me from getting entangled in a relationship with someone worse than treacherous Jeremy. Possibly far worse.

Except there never had been any possibility of my getting entangled, had there?

There was a girl whose name began with an *L.*

Late the next morning, I was not surprised to hear the Harley roar up outside. He was still enraged, I imagined, and I steeled myself for the confrontation. I would stand my ground. For Sophia's sake. She had begun to bond with me. She was still raw from losing her mother, and my leaving her right now would be a blow to her. He could banish me from the rest of the estate, but I would not abandon her, at least not until she was back at school.

I flung open my door. Ready to face his fury.

He was riding without a helmet. He pushed his goggles over his forehead, brushed wind-tossed curls off his face. His eyes were no longer black. "You were right. There were nineteen more pills hidden in her shoes. Nunci and I did a search. We had a witness, a lawyer who does no business with me. Beatrice had been off her meds for at least two weeks."

I felt a tick of relief. "Was that enough time for her symptoms to come back?"

"Yeah, it was."

"So it could have made her suicidal?"

"Definitely."

"Why didn't the police ever find the pills?"

"The police never searched my house. They had no grounds for a warrant. No crime was committed."

"Oh," I said.

He remained straddling the idling bike. "Do you want to take a ride?"

"A ride?" I repeated with surprise. "Where to?"

"Nowhere. Just a ride. Or actually, yeah, to somewhere. I want to show you something."

"Like what?"

He gave a huff of impatience. "It will be a surprise. A nice surprise, I hope."

"I expected you to be angry I was snooping in your wife's room."

"I'm furious." But he was smiling at me in a way that was not furious.

I couldn't resist. I slipped out the door and straddled the back of the bike. Wrapped my arms around his lean waist. The Harley shot off.

We rocketed up the moss-covered steps to the compound, then veered up one of the bluffs, steep twists, gravel spraying beneath the tires, ascending up and up above the redwood line. The bike leaped over the crest of the bluff, and just as I thought we'd go sailing out over the thrashing sea far below us, it fishtailed to a stop. Evan swung himself off, and I followed, a little wobbly legged but exhilarated. "That was really fun."

"I thought you'd like it."

We moved toward the edge. We were above the fog line now, looking down at a thick cloud bank, the top lit brilliant orange, the sky a blue bowl above. The ridgeline stretched for miles in either direction. There was no sound but the sweep of wind around us.

"This is one of my favorite places," he said. "I come up here when I need to escape. Even for a few minutes, it makes all the difference."

"It's wonderful." I flung my arms in the air, let the fresh breeze rush over and through me. "It must be what it's like to fly."

"It is, somewhat. You should learn how to fly." He added in a murmur, "I could teach you sometime."

I glanced up at him. There was an expression on his face that made my heart turn over. All I had to do, I thought, was just make the slightest move, one tiny step closer to him, and I'd be in his arms and he'd be kissing me. And I'd be kissing him back.

And yet the thought of his face the night before, so cold, and, yes, maybe even dangerous, came back to me. I didn't make that slight move. And then he motioned for us to get back on the bike, and we did, and it was another adrenaline rush down the bluff. This time, he skirted the compound and drove directly around to the washed-out road behind the cottage. He stopped, and I swung myself off.

"Thanks, that was great," I said.

He nodded, then gunned the bike, and I watched it gallop up the mossy little steps.

I thought: *Shit, shit, shit.*

I didn't trust him. I believed he was involved with another woman.

I wasn't totally sure he hadn't harmed his wife.

But I couldn't deny it any longer. I was falling desperately in love with him. It was going to take all my willpower to keep looking for those missing pieces of the truth.

Two nights later, there were violent winds. Shaking my doors. Stomping and banging on the roof. The next morning, branches of pine and redwood sailing through the air like jousting witches on broomsticks.

Otis called early. "There's a fire six miles down the coast. With these gusts, it could easily become an inferno. Evan's in the volunteer brigade. He's already gone to report in."

"Is he in any danger?"

Otis sniggered. "Of course. Why do you think he volunteers?"

I'd planned to meet Ella at the Vinyasa Center, but she called to report that a eucalyptus had toppled and closed Highway 1 into Carmel. She added breathlessly, "And a tree next door to me fell and killed my neighbor. An older man, crushed him in his sleep, poor guy."

Sophia couldn't get to school or tennis, though all her friends who lived in or near town could. "Why do we have to live in the middle of nowhere?" she pouted. I called for an early tutoring session. And afterward, attended by Pilot, we gave ourselves mani-pedis in the library. When the polish had dried, I played the two pieces I knew by heart—*Für Elise* and an easy Czerny étude—on the Steinway grand, and then the two of us banged out a "Chopsticks" duet.

I had noticed before that the piano's ebony finish was bubbled and warped. "Did the sprinklers ever go off in here?" I asked her.

"Not while I was here. Maybe when I was at St. Mag's." Her text sounded. Peyton, her classes over. Sophia began texting photos of her pedicure; more texts came in fast and furious, and she and Pilot headed back to her room.

After twilight, the winds died as quickly as they'd sprung to life. Evan returned, covered with soot and ash. Otis fussed over him, and Sophia peppered him with questions. He was exhausted but clearly exhilarated, and he swept us all out for pizza at a roadside joint and told us about the rains of fiery sparks and the heat that felt as solid as a brick wall.

His eyes continually sought out mine. And I fell even more dangerously in love.

❧

The highway was cleared by the following day. Fortunately, because Wade and his family had arrived in Monterey the night before and this was the day I was meeting them for lunch. I set out shortly before noon.

It was a city I had grown to really like. Parts of it still had a grungy, lost-in-time quality: I could imagine gin-soaked joints where platinum blondes chain-smoked Tareytons and cracked wise to men in fedoras. But I was not having lunch with the O'Connors at any such louche establishment. With a five-year-old in tow, they'd sensibly chosen a Bubba Gump.

It was on the main tourist drag of Cannery Row. I parked in a usuriously priced lot near Steinbeck Plaza, then walked down the waterfront, old sardine factories transmogrified into wine bars, boutique hotels, and shops selling scuba gear, stuffed dolphins, novelty socks. The restaurant was large and clamorous. It took me a second to spot the O'Connors at a table with a harbor view. Wade, sporting a new beard, waving at me sideways like the queen of England. Keiko, elegant in flowing earth tones, dark hair cut geometrically. Benny hopping up and down on the seat of his chair. I felt a great burst of love. I hurried toward them.

Hugs, shrieks, kisses. I'd put another sizeable dent in my Visa with a present for Benny. "A Zoomer Dino!" he crowed and plopped himself on the floor with it. Wade helped him take apart the packaging and put in the batteries. Then we grown-ups settled at the table.

"You look amazing, Janie!" Keiko said. "We expected to find you all thin and pale and haunted looking."

"It's true, m'dear," Wade said. "You look great. There's a bloom on you."

I flushed with pleasure. It did seem to me that the old gilt mirror in my cottage had been smiling at me lately. "It must be the fog. It's great for the complexion."

"Whatever it is, we should package it." Keiko laughed.

A harried server tossed down huge and glossy menus. We ordered. Popcorn shrimp. Mac and cheese. Candy-colored tropical fruit drinks.

"We got in late last night," Keiko told me, "and everything was misty, the hotel covered in a swirling mist like a haunted castle. And I thought it seemed so Gothic. Perfect for Jane."

"Speaking of Gothic," Wade said to me, "do you still have ghosts peeking in your window?"

Keiko leaned toward me, a frown grooving her forehead. "Yeah, let's get right down to it. Do you still feel you're being watched?"

"I really didn't mean to alarm you. It's just an occasional feeling." I gave a laugh. "My superactive inner life."

"I wouldn't be too sure," Wade said. "It could be the late Mrs. Rochester. Haunting the husband who got away with her murder. You're just an innocent bystander."

"I wouldn't blame her for haunting the hell out of him." Keiko furiously bit into a breadstick. "I would. I mean, first he kills her, and now he's about to make a financial killing as well."

"So you think that's going to happen?" I asked. "A financial killing?"

"Pretty sure. My firm doesn't really track tech, but since you've been living at his place, I got curious about him. He's poured a lot of money into a start-up called Genovation Technologies. Biobased tech."

Wade brightened. "Biobased, like androids?"

"More like algae," I said. "Extracting natural chemicals from it."

"So you know about it?" Keiko asked.

"The basics. Like you, I've been curious. I've read a few things online about the deal. But the jargon starts to make my eyes cross. I do know Evan's been trying to raise more money for it."

"Yeah, he's leading a Series C funding round. Oops, sorry. More jargon." Keiko slapped her hand to her mouth, eyes grinning at me. "Anyway, this company, Genovation Technologies, has patented software that's apparently got huge potential. But they've had trouble getting it to the market. Rochester was in serious danger of losing his entire investment in the company. But now Dillon Saroyan is about to invest something like a quarter billion dollars in it."

Wade gave a whistle. "That's a lot of dough."

Dillon Saroyan. Otis had mentioned the name. So had Evan's lawyer, Malik Anderson, at the fireworks party. "Who exactly is he?"

"Huge venture capitalist, based in LA," Keiko said. "If Saroyan comes in with that kind of money, it should guarantee Genovation Tech's success. And, of course, Evander Rochester's."

Our drinks arrived. I took a deliberately long sip of mango. Then I ventured a guess. "I might have met someone who works for Saroyan. A woman named Laura? Or maybe Lily somebody?"

"You mean Liliana Greco?"

The name cut through me. "Could be. Young, dark haired. Extremely good looking?"

Keiko nodded. "One of Saroyan's principals. A real go-getter. Forever popping up in articles in *Forbes* and *Bloomberg* with titles like 'Thirty under Thirty to Watch.' And now that I think about it, she was the one who brought the Genovation Tech deal in to Saroyan. If it works, it's her ticket to making partner."

I made another guess. "Have you ever heard anything about her being involved with Evan? I mean on a personal basis?"

Keiko raised her brows. "Have you?"

"No," I said quickly. "But she's very pretty, so I just wondered."

"It would be hard to imagine. I mean, it would be a huge conflict of interest for both of them. It could be career suicide for her. And he'd risk losing the funding." She shook her head. "I'm sure they're both far too smart and way too ambitious to take that kind of risk."

Large plates clattered onto the table. Keiko coaxed Benny up from the floor to have a few bites of mac and cheese. We busied ourselves for some moments passing around the platters, serving ourselves.

Wade dipped a shrimp in cocktail sauce. "But you still haven't given us the inside scoop, Jane. Do you think Rochester is guilty?"

I busied myself with a serving spoon. "He hasn't confessed to me. And, as you've been quick to point out, I haven't stumbled on any bodies."

"I'm positive he did it," Keiko said. "I think he's guilty as hell. He's always had a reputation for being ruthless."

I glanced at her. "Like how?"

"Manipulating his numbers. Stealing patents. There've been rumors about physical intimidation. A kid who wouldn't sell him his app got sideswiped by a hit-and-run shortly afterward. Then he *had* to sell to Rochester to pay his medical bills."

"But just rumors, right?" I burst out. "Nothing was ever proved."

Both Keiko and Wade stared at me, startled by the force of my outburst. They exchanged quick glances.

I added quickly, "I wouldn't want to just believe rumors. He's been very generous to me."

"And have you ever wondered why?" Wade asked.

"For being generous? It could be a lot of reasons. I think I've been good for Sophia. I've made real progress with her. And I've been helpful to Otis too. I'm sure he appreciates all that."

"And that's it? Nothing more?"

I looked at Wade levelly. "What else would there be?"

Wade and Keiko exchanged another glance. Wade said, "Nothing, I guess."

Benny wriggled off his seat to go back to his dinosaur. Keiko said, "Wade, it's time to tell Janie your great news."

"News?" I said. "Wait, let me guess. You've got a new gig!"

"Yeah." He grinned. "Actually, even better than just a gig. I wrote a spec pilot for a series. It's about Edgar Allen Poe—he's a present-day horror writer who consults with the police to solve particularly grisly crimes. And, well, I sold it to FX."

I whooped. "That's terrific. I'm thrilled. I really am!"

"They seem really high on it," Keiko put in. "I'm sure it will go to series."

"It's a great idea, and they've got a great writer," I said. "I'm sure it will too."

"And if it does," Wade said, "I'll be bringing you on board, Janie. You'll be back in the writer's room."

I felt a tick of excitement. All those months knocking futilely on doors. And now the real chance of a writing gig . . . and of working with Wade again. But a split second later, another thought: *Is this really what I want to do with my life?*

So much had changed for me now.

And it would be twenty-five thousand miles away from Thorn Bluffs.

"I guess we'll just have to wait and see," I said.

"Yeah, you're right, I shouldn't go jumping the gun. Getting your hopes up too high. But I wanted you to know because if it happens, things will go quickly."

"And if you need to come back early, I think I've got a place for you," Keiko said. "A woman at my firm, Kristin Halstead—she's just bought a two-bed co-op in Morningside Heights. She travels a lot and wouldn't mind having a roommate. It's a small room, but it's got its own bath."

"And if you ever really need it, our couch folds out," Wade added.

"Oh God, she'd break her back on that thing," Keiko said. "She'd be far better off at Kristin's."

Benny sought our attention, wanting to start making his dino walk and talk. Wade scooted down to help him. Keiko began talking about the Montessori Benny would be attending in the fall. And when Wade came back to the table, we reminisced about *Carlotta Dark* and where all our friends had ended up.

And then we were leaving, hugs and kisses on the wharf. Keiko pulled me a little to the side. "Seriously, Janie. I want you to be straight with me. Is there anything going on between you and Rochester?"

"No," I said. "There isn't."

"Good. I hope it stays that way. He's rich and kind of glamorous, and that can be pretty irresistible. But I really think he could be a dangerous guy. And if you let yourself give in to rushing endorphins—you know, they can really scramble your brain."

"You don't have to worry. I don't think I'm in his league. Particularly once he becomes filthy rich."

She gave a snort. "He's not in *your* league."

She hugged me again, and I watched them all leave with a pang. I missed them already.

And then I turned in the opposite direction and walked down the wharf until I came to a shaded bench where I could see my phone screen.

I googled *Liliana Greco*. I clicked on the first hit, a headline from *Fortune* magazine:

"A RISING STAR IN VENTURE CAPITALISM: At Twenty-Nine, Liliana Greco Is on a Rocket Track to General Partner at Saroyan Capital."

There was a headshot of a stunning young woman with a boy-short bob of dark-brown hair. Dark almond-shaped eyes. A pale oval face tilting with a hint of arrogance.

My stomach clenched.

Definitely her. The young woman at Evan's fireworks display.

I skimmed the article. Princeton BA. Wharton MBA. Early success as a partner in an online company called BestBride.com—a kind of Airbnb for weddings, hooking up brides with homeowners willing to rent their gardens as wedding venues. It was sold the following year to the actual Airbnb for $17 million, of which Liliana raked in a good share. She then joined the giant venture capital company Saroyan Capital.

I did a new search: *Liliana Greco + Evan Rochester*.

Page after page of hits on Saroyan Capital's impending Series C funding of the biotech start-up Genovation Technologies. Liliana's name was never prominent but often somewhere in the articles. I would have discovered it if I had ever dug deeper into the articles I'd looked up.

I continued scrolling, until seven pages in: an article not about the Saroyan deal. The headline read: *BRAVE NEW MONEY*. Dated March of last year.

A press release about a Bitcoin conference in Montreal. There were twenty-odd speakers listed. One was Evan Rochester. Another was Liliana Greco.

Nearly a year before Evan became involved in the deal with Saroyan Capital.

But just a few weeks before Beatrice Rochester was locked up in a mental health facility.

Meaning what?

Maybe nothing.

I clicked back to Liliana's company page profile. Enlarged her headshot. That feeling I'd had at the fireworks—why did she look familiar?

It struck me: the Modigliani!

The hair, the swan neck. The high cheekbones in an oval face. She bore a distinct resemblance to the slashed-up Modigliani portrait in the tower.

My pulse raced.

That couldn't possibly be a coincidence, could it?

BEATRICE

I am still in my bedroom, I am dressing very quickly. A big red pullover that says *49ers* on it with a hood in back. Gray pants that bunch at my waist and a pair of brown shoes that are too big even for my special feet.

I pick up my Neiman Marcus shopping bag. I put a *Vogue* magazine on top of the other things inside it. I go into the hallway, where Annunciata is waiting for my private time to be over.

She looks at the clothes I'm wearing with a frown on her face.

I am nervous of her frown, but I walk past her, and I descend the stairs. I listen for my jailer's voice. I don't hear it anywhere.

Annunciata stays right behind me, all the way down to the Ocean Room.

"Do you want your tray in here, Mrs. Beatrice?"

His hairs, Beatrice, Mary reminds me. Her voice in my mind soothes me gently now. *You need to get his hairs.*

I find my own voice to use to Annunciata. "Where is my husband?"

"I don't know, señora. You want I find him?"

"Yes."

She goes away. I sit down on my white chaise lounge. I begin to bite at my fingernails. My jailer sends a woman every week to cut them off, but there's still a little bit left, and I bite at what's left until they are all sharp and ragged.

"Why are you wearing my clothes, Beat?" My jailer is here now, and he has a tray with my lunch in his hands. He stares at me with his inky all-night stare.

I say nothing. My heart is going fast.

"They're comfortable, aren't they? But you'll have to change for dinner. Remember, we're going to Sierra Mar." The tray he's holding is black with Japanese designs on it. "Otis has got Kendra coming here at four o'clock to help you get dressed. You always liked her, didn't you?"

I see his plot. To make me think he is kind and gentle. To hide what he intends to do. I say nothing.

"Nunci said you needed me for something?"

"I don't know," I say.

"Okay. You can tell me when you remember."

He thinks I swallowed the extrastrong poison pill. That I can't remember anything at all.

Not even her voice. The voice of the girl Lilies on his mobile phone.

He keeps on talking. "Otis had to leave. But he made your favorite crab salad for your lunch."

He thinks I don't know. That I didn't see the boy go away in the Land Cruiser just a short time ago. That I didn't know the girl was back inside her picture frame.

I keep my face very still. I'm a perfect mannequin.

He sets the tray down on the end table beside me. There's no knife or real fork on it. Just a plastic fork. There's a can of my Dr. Brown. The white plate has a very small amount of pink-and-white crab salad on baby spinach leaves.

"Nunci only gave you a little because we're eating early tonight. Reservation at five thirty, remember? Are you okay with that soda? Would you rather have lemonade? Or a Perrier?"

I close my hand around the frosty can.

"Okay, Dr. Brown's it is." My jailer looks down. He spies my Neiman Marcus shopping bag. The *Vogue* magazine that I put on top. "You're reading *Vogue* again? That's great, Beat. Taking an interest in your field."

He starts to pick up the *Vogue*.

Quick as a cat, I spring to my feet. He turns with a puzzle in his eyes.

I step close to him. I reach and touch his twisty hair. I can sense his body go stiff all over. He hates it now when I touch him.

He wants you dead, Mary Magdalene whispers.

I slide my fingers in his hair, and I scrape my ragged fingernails into his scalp.

"Hey, what the fuck!" he says.

He grabs my wrists and pushes me back down on the chaise. He's not acting kind now. "Just sit down and eat your lunch."

He wants you dead. The voices all rustle together. *He's going to kill you. You can't let him do it, Beatrice. Make him pay.*

I curl my fingers into tight fists, so he doesn't see what I'm hiding in them. I see Annunciata hovering near us. "Tell her to go away," I say.

"She'll wait for you to finish."

My voice goes higher, very high. "I don't want her to watch me eat. Tell her to leave, now!"

"Okay, okay." He talks to Annunciata in their secret witch language. Then he talks to me again. "Use the intercom, Beatrice, if there's anything more you need." And he takes the Braidy Witch out of the Ocean Room.

I open up my fists. In my fingers, there are several twists of his hair, and I have scraped his scalp with my nails. I dig into my shopping bag and take out pieces of the Christian Dior dress, and I wipe the hairs on them.

I take out the blade and use it to scrape underneath my fingernails. I bury it all back beneath the *Vogue* magazine.

I pick up the shopping bag. Stealthy as I can be, I go outside.

I walk as fast as I can in my jailer's too-big brown shoes. I'm breathing hard. If Hector catches me, he will report me to my jailer, and he'll come for me before I can finish the plan.

I am very, very frightened.

SEVENTEEN

In the following week, I saw Evan only rarely. Once for a brief walk with the dogs. He looked exhausted. Spoke in a way that made it seem his mind was elsewhere. After that, it was only brief conversations in the motor court as he was about to leave either for LA, where Dillon Saroyan was headquartered, or to his own offices up in Los Gatos.

Los Gatos is near San Francisco, I couldn't help thinking.

Where Liliana Greco is based.

I continued compulsively to dig up articles about her. She was accomplished. Successful. And unquestionably beautiful. Though not quite as gorgeous as Beatrice. Liliana's was more of a hard beauty. *Like a hard currency,* I thought. Gold or silver. Something to be traded for like value.

Or maybe I just wanted to think that.

Then I did notice something. Beginning a year ago June, she was always pictured wearing a scarf or turtleneck, like the gauzy scarf she'd sported at the fireworks party. Something to cover up that ugly burn scar. Before last June, she had flaunted her swan neck, favoring scoop tops or deep V-neck jackets.

The Bitcoin conference she and Evan had both attended had been in March of last year. Beatrice was hospitalized just a month later, at the end of April. I could find no photos of Liliana at all in May.

And then there she was in June, sporting scarves. And dowdy turtlenecks.

A connection?

I absolutely needed to look at the Modigliani again. To be sure there really was a resemblance to Liliana. And that the slashes really did look like that scratchy writing in the margins of Beatrice's art book.

I had to go back to the tower, even at the risk of getting caught by the ever-spying Sandovals.

An opportunity finally arose. I'd just wrapped up a session with Sophia. She had translated the last chapters of *Le Petit Prince* and was teary-eyed. "I didn't know he dies. When we did it at St. Mag's, we didn't get to the end."

"But his body disappeared," I told her. "So it's possible he didn't die but went back to his asteroid."

She rolled her eyes. Her mom had never returned from Africa. And unlike me, she had no use for imagining the dead might not stay dead.

Otis's voice floated on the intercom: "Jane? Can you come up when you're done?"

Sophia jumped to her feet.

"You did a great job on the translation, Sophia," I told her.

She glowed. Then scooted upstairs.

I gathered my things and went up to the kitchen. Otis was sharpening a boning knife with an assassin's skill. A whole salmon glistened on a cutting board. The mouthwatering smell of baking chocolate wafted from the oven. "What's up?" I said.

"Evan's in Los Gatos, but he's coming back with Malik Anderson and another lawyer. So it's a last-minute dinner for three." He raised the salmon's glassy-eyed head and stabbed it behind the gills. "Listen.

Those detectives were here today. You know, the ones who questioned me before."

"What did they want?"

"I don't know. They wanted to talk to Ev, but he was gone. But why now? It's the first time there's been any cops here since December."

"Maybe it's nothing. Just something routine."

He began to filet the salmon, knife sliding expertly through the flesh. "Maybe. But what if they start questioning me again?"

"What if they do?"

He kept his eyes on his work. "Well . . . maybe there is something I didn't tell you."

My heart sank. "Shit, Otis. What?"

"I was arrested once before."

I stared at him. "When?"

He set the butchered filet on a platter. Heaved a sigh. "It was back in New York, at the Clown, right after you left. Remember that baseball bat I kept behind the bar?"

A Louisville Slugger. He'd wave it around occasionally when a drunk got out of hand. "Yeah, I remember. What did you do?"

He pushed his glasses up the bridge of his nose with the heel of his hand. "There was this guy who wouldn't leave this one girl alone. So I got out the bat, just to threaten him. But he came at me. Big beefy dude. I took a swing at his body but got his head. I mean, he had this gigantic head—you couldn't miss it. He went down, and then . . . well, maybe I hit him again, like on his shoulder, because I was worked up. Somebody called the cops, and they put me under arrest."

"Oh shit, Otis. Did you go to jail?"

"Just overnight. The guy was basically okay. You could run him over with a tank and he'd be okay. They let me plead guilty to a class B misdemeanor, and I got six months' probation. But it's on my record, and those detectives know about it." He flipped the salmon over and began fileting the other side.

"Well if they do question you, you need to tell them the truth this time. About not being in the bar in San Francisco the whole time that night. It'll be okay, I'm sure."

"You'd vouch for me, wouldn't you? Tell them I'd never really try to hurt anyone?"

"It's true, isn't it?"

"Of course it is," he said vehemently.

"Then, of course I'd back you up," I said. "We're family. You know that."

A timer pinged. He went to the oven, slid out a tray of biscotti. Prodded one to test for doneness. "I never told Evan either," he said. "He wouldn't have wanted me around if he knew. He's got to keep a pretty clean nose. He can't have criminals working for him."

"You're not a criminal, Otis. You made a mistake. And got probation."

"Still." He began to spatula the cookies onto a black lacquered tray.

"Hey, Otis?" I said after a moment. "Did Evan ever own a Modigliani?"

"Modigliani?"

"Yeah, a French painter of the 1920s . . ."

"I *know* who he is. Why?"

"No reason. I just heard he had one, that's all."

That tick of hesitation. Of not quite telling the whole truth. "Yeah, he used to." He turned, wiped his hands on his apron. "Listen. If I tell you something, will you swear to keep it a secret?"

"Another secret?"

"This is really important. It's about the day Beatrice drowned. There was something I also didn't tell the cops."

Shit, I inwardly screamed. "What?"

"That morning, Evan had me take something down to San Jose. He told me I had to keep it a strict secret. And that's what it was. The Modigliani painting. He and Hector nailed it up inside a crate and put it in the Land Cruiser, and I drove it to this gigantic warehouse with no windows and lots of guards and huge gates. The guards took it, and then I went on up to San Francisco. Like I said."

"Was it all slashed up?" I said. "The painting, I mean. Did it look like somebody had slashed it with a knife or something sharp?"

"What? No. It was just a regular painting. Of a girl with short dark hair. And, you know, a long neck."

"And that's what you meant, isn't it? When you said Evan makes people do things they don't want to?"

He shrugged. "I figured it must be something illegal—otherwise why would I have to keep it so secret? And then Beatrice getting drowned that exact same day." He glanced at a clock. "They're all gonna be here at seven o'clock. Plus I promised Sophia an acai bowl. I better get cracking. Swear you won't tell Evan I told you, okay?"

"Okay, I swear."

"Good. Hey, take some biscotti. Chocolate hazelnut."

I grabbed a couple of cookies and, hooking my tote over my shoulder, went outside. A heavy fog had begun to come in, tendrils of mist weaving into an opaque veil. I could barely make out Hector's truck idling in the motor court, Hector a phantom shape in the driver's seat.

A second phantom, Annunciata, glided up from the office path and got into the seat beside him. The gears engaged.

They were leaving early today. I had a thought: *There's enough light for me to get to the tower.* I'd have just enough time to get there and back before Evan and his guests arrived.

I waited, polishing off both the biscotti, until I could no longer hear the engine grumble. Before I could lose my nerve, I clicked open the middle garage door. Hoisted myself into the Land Cruiser, backed it out. Drove it around to the washed-out service road.

My heart was in my throat. The Cruiser jolted and jounced on the broken asphalt. What if I blew out a tire? Or broke an axle? The farther I got from the compound, the more misted the road became. And around every bend, I expected Hector's truck to appear. If he could materialize himself out of thin air, why not his vehicle as well?

In about twelve minutes, an outline of the tower shimmered into sight. The fog gave an eerie illusion—it looked in ruins, half the structure crumbled away, the other half just a jagged section of stone. I pulled up closer.

It wasn't an illusion! The tower was half-demolished. The violent winds must have taken a heavy toll.

I stepped down from the Cruiser. What was left of the structure rocked and groaned in the gusts of breeze, as if any moment it would completely crumble away—fall into the sea that was thrashing so dismally on the cove below. The heavy wood door was still attached to its hinges, and it creaked open and shut. I had a sense of being a child, being read a horror story—feeling that same sense of dread but also fascination. I stepped cautiously closer. The door creaked, and I half expected it to reveal that ghostly white shape inside.

But nothing was inside. All the furniture, the crucifixes and saints—all gone. The interior was empty except for that circular staircase rocking and swaying in the open breeze.

The horrific portrait gone as well.

And now I noticed a small machine parked beside the demolished wall. A long metal arm extended. The claw still grasping at the jagged remnant of stone wall. It hadn't been the winds. The tower was being deliberately torn down.

Because of me? I wondered.

I swept my phone flash around what was left of the interior. One of Jasper Malloy's old architectural drawings remained tacked to a piece of the wall. The structure suddenly groaned as if in great pain. I made a dash, ripped the drawing off the peg, and bolted back to my car. I hoisted myself back in and started the engine.

A rock hit the windshield with a loud crack. I jumped.

Someone was there. Hidden in the dark foliage. Someone who'd been watching me. Wanted me gone.

I slammed the accelerator.

As I sped away, I heard that shriek—that unearthly call of whatever bird or creature—coming from those dark woods. I felt a thrill of terror.

I didn't look back.

I made it to the compound before Evan or any of his guests had arrived. I stowed the Cruiser in the garage, grabbed my things and the drawing, and hurried to my cottage.

I pushed my dresser against the glass doors. And I piled books, shoes, dishes on top to give it more weight.

I poured a glass of my latest bargain-bin wine. Began to relax.

I'd let that ruin spook me. The rock on my windshield—just an acorn tossed in the breeze. That shriek was whatever woodland animal sometimes also roosted behind my cottage. Nothing malignant or supernatural.

And with my rational senses returning, disappointment set in. I'd lost the chance of ever examining that portrait again.

I thought of what Otis had said—he'd taken it to a guarded warehouse the morning of the day Beatrice drowned. And that it had not been slashed up then.

Which meant Beatrice could not have been the one to destroy it.

Unless she hadn't drowned. If she had still been alive. Hiding in the tower. And had slashed the portrait afterward, when Evan had got it back from the warehouse.

Hiding without ever being detected in there?

I smoothed the architectural drawing out on my table. It was a rendering of the entire Thorn Bluffs site, exteriors and cross sections of the interiors. It was darkened with age and heavily splotched with mildew. I could only faintly make out the main house and guesthouse.

My cottage was a little more distinct. It had a strange sort of symbol behind it. A small circle enclosing a spiral. It reminded me of a hex sign—like the ones painted on barns in Pennsylvania Dutch country.

The hatch I had stumbled on! The shaft enclosing a spiral staircase. Jasper Malloy's escape hatch.

I looked at the cross section of the tower, almost too mildewed to make out the details. I could barely see crossbeams defining two floors. One never built.

I made out another spiral symbol in the lower floor. Not enclosed in a circle. It was the circular staircase that stopped in midair. Spiraling up to a floor that was never built.

There were no hidden chambers or passages. No place for Beatrice to hide without being found. And she could not have survived outside it. Not all winter in that wild foliage.

It was impossible.

No, she had to have been dead by the time the painting got slashed. But if it wasn't Beatrice, then who?

I put on music. Bouncy pop stuff to drive away the last of my willies. I ached to have someone I could trust to talk all this over with.

Otis kept too many secrets from me. Wade and Keiko? They'd just insist I get out. I thought of Ella Mahmed. But she loved to dish. And she knew Rick McAdams; I couldn't be sure what she might let slip to him.

I'd have to keep searching for answers by myself.

EIGHTEEN

The landline shrilled me out of sleep. That old desk phone that some-times worked and was sometimes dead. It was later that night, almost one a.m. With a flash of alarm, I picked up. "Otis?"

"It's me." Evan's voice low, urgent. "Are you dressed?"

I felt a moment's confusion. "No. I was sleeping. Why are you call-ing on this phone?"

"You've got no cell connection. I need you to come to my office."

"Now? Why?"

"Please, Jane. I need you. You'll know when you get here."

The urgency in his voice heightened my alarm. "Okay, I'll get dressed."

I glanced at my cell. It flickered on one bar, getting no help from the too-cheap booster. I pulled on jeans, a thick sweater. Quickly combed my bedhead hair, then went out, taking care to lock the door securely behind me.

The fog had completely dissipated. The moon was now just a thin sliver of gold very high in the dark sky. The wind rushing through the tall pines sounded like traffic on an expressway. I made my way by the dim ground lights to the motor court. A vehicle was parked there. *Malik Anderson still here?*

But it was an SUV, not Malik's Porsche. A Range Rover. Black or maybe blue.

A feeling of trepidation crept over me.

I continued down the dark path to the office. The door was partially open. A dim and flickering light inside. Minnie and Mickey were crouched in front of the door, fixated on the interior, growling low in their throats. Their attention didn't waver as I walked past them. I stepped inside.

"Jane." Evan emerged from the shadowed far end of the room.

I gasped. His white shirt was covered with blood. "You're hurt!"

A thin voice spoke behind me. "No, he's not."

I swung my head.

At the opposite end of the room, three flat-screen monitors were mounted on the wall, tuned to financial programs—talking heads muttering low, stock quotes streaming—and below the streaming quotes, Rick McAdams lay sprawled on a couch.

I gasped again.

His face was a gory mess. Blood soaked his jacket, spattered his pants and shoes. He clutched a towel sopping with blood to his head.

I started toward him. Evan seized my arm. "He says he knows you. Is that true?"

I looked wildly at Evan. "I met him once. What's happened to him?"

"When did you meet him?"

"Last month. He recognized the Audi and followed me."

"Why didn't you tell me?"

"Why would I?" I glanced back at Rick. "He needs help."

"Hurts. I'm really fucked up," Rick said. "I told him to call you. You're a witness."

"She should be a witness." To me, Evan said, "He was trespassing on the grounds in violation of a restraining order. The dogs went after him. He tripped and fell and cracked his head."

"Not true," Rick muttered.

"When I found him, he was out cold. I got him into his car and brought him here. He didn't want EMS."

"He looks seriously hurt." I broke from Evan and went over to Rick. His glamorous blond hair was encrusted with blood—black at the ends where it had dried, dark blue near his scalp where the wounds were still oozing. "He needs an ambulance right away."

"Nuh-uh," Rick said. "No ambulance. Take me to the hospital." He drew the towel off his head. "Shit. I'm bleeding to death."

"You're not," Evan said. "Head wounds bleed a lot. It's not that bad." He turned and strode into another room and emerged with a fresh towel. "Keep the pressure on. I'll drive you to the medics."

Rick exchanged the gory towel for the fresh one. He struggled to a sitting position. "Not getting in a car with you," he said. "She takes me."

"No." Evan moved as if to shield me. "I won't have her involved."

Involved in what?

"She takes me, or the deal is off."

"Then it's off." Evan's tone was low and dangerous. "I'll call an EMT. They'll bring the police. We'll both take our chances."

Rick mumbled something inaudible.

I became exquisitely aware of all the mundane office sounds around us: a phone ringing even at this hour of the night, computer messages pinging, financial shows muttering. The flickering light added a layer of unreality, like a scene from a black-and-white movie. "It's okay, I'll drive him," I said.

"I can't let you do that," Evan said.

"It's not your decision. It's mine." I turned back to Rick. Clutching the towel to his head, he staggered to his feet.

Evan strode over and supported him. "There's an urgent care in Pacific Grove," he said to me. "Use his car. I'll follow."

"No doc in a box," Rick said. "The real ER in Monterey. And no following." He began with Evan's help toward the door. Then shrank back. "The dogs?"

"They won't hurt you. You're with me."

I followed them out. The shepherds sprang to their feet, barking fiercely. "Quiet!" Evan snapped. They fell mute, except for that ominous rumble in their throats.

He pulled open the passenger door of the Range Rover. Rick collapsed heavily onto the seat. "You fell at your own place. Are we straight on that?" Evan said.

"I *got* it. I said I'd say that."

Evan turned to me. "Are you sure you're okay with this?"

"Yeah, I am. He needs help."

His voice softened. "Listen. If he gets any worse, stop and call the paramedics. If not, when you get to the ER, leave his car there. I'll send a car to pick you up."

"I'll do whatever I think is necessary." I slid in behind the wheel. Pressed the starter.

"Take the 1 to the Pebble Beach exit," Rick said. "Hospital's right off it, you'll see signs. Go fast. I'm in excruciating pain."

I drove out of the compound and began navigating the looping private road. My throat felt tight. There were knots in my stomach. Rick whimpered at every rough patch. We were halfway around the first hairpin when suddenly he said, "Stop!"

I braked. "Do you want to go back?"

"No. Not going back there. This is where it happened. Where he attacked me." He pointed out into the woods. "I saw him. White shirt. Flashlight. There was a trail—I went after him."

"By yourself in the dark?" I said.

"Used the flash on my phone, okay? Just a short way. There's a cross out there. Red cross stuck on a burial mound. He's got a grave hidden."

I shot him a doubting look.

"He didn't want me to see. He came up from behind and hit me."
Another groan. "Shit, this hurts. Keep driving."

He lapsed into silence until we came to the highway, and the smoother pavement revived him. He hoisted himself a little straighter.

"What were you doing at the estate so late?" I said.

"Looking around. It's a big wild place. Evidence could be anywhere. Had to be late or that freak Hector would be on me."

"How did you get in?"

"I can get in," he said evasively. "I got a right to be there. Half belongs to my sister. Community property, it's law in California. All gets split half and half." He pulled down the sunshade mirror and lifted the towel. "This looks bad. Go faster."

I pressed the accelerator. Everything he said seemed dubious. But maybe I could coax something more from him. "There's something you should know," I told him. "Your sister had stopped taking her meds. She wasn't swallowing them—she was hiding them in her shoes. That would have made her suicidal."

"He tell you that?"

"I found one in one of her shoes. Clozapine."

"What were you doing with her shoes?"

"Snooping in her closet," I said bluntly. "And then Evan and Annunciata found a lot more pills in them. They had an impartial witness with them when they made the search."

"How do you know he didn't plant them there himself? Before he killed her. As an alibi."

I paused. I didn't know.

Rick gave a croaking sort of laugh. "He comes up with easy answers for everything. He's a psycho—they're good at that."

"So you're promoting him from sociopath?"

He swiveled his head. "Be sarcastic if you want. But you've got no idea what he's like. You think my sister was the first?"

"What do you mean?" I said warily.

"His parents. You know about them?"

"They died in a plane crash. While he was at college."

"Nuh. He was on spring break with them. In Peru. He was supposed to be on that plane. They disappeared. He got the money. Sound familiar?"

I felt a cold chill race through me. "It's possible to have more than one tragedy in your life."

"Yeah. He's just got really fucking lousy luck."

I was silent a moment. "Were you out prowling around the tower earlier? Before it got dark?"

"No. Told you, I just got there when he hit me."

"What about other times? Were you ever just looking around at night? Maybe behind the cottage?"

"I don't want to talk anymore. This hurts like shit." He scrunched down in his seat and was silent.

After about thirty minutes, I saw the exit for Pacific Grove/Pebble Beach and merged onto it. A sign for the hospital directed me to a smaller highway. As I turned, Rick let out a groan, a sort of death rattle. I glanced at him with alarm. Blood was streaming down his face.

And then his eyeballs rolled up, leaving just the whites visible, and he slumped unconscious against the door.

"Rick!" I gasped.

The sprawling white hospital complex appeared. I slammed to a stop in front of the ER. Leaped out, yelling for help. An orderly quickly appeared with a gurney, with a second orderly in tow. To my relief, Rick appeared to be swimming back into consciousness.

"Don't look too bad, man." The first orderly eased him onto the gurney. "Cuts on the head always bleed a lot. The docs will get you stapled right up."

"Do you want me to stay with you?" I asked Rick.

"Nuh. Leave me alone."

I parked the Range Rover in the visitor lot, then went back to the ER to give him the key. He was just being wheeled inside. He gave a ghastly grin and pointed to a corner of the ceiling. "Smile. You're on camera."

I glanced up. The blinking security camera. *So what?*

He disappeared into the examining rooms. I went back outside. An ambulance shrieked from around the back of the ER. What if Rick really was seriously injured and had died on the way? My heart beat violently. I took out my phone.

But now a black SUV glided up to the curb, and the driver spoke my name. He leaped out and opened the back door. I sank into the luxurious seat.

There was blood on my hands and sleeves. I shuddered. I reached for a bottle of water in the pocket of the door beside me and a tissue packet, and I scrubbed the blood off as best I could.

I must have dozed, since it seemed only minutes later we were turning into the Thorn Bluffs compound. The spark of a lit cigar twirled in the dark motor court. Evan pacing in agitation. He crushed the cigar under his heel, strode up, and flung open my door. "Are you okay?"

"I'm fine."

He spoke briefly to the driver. The SUV pulled away. He turned back to me. "I had a doctor friend call the ER. They told her McAdams had a concussion. Not life threatening, but you were right. I should have had the medics here immediately. And you should never have been a part of this."

"What was the deal you talked about?" I said. "Why did he agree to say he fell at his own home?"

"He was disbarred in Florida last year for trying to bribe a judge. He did not want to be caught trespassing in violation of a restraining order."

"Restraining order?"

"He'd been following delivery people through the gate when I wasn't here and nosing around. Badgering my workers. I don't know how he got in tonight. I intend to find out."

"Then why did you want to cover up for him this time?"

"I'm under suspicion of murdering my wife. To have her brother found bleeding on my couch would just make things more complicated for me."

I fixed my eyes on him. "Did you attack him?"

"No. I was in the Great Room reading documents. Fairfax brought me a beer about thirty minutes before. You can ask him. And why would I have attacked McAdams? The dogs had cornered him. If he hadn't cracked his head, I would have called the police."

"He said there's a grave out there. With a red cross on it. You wanted to stop him from seeing it."

He gave a mirthless smile. "It's where I buried my old dog, Delilah. She ate snail bait. She was old and addled."

"So she wasn't poisoned by . . . anybody?"

"By Beatrice, you mean? No. My wife was fond of dogs."

I was silent a moment. The ground lights flickered in the breeze; our shadows on the cobbled courtyard writhed and twisted together.

He said softly, "You've heard a lot of bad things about me, haven't you?"

"Yeah," I said. "I have."

"Do you believe them?"

I hesitated.

"I'll answer anything you want to ask me. Not now, you're dead tired—and I've got some business issues I need to deal with before the morning. But tomorrow, I will."

"Why?" I said.

He smiled. Brushed a wisp of my hair back from my forehead. I turned my face up to him, and he drew me into his embrace. His lips met mine, a kiss that deepened, and my entire body turned to fire.

But then an image flashed in my mind. A girl who looked like a Modigliani. I pulled back from his arms.

He smiled again. "Okay. I'll see you tomorrow. Good night to you, Jane."

And I watched him disappear down the darkened path.

BEATRICE

It's Ricky's plan that I have to do.

In the foster homes Ricky always made plans for us. He planned how we could steal watches from the Cartier in Boca Raton or diamond necklaces from the Tiffany and run away to Wyoming. But then I began to make us lots of money, and he didn't need to make the plans anymore. Not until the new girl from St. Petersburg. The one who became a sabertooth on the catwalk and I took her down, and Fiona from the agency cawed and crackled at me on my phone.

And then Ricky went back to making plans.

"Face it, Beatie June, you're getting worse. You got maybe two good years of work left if you're lucky. We've got to marry you off. Some rich older guy. Quarter of a billion minimum. You've already got a bunch of them to choose from."

"I don't like any of them, Ricky. I don't want them."

"Tough shit, BJ. You gotta pick one. And if it comes to it, we can always get rid of him."

"How? Tell me, Ricky."

"It's easy. There's a million ways."

And then he made up a new plan. "First thing you do, BJ, is you collect evidence." He told me about the blood. The blade. The hairs. "You hide it all in some secret place."

The Secret Place. Mary's voice hisses angry. *What the frig are you waiting for? Get to it now!*

I start walking faster to the Secret Place. Down the green-moss steps to the old wooden cabin. My feet go clump, clump in my jailer's shoes. I take the hidden path around to the back. I give a very nervous look at the glass doors. But it's all dark inside the cabin.

Not like it was that day in last April.

Hurry, Beatrice! Mary hisses.

I pull the hood of the red 49ers shirt up so it will protect my hair and some of my face from all the tangles of bushes and weeds. I keep going on the hidden path, and it takes me to the Secret Place.

The top is all covered in dirt and leaves. I wipe off the handle, and then I pull it open all the way. I lower myself down onto the stairs inside. They go around and around but not very far, and then they get buried up in rocks and dirt.

I take the evidence out of the bag. The hairs. The bloodied-up pieces of silk chiffon and bra. I scatter them on the rocks and dirt. I take out the little knife that has my blood and the parings from underneath my fingernails, and I throw that in the dirt as well.

Then I reach into my too-big-for-me pants and scratch at the tiny cut I made down there. And now I have blood and pubic hairs on my fingers. I swipe my fingers on the railing as I go back up, bringing my Neiman Marcus shopping bag with me.

I hoist myself out of the Secret Place. I pull the top back closed, and it falls with a sound like a loud church bell. For a moment I'm scared it will bring the witches.

But it doesn't. I go back up the path around the cabin, and I continue walking to the side of the house where there are sheds and machines. I go to the mulching machine. It's big and red and has a large hungry mouth. I feed the *Vogue* magazine into the mouth, and it crunches it up like an ogre eating crackers. *Grrrrunch* it goes. And again, I'm afraid it will bring the witches. Quick, I feed the shopping bag with the pieces of silk chiffon wrapped up in plastic into the mouth, and the ogre crunches that up too.

Quick, quick, I go back to the Ocean Room. Before I go inside, I push the hood of the 49ers shirt off my hair, and I slap off as much of the thorns and leaves and dirt from myself as I can.

My tray is still on the table next to my white chaise. I don't feel scared now. I'm very hungry. Hungry like an ogre.

I sit on my chaise and take the tray onto my lap. I scoop the plastic fork into the crab salad and start to eat. I taste salty fish and baby spinach leaves. It gives me a memory.

It reminds me of the taste of blood.

Yes. I remember. That day in the month of last April.

The taste of the girl's blood in my mouth.

The girl named Lilies.

NINETEEN

In the morning, I called the hospital in Monterey, asking to be connected to Richard McAdams's room, and was told he'd been released. I texted him. Are you ok?

Twenty minutes later, a response. Feel like shit. Six staples. Head exploding.

I'm sorry. But glad it was nothing worse.

It's bad. Actionable. Suing him. Calling u as witness.

I witnessed nothing. The grave you saw is for a dog that died. Delilah.

Old trick. Bury animal on top of other buried evidence. Nobody digs farther. I'll get court order to exhume.

He texted again immediately: Might sue u too. Yr a party to it.

I felt a flare of anger. Nonsense. You asked me to take you to the ER.

Not so. He got u to do it. So not to look involved. Conspiracy.

That's a lie and you know it. I pressed "Send" and blocked his number again.

I'd heard nothing this morning from Evan. I texted him: Can we talk now?

He replied: Still putting out fires. Maybe later.

How long was I supposed to wait? Unless he never meant to answer all my questions and was just stringing me along. He had to know what my feelings were. One look into my tell-all eyes would give it away.

I went up to the house and gave the dogs their midday snacks, making sure Hermione didn't nose in on Julius's special kibble after she'd inhaled her own. I wrestled with Julius for him to swallow his asthma medicine. Another wrestle, with Pilot, getting him to stay put while I combed out his freshly clipped coat, keeping a close eye out for ticks.

Otis burst into the service porch. "Do me a huge favor? Sophia's going to spend the weekend at Peyton's and forgot her overnight bag in her room. Could you bring it to her at tennis?"

"She's been spending a lot of overnights there. Did you give her permission?"

"She asked Evan. He was probably on about six phones at once and just said yes. And I don't see why not."

I didn't know exactly why it made me uneasy. "Okay, I'll take it to her."

"Great, because you know I'm going up to Berkeley." He yawned. "The damned German shepherds were barking outside last night. Evan must have been having one of his insomnia spells. Pacing around out there."

"I heard them too," I said simply.

I went to Sophia's room to fetch her bag. A knapsack—orange, emblazoned with tiny skulls—sat on her bed amid a tempest of sheets, beach towels, bras, and assorted junk food wrappings. I paused to peer at the little ball python, Niall, in his tank. A glistening black-and-gold comma. A pretty thing, really. Hard to imagine the fearsome Annunciata being scared of him.

At the tennis club, I took my usual seat on a courtside bench while Sophia finished out a set. She won with a smashing backhand return of serve. I put up a hand, and she came loping over. Snatched the back-pack. "Thanks for bringing," she said. "I was stupid to forget."

"No, you weren't," I said. "Are Peyton's parents going to be there the whole weekend?"

"Her real mom lives in Copenhagen, but Kelly, her stepmom, will be. And maybe her dad, except sometimes he's not."

"What about her brother? Alcott—is that his name?"

"Yeah, he'll be there."

"If he's smoking, please don't stay in the same room with him. Secondhand smoke is just as dangerous."

The mother of all eye rolls. "I *know* that."

"Okay, good. I'll text you later. Oh, and Sophia?"

"What?"

"Your room is such a mess. If Annunciata won't clean it, why don't you let one of her helpers?"

"I don't want them to. They take things."

"Those nice ladies? I don't believe that."

She shrugged. "I had this teddy I really liked from Victoria's Secret. It was white lace with a push-up bra, and now it's gone, and I can't even buy it again because it's been discontinued. And also my mermaid-tail snuggly that my mom crocheted for me."

"Oh, Sophia, I'm sorry." I flashed on my nightshirt—the one that had gone missing my second night at Thorn Bluffs. "Are you sure they're gone? Maybe they're just lost in that mess."

"They're not. I left them when I went back to school in January, and all the time while my dad was living in San Francisco. The cleaners were the only ones who ever came to our house here back then. Once a week."

"Not Annunciata?"

"She went up with my dad. She just came sometimes on weekends when he did."

"Tell you what. I'll help you clean your room, okay? We'll do it together when you get back and look for your stuff. Have a good weekend. I'll text you."

She smiled suddenly, in that heartbreakingly sweet way she sometimes had. I watched her jog back to her teammates. Gangly, fidgety girls with scrunchied topknots and shrieky voices. I felt a tug in my chest—some aching emotion I couldn't quite identify.

When I got back to Thorn Bluffs, I found the gates opened and a workman fiddling with them. Otis was waiting at my door. "I thought you'd already be gone," I said.

"I'm just about to leave." He followed me inside. "We've got a new security company. Home Protect. Evan found out somebody at Guards Plus was giving out the codes."

That must have been how Rick had managed to get in. Bribed a Guards Plus employee. Like he'd once tried to bribe a judge.

Otis handed me a remote and a piece of paper. "Here's the new codes and emergency call number. The remote's programmed."

"Okay, thanks."

"And Evan says you want to talk to him? He's at the pool, so you can catch him there." He eyed me with narrow suspicion. "What's that about?"

"Nothing. About Sophia. Just bringing him up to speed."

"Well, you better get him before he leaves."

"He's leaving too?" I said.

"Yeah. He's going up to SF, then tomorrow to Los Gatos. He had me order a car to drive him."

"So I'll be alone here tonight?"

He bounced a little on the balls of his feet. "Yeah, I guess so. I know it might seem weird. But I've done it lots of times. It's no big deal. There's not a lot of criminal activity around here. Beatrice was, like, the crime of the century." He gave a strained chuckle. "Hector will take the big dogs home, and the rest can stay in the house. Hector will come back early to take care of them, so you don't have to worry."

"I guess. But it does feel weird."

"Well, don't forget there's the security. They come pretty fast if you call." He took a step toward the door. "I better get moving. The traffic gets bad early going south."

"I thought you were going north. Up to Berkeley."

"No, San Luis Obispo . . . um, my friend Jake, I worked with him at that vegan place in Berkeley until it went belly up. He's having a birthday—it's a, like, surprise . . ."

"For God's sake, Otis!" I said. "Why are you acting so peculiar?"

"I'm not. Or maybe I just feel kind of guilty. About leaving you alone."

"So I should be worried?"

"No! You're twisting everything I say. These new security guys are really good—you'll be fine."

I paused. "Tell me something. Why did you really want me to come here?"

"What do you mean?"

"I mean, the way you practically begged me to come. And how you lied to Evan about us growing up together. And after I got here, you turned in my rental car, almost like you were trying to keep me from getting away."

"I wanted to save you money. That's what you wanted, right?"

I sighed. "Just level with me for once, okay?"

"I am leveling with you." He bounced a little again. "But okay, I did really want you to come. Because sometimes I get a little freaked by things that go on here. Like Hector and Annunciata, I think they're into voodoo, or okay, maybe not *voodoo*, but they're weird. Especially Annunciata, I don't know, it's like she's not quite right in the head. And it's, like . . . sometimes I think there really *are* ghosts here like people sometimes say. And I thought your being here would take the weird-ness away."

"Why didn't you just quit? You can always get a restaurant gig somewhere else."

"I don't *want* another restaurant gig. Crappy chefs screaming at me like they think they're Gordon Ramsay and asshole managers bossing me around. But when Evan's deal goes through and his biotech com-pany gets off the ground, there'll be a huge new campus with a cutting-edge cafeteria. And he's going to put me in charge of the menus."

I raised my brows. "That sounds like a big job."

"It is. My dream job."

"Is that how he got you to take the painting in secret to the ware-house? By promising you this job?"

He sidled a glance from under his glasses. "No. He happens to think I'm an amazing cook. Even if you don't think so."

"I do. You *are* an amazing cook."

"Yeah, I am. I can do all sorts of menus—vegan and paleo and flexitarian. And I'm really good, and I don't know why you can't be supportive of me."

"I *am* supportive of you, O."

"No, you're not. You think I'm this total screwup and can't do anything right or ever be any good. But I'm never going to get a chance like this again, ever, so why can't you just be on my side?"

He spoke so bitterly it caught me by surprise. And it occurred to me: I was keeping some things secret from him now as well.

"I am on your side," I said. "And I do think you're a good cook, a really great one. I want to be supportive of you."

"Then why aren't you acting like it?"

"Because you keep telling me things that sometimes aren't exactly real."

"Well, *this* is real, and I don't want to fuck it up. I really and truly want it to happen, okay?"

"I really want it to happen for you too. You know I do, right?"

"I guess." He paused. "Look, if you're really nervous, I guess I could stay."

"No, it's okay. I don't want you to miss your weekend off."

We hugged. And his face became Mr. Raisin Bran Sunshine.

Like we'd never argued at all.

The infinity pool was built along the southwest bluff of the promontory and made of local stone, giving it the look of a natural grotto, the water spilling perpetually over the edge. Pilot galloped up to me in a delirious yapping frenzy and escorted me to the pool. Evan was doing laps, easy, powerful strokes. Pilot crashed into the water, and Evan looked up. Saw me. Pulled himself fluidly onto the deck.

He shook streaming curls from his eyes. "Toss me a towel, will you?"

I handed him one from a stack, and he began to briskly towel himself off. He had another tattoo, on his back, just below his left shoulder blade—a pre-Columbian bird with fierce claws gripping a branch of thorns. I had as fierce a desire to touch it. To trace the inked lines with my fingers.

He dropped the towel on the deck. Picked up a linen shirt from a chair and shrugged it on. Motioned to the umbrella-shaded table. "This okay?"

"Sure." I sat down, and he sat across from me.

"Did you get all your fires put out?" I asked.

"The ones that mattered."

"Otis said you're leaving later."

"For a couple of days, yeah." He put on a pair of dark glasses. Fixed his obscured eyes on me. "I didn't kill my wife," he said abruptly.

I gave a start. "I didn't say that."

"A lot of people have. Rick McAdams. He must have accused me to you last night."

"Yeah, he did. And also before, the time we first met."

"Did he claim that I abused her? Beat her? That I staged her first suicide attempt as an alibi for murdering her later?"

"Yeah," I said. "All of that."

"And that I killed her to get her half of the assets?"

"Yes. He said she owned half of everything. Community property laws."

He smiled mirthlessly. "Did he mention that it works both ways? That I also own half her debts?"

"No. Was she in a lot of debt?"

"In her manic stages, my wife blew through millions. Clothes, jewels, anything expensive that caught her eye. And drugs. An entire fortune went up her nose."

"Cocaine?"

"Mostly, but other drugs too. Go backstage at a fashion show, it's swimming in hard drugs. But coke was her favorite. She called it snow white. And her brother was her chief supplier."

I felt a shudder. "Rick!"

"Yeah, brother Ricky. He supplied the snow white, and she kept him in style."

His pricey clothes. Expensive haircut. The tricked-out Range Rover.

"What else did he accuse me of? That I locked my wife in a psych ward and tried to keep her there?"

"Yeah," I acknowledged. "That too."

"Beatrice had a psychotic break. A year ago. She was bipolar, but it was the drugs that pushed her over the edge. Hearing voices, seeing hallucinations. She had violent outbursts. Sometimes in public."

"I've heard that she did."

"I got her to a good psychiatrist, and she began getting injections of Haldol. It controlled the psychosis, but there were side effects. She put on weight. She thought bugs were crawling under her skin. She was switched to oral meds." He glanced out at the slate-colored cove. "The mistake, *my* mistake, was trusting her to take them on her own. She quit without my knowing, and it led to her worst episode yet. When I tried to restrain her, she went wild on me. Biting, clawing, kicking. I tried to hold her down, but she broke away and ran to the stairs. She threw herself down."

Could that be true? "And so that was when you had her committed?"

"I never had her committed," he said. "I called EMS, and they took her to the hospital. She was kept three days for observation. That's the limit of the law in California. After that, she agreed to be hospitalized."

I glanced up in surprise. "She agreed to it?"

"She had to give her consent. At that point, I got her into the best facility in Northern California. The Oaks, up in Sonoma. A beautiful place with a top-rated staff."

Easy answers. But it all sounded credible. "How long was she there?"

"Five months. They got her stabilized. When she came home, I made sure she took the meds under supervision. I'd be there or Annunciata. For a while, it seemed to work. Her blood tests checked out." He paused and glanced again at the water, then back at me. "Then she started to get erratic again. Nunci noticed it too. I kept hoping it was just a temporary setback. That last day—she seemed better. It was our anniversary. I thought taking her out for a nice dinner—maybe it would help. I was miserably wrong." He gave me a small smile. "She had stopped taking her meds. You know that."

Rick's words: *How do you know he didn't plant the pills himself?*

I said, "There were police here yesterday."

"Yeah. They wanted to look at my guns. Two Remingtons locked in a safe in my study and a handgun by my bed. They'd looked at them before. They were fishing. Hoping to luck into something."

Easy lies. Sociopaths are good at that.

But Rick was a liar too. And he had pushed hard drugs to his sister.

"Is it true . . . ," I said hesitantly. "Rick told me you've already filed to have Beatrice declared dead?"

"Yes," he said emotionlessly. "It's true."

I stared at him.

"Christ, Jane, what am I supposed to do?" he burst out. "I'm at my wit's end. I'm under suspicion of murder. I've already been tried and convicted of it in the media. My remaining assets, everything I held jointly with my wife—they've all been frozen because I can't prove she's dead or alive. If I could find her—her body, any trace at all—to prove she's gone, don't you think I would?"

"Are you so sure? I mean, that she is dead?"

"Yeah. I'm sure."

"There's no chance at all she might have survived?"

He stared at me a moment. Then stood up and slipped his feet into canvas shoes. "Let's go down to the beach. I want to show you something."

"Right now?"

"Yeah. Come on, before the tide comes in."

I rose hesitantly. But he had already stepped off the pool deck, and I followed him to a gate in the stake fencing that bordered the edge of the promontory. He opened the gate. Pilot bounded up. "Stay!" Evan ordered. The poodle wound himself in an agitated circle but obeyed.

We began to descend a weathered set of wooden stairs. I had been tempted to go down them before, but the cove looked a long way down and the steps exceptionally rickety and rotten. And they were, hugging the edge of the bluff, gaping holes where the wood had rotted completely away. I clung to the wobbling rail, keeping my eyes fixed on Evan, who took the steps easily.

At the bottom, we stepped onto a long, unstable slope of broken rock. He took my hand to help me down to the crescent of damp sand that constituted the beach. He kicked off his shoes, and I did too.

We began walking between craggy slabs of black rock ragged with lichen and coral and tiny green-black mussels. The thunderous surf reverberated in my bones. With each surge, water seethed and threw up furious spouts between the rocks, and tiny translucent crabs scurried to bury themselves. The wind flapped my shirt and tossed my hair.

About halfway around the crescent, he stopped. "This is where I saw her," he said. "Where she went in."

I gazed out at the water. Waves clashed furiously from every direction. That immensity of power—that war of surf—I'd so often watched from my terrace. How much more powerful and terrifying it appeared up close.

"You can't imagine the strength of these currents." Evan spoke loud above the thunder. "Thousands of tons of water gathering force all the way from China. Every minute of every day and night, slamming into this cove."

I nodded mutely. Pushed whipping hair from my face.

"This is still fairly low tide. In a rising swell, the beach disappears completely. There's no shelter. No place to hide."

I pictured Beatrice. Dressed up for their anniversary dinner. Her cocktail dress. Wading into that violent war of water in high-heeled shoes.

She had to be delusional. Suicidal. The only explanation.

If that's what actually had happened.

"By the time I got down here, she was gone," Evan continued. "I went in after her anyway. It was impossible. I barely survived."

"But you did," I said.

"Dumb luck. I had on a watch. The band caught on a sharp rock, and when I unsnapped it, it gave me enough leverage to get in front of a surge and ride it to the beach. I was half-drowned when I crawled back onto the sand." He turned and pointed to the jutting rock face at the far point of the cove. "See there? That point."

Steel-colored waves surged and crashed against the rock with the noise of a hundred doors slamming and then ebbed in hellish-looking whirlpools.

"That's where the currents would have swept her body. If she wasn't already drowned, she would have been ripped to shreds."

I thought of that eerie little cove on the other side. Where I'd seen the ghostly shape. The firefly sparkle. "Can we get around the point to the other cove?"

"No. It's impossible." He looked back to the cove, the jagged black rock that dominated it. "That outcropping? Beatrice was obsessed with it. In her delusions, she talked to it."

"I know," I shouted to make myself heard. "She called it Mary. I think she meant Mary Magdalene."

He looked quizzically at me.

"There's a sculpture in her art books. Mary Magdalene as an old woman. Her hands touching like this." I made a steeple of my fingers, the tips not quite touching. "Beatrice had circled them. I think maybe she thought they looked like that rock."

"Jesus." He stared back out at it. "I know that sculpture. Donatello, in the Duomo. We were in Florence on our honeymoon. I bought her the damned books." His voice lowered. I barely caught his words. "I should have thought of that."

Frigid water suddenly frothed up at our shins.

"Shouldn't we go back?" I shouted.

"Yeah, the tide's coming in. Let's go."

He grabbed my hand and began striding back at a quicker pace. We were heading into the wind now, and the rocks, half-submerged, were slippery and difficult to avoid. I had a hard time keeping up with him.

And then something terrifying happened.

I stepped on what looked like a large flat stone. It was slick, sloping, and I lost my balance as well as my grip on his hand. My foot dropped into churning sand. A wave slammed me from behind as the sand ebbed out from under my feet.

And suddenly I was underwater, and I was being dragged by a cold and powerful force I couldn't resist. Salt water and sand stinging my eyes, blinding me, and there was sandy water in my nose and mouth. I flailed, but the force dragged me sideways, kelp entangling my arms and hair, and I thrashed some more, helpless, panic rising as I felt myself being sucked relentlessly out into the cove.

And then arms encircled my chest. Lifted and carried me, still flailing, to a patch of sand. Steadied me on my feet.

I turned and pressed my cheek to his chest, felt the beating of his heart. His arms wrapped me tight. "It was so cold," I said. "So very strong."

"It's okay. I was right there."

I still felt that force. Dragging me out to sea. If he hadn't been right there . . . I'd have been powerless. I could not have escaped. Nor could Beatrice have.

I looked up at him. "She's really gone, isn't she? She's got to be."

"Yes," he said. "She's gone."

I was shaking uncontrollably. With shock and cold.

With pity for Beatrice. And all her delusions.

"You need to get back." He took my hand again, gripping it firmly, setting a more careful pace back to the stairs. Most of the rocks were totally submerged now, and water roiled to our knees and slapped partway up the slope.

"My sandals?" I said stupidly.

"Gone." He kept tight hold of my hand as we climbed the slope, rocks digging painfully into my bare soles. At the foot of the stairs, he said, "I'll have to carry you up. They're full of splinters." He scooped me up in his arms, and I clung to his neck, not daring to look down as we ascended the steep, rickety flight.

I heard Minnie and Mickey barking and Pilot yapping too. All three waiting at the top of the stairs. Evan set me down at the top, and I unlatched the gate. The dogs milled and snuffled protectively around us as we stepped onto the bluff.

The breeze wicked moisture from my skin. I shivered uncontrollably.

"You need to get warm immediately," he said. "We both do."

He took my hand again and led me to the house, through the doors of the Ocean Room. I walked painfully on sand-coated feet, shivering, unwilling to let go of his hand. Still not letting go as he continued to lead me upstairs, to the main level, and then up again to the top, and I gripped his broad, warm hand tight as we turned into his bedroom. I registered a suite that mirrored Beatrice's but this one done in a palette of sage and dove gray. Large-scale modern furniture. Hillocks of books everywhere. Two walls of glass—not curtained like Beatrice's windows but giving onto a panorama of cliffs, sky, sea.

My heart beat fast as we approached the large bed. But he led me past the bed and into the connecting bathroom—an alcove containing a vast semienclosed shower built of the same grotto stone as the pool. He pulled me in beside him. He pressed a panel, and a hot, steamy waterfall cascaded down, drenching our hair, our skin and clothes, in soft and luxurious warmth.

I let out a gasp of pleasure. The delicious sensation. Melting the bone chill inside me. I felt like a marble statue being warmed into real life. *Pygmalion*, I thought. Or, no, that was the name of the sculptor, not the statue he was in love with.

And then I laughed at my silly thoughts and let the spray wash away the gritty sand and scraps of kelp that clung to every inch of me. He laughed, too, shaking his hair like a wet animal, like Pilot shaking out his coat after he'd jumped in the pool. The steam rose around us like mist in a rain forest, creating tiny rainbows on the stone.

"Better?" he said.

"Much better."

He stroked my drenched hair with both hands, pushed it over my shoulders. The water rained gently around us. I gazed up into his eyes, black eyes gazing back down at me from beneath lashes beaded with sparkling droplets. My heart gave a somersault.

It was the most handsome face I'd ever seen.

I couldn't stop myself. I reached up and cupped his face in my hands, and I drew his mouth to mine. I kissed him voraciously. Devouring his mouth, his tongue, all I could get of him, with all the passion that had been building up inside me.

Those rushing endorphins. Scrambling your brains.

To hell with Keiko's warnings. To hell with anything that wasn't now, this moment.

He kissed me back with equal hunger. Greedily, I began to pull at the buttons of his wet shirt. Ran my hands over his naked chest, wet warm skin, taut muscles beneath it. His arms tightened around me, and he pressed close and hard against me.

Then he grabbed my wrist and pulled me out of the shower and back into the bedroom. To that king-size bed. We went tumbling onto it, grabbing desperately at each other's clothes, mouth on hungry, greedy mouth.

A phone burred beside us. As if by reflex, he glanced at it.

I tensed.

Another phone rang, from a desk across the room. "They're calling for you," I said.

"They're always calling. I'll turn them off."

He's leaving soon, I thought. To San Francisco.

Where Liliana Greco is based.

I sat up and drew my shirt closed around me.

"What?" He grasped my shoulders. "I said I'd stop them ringing."

I shook my head. "It's not just that."

"Then what?" he said.

Still so many questions. So much I still needed to know.

"Hey," he said softly. "There's no obstacle to us, Jane. My wife is dead. She took her own life seven months ago. I'm free to want someone else. And you're free to want me. If you do."

"It's not that. It's just . . ." I couldn't find the words.

His face hardened. "You don't trust me."

"No, I don't," I admitted. "I can't. Not yet."

Two phones were ringing simultaneously.

"Fucking hell!" He grabbed one and threw it violently at the wall, where it shattered into shards. He turned and glared at me, and I looked defiantly back at him.

"Okay, I get it." He got off the bed and strode back to the shower alcove. The water stopped. He reappeared wearing a terry robe, and he tossed a second robe and towel on the bed, then turned and disappeared into another connecting room.

I wrapped myself in thick terry cloth and roughly dried my hair. I heard a drawer yank open, slam shut, and he came back, holding a pair of thick black socks.

I stood up.

"Sit down," he said.

"Why?"

"For Chrissake, can't you just once in your life do one goddamned thing you're asked?"

"If I'm asked, maybe. Not if I'm ordered."

"Oh, for God's fucking sake. *Please*, sit the fuck back down, and please put on these goddamned socks. Because there's still sand on your feet, and it will be fucking painful for you to walk barefoot back to your place."

"Fine." I sat rigidly on the edge of the bed.

He knelt down. Rolled open one of the socks. Made a "gimme" gesture toward my right foot. I couldn't help but smile. I lifted it, and he rolled the sock over my heel with that same surprising tenderness he'd shown when he'd tucked his denim jacket over me in Hector's truck. It seemed so very long ago.

He smoothed the sock up. Repeated with the other sock. Putting it on my left foot in that same tender way. "They're big, but it's all I've got," he said.

They flopped clownishly from the ends of my toes, but they were warm and soft. "They'll do fine." I stood up. The desk phone was jangling. The cell phone purred.

I began toward the door.

"Wait," he said. "I want to ask you for a favor."

"What?" I said warily.

"To come with me to something. An event. Black tie, a benefit kind of thing down in Los Angeles. It's in a couple of weeks. I forget the exact date. We'd fly down the afternoon before, come back the next morning."

I stared at him.

"We'll stay in a hotel," he added. "Separate rooms."

I was too astonished to speak for a moment. Then said, "What's it for? I mean, the benefit. What's the cause?"

"Doctors without Borders."

"Oh. They're a great organization. I've given money to them."

"Yeah, so have I. But this will be business. There's an investor, a VC, who's about to put money into Genovation. He and his wife are hosting the event."

"Dillon Saroyan?"

He smiled wryly. "You've been doing your homework."

"A little." I kept my eyes fixed carefully on his expression. "I met one of his people at your fireworks party. Liliana Greco. She came late and was looking for you. Did she ever find you?"

There was no change in his face. "Yeah, she did. She's one of Dillon's principals. It was nice of her to stop by."

"I suppose she'll be at the benefit?"

"No idea. She travels a lot."

"She's very attractive."

"Yeah, she is. Look, do you want to come to this goddamned thing with me or not?"

He'd shown no change of expression at all talking about her. I was wrong, then. He wasn't involved with her, except as a business colleague. I felt a ridiculous surge of relief. "I didn't pack for black tie," I said.

"Then buy yourself a dress. Fairfax will give you a credit card."

"No. I won't let you buy me an evening gown."

"There's an entire closet filled with fancy dresses down the hall, most of them brand new. Nunci can alter it for you."

I recoiled at the thought. "God, no! I definitely can't do that."

"Then wear jeans. Or come stark fucking naked if you want. Just say yes or no. Though I would prefer it if you said yes."

I was still muddled with confusion. He was not involved with Liliana. Beatrice had drowned herself in that monstrous current. Could it all be true?

"You don't have to tell me right now," he said. "You can let me know."

"Okay, I will. Let you know, I mean."

"Do you want me to help you back to the cottage?"

"No. I'm okay." I left the bedroom and padded out to the hallway in the floppy socks. I paused to glance down the hall.

Beatrice's bedroom. The discolored rectangle on the wall. The size of that slashed-up Modigliani.

There were still too many questions I had no answers to.

Not yet.

BEATRICE

I take another bite of my crab salad from the tray I have on my lap, and I remember everything that happened that day in the month of April.

The girl named Lilies was still living in the painting by Amedeo Modigliani, and she was still hanging on my bedroom wall.

It was before the boy with the golden spectacles came here. But there were always lots of other people here, and I could always hear their voices everywhere in the house.

There was the voice of the smiley man whose name was Raymond. Raymond was very skinny. I could see his bones sticking through when he wore a polo shirt, and he talked like a kangaroo. He lived in the smaller house behind the garage, and if anybody called him a butler, he stopped being smiley and the tips of his ears became very red. "Estate manager, mate," he would say in his kangaroo voice.

I remember once I played a joke. I put my hand between his legs, just to see what would happen. But nothing did. He gave me a wink. "Sorry, Mrs. R., wrong tree," he said. "I'm gay as pink."

And there was also the laughing voice of the brown-skinned lady named Cecily who was our cook. When she laughed it was like she was saying her name over and over again. CecilyCecilyCecily. She always came with us when we went up to the house on Lombard Street in San Francisco.

That day in the month of April, I could hear her in the kitchen, talking to Raymond and going CecilyCecilyCecily.

There was also the voice of a very crinkly lady named Muriel, with a hat wide as a flying saucer. She told the gardening men where to plant the bushes and which poison to use to make the snails die.

And the girl named Kendra with rubies in her nose. She brought clothes for me to choose after the witches put a hex on my black Amex card and it stopped working. And Lawrence, who was beautiful and Chinese and made appointments for me and for my jailer. Lawrence also came up with us to the tall house on Lombard Street.

All those people were there that day in last April. Their voices and their footsteps everywhere.

It was Cecily who brought me my lunch that day. It was in the dining room. Lunch was crabs that day too. But not a salad. Tiny crabs with heads and legs but no faces. And there was only one place setting.

I asked Cecily, "Where's my husband?"

"He's got a lunch in Monterey, but he'll be back for dinner. These are the first soft-shells of the season. I'm saving him some."

"Where are their faces, Cecily?"

"I cut 'em off. You don't want your lunch staring up at you, do you, Beatrice?" She laughed her laugh. CecilyCecilyCecily.

I wasn't hungry that day. I bit off some of the legs so it would look like I had eaten some. There was a glass of my Dr. Brown. And next to the glass was a tiny paper cup with a poison pill.

I put the pill inside my bra like I always did. But I drank up my glass, so it looked like I had washed the poison down my throat.

And then I went up to my room, and I flushed the poison pill down the toilet.

It was before my jailer started testing all the water.

Back then, I always took a nap in my bed after my lunch. The girl Lilies looked down at me from the painting hanging on the wall, with her head tilted to one side. I didn't know yet that she was watching my dreams.

I didn't know she was plotting to come down from inside the picture frame.

Plotting to replace me.

I napped for a long time that day. When I woke up, I felt jumpy and strange. I had some snow white left, hidden in the Secret Place. I really needed some, and I went downstairs and then outside to go get it. I remember. The smiley skinny man named Raymond was in the courtyard washing the new silver car that had no engine. The one my jailer made run on his thoughts alone.

"How do you like the new Tesla, Mrs. R.? Smooth ride, yeah?"

"Yes," I told him.

"Looks like the fog's rolling in early today. It's come in pretty strong already."

Raymond went back to washing the silver car. He began to hum opera songs, like he did all the time.

There were white fog fingers wriggling into the redwood trees, and I was scared of them. But I needed the snow white, so I kept on going to where I had hidden it in the Secret Place. Just like I did today, that day in last April I went around to the hidden path in back of the wooden cottage.

I heard something inside the cottage, and I stopped.

I could see a tiny glow inside through the doors made of glass. I was all jumpy, but I wanted to see what was making that glow. I crept through all the ferns and bushes to the brick steps, and I walked up them. I looked inside, through the doors.

The glow was a light from a tall candle. A flickering candle. And in the flickering light, I could see other things.

The old bed with four iron knobs. And there were two people on top of the bed.

One of them was my jailer. He was lying on his back, and his pants were all in a crumple around his feet.

The other one was a girl, and she was sitting on top of him and bouncing up and down, up and down. She had on a yellow dress with buttons on the front, and the buttons were opened up, and her tiny breasts were bobbing naked as she bounced up and down.

She turned her face a little way to me. She couldn't see me outside, because the white fog fingers kept me secret. But I could see her face.

And I could see she was the girl in the picture by Amedeo Modigliani.

You see things that aren't real, Beat. My jailer's voice now comes up soft in my mind. *You hear voices that aren't there.*

No. She was real. She was there. And I remember I was very frightened.

How did she get out of her picture frame?

I kept watching through the glass doors. Up and down she bounced. Up and down.

And then I heard steps, little steps, coming toward me.

They were dog steps. It was the old dog, Delilah.

I stood still as a statue.

She was keeping guard, like she always did. She'd bark and let my jailer know I was spying on him. And then he'd give me extra poison, so I'd no longer be able to move my arms or legs or talk at all.

I took two very soft steps away. Delilah watched me with her runny eyes, but she didn't bark.

And then I was walking away very fast. I was on the old road in the front of the wooden cabin, and I kept walking and walking, and after a while, I began to scream.

But that was a mistake, because it brought the two witches. They came for me in the brown truck, and Braidy Witch had put me in the front seat next to the witch husband, Hector, and they took me back here.

The Ocean Room, where I am now.

That's when you did the terrible thing, Beatie. The voice of the very young one, called Beatie June, whispers in my mind.

Liar, liar, liar, Mary hisses at her. *It was a very good thing.*

What was it that I did that day in April? Why can't I think?

I finish my crab salad that has the taste of blood, and I lick the plate.

And then I go on remembering.

TWENTY

I showered again in my own primitive stall to scrub the sand that still clung tenaciously to my scalp and between my fingers and toes. The showerhead emitted a cold spurt of water. I had a sudden and traumatic flash of being submerged in that frigid current, my thrashing panic as I felt myself being sucked out to sea.

I imagined Beatrice Rochester grabbed by that current. That monstrous force, clutching at her flimsy blue party dress. At her long silvery hair. The icy silted water filling her nose, blinding her eyes, replacing the air in her lungs. She would have been helpless. Unable to resist.

She had been off her meds. Hallucinating. Driven by suicidal impulses.

Maybe not suicide. Maybe in her delusions she'd harbored some idea of swimming to Mary Magdalene's praying hands. She had been a champion swimmer once. Maybe her madness had led her to try it.

She could not have survived.

Evan had done everything in his power to save her. He'd put his own life at risk.

It all made sense. He was innocent.

And yet . . .

Beatrice had taken her life just when he most needed her out of the way.

The shower turned scalding. I leaped out of the stall. Wrapped myself again in the thick terry cloth robe.

My mind revolved on that nagging question. How did a painting that Otis brought intact to a guarded warehouse end up in the tower slashed by Beatrice—who was already dead and gone?

Unless she wasn't.

And what did it mean that the painting resembled Liliana Greco?

But Evan had displayed no emotion when I mentioned Liliana's name. Keiko had insisted they'd be crazy to risk having a sexual relationship. That it would be a gross conflict of interest. Jeopardize the deal that was about to make both their fortunes.

Evan loved taking risks. But that great a one?

Or the even greater risk of murdering his wife?

I shrank from the thought. Began combing out my wet hair. I thought of Liliana. Her lovely long neck disfigured by that ugly scar on the nape. The scarves and turtlenecks she wore to hide it. Beginning in June the year before.

I pictured the scar as I remembered it. Red and faintly puckered. Shaped, roughly, like two facing horseshoes. If it were a burn scar, what could have caused it?

A branding iron? Like for some kind of ritual?

Demonic rituals. I laughed at myself. Still writing episodes of *Carlotta Dark.*

But that led me to another thought. About one of the *Carlotta* characters: the prim banker's wife who'd been bitten by a vampire and always wore high lace collars to disguise the marks.

Okay, now I was just getting silly. Liliana's scar didn't look anything at all like vampire fang marks.

Though maybe a bite of some kind. Like from a large animal.

A German shepherd.

I thought of the old dog, Delilah. Mickey and Minnie's mother. The one who had died from eating snail bait.

Or maybe not. Maybe she had been put down after attacking someone. And then I wondered: *Has Liliana ever been to Thorn Bluffs?*

The tide outside was very high now, and it crashed and roared frenetically. The mist was gathering, and it was getting dark.

I'd be alone here tonight.

Maybe I should have let Otis stay. Or maybe I could try to get a hotel nearby? A Friday night at the height of tourist season? Unlikely.

I thought of Ella. Maybe I could crash on her couch. I called and explained my situation. "I'm not scared exactly. It just seems a little spooky."

"Hell, yeah, I can believe it would be spooky as shit. Absolutely you can stay, no problem. The only thing is, I've got a date, a gal I met the other day. She raises mohair goats—kind of looks like one, too, in a sexy kind of way." A bright peal of a laugh. "But I'll leave a key in my mailbox. Help yourself to anything—there's eggs in the fridge, a couple bottles of Fat Tire. Sheets and blankets in the hall closet. I've got to warn you, I've got two cats. The ginger one, Furrier, she'll try to sleep on your face, and Mr. Handsome, he's a sphynx, a yowler. And if my date goes okay, well, we might be back, but we'll try to keep it quiet."

"Oh, hey, I don't want to intrude on your date."

"Absolutely no problem. Come whenever. I'm heading out now."

I felt better after listening to her chatter. And her offer to stay. I threw some overnight items in my tote. Then texted Sophia: Everything ok?

K
Peyton's parents there?
Kelly is. She just ordered sushi. We're gonna watch Annabelle 2.

Sushi and a horror flick. Reassuringly normal. Ok have fun.

I locked up and headed out to the garage. Decided not to go straight to Ella's. I'd treat myself to dinner first. Someplace lively, a lot of other people around. A burger and beer wouldn't bankrupt me. I clicked the garage's middle bay open.

Footsteps came from the office path. My heart gave a little leap. *He didn't go after all!*

It was Hector who appeared through the fog. He headed directly toward me, as if knowing all along I'd be standing in that precise spot, at that precise moment. "This for you." He handed me a manila packet.

"From Evan?"

"For you," he repeated. Then, in his shaman-like way, he vanished again.

The packet was sealed tight. I wanted to get on the main road before dark, so I crammed it in my tote and climbed into the Land Cruiser. I drove to the rustic roadhouse just past Big Sur Village that I sometimes lunched at with Otis.

It was raucously crowded. An overmiked eighties tribute band performing. I nabbed a small table in back. Flirted with my waiter, a lanky twentysomething with a frizzy man bun. His name was Clinton. He hated being called Clint. I ordered a bison burger, sweet potato fries, a glass of the house zinfandel.

The band's female lead began to belt out "What's Love Got to Do with It?" and an image of Mom came into my mind. Blasting music in the living room—Tina Turner, Rod Stewart, Debbie Harry. Dancing with almost frenzied abandon, shaking her hips and hair, snapping her fingers.

Always dancing alone.

Was that my fate too? In the end, always dancing alone?

Poor orphan girl.

Mom hated self-pity. She had refused to give in to it. I wouldn't either. Not now; not ever.

Clinton-never-Clint brought my burger and fries, and I ordered a second zin. I hungrily polished off half my food. The band finished its set and took a break. I swallowed some more wine and then remembered the sealed envelope in my tote. I fished it out and ripped it open.

A manila file with maybe half a dozen documents in it. I looked at the first one. A copy of a birth certificate. I stared at it, puzzled for a moment, and then realized.

My birth certificate.

Confirming I was born at 12:01 a.m. on February 26 at Children's Hospital of South Orange, New Jersey. That I was female. Weighed six pounds, seven ounces.

I drew a breath. It was the report on me from Evan's investigators. The one he had said wasn't possible for me to see.

I turned to the next document. A list of my known addresses since college. The Williamsburg roach paradise I'd shared with Holly Bergen. Jeremy Capshaw's freight elevator loft in Bushwick, where he'd had sex with Holly while I tended to my dying mother. My snapped-up-in-desperation Carroll Gardens apartment after I'd caught them together.

The next document: my employment contract for *Carlotta Dark*. I felt a flare of anger: *How the hell did they get that?* My bruising credit reports from Experian and Equifax. Last year's Amex and Visa year-end statements with their dismal balances.

I gulped down the second glass of wine, kept turning documents. Mom's death certificate, signed by her oncologist, Dr. Cheryl Aminpour. Cause of death: small-cell lung cancer. I felt a sharp pang.

And then another death certificate. I gave a start. My father's.

Date of death: September 12, 1994. Occupation: Mechanical engineer.

Cause of death: Multiple traumatic injuries resulting from a car crash. Ruled by a coroner's jury as a suicide.

I stared at the word. *Suicide.*

Stapled to the certificate, a copy of the coroner's jury report. Witness statements. He'd been recently diagnosed with depression. His car had accelerated suddenly at a ninety-degree angle from the right lane into the left highway abutment.

Self-inflicted death.

And Mom had kept that a secret from me. Had let me think it was an accident.

She had let me believe a lie.

There was one last document. A copy of an email to Evan dated just six days ago:

> Joanne Patricia Meyers, a.k.a. Froggy, born 11/26/1959, was issued an Arizona driver's license on Dec. 1, 1998. No immediate record of the name after that. She could have married or otherwise changed her identity. Let me know if you want us to pursue further.
>
> Norris Laughlin, president
>
> Laughlin Group Investigation

So Evan was still checking up on me. My temper flared again but just briefly. It didn't feel like that. It felt like a gift. A head start in finding Aunt Joanne. And now I felt a warmth of gratitude to him.

I'd given up too soon on looking for her, I realized. And I'd let myself become so preoccupied by the mysteries of Thorn Bluffs that I'd neglected those of my own family.

I texted Ella: Hey don't need to crash with you. I'm okay staying put. But thanks a million for the offer.

She texted instantly: Did I scare u away with goat girl?

No!!! Got over my jitters.
If u change yr mind, key still in box.

I stuffed the file back in the envelope. Paid the check, left Clinton a whopping tip, and climbed back in the Land Cruiser. I began negotiating the winding highway through patches of dense cloud: *That second glass of zin, stupid.* I slowed to a snail's pace. Cars honked fitfully as they swooped around me. I steered with superhuman concentration between the two white boulders onto the Thorn Bluffs private road. The road seemed spooky to me again, shadows dancing on the car, glistening ferns beckoning between glowering black tree trunks. The glow of the compound became visible, and I sped up into it.

An animal stepped in front of the car. I slammed the brakes.

It was Julius, the old bulldog. Standing stock still in the headlights, staring up at me.

What is he doing outside?

I grabbed my tote, lowered myself out of the Cruiser. He trotted up, flat nose snuffling laboriously. "Hey, boy. How did you get out?" I patted the thick folds of his head. "Did everybody go away and forget you?"

I whirled at the sound of freaky-sounding footsteps coming from the foliage. Patter, click, patter, click.

Hermione. The click of her hind leg prosthetic. She had a small animal clamped in her jaws.

I felt a shiver. Why were they both out here, wandering in the dark?

Hermione came up to me with her prize. Not an animal. A rag of some sort. I tried to pry it from her jaws, but she held on fast, growling playfully, a game. "Bad girl, bad Hermione!" I tugged it hard, and she relinquished it, barking.

A thin piece of fabric, linen perhaps, or a synthetic. Filthy and damp. White or beige originally, it was hard to tell.

My disappeared nightshirt.

A frightening thought. I let go of the fabric, and it fluttered off in the breeze like a small white bat. Hermione barked again, strenuously.

"Come on, guys," I crooned. "You can't stay out here. Come with me." I tried to herd them toward my cottage steps, but Hermione obstinately turned toward the main house, and Julius, after a moment of split loyalties, waddled after her.

I clapped my hands. "Hey! Guys! Not that way."

Julius stopped. His stumpy curl of a tail quivered. Hermione continued into the covered walkway that led to the side service porch. I hurried after her and then stopped.

The service porch door was wide open.

The Sandovals were the last to leave. How could they have been so careless?

Unless someone else had come back?

I could see no lights on in the house except a low one in the service porch. I peered inside. Bowls of kibble and fresh water on the floor. Night lights glowing softly from the kitchen.

I called out, "Anybody here?" No response.

If anyone were here, the dogs would know. They'd be barking like crazy. I shooed them inside and closed the door behind them, making sure it was firmly latched. As I walked away, I heard Julius woofing plaintively. It gave me chills.

I hurried down the steps to the cottage. Turned the key as fast as I could, locked it securely from the inside, felt relieved to see that all was homey and cozy, just as I'd left it. Bed lamp burning. My down vest still flung over the chair. Half-finished mug of tea, Vanilla Spice Energy, still on the table.

Except for one thing. One of the glass doors seemed more askew than usual.

Like someone had forcefully tried to get in here.

I felt a sudden sense of dread. *I could still go to Ella's,* I reminded myself.

I stepped to the door and rattled it. A little wiggy on its track but still locked tight. And probably no wiggier than usual.

I was spooking myself. Everything that had happened today. Those documents. And the dogs roaming outside. So creepy.

I lit Annunciata's votive candle, and that sweet churchy scent spiraled into the air. I poured another glass of wine, a South Australian Shiraz. Took a sip.

And now I began what I had come back to do.

I opened my laptop. I googled *Joanne Meyers*. The sheer volume of hits—people with that name—overwhelmed me. Not to mention Joanna Meyerses and Joan Meyerses and J. Meyerses. I added her middle name, Patricia. Still hundreds of hits.

She could have changed her name. She might well be dead.

I added more search terms. Arizona, where she'd applied for her last driver's license. Dozens and dozens of results. I scrolled, but none of them fit Aunt Jo. I kept trying other combinations of terms and getting dead ends. I lost track of time. I was starting to get logy. I got up. Paced a little.

A phrase from the investigator's email swam into my mind: *A.k.a. Froggy.*

I added *Froggy* to the search box, along with *Joanne Meyers* and *New Jersey*. One hit with all the terms except *Meyers*. An article from eight years before from the *Santa Fe New Mexican* that was about a shelter for abused horses—Happy Trails. In the third paragraph: "A volunteer, Joanne, said, 'I'm originally from New Jersey and never even met a horse before I started working here. I've got this froggy kind of voice that seems to calm them down. It's been as much a healing process for me as it is for them.'"

I felt a quick thrill. Could I actually have found Aunt Jo?

I grabbed my phone, tried the number listed in the article—it was late, but I could leave a message. The number was out of service. I googled *Happy Trails*. Several items but none dated sooner than eight years ago.

It must have closed. Another dead end.

There was also an email address in the newspaper article. I banged out a quick message and sent it. It didn't get bounced back. I had a tick of hope.

The wine, the candle's incense, all the extraordinary events of the day . . . they were making me feel light headed. My eyes were swimming from staring so intensely at the computer screen.

I got up from my chair. Stretched my neck and shoulders. Finished the glass of Shiraz.

And I suddenly got that prickling sensation I always did when I was sure I was being watched.

I turned and looked at the glass doors, out through the shimmering reflection of my room to the dim terrace outside.

And I locked eyes with Beatrice McAdams Rochester.

BEATRICE

That day in April, the witches had picked me up on the old road and taken me back here to the Ocean Room and put me onto my white chaise. The smiling skinny man, Raymond, brought me tea. He winked at me. "Annunciata's herbal, Mrs. R. It'll calm ya right down. Did you take your med today?"

"Yes, Raymond. When I ate my lunch."

"Good on you, Mrs. R."

The tea he brought me had a potion in it to put me back to sleep. But I wanted to go to sleep, so I drank it down.

And I remember that later when I woke up, I couldn't hear any more steps anywhere in the house. Everyone had gone away. The light had become so low. I could hear the ocean way far below breathing in and out. So soft and very slow, in and out. The ocean was still asleep.

But I was awake. And I could still remember in my mind the candles dancing inside the old cabin.

And then I did hear some steps. Tapping light on the stairs, and I thought maybe it was the old dog again. But they were not dog steps.

These were very light and fast footsteps, and they were coming down and down.

I sat up very straight. I was very nervous and frightened.

I waited as the footsteps came for me.

I heard a voice calling out something. A voice that had cobwebs in it.

And then she came into the Ocean Room. The girl. The one who had come down from the painting by Amedeo Modigliani. Her face was shaped like an egg, and her hair was chopped off like a little boy's. And there were the eyes that were the shape of diamonds, that glittered like diamonds, the same eyes that always looked down at me from the painting on the wall in front of my bed.

She made a sound of surprise. "Oh!" she said in that cobwebby voice. Living in the picture frame had kept her face young and smooth. But not her voice.

I kept still as a statue, just like I had with the old dog, Delilah.

"You must be Beatrice," the cobweb voice said to me.

I said nothing. I watched her.

She made her mouth into a cherry. She came up a little closer to me. "It's nice to meet you, Beatrice. I've heard so much about you. My name is Lilies. I'm a friend of Evan's."

She had watched me from the wall while I was sleeping. She had spied on all my dreams. She had reported my dreams to my jailer, and they had plotted to have her come out of the picture frame and replace me.

I was silent, but she could hack into my thoughts.

"I didn't mean to disturb you, Beatrice. I just wanted to get a peek down here."

I made the words come out. "How did you get down from your picture frame?"

Her face swayed to one side on its long stalk of a neck, just like it did in the picture. "I'm sorry. What did you say?"

"The picture by Amedeo Modigliani. How did you get out of it?"

Her diamond eyes went glittery.

"You are crazy as a bedbug, aren't you, Beatrice?"

I whispered low, "Are you going back into the picture frame?"

A laugh came out of her, like egg yolk oozing out of a cracked eggshell.

"Yes, Beatrice, I am. I'm going to jump right back into the Modigliani. But not for long. I'll be coming back again soon." Her cobweb voice was weaving strings around me to hold me in a web. "But don't worry, Beatrice. Evan will take care of you. He'll put you someplace comfortable. He'll be able to afford it."

All the voices are whispering in my mind now, and they are laughing because they remember, too, because that's when it happened.

The very good thing that I did on that day.

TWENTY-ONE

I kept my eyes fixed on the figure outside the glass doors. She was indistinct in the terrace light. More ghostly than corporeal—standing, or perhaps hovering, ten feet back from the glass doors.

A figure as haunted looking as it was haunting. Matted snakes of flaxen hair framed a wild, pale face. Her body through the glass seemed attenuated, well over six feet tall, stretched thin and encased in layers of ragged garments.

Is it real? Or just a product of my overinflamed imagination?

I set my glass down on the table, and when I looked back, the glass-distorted reflection of my room took over my view outside so that I now saw only myself in the glass, lit by the ghostly blue glow of the computer and the flickering candle. My own image looked as spectral in this reflection as the one I thought I'd seen outside.

I moved my head slowly, slightly, to the side. The reflection of the room in the glass shifted with my motion.

And now there it was again, that dim, attenuated figure.

For a moment, the reflection of my room became overlaid with my view of the terrace, giving the illusion that we were occupying the same space—that the ghostly figure of Beatrice Rochester was inside the cottage with me, and simultaneously, I was standing beside a table outside on the terrace with her.

That feeling of light-headedness came over me again.

The figure outside shifted its gaze to the flickering votive candle on my table.

I picked it up and lifted it to her. Her eyes followed it.

In a sort of trance, I raised the candle even higher. I felt the glow of the tiny flame suffuse my face. The scent of incense heavy in my nose.

The figure outside emitted a shriek. Like that shriek of torment I sometimes heard late at night and that sometimes reverberated through my dreams.

Icy tendrils of fear ran through me. I hurled the candle at the door.

The fragile votive shattered in a rain of splintered glass, and the candle with its burning wick rolled onto the old braided rug and began to singe it. I watched, still in a semitrance, as the rug's fibers flared into a tiny dancing flame. Then, as if a hypnotist had snapped fingers, I darted to the flame and stamped it out until every spark was extinguished.

I looked back outside.

The spectral figure was gone.

I moved cautiously to the glass door, the broken glass and wax shards crunching under my feet. I cupped my hands on the glass and gazed out beyond the wavering reflection of my room.

Nothing out there but the crumbling brick terrace, lit by one low-wattage ground light. The breeze was suddenly still: not even a swaying branch to explain away the vision.

Had it been real?

Had I actually seen Beatrice Rochester? Returned—or maybe escaped—from wherever she had vanished to?

Or her ghost?

Or nothing at all?

The light-headedness now expanded to encompass my entire body. I had the feeling I was about to rise off the floor and float as weightlessly as any ghost.

I gripped the edge of the table.

Abruptly, the feeling of weightlessness shifted back into agitation. Jumpiness. I felt ready to jump out of my skin. A hot orange comet streaked in my eyes.

And then it came on full force. A visual migraine. A sea of urgent neon zigzags, the aliens messaging me: *Warning, warning!*

What were they warning?

I groped for my phone. Through the riotous flashes and patterns in my eyes and in my brain, I managed to hit a number.

He answered on the third ring. "Jane? What's wrong?"

My breath came harshly. I couldn't speak.

"Jane? Talk to me." Music, chattering voices behind him. He was at a restaurant. Or a party. "Jesus Christ, Jane, what is it?"

I found words. "I saw her."

"Saw who?"

"Beatrice. She was here."

"Where? Where are you?"

"Here. In the cottage. She was outside, at the doors."

"Jane . . ."

The migraine was really strong, every nerve in my body jitter jumping. The patterns in my eyes, the alien texts, all intensifying. *Warning! Warning!* "She was there. She looked wild and savage and maybe not even alive. Maybe she was something else."

"You don't sound well. You're not making sense."

Behind him, through the music, I heard a woman laugh. A musical laugh. She said, "You can't possibly be on that phone again."

He's with her.

"Jane?"

My own voice sounded far away. "You have to believe me. She was here, I saw her. I threw a candle. She disappeared."

"Listen to me. You're not making sense. Were you asleep?"

The phone emitted an electronic pulse and the connection went dead.

Oh shit, shit, shit.

A buzzing began to swell in my ears, an insect swarm, inside and outside my head. *This must be what it's like to lose your mind,* I thought. To feel yourself going crazy. I let the phone drop from my hand and collapsed onto my bed and gave in to the migraine, the hot flashing colors, the jagged banners, just letting the aliens have their incomprehensible say.

It might have been thirty minutes, it might have been hours, but finally, finally, the buzzing ceased. The lights and patterns faded from my eyes, and I felt like I was no longer jumping or floating out of my skin.

I sat up. Found my phone tangled in the bedspread. It flickered between one and two bars. I looked at the recent calls.

He hadn't called back.

Why would he? I'd probably sounded hysterical. Half-deranged. And he was with Liliana.

I still felt very disoriented. I took several deep breaths, struggling to get back my bearings. I had a crazy thought: *Someone's coming to the front door.* I tried to process this, but I couldn't.

A pounding on the door. "Home Protect!" A male voice, loud and stern.

Home Protect. What does that mean?

"Ma'am? Security. Are you in there?"

The new security company. I stood up, feeling slightly less light headed but still wobbly on my feet. I went to the door, turned the iron key.

A short, massively built man seemed to fill the entire doorframe. "We got a report of somebody trying to break in here." He had a vaguely military aspect. Olive uniform, black vest. Close-cropped hair. A two-way in his hand.

"Did I call you?" I might have in my disoriented state.

"Mr. Rochester did, ma'am." The guard's name tag read ESTEVEZ. He craned his head to look inside. "Okay if I come in?"

I moved aside to let him enter. He strode in briskly, bringing with him the chill night air and a fug of fast food. Ketchup. Fried meat. Onions. He glanced at the glass doors. "Is that where the intruder was?"

"Yes."

He went to the doors, peered through the glass. Tried the locks. "These seem secure. Did you have them locked?"

"Yes. I haven't touched them since."

"You didn't go out after the intruder?"

"No."

He rattled the metal pulls. "One of these doors looks like it's jumped its runner." He gave the pull a strong tug. "Still secure, though. Did they try to break in through the glass?"

"No."

He looked at the shards of candle glass.

"I threw a candle at her, and it broke against the door. It started a little fire on the rug, and I stamped it out. And then she was gone."

"So it was a she?" Estevez said.

"Yes."

"You get a good look at her?"

"Just hazy. I had the light on in here, and it was hard to see through the reflection in the glass."

"Can you describe this lady?"

I hesitated. How much had Evan told them about my state of mind? "She was very tall. And gaunt and thin. She looked like a wraith."

"A wreath?"

"No, a *wraith*. Like a . . . a phantom."

"You mean like a ghost?" The humorous skepticism on his face was perhaps natural to his snubby features.

"Well, ghostly. And wild looking. A lot of long pale-blonde hair that was all matted and tangled."

"So more like a homeless person?"

I hesitated. "I suppose. Like a wild homeless woman."

"She rap on the glass? Call out to you?"

"No."

"So what then?"

"She watched me."

"Just stood there and watched you?"

"Yes. I had been working on the computer at this table. I sensed something out there, so I turned to look. I don't know how long she'd been watching."

"Peeping Tammy, huh?" Humorously skeptical. "Did you yell at her to go away?"

"No. I was in shock. And then she made this howling sound that scared me, and that's when I threw the candle at the glass. And that's when the wick started to burn the rug."

Estevez took in the burn mark on the braided rug. The wineglass on the table. "You have a lot to drink tonight?"

"A few glasses. Over a few hours. I was by no means drunk, if that's what you mean."

"You said you were on the computer? Watching anything exciting?"

"You mean like a horror movie?" I gave a wobbly smile.

"Whatever. Something that might have got you going?"

Before I could answer, his two-way crackled. "Yeah?" he answered. A voice squawked. "Okay, keep me posted." He said to me: "We've got another car at the main house. My colleague says looks like somebody's inside."

I drew a breath. "Is it her?"

"They'll check it out. I'll take a look out here meantime."

He unlocked one of the glass doors and slid it open. "You just sit tight. I'll do a recon." Estevez stepped out, slid the door shut behind him.

I sank back onto the bed. Drew my knees tight to my chest, listening to the sound of his steps roaming the perimeter. The light of his flash sliced the dark. I heard him talk, the two-way squawking back, the words indistinguishable.

His footsteps receded. Then returned and circled to the front.

Minutes later, he burst in the front door. "We found her, ma'am. She's up at the house."

My eyes widened. "So she's back? She's alive?"

"She's got a pulse, far as I know. They found her in her own room, passed out drunk. Come on, I'll run you up there."

My heart started beating fast. "She's in a terrible state. She might need a doctor."

"She's being taken care of."

I grabbed a jacket and accompanied Estevez to his car parked on the service road. I got in beside him, and he drove us around to the main compound. "My colleague says she looks pretty wild. Long white hair like snakes, he says. Fits your description. Funny, though, you didn't recognize her."

"I did," I said. "I just wasn't sure. Where has she been?"

"I think she's too impaired to say, ma'am. Probably just wandering around."

"All this time?"

"Don't know yet how long."

"Does Evan know?"

"Mr. Rochester? Yes, ma'am, we've been keeping him informed."

"He must be stunned."

"I didn't speak to him personally."

Estevez pulled up behind another Home Protect car. His radio crackled again. The voice on the other end rasped: "We got her back to the land of the living. Looks like she killed at least a bottle of Don Q. The husband's on his way."

So I really was about to meet her. My heart pounded in my throat. I was shaking as I got out of the car.

Estevez continued to trade remarks on his radio as we went in the front door. The main floor was ablaze with lights. I followed him to the central stairs. He began going downstairs instead of up.

"Her rooms are on the top floor," I said. "Both Rochesters have suites up there."

"Mr. and Mrs. Sandoval, ma'am. I was told downstairs."

Sandoval?

As we descended, I heard music playing low. Haunting guitars, a mournful Spanish contralto.

My mind swam in confusion.

The lower floor also was brightly illuminated. We passed the screening room, the gym, went toward an opened door at the far end of the corridor. The music was coming from inside. Under the music, a low persistent wailing.

A sound of unfathomable agony.

I followed Estevez into a darkened bedroom. Candles flickered. A smell of dark rum, black coffee, singed aromatic herbs. Another security guard bent over a woman hunched on a chair. She held her face in her hands. A cyclone of tangled white hair streamed over her hands, face, blanket-draped shoulders. She rocked rhythmically, emitting that steady, terrible low wail.

I stepped quickly to her. Knelt beside her.

"Annunciata." I spoke softly.

She lowered her hands, lifted her eyes to me. Eyes wolfish with the ferocity of her grief. Her keening continued unabated. I thought of her tragic life. Witness to the execution of her son and daughter-in-law. The unimaginable horror.

I took her hand. It was large, rough with faint scars. It squeezed mine in rhythm with her tormented rocking.

"*Lo siento*," I whispered. "I'm sorry." I felt an almost overwhelming sorrow for her.

But she was not the one I had seen outside my doors.

TWENTY-TWO

I remained kneeling beside Annunciata for some time. And then a dog barked upstairs. One of the German shepherds. Moments later, Hector appeared in the room. I relinquished his wife to him and retreated into the corridor.

I found Estevez in the gym, perched on the end of an incline bench, phone clamped to his ear. "Yes. Yes, sir . . . he just arrived with two dogs, yes. He's in with her now. I will, sir, no problem." Estevez hung up. "That was Mr. Rochester. He wanted to make sure everything had settled down. I told him we got everything under control."

"Is he going to call me?" I said.

"He didn't say, ma'am."

The second guard—Hendricks, according to his name tag—appeared in the room. "You okay, miss?"

"I think so."

Hendricks had the bulging build of a gym rat. He picked up a weight in his left hand—thirty pounds—and pumped it absently. "You've had quite a night," he said to me.

I nodded. "Where did you find her?"

"Sitting outside the house at the side door. In a disoriented state. Seems she'd been wandering around the grounds for a couple of hours. She had a bottle of Don Q with her. It was down to the dregs. She couldn't get back inside. The door must have blown shut while she was wandering around and locked automatically. She didn't bring a key."

"I shut it," I confessed. "I noticed it was open when I came back a few hours ago. Two of the small dogs had got out, so I put them back in the house and shut the door. I didn't know she was here."

Hendricks nodded. Transferred the weight to his right hand and pumped double-time.

Estevez said to me, "She must've given you quite a scare. Coming up outside your windows like that."

"Yes." I saw no use in trying to convince him it had not been Annunciata I had seen.

Hendricks slotted the weight back on the rack. "Are you okay with going back to your place? Estevez is gonna stay on the grounds till the end of his shift."

"I'll be in my car," Estevez said, hoisting himself to his feet. "I'll do a sweep every half hour. If you're okay with that, I'll run you back now."

I was bone exhausted. "Yeah, thanks."

He drove me back around to the cottage. Did a final check inside. Rattled the glass doors again. "Pretty easy to jimmy." He assured me again he'd be on constant patrol and left.

I shoved my bureau in front of the glass doors. I picked up some of the glass shards from the rug, my eyes constantly darting to the doors, the hazy terrace outside. I couldn't get that spectral figure out of my mind. That face, pale as ash, wild as a forest creature. That matted cyclone of white-blonde hair.

I'd scrutinized Beatrice Rochester in photos and on YouTube; I knew her face intimately, the shape of her eye sockets, the formation of the bones beneath her skin. I'd know her even as a skeleton. Just as I had known Mom in her ravaged last moments, wasted to a skeleton, just a parrot's beak of a nose.

It had been Beatrice McAdams Rochester. In some form or other. Alive or dead. Corporeal or ghost.

I was sure of it.

I wouldn't be able to sleep. The last hour replayed over and over in my mind on an endless loop. If I weren't careful, I'd have another migraine, and maybe I was having one already, because I was hallucinating the sound of Evan's voice outside my door, calling out my name.

It wasn't a hallucination. He really was there. My heart gave a bound. He gripped my arms. "Are you okay?"

"Yeah. Almost. I will be."

"Didn't you know Nunci was here?"

I shook my head. "No, I had no idea."

"Did you think I'd let you stay alone? I told her to spend the night. I thought she'd let you know. I should have known she'd start drinking."

"Such terrible grief," I whispered. "I could never imagine . . ."

"Yeah," he said softly.

"I'm so very sorry for her. Her terrible pain." I looked up at him, unable to say anything more.

And then somehow I was enclosed in his arms, and he was holding me tight, and I never ever wanted him to let me go. And then I was kissing him, a kiss that went deeper and deeper, and I felt I'd perish if he let me go. If I let *him* go. Still locked in an embrace and the deepest of kisses, I pulled him toward the bed, and we fell onto it. "You sure you're okay with this?" he said, and in response I pulled him closer still, kissed him, tasted his mouth with my tongue, inhaled the scent of him. "I'm sure," I murmured, and we kissed again, and we began to pull and tug at each other's clothes, flinging them off the bed. I felt desperate to have nothing between his body and mine. And finally, finally, there wasn't, just naked skin against naked skin. The sheer luxury of his body, both hard and pliant, and the delicious warmth of it. Every nerve in my body was rejoicing.

I heard him whisper, "Dearest."

And then I forgot where I began and where he did. And I let myself drown in pure sensation.

Sometime before dawn, I stirred half-awake, aware that he was getting dressed. No, undressed. He slipped back into bed. His body carried a moist chill and the scent of juniper and pine.

He's been outside, I thought. *Searching for her.*

I raised myself on my elbows. Looked questioningly at him.

"I was just out checking with the guard," he said. "Everything's under control."

"She hasn't come back?" I said.

"Nunci? Of course not."

"Not Annunciata. I don't think she was the one I saw."

His eyes narrowed. "Who did you think it was?"

I hesitated.

"Beatrice? Is that who you mean?"

"You don't believe me," I said.

"I believe you thought that's who it was. Nunci gave you a bad shock. I've done the same thing, jumped to senseless conclusions. It's easy in a heightened emotional state." He stroked my hair. "Hey. Don't think about it now. It will all be clear in the morning."

I wanted that to be true. I let him gather me, and we made love for the second time, slower now, lasting longer, and with that exquisite tenderness he'd shown to me before. And afterward, I traced every line of his tattoos with my lips, the way I'd yearned to. That silly band of gibberish encircling his forearm. The fierce thorn bird on his back.

And then I drifted back to sleep in his arms.

When I awoke again, it was to the sound of coffee grinding. I sat up. Evan was in the kitchen, fully dressed. "What time is it?" I asked.

"Just past seven o'clock. I've got to get up to Los Gatos." The coffee machine spluttered, and a delicious aroma filled the air. I got out of bed and pulled on a robe. "You don't have to get up," he said.

"I'm a morning person, remember. And you're a night person. Who's afraid of the dark."

"Exactly right." He smiled. Poured coffee into mugs and brought them to the table. And then a jar of honey.

"How did you know I like honey?" I said.

"I notice things. About you." He took a deep sip of black coffee. "You scared the hell out of me last night. I thought you were sick. You sounded feverish."

"I was sick, in a way. There's a condition I get—it's called visual migraines. It's not serious, but it makes me feel strange and disoriented."

"I've heard of it. Kind of psychedelic, isn't it?"

"Yeah, it is. Lights and patterns go flashing in my eyes. My mother had the same thing. She used to say it was like getting messages from Mars."

"Just what I'd expect from you," he said. "Communicating with alien planets."

I gave a laugh. "I thought I was a pretty down-to-earth person."

"No. Not down to this earth. Not entirely."

"Is that what you meant last night?" I said. "About my jumping to a senseless conclusion? That I'm spacey?"

"No. I meant I knew what you were feeling." He drained his mug and set it down. "I thought I saw Beatrice once. About a month after she drowned. I couldn't sleep one night, and at first light, I went out to the deck. And I saw her. At the edge of the bluff, walking in a wild sort of way along the fencing. The light was pretty dim, but I felt sure of what I saw. Positive. I took the dogs and went outside, but she'd vanished. I called security and had four cars at the compound in half an hour. We spent the rest of the day searching. There was no trace."

"But you did see her?" I said excitedly. "She was still alive?"

"No. I saw what I wanted to see. An illusion. That's all."

I was silent a moment. "You must have loved her very much."

"I suppose I did at first. She was stunningly beautiful. But more than that. She had a quality about her . . . some lost quality that made me want to protect her. To come to her rescue." A bitter grimace crossed his face. "That was another illusion. When she went insane, she revealed something twisted that must have been there all along. I'd fallen in love with a perfume ad. What I'd married was a monster."

"I don't believe that," I said. "Whatever she became in her disease, I can't believe it was there all along."

"You never knew her. The monstrous things she was capable of."

"Like what?"

He paused. "You asked me if she had poisoned my dog, Delilah. I can't say for sure. But it's possible." He shook his head, then stood up. "I've got to get going. I'll call you later."

"Back to San Francisco?"

"Yeah. For another couple of days."

The tinkle of music and laughter. That teasing voice: "Are you back on that phone?"

"It sounded like you were at a party last night. I'm sorry I pulled you away."

"Hardly a party. It was a very dull dinner in a bad restaurant with some members of the Genovation Tech board." He picked up his jacket. "I'll be back day after tomorrow. I can come down here later that night if you want."

"Here?" I gave a wry smile. "This shack?"

He smiled. "Yeah, this shack. I think we should keep this to ourselves for right now."

I stiffened. "Why?"

"Financial people are extremely skittish. I don't want anyone to think my entire focus is not on this deal. That I'm being distracted. But we don't have to, if you don't want to."

I hesitated a moment. "Do you want us to keep it a secret from Otis and Sophia too?"

"It would be better. Fairfax can't keep anything under his hat. And I've realized that Sophia is a lot more fragile than I knew. I'm not sure how she'd take this."

"It's true, she might feel threatened," I conceded. "It might be too sudden a change. But Hector and Annunciata will know. They seem to know everything that happens here."

"Whatever they do or don't know, they'll keep to themselves." He came over to me and lifted me gently into his arms. "Hey, it would just be a couple of weeks. Three at the most."

"I need to ask you something." I drew a breath. "Are you involved with anybody else?"

He released my arms and looked down at me with a puzzled expression. "Of course not. I've been working round the clock for the past eight months. How could I be?"

"With somebody you're working with. Around the clock."

"I have always kept my work and private life strictly separate. Why are you even asking me this?"

"Because I want to know. You've made no promises to me, and you've got no obligation to me. But I want to be clear where things stand."

"Well, now you are." He drew me back and kissed me. "And I really need to go. I want you to keep one of the dogs with you at night. Minnie. She's the best protection."

"Protection from what?"

"From your own goddamned imagination, if nothing else."

I gave a quick laugh. "Okay, I'll keep Minnie with me. To protect me from my own damned imagination."

He was gone. And I was suddenly ravenous. I poured a bowl of Grape Nuts and scattered blueberries on top and began to wolf it down. The mist was clearing early. The day promised to be bright and warm. My head was quickly clearing as well.

And doubts crept back into my mind. My frantic call to him—the sound of music, laughter behind him. The teasing voice: "Are you back on that phone?" The musical laugh.

I finished the cereal, dumped the bowl in the sink, and opened my laptop. Googled the board of Genovation Technologies. Five men and a sensible-looking woman in her midsixties. Who might have had a throaty voice and musical laugh.

Though I tended to doubt it.

About an hour later, Hector Sandoval appeared at the glass doors, accompanied by two men wearing work shirts and carrying toolboxes. "These men fix the doors," he announced.

"How is your wife?" I asked.

"She is sorry she frighten you." His expression seemed to declare that neither he nor she was sorry at all, and whether or not I'd been scared out of my wits was of absolutely no concern to either of them.

He vanished. The men set immediately to work removing the wiggy doors. An electric screwdriver screeched. Minutes later, a trio of bearded techies from Geeks on Wheels arrived at the front door. Tasked, they informed me, with jacking up my cell reception and Wi-Fi.

I grabbed my bag and laptop and escaped to the sanctuary of the Ocean Room. I set the laptop on the card table. One of the legs wobbled.

That silver medallion still under there.

I knelt and again rolled the rug back. That amoeba-shaped stain on the hardwood floor. There was little light in the room right now, so it didn't look as red tinged. Just heavily scrubbed. And it wasn't quite as large as I remembered. Just a foot or so in diameter.

Still, I couldn't shake the idea it was blood.

And that something terrible had happened here in this room.

My thoughts traveled to the hideous scar on Liliana's neck. The scarves she had begun wearing just this June.

The idea of a bite scar came back to me. The old and addled dog, Delilah. Again, I wondered if Liliana had ever visited here.

I sank down on the white chaise that Beatrice had often lounged on. Its view out into the cove. That jagged rock, like hands making a steeple. The Donatello Mary Magdalene. And then I flashed on the slashed-up Modigliani portrait in the tower. How those slices and slashes had seemed personal to me—like whoever had viciously destroyed it had wanted to actually kill the real girl who'd posed for it.

Or a girl who resembled that one. Like Liliana.

And now another idea crept over me . . . that Liliana's scar was not from an animal.

Or from a vampire.

From something too grotesque to even consider.

BEATRICE

"You are crazy, Beatrice."

I remember. The girl named Lilies had said that to me that day in last April. She had spun cobwebs from her cherry mouth to keep me pinned down. "He'll put you away someplace, Beatrice."

Then she gave a jingling kind of laugh, and the cobwebs broke away.

And that's when it happened.

I sprang up from my white chaise, and I pounced.

I was a cheetah with my prey, and my prey was the girl with the name Lilies. I got her in my claws, I heard her howl, I felt her squirm. She kicked at me with her hind feet. She was a scared beast, squeal screaming, and she used her scared strength to get away, running for the door.

I pounced again with all my claws unsheathed, and I ripped her breast in my claws, and then I held her fast, and I bared my cheetah fangs. I sank my fangs into her skin, the soft part where the back of her neck met her shoulder, and she flapped like a bird with a broken wing and made the sound that a rabbit makes when the coyotes are on it. I sank my fangs deeper, and my mouth filled up with the salt and baby-spinach taste of her blood. Her blood spilled from my mouth and onto her breasts and nipples and onto the floor, and still I kept her in my jaws, until I felt her not squirm and flap anymore, and she just hung limp.

And then he was there. My jailer. He grabbed at my hair, and I jerked my head back, but I kept my fangs sunk into her skin.

His arm came underneath my chin and tightened up, it cut out the air from my throat, and I became afraid because I couldn't breathe. I let the girl fall to the floor and struggled to get air. But I still couldn't breathe, he kept strangling the air from my throat, and I was very frightened.

And then Raymond, the skinny man, came into the Ocean Room. He made a kind of shrieking sound, and my jailer loosened his arm around my neck, but he kept his arms gripping around me. I could see the girl lying dead on the floor with blood all around her, and Raymond was hopping like a kangaroo.

And then there were a lot of people in the room. They were all talking on their mobile phones or kneeling to do things to the girl.

My jailer took me out of the room. But he was no longer rough with me—now he was speaking gentle. Like I was a child. "It's okay, Beat. Settle down, it's all going to be okay."

"How did she get down?" I said that even though it was hard for my voice to come out. It still felt like his arm was squeezing my throat.

"She came for work, Beat. She came here to talk about a deal. We had a business meeting in the Great Room. That's all it was."

He couldn't fool me. I'd seen her bouncing on top of him in the wooden cabin. I could smell sex on him. But I couldn't let him see I wasn't fooled, because he would squeeze my throat again until I couldn't breathe at all.

I tipped my face up to him. And I made myself smile.

His face went black with horror. He took a step back away from me. "Christ, you're a fucking ghoul!" he said.

There was blood on my teeth. The girl's blood.

I licked at it with my tongue.

He took another step away from me, and his eyes were black with hate. He wanted to kill me. I could tell he did.

You saw then that he wanted to kill you, Beatrice. Mary's voice cackles to me now. *He still wants to. He is going to.*

Yes, I remember. He wants me dead.

I can still see it in his eyes.

TWENTY-THREE

I spent the rest of the morning distracting myself by catching up on messages and emails. I checked in with Wade, who was in high spirits. His new show still on track. "With any luck, I'll have a job offer for you soon after Labor Day."

So much had changed in just the short time since I'd last seen him. So much I couldn't tell him about. "How's Benny? Does he still like his dino?"

"Crazy about it. It's the only toy he'll play with. He just learned how to make it chew on a bone and then belch."

Around noon, Otis came clomping downstairs. Sucking on a joint. Looking pissed off. "Shit, Jane! I *told* you the Sandovals were freaky. I told you Annunciata liked to drink rum. Why'd you freak out like that?"

"She gave me a shock. I didn't know she was here."

"Did you really think it was Beatrice? What the hell? You're the one who's supposed to be always in control."

"Me?" I said with surprise.

"Yeah. You're the one who always knows what to do in a weird situation. I mean, if you'd still been at the Clown when I hit that guy, you'd have stopped me from hitting him again."

"Yeah, Otis, I probably would've. And like I said, last night was a shock."

"Jeez. First you think you see Beatrice chasing you around in a Range Rover, and it turns out to be her brother. So now you see her ghost haunting you outside your door. And *that* was Annunciata."

I sighed. "Why are you back so early?"

"Evan hauled me back to supervise all this work he's having done on your cottage. Just because Annunciata gave you a boo."

"Don't talk like that. She was in terrible shape last night."

"Yeah, I heard. Drunk as a freaking skunk."

"No, much sadder than that. Terrible misery. It was horrible." I felt a grip of horror remembering it again. "I'm sure she's still in bad shape today."

"No, she's not. She's upstairs vacuuming the Great Room."

"Really?"

"Yeah, really. And I certainly don't blame *her* for my having to come back. I blame you for making such a big deal about it."

"I'm sorry. But you could have called me. I can supervise the work."

"Evan didn't leave me a choice." Otis huffed out a stream of pungent smoke. "He sure seems concerned about your welfare."

"He probably doesn't want to be responsible. In case somebody really does break in."

Otis made a dubious sound.

"Let me make it up to you," I told him. "I'll treat you to lunch. Anywhere you want to go."

"Yeah? Then, okay . . . Ventana."

I hesitated. "Okay. Sure."

"Joking. It would cost you a week's tutoring money. Why don't I just throw a salad together, and we can picnic alfresco."

He assembled a stunning salad of arugula, radicchio, and fennel, with white sardines and toasted slices of sourdough. He spread a checkered cloth on the mossy ground beside his herb garden, and we ate overlooking the cove, the scent of sage and thyme and rosemary enhancing the meal. I told him about the file Evan had given me last night.

"A dossier." Otis gave a snort. "Doesn't surprise me one bit. I'm sure he's got one on me, too, even though we're family."

"The amazing thing," I said, "is I found out something I didn't know about mine. Mom always let me think my father's death was a car accident, but he actually committed suicide. He deliberately crashed his car into a highway barrier."

Otis widened his eyes. "That was in the dossier?"

"Yeah, it had the coroner's jury report. I don't know why Mom kept it a secret from me. Maybe she thought she was protecting me from something terrible."

"I never thought of your mom as someone with deep, dark secrets. She was actually kind of bubbly. Though maybe sometimes she did seem kind of sad."

"I think she was sad a lot of the time. And I think that's why she loved being on stage. So she could dissolve herself into somebody else, the character she was playing, and take on their tragedy instead of her own." I dabbed a stray piece of arugula off my chin. "And it wasn't the only secret she kept from me."

"Whoa," Otis said. "More from your file?"

"No. Something she told me herself right before she died." I filled him in about Aunt Jo, the letter that had come for me that Mom had ripped up. I decided not to tell him about the email from Evan's investigator. "Last night, when I came back from having dinner and reading all this stuff, I began to try to find her. That's what I was doing when I saw something outside the doors."

"Investigating your family ghosts. No wonder you thought you saw one outside. That's like raw material for you. I'm surprised you only thought you saw one ghost, not a whole mob of them."

I laughed. Otis sometimes displayed remarkable perception. "You know, maybe sometimes I do treat you like a screwup. From now on, I promise to give you a lot more credit. I think you're a superb cook, and you're going to have a brilliant career."

"I sure hope so." He gnawed meditatively on a heel of the sourdough. "I've missed this. With us, I mean. Being straight with each other. Telling each other everything."

Not everything. I felt a twinge of guilt.

"Let's not ever argue again," I said quickly.

"Never," he agreed.

Later in the afternoon, an email popped up from a woman named Melinda Cartland. The subject line read: *Happy Trails.* The shelter for abused horses listed in the *Santa Fe New Mexican* article.

She wrote that the shelter was now Happy Trails and had moved to Abiquiú. It's where Georgia O'Keeffe painted many of her best paintings. She said she'd been the director for over three years and had not known a volunteer named Joanne. She sympathized with my search for my long-lost aunt and would be happy to inquire among longtime volunteers to see if the name rang any bells. Thank you for your offer of a donation. So many beautiful animals are shockingly abused.

Disappointing. But not yet a complete dead end.

I rounded up Pilot and the two German shepherds and took them for an early walk. Otis met us upon our return to the house. "The work's all done at your place. You've got cell reception to the moon. And if anybody even breathes near the cottage, it lights up like a prison yard. And you've got drapes on your doors. They're ready made, so they don't fit so hot, but they cover up the glass." He gave me a shiny key. "New dead bolt on your door. The guys left a mess, but Annunciata tidied up. She just left."

"Did she seem okay?"

He gave a snort. "You think I can tell?"

I went to check it out. The bed freshly made, clean sheets, blankets tucked with army corners. (*What could she have thought about that telling disarray of sheets?* I wondered with a flush.) A fresh votive candle flickered on the bed table. The old landline—the one that was sometimes dead and sometimes alive—was gone, as was my cheap booster, replaced by a Linksys Wi-Fi range extender.

Opaque navy curtains blocked out the glass doors. I drew the curtains open. Tested one of the doors. It glided straight and true on new runners.

I stepped outside, and motion-detector lights flooded the terrace. The dangling pine branch that used to brush against the doors was now pruned back. Something shiny dangled from a branch. I stood on tiptoe and pulled it down to look.

A medallion on a leather string. Beaten silver, with religious symbols embossed on both sides. Identical to the one under the rug in the Ocean Room. Set on that large reddish stain.

I let it go. It swung back up high on the branch, glinting in the floodlights.

Evan noticed it at once when he came two nights later. "What's that?"

"A religious medallion," I said. "Annunciata hung it there."

He went out and unhooked it from the pine branch. Turned it over in his hand. "In the part of Honduras she comes from, they put these in places of misfortune. At deathbeds and at the scenes of accidents and violent crimes. It's supposed to sanctify them."

"Why did she put one here? There was no violent crime."

"She got drunk and scared you half out of your wits. That calls for sanctifying in her book."

"There's one in the Ocean Room," I said. "On that wine stain underneath the rug."

A flash of something crossed his face, then vanished. "When Beatrice threw the bottle at my manager, Raymond, it knocked him

265

out cold. It cost my insurance a lot of money. And it cost me a very good estate manager." He smiled. "I suppose Nunci considered that also worthy of a charm."

Minnie trotted out and nosed his leg. He nuzzled her head. "She been behaving herself?"

"Beautifully. I feel very protected having her here at night."

"Good." He hooked the silver medallion back on the branch. "Nunci's superstitions are a comfort to her. Let her have them. And let's us go to bed." He took my hand and led me back inside; he unbuttoned my shirt, and my heart quickened. He began to kiss my breasts, and then his lips moved downward; he undid my jeans and continued down between my legs, softly kissing, and I just let the endorphins scramble my brains.

BEATRICE

Braidy Witch came running down to the Ocean Room that day in April, and my jailer said something in the witch language to her. She tried to take me by my arms. I snarled at her, the girl's blood still on my teeth. But she did not back away from me the way my jailer did. She talked to me in a gentling way. "Come up to your room, Mrs. Beatrice. Come up the stairs, and I clean your face."

She's as big as me and very strong, and that day she began to pull at me to go upstairs. But I was even stronger than she was, and I sprang away from her, and I ran like a cheetah up the first stairway. I could hear my jailer and also Annunciata come running after me. I ran up the second stairway and into my room, and I locked the door behind me.

And then I turned around, and I saw that the girl had gone back inside the picture by Amedeo Modigliani.

You failed that day, Beatrice, Mary hisses at me. *You didn't kill her.*

The girl had jumped back up into the picture, and now she was watching me with her head swayed over to one side.

Why wasn't she dead? I could still taste her blood in my mouth and on my teeth.

My jailer was pounding at my door. "Beatrice! Open the door."

I got a pair of manicure scissors from my dressing table. And then I stabbed and stabbed. I stabbed out the girl's superior eyes and slashed away her blue cherry mouth and I sliced her little breasts in half and then in half again, and then I wrote her name with the scissors all around her. Lilies. I wrote it over and over so everyone would know that she had given herself a name. *Lilies, Lilies, Lilies.*

The key turned in my bedroom door. I heard my jailer roar deep like a lion in the dark jungle.

But I did not stop writing the name of the girl in slashes all around her.

And then the lion got me in his paws. He was going to tear out my throat, he wanted to rip me apart and eat me alive, I could see that in his eyes. He had the hate of the hunter in his eyes, and I was his prey now.

I stabbed him with the scissors, like I had stabbed the girl in the picture frame.

He roared again. He cuffed my wrist with his giant paw, and the manicure scissors dropped out of my hand. He got me in his paws again, and I snarled and spit and clawed, and I got away.

I was a cheetah. I ran fast as a cheetah away from him.

The lion roared even louder, loud and fierce. He came running on all fours after me.

I got to the staircase, and at the bottom, Mary Magdalene was waiting for me. I could see her fingers pointed up in prayer.

I remember now. That day in last April. I leaped like a cheetah off the top of the staircase into Mary's praying hands.

TWENTY-FOUR

What was it about secret sex that gave it an extra spice?

The soft rap on my door late in the evening, making my heart beat furiously and lighting a fire in every nerve. The exquisite bouts of sex, exploring every inch of each other's bodies. And, afterward, munching pistachios and croissants in bed, talking, laughing incessantly until we fell asleep in each other's arms. And then at dawn, waking to make love again, crumbs sticking to our damp skin as we tumbled naked together.

The thrill of secretly watching him when we were not in private, thinking of our bodies together, and every so often his eyes catching mine, a smile playing on his lips that told me he was thinking the same thing.

But a major part of me rebelled against the secrecy. I wanted to shout about us from the top of the bluffs. To grab random strangers on the street and tell them how dizzyingly, ridiculously alive I felt.

I hated concealing it from Otis and Sophia.

It was now the beginning of August. There was less fog, more heat and brilliance in the afternoon. Sophia's tennis clinic ended, and she stopped going for sleepovers at Peyton's. Peyton must have taken her up as a convenience—somebody to hang out with in summer school.

I tried to draw out Sophia on the subject. "She's busy with stuff," Sophia said.

"Are you upset about it?"

A shrug, one shouldered. "It's okay. I don't care."

She aced her algebra final, as I knew she would. Evan rewarded her with a ride on the Harley and a pizza afterward, and for a day after that, she snapped out of moping.

But he was gone the next morning, and she sulked through tutoring that afternoon. "*Je m'emmerde*," she muttered.

"Bored to shit." She hadn't learned that one from me.

Evan began spending most of his time up in Silicon Valley. I walked Pilot alone, the earlier-setting sun slanting through the redwoods in broad rays, like a child's drawing of tree trunks and sunbeams. I still kept Minnie in my cottage at night. Sometimes she'd rouse herself and grumble low in her throat, waking me, but she'd quickly settle back down.

But I'd lie wide awake for hours and think of Evan's answers to all my questions. Easy answers. Some nights I'd conclude he was telling the truth. Beatrice was a suicide. Plain and simple. It all fit together.

Other nights, I'd be sure there were still missing pieces to the puzzle. And if I found them, they'd reveal a different result. One that made me shudder.

The end of summer was approaching.

I wondered, *What will happen then?*

On August 4, I received an email from Khalim, the intern at Evan's office in Los Gatos. An itinerary for the Doctors without Borders benefit in Los Angeles.

Thurs., 8/10 1:00 p.m.: Depart by car from Thorn Bluffs for the airfield. Please be in the motor court by 12:45 p.m.

Thurs., 8/10 4:00 p.m.: Check in to Shutters on the Beach hotel.

Thurs., 8/10 6:30 p.m.–11:00 p.m.: Cocktail reception and dinner at home of Mr. and Mrs. Dillon Saroyan. Please be ready in hotel lobby to depart at 6:00 p.m.

Fri., 8/11 7:30 a.m.: Depart from Shutters for the airport. Please be ready in the lobby by 7:15 a.m.

The dress is black tie. Feel free to contact me with any questions.

I asked Evan on the phone that evening, "Do you still want me to come to this benefit?"

"I'm counting on it."

"What about keeping us a secret?"

"It won't be an issue. You're accompanying me to a tedious business affair. We'll behave professionally."

"I never said I would go," I told him.

"That's true. I'm still waiting for an answer. Yes or no?"

"Yes," I said. "I would very much like to go with you."

"Good. Because I would very much not like to go without you."

I did not intend to go in capris. Or naked. But it left me just a few days to come up with an outfit. I recruited Sophia to help me pick out a dress from Rent the Runway. "Nothing black," I told her. "Yeah, it's not your color," she agreed—a little too readily. She picked out a lovely pink dress. I had a pair of dressy sandals I'd brought from New York. I bought a long scarf to serve as a wrap and borrowed a beaded ivory clutch from Ella Mahmed.

She brought it to me when we met for drinks at a café off Junipero. We sat at a table beneath olive trees in the courtyard, sipping strawberry-and-kiwi tonics.

"Can you recommend a hair stylist?" I asked her. "Somebody who does, like, classic cuts."

"You mean you don't want to get scalped like me?" She grinned.

"I'd love to get a Mohawk, but I'm not sure I could pull it off."

"Ha, no, you've got your own style, and it suits you. My lady is terrific. You can trust her to do what you want. Her name's Jamaica. She's in high demand, but I can get her to fit you in." She suddenly glanced over my shoulder. "Hey, there's Rick McAdams."

I turned. He'd just emerged from the café into the courtyard. He wore a snappy cream-colored blazer, spotless white pants, and a straw fedora pushed rakishly back on his head to show off a wide gauze bandage. He steered himself instantly to our table.

He knew I was here, I thought. *Still stalking me.*

"Ella, marvelous to see you." He kissed her demurely on the cheek. "And, Jane, always a pleasure."

He bent to give me a similar kiss. I shrank from him, and his kiss landed in air. "Mind if I join you?"

"Please," Ella said.

He appropriated a stool from a neighboring table. Ella glanced at his head. "What happened to you?"

"I was mugged." He stroked the bandage gently, as if even the slightest pressure would be excruciating. "I got a very significant head wound. Like a month ago and it's still bad."

"Oh my God!" Ella said. "Did it happen anywhere around here?"

"Yes, in fact. Fairly near here." He sidled a look at me.

"I thought we didn't have much in the way of muggings," Ella said. "How did it happen? Was it at night?"

"Yeah, it was night. A man attacked me viciously from behind. Knocked me cold with some sort of hard object."

"Oh my God," she exclaimed again. "Did he rob you?"

"He definitely robbed me. He took just about everything I had."

"So what do the police say? Any chance of this guy getting caught?"

"As a matter of fact, yes." Rick now directed a triumphant look at me. "The police tell me he's definitely going to be caught and very soon. But, Ella, didn't Jane tell you anything about this?"

Ella turned a surprised face to me. "You knew?"

"She did. She was actually my angel of mercy after this vicious attack," Rick said.

"I gave him a lift to the ER," I said quickly. To Rick, I said, "It was weeks ago. I'm surprised you still need a bandage."

"It was quite a serious injury. Ella, Jane came to me as soon as I called even though it was the middle of the night. You should have seen how much I was bleeding. I sincerely thought I was going to die. But Jane took mercy on me and drove me all the way to Monterey for treatment. She even came into the ER with me."

"Just to give you your car keys," I said.

"But it was so extraordinarily kind. And I remember lying there in the ER, looking up at the security camera blinking away and thinking, *How nice it's recording this moment, me bleeding half to death and Jane, my angel of mercy, right there by my side.*"

I recalled him pointing at that blinking light. And again wondered what he had meant by it. "I'm glad to see you're all right," I said. "With no permanent harm done."

"No, no permanent harm to me." His pretty lips slid into a grin. "Too bad I can't say that about all parties involved."

Ella glanced from him to me. "I hope they catch this guy. I hate to think he's still on the loose."

"Trust me, it won't be for long." Rick jerked his head in that puppet-on-strings way. "Well, I'll leave you gals to your coffee klatch. Ella, you're looking absolutely stunning as always. Jane, well, words can't express how I feel." He got up, smiled now with that mockery of boyish charm that gave me the creeps. He left the courtyard.

Ella leaned to me with an eager gleam. "So *that's* who it is! I knew you were having a thing with somebody! So it's Richard McAdams!"

"Oh my God, no," I said.

"You're outed, kiddo. You and Ricky."

"I am *not* having any kind of thing with him. I'd never even consider it. I find him repulsive, really and truly."

"Oh, please. He obviously came in here just to see you. And he sure ain't repulsive. A little on the squirrelly side, maybe, but he's pretty gorgeous. You know what? He looks a lot like his sister."

I shook my head vehemently. "Seriously, Ella. I am not in any way involved with that man. He's a liar and a cheat, and I would never have anything at all to do with him, ever."

She frowned. "So what was all that about, then? All that angel-of-mercy stuff?"

"He fell, and he cracked his head. And for some strange reason, he called me. And now he's trying to turn it into some drama about being the victim of a mugging."

"Okay, whatever. You've got no interest in a handsome, charming man—who, out of all the people in town, decided to call you to ferry him to a doctor in the middle of the night."

"Maybe I'm the only person who would take his calls. He made it sound like he was dying. I couldn't refuse."

"You don't think he was really robbed?"

"No, I don't. He's just trying to get pity and sympathy for himself. He really is a creep." I paused. "I'm sorry. I know he's a friend of yours."

"No, just an acquaintance. I rarely see him. The last time was about a month ago when he came into the gallery. Oh, and funny, he was asking about that Grayson Perry vase—the one Beatrice Rochester broke accidentally on purpose." She shot me another significant look. "The one you were so interested in."

"Did you ever tell him the story about her?"

"Can't remember. Though I've told enough people that he could have found out anyway. He said he had a client who collected Perry and might be interested in it. He wanted to know the price. I told him I wasn't sure because it had been reconstructed. And, like I told you, it still technically belongs to Evan Rochester."

"Did you think he really had a client?"

"Nah. I thought he was just killing time. People do that—they come in with or without an appointment and pretend they're high rollers." She meditatively scratched her nose. "Now that I think about it, about a week later, a couple of cops came in. *They* wanted to hear the story about Beatrice Rochester. They took pictures of the Perry vase."

"Rick must have put them up to it."

"Maybe, but not necessarily. There's been some buzz around town that the cops are gearing the investigation of Beatrice back up. I've had other friends who've been questioned. You know Terry, at yoga? She was questioned. And so was Pam."

The Semi-regulars. Always willing to share their stories about the Rochesters, accurate or not.

"By the way," Ella said, "there's a jazz concert Thursday night that I'm going to. Outdoors in a park just outside of town. I'm going with my goat lady and a couple of other pals."

I grinned. "So goat lady was a hit?"

"So far so good. Do you wanna join us?"

"I'd love to, but I won't be here. I'm going to LA for a couple of days. I'm attending a benefit." I couldn't keep a hint of excitement from my voice.

"Aha. That explains the haircut. Where are you staying?"

"A hotel. Shutters on the Beach in Santa Monica."

She raised her brows. "Fancy. Don't suppose you're going alone?"

I hesitated. "No. Not alone."

"But not with Rick McAdams."

"No."

Now she looked at me with a dawning thought. She started to say something but then snapped her mouth shut. "Okay. I'll catch you when you get back."

I lingered at the café after she left and sent a text to Rick: Ok you got my attention. Let's talk. I'll wait here.

He replied immediately: Don't need u anymore. I got him. He's going down.

My stomach tightened. What do you mean?

New evidence.
What evidence? About the Perry vase?
Not that. You'll find out. Free advice. Always check old messages.
What do u mean? Did u leave me a message I didn't return?

No reply. I texted again.

What do u mean about a message??

Still no reply. I texted several times more.

Seriously, Rick. What new evidence? Talk to me please.
Don't ghost me!! Please let's talk. I want to help.

Radio silence.

BEATRICE

I remember. I had leaped down the staircase to Mary Magdalene's praying hands, and she had stopped the lion from tearing me apart. But he took me to the dungeon after that, and the fat dungeon master fed me poison with a tube, and I got fat, too, all puffed up.

Like the puffer fish Ricky caught. With deadly poison inside it.

And after I came home from the dungeon, I started hiding the poison in the shoe, and now I'm no longer so puffed up.

I am finished with my crab salad now, and Annunciata has come back. I let her take me up to my bedroom. A model prisoner, I lie down for a nap.

And now I'm awake again. My eyes open and look up at the wall in front of my bed. I look to make sure the girl is not there anymore. She no longer looks down while I'm sleeping to watch my dreams.

I get up and go into my dressing room, and I sit down at my table and put on lipstick. It's Rose Celebration, by Yves Saint Laurent. It gets on my teeth, just like the girl's blood that day in the month of last April.

But it's not red like the girl's blood. It shimmers pink and pretty.

"Hey, Beatrice, happy anniversary!"

Another face floats behind mine in the mirror. Skinny eyebrows and black hair that's cut short on one side and droops long on the other. A nose with a little bump on it.

"Oh my God, don't you know who I am? I'm *Kendra*, Beatrice! Kendra Hayman?"

I remember. She had brought me clothes after my black Amex got a hex on it. She used to have jewels in her bumpy nose. "The holes are still there," I say.

She grins and taps the three holes on the nostril. "You mean these guys? Yeah, I took out the ruby studs. I'm waiting for the holes to close up, and then I'm gonna do a septum piercing." She goes on talking. "So a lot of changes since I was last here, huh? No more Raymond, huh? Or Cecily, or Lawrence Cho? But your new guy, Otis, seems like a real sweetheart."

In the doorway behind her, I see a shadow.

My jailer's shadow. The arms are crossed.

Kendra Hayman glances quickly at the shadow too.

He got her here to be a witness, BJ. Ricky's voice talks in my mind. *To help establish his alibi.*

Yes. His alibi so he can hide what he is plotting to do to me.

I won't let them see that I know.

Kendra talks in an extra cheerful voice. "You've dropped a lot of weight, haven't you, babe? You look amazing! Su-per mod*el*, right? Scoot around a second."

I am obedient. I twist my back to her.

She lifts up my hair with both her hands. "You sure do have gorgeous hair, Beatrice. And it's so long now." It falls from her hands in golden wings to my shoulder blades. "You've got some twiggy stuff tangled up. Have you been in the woods?"

Scared, I glance again at the shadow in the doorway.

It's gone.

"But no problem, Annunciata will do a deep shampoo. Meanwhile, I'll browse the closets, pull a few dresses." Kendra looks me up and down. "Ice blue. Cold colors, that's always been your color palette. Winter is definitely your season."

And now I am sitting with my head tilting back at the biggest of my sinks, and Annunciata's thick fingers scrub in shampoo. Hot water washes away the foamy suds, and Annunciata combs my hair, not gentle like the brushing this morning. Now she makes the teeth of the comb bite into my scalp.

The hair dryer blows stormy around my face. Hot rollers snuggle warm against my head.

I'm a mannequin. They may do whatever they want with me.

Kendra opens up her makeup kit. She smooths my face with foundation. She draws cat eyes and paints my eyelids. She scrubs the Rose Celebration off my lips and paints them darker pink. She unwinds the hot rollers and then uses the blower again.

She holds up two blue dresses on hangers. She first holds one up high, then the other. "Definitely the Alexander McQueen. Handkerchief hems are back this season."

Annunciata unties my robe. She gives me silk panties to step into. She fits a silk bra onto my breasts and hooks it up in back. Size 34B.

The water is going down in the cove, Mary whispers to me. *Listen to the sound, Beatrice. There's not much time left.*

Light-blue silk falls over me cold like winter rain. The kerchief hem drips like melting ice down my thighs.

And now Kendra is at my shoe closet. She's making the racks go around and round.

Ricky's voice yells in my head. *You're letting her into your shoes? What are you, brain dead, Beatie June? She'll find the poison pills.*

But Kendra has picked out high-heeled sandals with open toes. There can be no poison hidden in them. "You've got such amazing feet, Beatrice," she says to me. "So long and aristocratic."

Annunciata squats down to help me put the sandals on. A sparkling bracelet snaps onto my wrist.

"Oh! My! God! You look ravishing, Beatrice! Check yourself out."

Kendra turns me to look in my long three-way mirror. My painted face and the white-gold cloud of my hair. My body drips sapphire blue.

The bracelet around my wrist is getting tighter. It has a spell on it. I squeeze the bones of my hand together and slip my hand out of the bracelet, and I put the bracelet down on the dressing table.

"Oh my God, you're right. With the earrings, too much bling." Kendra starts packing up her paints and hot rollers into her makeup kit. "You really should go back to work, babe. You've still got it. You could be totally back on top in no time."

Stupid girl. What is she talking about? I am Beatrice McAdams. I'm the most famous girl. The one who always wears the white dress at the end.

I cannot be replaced.

You will be, Mary whispers. *The girl Lilies. You heard her voice on his phone last night. You saw her face today.*

"No!"

"What did you say, babe?" Kendra looks up from packing her makeup kit.

Mary's voice hisses loud. *He's going to get rid of you tonight, Beatrice. You heard him say so.*

Kendra's voice says, "Something wrong, Beatrice?"

There are too many voices. I shake my head.

"Okay, then, you just chill for a little bit. Annunciata went to tell Evan you're done, and he'll be back up soon with your medicine." Kendra picks up her makeup kit and slings the strap over her shoulder. She shoots both her thumbs up. "You look freaking out of this world. He's going to fall madly in love with you all over again."

And then Kendra Hayman is gone.

The ocean is low, Beatrice. Mary whispers very low. *Listen to the way it's crying. You need to finish the plan before he comes back with the poison.*

No. I am Beatrice McAdams, he'll fall in love with me again like he did on the island of Barbados.

Mary whispers low. I can't hear her at all. Too much of the poison pill seeped into me this morning before I got it out. I can't hear any of the voices.

I don't know what to do.

TWENTY-FIVE

I texted and tried calling Rick multiple times over that day and the following one, but he continued to ghost me. I scanned all texts I'd received for the past two months as well as voice mail and email. Nothing from him or anything else important that I'd overlooked. So what did he mean about checking old messages?

I reread the texts from him that I'd got before blocking his number. From the day after the ER, and before that, after my first Vinyasa session, when I had told him to stop stalking me or I'd call the police. His reply: *I have friends in the police.*

So maybe he had bribed one of those friends to reactivate the investigation?

Or did he really have some new evidence? Something he might have given those same cop friends?

Should I tell Evan about it? We were flying to LA the next day. I was looking forward to the benefit, and I didn't want anything to ruin it. If I still hadn't heard from Rick by that night, I'd show Evan his texts directly after the event.

I presented myself in the motor court at 12:45 p.m. per the intern Khalim's itinerary. Otis was backing the Tesla out of the garage. He parked and got out.

"Are you driving us to the airport?" I said.

"No, Evan is." He regarded me balefully. "You sure you know what you're doing?"

"Going to a benefit with him in LA. It's a business event. Not a big deal."

"Overnight. And it's twenty grand a plate."

I widened my eyes.

Otis tossed my bag with emphatic overexertion into the back seat. "I know what's going on. I'm not an idiot, you know."

"I know you're not."

"So let me ask you again. Do you know what you are doing?"

"Okay, listen. It's not very complicated. I like him. I think he likes me."

He gave a snort. "You don't even know him. I mean *really* know him."

"I think I do well enough."

"You have any idea how rich he stands to be?"

"Yeah, I do. And I really don't care."

"Maybe. But you think anybody gets there by being nice and kind and good?"

"What are you really trying to say, O.? Is it still about that painting he made you deliver? Or are you accusing him of something else?"

"I just don't want you to get hurt. I mean, like, with Jeremy, he hurt you—he was a shit and cheated on you, and you were miserable. But he was nothing compared to Evan, believe me."

"You talk about him like he's a monster," I said. "But you got me here, remember?" I gave a quick laugh. "You assured me I wouldn't get my throat cut."

"You were the last person I thought would be taken in by him."

The front door of the house opened and released a gust of dogs, followed by Evan in a heavy aviator jacket, a garment bag slung over his shoulder. Sophia trailing him, carrying his bag.

"Just don't let him play you," Otis muttered. "I mean it."

"I won't. I mean that too."

They came closer, and I could hear Sophia complaining in a high voice, "It's not fair. Why does Jane get to go and not me?"

"It's a work thing, Sophia. I can't bring my kid to it."

"You treat me like a little kid, but I'm not. I never get to go flying with you."

He took his bag from her. "I'm going to teach you how to fly. As soon as you're sixteen."

"That's, like, three years from now. Why can't you take me before I get sent back to that crappy school?"

He softened his voice. "Hey, okay. I'll take you up right after I get back."

"You won't have time. You never do. It's not fair." She turned and began stomping back toward the house.

Evan shot a what-can-I-do? glance at me.

I went after her. "Wait, Sophia."

She turned. "When did you and him get so wrapped up in each other?"

I looked at her with astonishment. Apparently, we had kept our relationship a secret from exactly nobody. "I'm just keeping him company on a business thing. We'll be back tomorrow. And then he'll take you flying."

"He won't. He'll say he's still got too much work. Because he doesn't give a crap about spending time with me."

She continued stomping back to the house. I sighed, but I had no time to try to mollify her further. I returned to the car. With a decidedly ironic motion, Otis swung the passenger door wide. Ignoring him, I slid in.

"Is she okay?" Evan said.

"She will be. Call her when we get there, okay?"

"Yeah, I will." He started the car and began pulling out of the compound.

"Are we taking your plane?" I said.

"Yeah." He shot me an amused look. "Were you expecting a private jet?"

"I don't know what I was expecting. Maybe the Alaska Air shuttle."

He laughed. The phone in the pocket between our seats began to buzz. I caught a glimpse of the caller ID.

Delilah.

The name of the old German shepherd. Whose grave Rick McAdams had seen out in the woods. The dog who might have been poisoned by Beatrice.

Not a very common name.

Evan didn't pick up. The phone buzzed again, a different number. This time he answered and began speaking on his Bluetooth.

I checked my own phone for a text from Rick. Still nothing.

We merged onto Highway 1, and Evan pocketed both phone and earpiece. In half a mile, he turned onto an exit that led inland.

"Where exactly are we going?" I said.

"A private airfield where I keep my planes."

"Do you have more than one?"

"Two at the moment, a Beechcraft and a Mooney. We'll take the Mooney. It's a four seater—it's fast and comfortable. You'll like it."

I nodded, a little nervously. I'd never been on a private plane before. "Were you sixteen when you learned to fly?"

"Eleven. I first soloed at twelve. It was in Bolivia. The backcountry. My parents spent their working lives in remote places. Sacred places, usually no access except trails for mules or llamas. It was crucial to know how to fly. It seemed natural to me, like riding a bike for other kids."

It was the first time he'd mentioned his parents. Or anything about his childhood. "It sounds like a good way to grow up," I said.

"It was. A very good way."

I was silent a second. "Can you fly a jet?"

"In theory, yeah," he said. "I'm not licensed. I'd planned to attend the Air Force Academy after college, but they revoked their acceptance. They said I'd become too unstable."

"Was it true?" I said.

"I'd just killed my parents. What do you think?"

I felt a chill race through me. "Do you mean that?"

"Yeah, I do. I knew their plane was defective. I didn't tell them."

"Why not?"

"No good reason." He steered onto a narrow two-lane road, and the surrounding vegetation became dusty scrub. "I'd taken it up the day before. A Piper Super Cub, great bush plane, rugged as they come. My seat slid back midflight, just a fraction, but for a split second, I lost my grip on the controls. I stayed out late that night, got trashed. In the morning, I was too hungover to drag my ass out of bed. They left for the dig site without me. And never came back."

"That's all?" I said. "A seat sliding back a fraction?"

"You lose your grip even for a split second, you can go into a dive. My parents were excellent pilots. But my father was seventy-two, my mother fifty-nine. Neither had the reflexes of a twenty-year-old."

"But you can't know for sure that's what happened."

"No, I can't." His voice was suddenly flat. Devoid of emotion.

I flashed on Rick McAdams's words: *They disappeared. He got the money. Sound familiar?*

We had arrived now at the gate of a cyclone fence. A sign: **ALTA VISTA AVIATION**. A small tower, some dozen aluminum hangars. A sleek-looking plane, white with teal-blue stripes, parked outside one of the hangars. Evan drove up beside it, and we got out.

A young guy with waist-length hair came over with a clipboard, and he and Evan walked a check around the plane. Evan helped me board and tightened a harness strap over me. He climbed into the pilot's seat. He gave me a headset. Strapped himself in and checked instruments.

His voice suddenly over the headset. "It'll be bumpy over the hills. Once we break through the rough air, it should be smooth sailing for the rest of the trip."

The engine roared; the propeller began to spin. The plane taxied into the wind. The nose lifted, and we rose, hard bumping and rattling, the wings seesawing with every gust of wind. I gripped the edge of my seat, white knuckled.

But then we broke above the ridgeline and began to glide over a sea that dazzled turquoise and silver, and I loosened my death grip on the seat.

"This is amazing!" I breathed.

Evan's face was as radiant as a young boy's. "There's nothing else like it. If I could live in the air, I would."

"You must have been a bird in another life. A hawk or an eagle."

"A vulture, more like it."

"No, not a vulture. They fly too low to the ground."

He laughed and lifted the plane's nose higher, and we soared upward, higher than eagles. I felt everything drop away, all my suspicions and questions, all of it left behind me on the earth below. Evan pointed out features of the ragged coastline: synclines and eroded volcanic cones and an earthquake fault line. "This is a spectacular earth science lesson," I told him. "I wish Sophia was here."

"She'll get the same lesson when I take her up."

Too soon, we began to descend over the LA sprawl. Evan spoke to air traffic control, and we put down at the Santa Monica airport. A thump on the runway, a short taxi to a stop.

We ducked into a waiting black Suburban. The hard rock-candy light of LA, so different from the mist-textured air of Big Sur. A short freeway drive to the hotel, a large multilevel building on the oceanfront. Evan checked us in and gave me a swipe card. "Separate rooms?" I said.

"And separate floors, I'm afraid. I'll see you back down here in two hours." He was already distracted, calls and texts sounding relentlessly.

My room was on the third floor: a small suite, prettily appointed, more Hamptons in decor than West Coast. A view of sugary white sand, a strip of ocean, the boardwalk in between.

I stepped out on the small balcony and watched the boardwalk parade. Strollers, cyclists. Daredevil skateboarders. I indulged in a fantasy: We'd skip the benefit and spend the evening on the boardwalk instead. We'd gape at the bodybuilders and buy silly hats. We'd eat curly fries and Cronuts and ride the Ferris wheel on the pier.

A Ferris wheel and Cronuts versus closing a deal worth hundreds of millions of dollars. A ridiculous fantasy.

I went back into my suite. I had less than two hours to get ready.

A luxurious soak in the suite's capacious spa tub. I washed my hair with a shampoo that smelled like Alpine flowers. I had gone to Ella's stylist, Jamaica, and she did not scalp me—she'd trimmed my hair blunt to my shoulders with thick long layers and painted in subtle threads of butter and beige. When I blew it dry now, it fell full and swingy, the highlights enhancing my natural light brown.

I took extra time with my makeup. Using techniques I'd picked up from the *Carlotta* makeup department, I blended highlights and shadows and a powdered blusher to emphasize my cheekbones and make the most of my wide-set eyes. I outlined my lips and painted them a deep coral.

I contemplated the results.

I blotted a quarter of it off.

I removed my Rent the Runway dress from its vinyl bag and shook it out. A rose-gold silk with a subtle lace pattern and a deep V neckline and a fitted bodice that belled out to midcalf. It had arrived two days before, and I'd tried it on in front of the blackened old mirror above the bricked-in fireplace. The mirror had smiled.

But like every oracle, it was capricious, and when I took a few steps back, it seemed suddenly to mock me. The V-neck was too plunging.

The rose gold too garish. A just-pretty-enough girl trying too desperately to please.

"The hell with you," I'd muttered to the blackened glass. I'd peeled off the dress and interred it back in its vinyl bag. And hadn't taken it out again until now.

I carefully wriggled it over my head. Smoothed the skirt and adjusted the deep-cut bodice. Contorted myself to zip the hidden zipper in back.

I didn't look in the suite's full-length mirror. Not yet.

I slipped on my sandals—dark gold, three-inch heels. I fastened my small diamond studs to my earlobes and clasped on the amethyst necklace Mom had given me for my sweet sixteen. It made my eyes violet, she'd told me. Like Elizabeth Taylor.

And only then did I turn to my reflection.

The dress was just the right combination of sexy and demure. The rose gold brought out roses in my cheeks as well as golden lights in my hair. And maybe there was a hint of violet in my eyes.

I felt a flush of pleasure. I looked more than just pretty enough. Almost a beauty.

I took a selfie and sent it to Sophia.

She texted back immediately. **OMG u look awesome!!!!**

Not too much cleavage?
No!!! U can totally rock cleavage!

I knew her brutal candor in such matters. I felt a pulse of pleasure. Maybe I did look awesome.

At six o'clock, I made my way down to the lobby. It swirled with activity. A Scandinavian-looking family checking in. A hip-hop star with an entourage. A clutch of bridesmaids in palest blue. And then I saw Evan. Standing kitty-corner to the reception desk, frowning at his phone. He looked impossibly elegant in his tux. His hair tamed, just a few black curls spilling into his eyes. Beard impeccably sheared.

He glanced up and saw me. He took a darting step forward, as if eager to claim a prize.

To claim *me* as his prize.

I felt such a rush of pure and heady joy that I thought my feet might leave the floor.

He came quickly to me. Gazed down, consuming me with his eyes. "You look . . . very nice," he said.

I laughed. "So do you. You look civilized."

"Yeah? Let me fix that." He tugged the end of his bow tie, undoing the bow. He pulled it off and stuffed it in his pocket. "I hate anything at my neck. I must have been hanged in a previous life."

I felt something pass over me—a dark shadow, the kind that felt like a premonition.

But then he leaned and kissed me softly on the lips, and all shadows passed, and I felt another burst of levitating joy. I slipped my arm through his, and we advanced arm in arm, past the hip-hop entourage and the shriek of bridesmaids, outside to Pico Boulevard. The black SUV was once again waiting. We slid into the back seat.

The 405 freeway took us to Sunset Boulevard, and then we wound east to the ornate Bel Air gates. A short distance up Bel Air Road to a gatehouse, the checkpoint for the snaking line of vehicles already arrived. We were finally checked through, and we cruised up a palm-lined drive to a gargantuan modern chateau.

"Do you think it's big enough?" Evan asked with a grin.

"Maybe it could use another wing. It's not quite as big as the Louvre."

"I'll suggest that to Dillon." A squadron of good-looking attendants of both sexes sprang to open our doors. "There'll be a lot of people here I'll need to talk to. I hope you won't feel neglected."

"I won't. I've been to these kinds of affairs before. I can fend for myself."

"I'll bet you can."

We entered a series of vast rooms, each furnished with only small islands of neutral-colored furniture accented by one or two contemporary paintings. How much money did it take, I wondered, to achieve this amount of emptiness in such staggeringly high-priced real estate?

An extremely tall young woman in a golden gown guided us into a salon. One wall opened entirely to a series of outdoor terraces. Inside and out, a crush of tuxes and jewel-colored dresses. The cityscape of Los Angeles stretched for miles beyond.

"Ready?" Evan said.

"Yeah, ready."

We plunged into the crush. The next hour was a whirl. Names, instantly forgotten. Handshakes, firm ones and limp-as-dead-fish ones. Champagne flutes and trays of elaborate hors d'oeuvres proffered by circulating waiters. Evan introduced me to the host, the venture capitalist Dillon Saroyan—a chubby-faced silver fox with a twentysomething wife who flaunted a baby bump beneath her clingy red gown. And then more faces, more names, more handshakes.

I kept on the alert for one particular face—a lovely oval framed by a short dark bob. *She isn't here.* I felt a silly tick of relief. A Cuban orchestra suddenly struck up on the terrace below, and the rhythms made my entire body itch to move.

I shot a mischievous smile at Evan. "I'll bet you don't dance."

"That is a bet you would lose. Don't forget I spent my formative years in Latin America." He plucked the champagne flute from my hand and set it on a waiter's tray and then led me out to a dance floor set up in front of the orchestra. He held me with feather lightness. Twirled me out, drew me back in. Dipped me in an exaggerated way. I laughed, giddy with happiness.

The musicians segued into a slower number, and now he drew me very close and led me in a sinuous step, expertly, his hand on my bare back. And I nestled my head in the hollow of his shoulder and thought of how later, after this was all over, I would go to his room or he would come to mine, and this was the way we would make love, slowly and sinuously, and I felt almost choked with desire.

We were keeping nothing a secret right now. Anyone who saw us, who noticed, would have no illusions about our relationship.

The number ended with a flourish. "I could use a real drink," Evan said.

"Me too," I said. "An extra dry Bombay martini with a twist. Stirred, of course."

"You read my mind."

We headed back up toward the long bar in the main salon. Evan was instantly besieged—faces, outstretched hands. I mouthed, "I'll get the drinks" and continued on to the bar.

Mobbed. Ten minutes to work my way to the front. I squeezed in next to a red-faced man in a noticeably too-tight tux. He was drunkenly berating the bartender, who looked like a moonlighting actress. "A fricking old-fashioned, baby," he slurred. "It's Bartending 101, not rocket science." He slammed his glass down. "This tastes like a frigging 7UP."

"I used the standard recipe, sir." The young woman's voice was on the edge of cracking. "Do you want me to do it another way?"

"Yeah, the frigging right way."

I said to the bartender, "Try using a sugar cube instead of simple syrup. It makes it a little less syrupy and sweet."

She glanced at the drunk, who made a "whatever" gesture. She turned to fix the drink, and he shifted his attention to me. "I saw you dancing with Evander Rochester."

I kept a neutral expression.

"Wanna piece of advice? Don't get too cozy with him. You think he's got Saroyan eating out of the palm of his hand? Don't count on it, baby. Ya know the saying: 'Fake it till you make it'? Rochester's been faking it too freaking long."

"How would you know?" I said coldly.

"Everybody knows everything in the Valley." The guy tapped his head with an index finger. "Everybody knows he's a fraud. A wife killer, too, but hey, who gives a shit about that, right?"

The bartender set down the freshly made old-fashioned. "I hope this one is better."

"Whatever." The drunk grabbed the glass and lurched off.

"Asshole," she remarked.

I nodded in sympathy. "I used to tend bar. I know the type. Nasty drunk."

I gave my order, two extra dry Bombay martinis, stirred, with a twist. She made them efficiently. I wove carefully back through the crowd, taking care not to slosh the drinks.

I spotted Evan still where I'd left him, near the opened-up wall. He was talking intently to someone blocked from my sight, bending slightly forward to whoever it was. I edged around a small knot of people and could now see his companion clearly.

I froze in place.

It was a woman. And even though her back was turned to me, I could tell it was Liliana Greco.

I watched her throw her dark head back in a laugh, and Evan leaned just a fraction closer to her.

And then I watched her grasp the collar points of his white shirt and playfully tug them together, teasing him for his lack of a bow tie. I felt a punch in my stomach.

It was a gesture somehow so intimate it seemed obscene.

Like watching them make love right before my eyes.

BEATRICE

All dressed now, I walk outside my bedroom, onto the deck by my Jacuzzi. I can't think. The sea is going way down, but it doesn't want to die, it makes a weeping sound that's very sad, that says it doesn't want to be taken away. The sun is going down, too, and the wind puffs and blows my hair. It blows away the fog in my mind. And now I'm trembling all over but not from the sound of the weeping sea or from the cold wind.

I'm trembling because I remember now about last night. About what I heard on my jailer's phone.

Yes, I remember. He had been in the Great Room. He thought I was upstairs in a deep poison sleep. But I hadn't swallowed the poison last night, just like today I didn't. So I was not asleep. I was prowling like a cat.

And I heard him in the Great Room talking on his phone.

His voice was soft, and it had sex in it. The way his voice used to be on the island of Barbados when he talked to me.

I crept closer to the Great Room, and I stood very still. And I listened hard.

"Yeah, I will. I promise." His voice murmured low. Then he said nothing for a moment. He was listening to his phone. Then he said, "Yeah. Tomorrow night."

Who was he talking to in that sex voice? I wanted to know very badly.

I thought of a plan to get him away from his phone. Maybe it was Mary who told me. I went to the kitchen and then into the big pantry with all its boxes and cans. I found the box that had fire lighters in it, and I took one.

I went back out through the kitchen and kept going to the library room on the other side of the stairs from the Great Room.

One of my books was on the piano. The one called *The Opera del Duomo Museum*. I opened it and turned the pages until I found the page I wanted, the one with Mary Magdalene on it, with her hands pointed up in prayer.

I clicked the fire starter. I set Mary on fire. She began to blaze, and then she made the rest of the book dance into flames.

The alarm bell began to ring very loud. I walked fast out of the library room just as water began to spray down from the fire sprinklers in the ceiling. It fell onto all the books and all over the black piano.

I went into the powder room that was next door, and I shut the door closed.

The dogs were barking all over the house. I heard my jailer's footsteps come running fast. He ran past where I was hiding and kept running to the library room where the bell was going off.

My jailer is always talking about fire danger. He says it is the most terrible danger, and he puts red fire extinguishers in every room. I knew that he would grab one and leave his phone behind. Quick as a cat, I leaped out of the powder room and went back to the Great Room.

And yes, there was his phone. It was on the sofa. And it was ringing.

I picked it up and looked at the screen.

It said *Delilah*.

The name of the old dog.

Men are all alike. They think they are stealthy, that they can hide things, but they can't hide things from me. I know all their tricks.

The phone stopped ringing. I pushed the button to call the number back.

And I heard her voice. Her cobwebby voice. "Oh, there you are. I was just leaving you a message." Her cobweb voice was saying that on his phone. I kept very still and listened. "I mean it, darling, you've got to get rid of that creature immediately. I want to be able to come see you in your own home. Be in your bed without worrying about being attacked by a monster."

I was breathing hard. I didn't talk.

"Evan?" The cobwebs of her voice came tangling out from the phone. "Are you there?"

And then a hand grabbed the phone out of mine.

It was my jailer. He pushed the button on the phone to turn it off. He stared at me. His eyes were black with hate. "You should be in bed," he said to me.

"Lilies," I told him. "I heard her voice."

"You hear voices in your head, Beatrice. You imagine them. They aren't real."

And then the boy with the golden spectacles came into the room. He was holding a fire extinguisher. "Jesus, Ev. Did she start the fire?"

"My wife is not in her right mind. Help me get her back to her bed."

My jailer's hand tightened around my wrist, tight as a python. He wanted to keep squeezing until he had snapped my wrist in two. I could feel that in him.

He was going to get rid of me. "I promise I will." He had said that to the girl Lilies on his phone. "Tomorrow," he had said to her.

I walk faster on the deck now. I remember all of it from last night. I pace back and forth next to my Jacuzzi.

He's coming with the poison soon, Mary hisses. *You have to finish the plan. Before he comes back to get rid of you.*

What is the plan? I can't think.

Get a brain, BJ. Ricky's voice speaks loud and harsh. *The next part of the plan. You call me after you've hidden the evidence. You leave me a message.*

Yes. I need to call Ricky. They've taken my phone away from me. And they locked up all the telephones in the house.

Except there is one left that they didn't lock up.

They think I don't know it's still working.

TWENTY-SIX

I remained frozen in place, clutching the stems of the martini glasses, watching Evan and Liliana.

I'd tried hard not to believe it. The story I had put together from the puzzle pieces I'd gathered—the story I'd tried to convince myself couldn't be true.

Dillon Saroyan approached them now, and they moved quickly apart. Saroyan introduced several middle-aged Asians, two men and a woman, who made formal bows. I watched Liliana gracefully extend her hand to each of them. She was lovely; I could not deny that. She wore a deceptively simple—almost severe—long black dress that fell fluidly over her lithe figure and accentuated her pale skin. Her diamond earrings, twice the wattage of mine, coruscated beneath her lustrous cap of dark hair. A wrap the color of storm clouds gusted at her shoulders.

I thought of the scar underneath that wrap. The telltale clue in that grotesque story I had pieced together.

Saroyan was now steering the Asians away. I summoned a semblance of composure and made my way to Evan and Liliana. He turned to me with an easy smile. "Oh, there you are. I've been waiting for that martini."

Liliana shot him an amused glance. "So you *did* bring a plus one after all!"

I felt another punch in my stomach. *They talked about it beforehand,* I thought. *His bringing a plus one.*

A decoy from what was going on between them.

"Jane flew down with me this afternoon," Evan said. That easy tone of voice. "Jane, this is Liliana. She's one of Dillon's principal executives."

"Mind if I steal one of those martinis?" Liliana said. "I'm parched. I just got off a seventeen-hour flight from China."

"Please." I held out one of the glasses.

She snatched it eagerly. "Ninety-five degrees in Shanghai and a hundred percent humidity. Thank God my last meeting finished early so I could catch an earlier flight, and thank *God* the firm managed to get someone bumped out of first class for me." She swallowed a greedy gulp of the drink. "Gin? I thought it would be vodka. Who drinks gin?"

"I do, for one." Evan took the glass away from her, signaled to a waiter with a tray of champagne. "You might like this better." He gave her a flute and sipped the glass he'd taken from her. "I think you and Jane have met before."

Liliana gave me a slightly condescending look. "Really?"

"Briefly," I said. "At the fireworks party. You arrived late and asked me where you could find him."

The oval face tilted just a smidgen to one side. "I remember asking somebody. Was that you?"

"Yes, that was me."

"Liliana has been very active in getting this funding round to close," Evan said. A studied, impersonal tone.

Liliana's smile was equally studied. "I suppose I can take some credit for it, but you've done all the heavy lifting. When you go after something, Evan, it's impossible for anyone to say no."

"And yet there are many who have."

"And a few months from now, they'll be kicking themselves. And you'll have the satisfaction of gloating over them."

"I'll try to keep all gloating to a minimum."

Pleasant professional repartee. Hardly different from the way Wade and I kidded around with each other. And yet I knew what I had seen. What I'd already suspected and now had confirmed. The Cuban orchestra began playing again outside, those erotic rhythms and melodies, and it seemed to underscore what I positively knew was between them.

An older woman in a satin tuxedo suit came up. "Evan Rochester, you owe me a lunch." He turned to her, and I was momentarily left alone with Liliana. Her eyes began shifting about the room, searching for bigger fish than me.

I felt desperate to keep her there. I needed to talk to her. To hear her confirm what I already knew. I searched wildly for something to hold her attention. "Did anyone ever tell you that you look like a Modigliani?"

She swung her gaze back to me. "I get that a lot. In fact, that's how I met Evan. We were at a conference together. He told me I looked a little like a Modigliani that he owned."

"The Bitcoin conference," I said.

"He told you?" She studied me a little closer, and I could see a shadow of a worry cross her face. Pretty girl. Pretty dress. A threat? "Remind me again what your connection to him is?"

"I'm staying at Thorn Bluffs for the summer. Helping with his daughter's schoolwork."

Her face cleared. "Oh, you're the nanny."

"No, not a nanny," I said. "Sophia's too old for that. If anything, I'm the governess."

She gave a startled laugh. "That sounds so Victorian. But poor you. I hear the girl's a nightmare."

"Did Evan say that?"

"Not in so many words. But I gathered."

"She's not. She's a thirteen-year-old who recently lost her mother and is still grieving and confused. And I'm very fond of her."

"Are you? Good for you." Her tone, so slightly condescending. "I suppose you'll be leaving soon, when she goes back to her boarding school."

A sharp reply was on the tip of my tongue. But I needed to draw her out—get her to reveal more than she had intended. I chose my words carefully. "I don't think Sophia's going back. I'm pretty sure Evan will let her stay at Thorn Bluffs and go to a local school. It's what she really wants."

"Oh, I can't imagine he will. She might want to, but he can't possibly keep her around." She might have been talking about a too-troublesome pet. "Once this deal goes through, he'll be taking full charge of Genovation Tech and working like a demon. He'll have to live close to the company's campus. He'll probably get rid of his tenants in SF and move back in there." She smiled with smug confidence. "In fact, I wouldn't be surprised if he gets rid of Thorn Bluffs too. It's a sweet hideaway, but he's going to want more of a showplace for a second home."

She had made a mistake, and I seized on it. "He will never give up Thorn Bluffs. He loves it with his entire soul. Both that gorgeous house and those wild, beautiful bluffs. It's like both sides of his own nature."

Again, a hint of worry in her face.

I took a gamble. "And besides, it's his last connection to Beatrice."

She gave a start. "What?"

I definitely had shaken her now. I pressed my advantage. "I sometimes get the feeling he's still not over her. Maybe he never will be. She was so incredibly beautiful, don't you think? Hauntingly gorgeous. How could any other woman measure up?"

"Please, that's ridiculous. She was good looking when she was very young, but she had lost her looks completely. God, you should have seen her! A freak. A bloated, vicious monster . . ."

I said, "Oh, so you met her?"

She caught herself. "No. I . . . no, never actually met her. I caught a glimpse of her once. I was staying with friends in Big Sur and stopped by to say hello to Evan. Beatrice was in the house, of course. One look at her and you could see she was totally insane."

"I don't think that really mattered to him," I said. "He wouldn't stop loving her just because she was sick. He's got a protective streak in him. It might even have made him love her more."

"That's crazy!" Her gauzy wrap slipped low off her neck. She quickly hitched it higher. She glanced over at Evan. He had turned away from the tuxedoed woman and was returning to us. Liliana instantly regained her composure.

But I had rattled her. And I'd learned all I needed to know.

"It looks like we're being summoned to dinner," Evan said. "Liliana, what table are you at?"

She curved her lips, that careful, professional smile. "Table two. Next to Dillon's."

"We're at twelve. We'll see you after the speeches."

"If I can stay awake that long. I'm still zonked from jet lag." To me, she said smoothly, "Lovely to meet you, um . . ."

"Jane," I said. "Very nice to see you too."

She moved rather regally away into the stream of people heading toward the banquet room.

I said to Evan, "I need to talk to you."

"Sure, but let's get to the table. Oh, by the way, there's been a change of plan tonight. I've got to meet with Dillon and his people after this thing is over. You can take the car back to Shutters since I'll be here for quite some time."

I looked at him without expression.

"And another thing. I'm going to have to stay down here for a few more days. You'll fly back tomorrow as planned but from LAX."

"Will you be staying with Liliana?" I said.

His face darkened. "What?"

"Liliana. Will you be sleeping with her while you're here?"

"What the hell are you talking about? Come on, we need to go in to dinner." He reached for my arm.

I drew back. "You haven't answered my question."

"The question is nonsense. But the answer is no, of course not."

"I don't believe you. I think you didn't know she'd make it back tonight, and now that she has, you intend to stay with her. I think you're involved with her and you have been for some time."

"Jesus Christ, Jane. You're being ridiculous."

"No, I'm not. And that's why you invited me to this, isn't it? If anybody had suspected you and Liliana, it would make them think otherwise. I'm a decoy to draw attention away from your affair."

"You're being irrational."

"I'm not."

He struggled to keep his temper. "We can't talk about this here. Let's go outside."

I swiveled and walked back out to the top terrace and continued to the far end. He followed. His face was an unreadable mask.

I said, "I need you to tell me the truth."

"I've told you the truth, Jane. I'd have to be insane to be sleeping with Liliana. It would be a gross conflict of interest for both of us. It would destroy all her credibility with Dillon and mine as well. It would sabotage this entire deal."

"I think you're lying. You've been involved with her since the time you first met at a conference. I can see it for myself."

"You see nothing but your own imagination. I have a working relationship with Liliana. It's a close one, a very friendly one, but it's business."

"I know she met Beatrice at Thorn Bluffs. I thought she might have, and she just confirmed it."

"Once, just in passing. She had been visiting people nearby and came by to see a painting of mine."

"Your Modigliani. The one that Beatrice slashed up." He stared at me. A frightening expression in his eyes. But I would not back down. "I saw it hidden in the tower. I'd gone there that night you came to get me out on the road. I should have told you. It's the only thing I've really kept from you."

"It wasn't hidden, Jane. It was just a fake."

I hesitated. "A fake?"

"A reproduction that used to hang in my wife's room. She destroyed it. She took a pair of nail scissors to it during one of her psychotic episodes, the same way she destroyed a lot of things. I told Hector to get rid of it. He stashed it in the tower with the rest of the junk."

"Why did you demolish the tower? Was there anything in it you didn't want anyone to find?"

"Of course not. It was a safety hazard. About to fall down any minute. Hector hauled away all the junk in it. I don't know where he took it. You'll have to ask him."

"That painting too?"

"It was worthless. It should have gone to the trash right away."

"But you did own a real one?"

"Yeah, at one time. But I'd already sold it when Liliana came to see it."

"I don't believe you."

He stared at me in that frightening way.

"I think Beatrice knew what was going on between you and Liliana. She saw the resemblance in the painting—the real one—and that's why she slashed it up." I felt I could hardly breathe. I forced myself to continue. "And I think she attacked Liliana too. There's a scar on her neck she tries to hide."

"Yes. She was bitten by a neighbor's pit bull. She's very self-conscious about it."

"It doesn't look like a dog bite," I said.

His face was black. "What in the name of God are you saying?"

"It looks like a human bite. Like someone attacked Liliana with their teeth."

He turned, took a furious step away, then whirled back. "You really try my patience sometimes, you know that?"

I felt a strong flush of anger. "Do I?"

"Yeah, you really do. You let your imagination run away with you. You see ghosts, you see goblins. You make connections that don't exist. You imagine ridiculous things."

"I did not imagine what I've seen between you and Liliana. Beatrice saw it, too, and one way or another it led to her death."

He shook his head. "I'm done talking about this. I've told you all there is to know. You can either come with me now and forget all these delusions and we'll have a nice dinner, or you can go back to Shutters."

"You can prove I'm wrong," I said. "If you're not staying with Liliana, then come to my room later."

"It's going to be an all-nighter. We're getting down to the wire now on this deal. It could go on until nearly morning."

"Then you can come then. I don't care what time. If you don't, I'll know you're with her."

His voice dropped low. "I don't take very well to ultimatums."

"And I don't take well at all to lies." I was shaking with anger now.

"I'll text the car for you now," he said. "And I'll have someone from my office book you a return flight for the morning."

"I'll make my own flight arrangements." I turned in hot rage and walked away. And kept on walking through the grandiose rooms and back to the front entrance of the house.

In the foyer, I felt my knees give way, and I placed a hand on a wall to steady myself. My rage dissipated into a feeling of numbness. I composed myself enough to get outside, and I told a valet that my car had been called. Some moments later the SUV glided up, and I got in and rode back to the hotel. It was dark now, and outside the car's tinted windows, the headlights streaming by were just a ghostly haze.

You see ghosts, you see goblins. You let your imagination run away with you.

A twirl of light on a cove. The blood-chilling shriek of a night bird. A ghostly figure appearing outside my glass doors.

You make connections that don't exist.

Could that be true?

I arrived back at Shutters and went up to my room. I peeled off my rented dress and zipped it back in the vinyl bag. Scrubbed the makeup off my face.

Was it just a story I'd spun to myself? About a beautiful, mad wife driven to greater madness by her husband's affair with another woman—one who resembled a painting that had hung in her room. A wife who then viciously attacked the other woman.

Sank her teeth into the other woman's long neck.

Stabbed and stabbed again the portrait that had looked like her.

A wife who couldn't be divorced without jeopardizing her husband's chance to become filthy rich. Who'd been kept shut up by that husband until she was driven to suicide.

Or possibly was killed by him.

Or was this just something I had fabricated from things that could all be explained otherwise?

I thought of my childhood yearning for the dead not to stay dead. To come back as ghosts or mummies or rattling skeletons. Or even vampires.

Was I still just conjuring up ghosts and vampires?

No. I don't believe that.

I took out my phone and booked a flight back in the morning. The earliest and cheapest flight.

The Alaska Airlines shuttle.

I knew that soon, shattering heartbreak would set in.

I also knew I wasn't finished looking for answers. The puzzle still was not completely solved.

BEATRICE

Thorn Bluffs, December 17
Late afternoon

I walk past my Jacuzzi on the deck and go down the stairs. I want to go fast, but the high heels of my shoes won't let me. I get to the bottom and continue to the mossy steps that go down to the wooden cabin. I'm very frightened that the witch Hector will catch me, but he doesn't.

I go around to the glass doors in back of the cabin, and I slide one open.

Here is the bed where I saw the girl Lilies on top of my jailer and her breasts bobbing up and down. I don't go to the bed. I go to the old telephone on the bureau.

I pick up the receiver. The line is dead.

But I know how to bring it back alive. I jiggle the cord, just a very delicate bit, and the tone starts buzzing in my ears.

I call up Ricky's phone number and listen to it ring. I know he won't answer. He never answers his phone anymore, he only calls people back.

I hear his voice on the message machine. There's a beep sound, and I start talking. My voice goes higher and higher until it sounds very far away to me. I leave the message that Ricky told me to, the words that are part of his plan. Then I hang up the phone.

I go over to the mirror that's on the wall over the old bricked-up fireplace. I want to look at myself again, to see that I am Beatrice McAdams, the most famous girl, the most beautiful girl.

I look into the darkened old glass. And I scream.

What I see is a ghost.

A ghost with great hollowed-out eyes and a black screaming mouth. I see white hair, ghost hair, floating in a dead-ghost cloud around its head.

I back away from the mirror. I'm shaking very hard.

Mary's voice is soft and whispering like a prayer. *You see, Beatrice? This is the way you will be forever. After he gets rid of you.*

I let out a howl. "NO!"

She's lying, Beatie. The voice of the very young one named Beatie June comes into my mind. *This is what you'll be if you finish the plan. You'll be a ghost, Beatie June.*

Liar, liar, liar! Mary screeches.

The voices all rustle together: *Finish the plan. Finish it, Beatrice. Make him pay.*

TWENTY-SEVEN

Otis picked me up at the Monterey airport. If he hadn't already guessed, one look at my face would have told him everything he needed to know. Sweetly, he refrained from saying, "Told you so."

Sophia came out of the house to meet us. She guessed too. "What happened? Did my dad dump you?"

"No," I told her. "It's nothing like that. We were friends, and we're still friends."

She knew bullshit when she heard it. "So are you going to be leaving?"

"I was always going to leave at the end of August."

"But I thought you wouldn't. I thought you were going to stay here with us." She was near tears. "I thought he was in love with you, but he's not. He's still wrapped up in Beatrice, isn't he? So why doesn't he just throw himself into the ocean and be with her, like Heathcliff did with Cathy's grave, so they can rot together."

"Heathcliff kept living a long time after Cathy died. Your father will too." I tried to keep any note of bitterness out of my voice. "And nothing has really changed, Sophia. I'll be leaving just the way I was supposed to."

I did my best over the next couple of days to present a cheerful face to her. Made our next tutoring session as lively as I could. She breezed through her earth science exam, and in celebration, I took her to the Carmel Plaza mall and let her go a little crazy at the Anthropologie sale.

I said nothing to Otis about what had happened, and he still didn't probe.

Only with Ella did I allow myself the luxury of tears. She invited me to lunch at her home in Del Mar, a charming stucco house furnished less austerely than her gallery. She greeted me effusively, wanting to know all about the swanky benefit, and suddenly I couldn't hold it back any longer. I found myself weeping uncontrollably. She sat me down on her couch and perched next to me, handing me tissues at frequent intervals. Letting me cry myself out. When I had, she said, "Do you want to talk about it?"

"There's nothing really to say. I simply fell in love with somebody I shouldn't have."

"It was him, wasn't it? Rochester?"

I nodded. "Yeah."

She rolled her eyes briefly to the ceiling. "I had a feeling. And I think you're better off out of it. But that's all I'm going to say." She made a zipping lips gesture.

She plied me with vegetable curry and carrot cake and ice-cold Stoli. Coaxed a few laughs out of me with stories about her own "Ms. Wrongs." Her first wife, Hallie: "Bitch on wheels." Her second, Frances: "Eye surgeon. Never trust your emotions with someone who regularly slices eyeballs with a scalpel." Her hairless sphynx cat, Mr. Handsome, flopped on my lap like a warm-blooded mummy. Purring. Occasionally yowling.

But when I returned to Thorn Bluffs, the full extent of my heartbreak came crushing back. I sat on my terrace steps, gazing at the cove. It was all such a part of me now. That view. The water. Even the huge jagged rock. It was impossible to think of leaving it forever.

But I would have to. The thought gave me a feeling that teetered dangerously on self-pity. I leaped up from the steps and began throwing myself into tasks. Pampering the dogs. Chopping vegetables while Otis made dinner. A double feature of French flicks in the screening room with Sophia: *Amélie, A Man and a Woman.*

I'd heard nothing from Evan. I hadn't expected to.

Still, when my phone rang the next morning, I felt an absurd tick of hope. But it was a number I didn't recognize, from Medford, Oregon.

"Hello . . . um, is this Jane? I hope I've got the right number—a friend of mine in Santa Fe gave it to me."

A woman's voice. A little bit croaky like a frog. I gave a start.

"Aunt Joanne?" I said. "Is that you?"

It was true. I had found her! We spoke for over an hour. Her name now was Joey Castigliani. She had married a man in Santa Fe—a biology teacher, fifteen years older—and she had worked as a physical therapist. "Larry passed from Alzheimer's six years ago. The next year I retired and moved to Medford, Oregon. It's cheap, and it's got beautiful scenery. And the winters aren't too bad."

She had followed my career, she told me. Had been a huge fan of *Carlotta Dark.* Never missed an episode.

I told her about Mom ripping up her letter and how sorry I was I hadn't tried to find her sooner.

"Are you married, sweetheart? Do you have a family?"

Sweethaht, she pronounced it. Jersey accent, like Mom's.

"No," I said. "Neither."

"Do you have anyone special?"

"No, not that either."

She gave a kind of surprised hum, and that, too, was like Mom. I thought of Mom keeping the letter a secret and the mystery of why Mom had never tried to find love again, rejected every suitor, poured her passion into acting, and maybe Aunt Jo could give me answers. But not on the phone. I was seized by an impulse. "I want to come see you, Aunt Jo. Soon. Tomorrow, I'll fly up just for the day."

"Wonderful, but stay longer. It's too far for just a day. And we've got so much to catch up on. Years and years."

"I can't take more time, not right now. I'll come back soon for a much longer visit."

I hung up in a swirl of emotion. It seemed like a miracle. I had found my aunt. She was still alive when I had thought she was dead.

I had a living relative.

I wanted to tell Evan. I knew he'd listen with total absorption and understand exactly what I was feeling, the way he understood everything about me . . .

I caught myself. That had been an illusion. It had just been charm. Manipulative charm.

I texted Otis about it instead.

I caught an early flight from Monterey the next morning and landed in Medford at exactly 10:30 a.m. Called a Lyft. I'd refused Aunt Jo's offer to pick me up. I needed time to orient myself before seeing her. It was only a short drive to her home—a modest house with gray clapboard siding and a blueberry-colored door.

I hesitated a moment before ringing the bell. I flashed on the giant frog in my nightmares and felt a residual tingle of dread. *Nonsense.* I pressed the bell. Hurrying footsteps inside, and the door flew open. And a shock ran through me.

It was Mom standing in the doorway.

She was slightly plumper. Her hair dyed strawberry blonde. But Mom's speckled green eyes and elfin chin. Her tiny waist she was always so vain about. Her infectious smile, the way it showed all her teeth.

It had all been a joke.

All this time, just a stupid joke. She hadn't died after all; she'd just been hiding out, waiting for me to discover her. Grinning now at the joke she'd played on me.

Then Aunt Jo's croaky voice broke the illusion. "You look so much like your father!"

I laughed. "And you look exactly like Mom."

"Yeah, I know. We were two peas in a pod." Aunt Jo hesitated, then reached out her arms, and I moved into them, and we hugged warmly. "It's so wonderful to see you, sweetheart." *Sweethaht.*

Just like Mom.

"Come in, come on in." She ushered me into a living room, with houseplants galore and far too much furniture and framed photos crowding every surface. She bustled about, providing snacks and coffee, while I made a tour of the photos. Mom and Aunt Jo as little girls. Yes, they looked almost identical. A photo of a kindly-looking bald man. "That's my Larry," Aunt Jo called out. "A real sweetheart. I wish you could have met him."

My parents' wedding day, feeding each other wedding cake. Looking young and radiant. And then me as a toddler, walking between them, holding their hands.

Aunt Jo came and looked over my shoulder. "I miss Rachel so much. And your daddy too. And all those years I missed seeing you grow up. I'll never stop kicking myself."

I turned to her. "What happened, Aunt Jo? What made you and Mom become estranged?"

"Didn't she ever tell you?"

"No. She never wanted to talk about the past."

Aunt Jo gave a deep sigh. "It was about her miscarriage. A stupid misunderstanding."

"What miscarriage?" I said with surprise.

"She didn't tell you about that either?"

"No." Another secret Mom had kept from me.

"Here, sit down." We sat down side by side on the couch. "It was when you were about three. Twins, a boy and a girl. She miscarried at twenty-seven weeks. Or not actually a miscarriage. They survived birth but were too tiny to be saved."

I drew a deep breath. A brother and a sister. Blinked out of existence right after they were born. "What was the misunderstanding?"

"She couldn't reach your daddy when she started to bleed. She finally found a neighbor to take her to the hospital. He was with me."

I looked at her with shock.

"Nothing was going on between us," she added quickly. "He'd lost his job when the factory he worked for got outsourced to China. He was depressed. A friend of mine had given me tickets to a Giants game. I thought a ball game would cheer him up—he was a huge fan. He didn't tell Rachel he was going. She was having a rough pregnancy and had to stay in bed. He probably felt guilty about leaving her alone."

I was suddenly close to tears. "She blamed you for his being away?"

"Not at first. But losing those babies made her almost out of her mind. And then, not long afterward, your father was killed in that car accident. I came to her immediately when I heard the news." Aunt Jo dabbed a tear at her eye. "She was in a terrible state. She accused me of having an affair with him. She didn't mean it—she was just crazy with grief. But pigheaded me said some harsh words back. We began yelling and screaming at each other."

"I think I heard you fighting," I said. "I remember hiding under my bed while you were yelling at each other. Your froggy kind of voice."

"Oh, I'm so sorry, sweetheart. I am so darned sorry. She told me to get out, and I did, and we never spoke to each other again. Then I moved away, and that was that. It was my fault, my pigheaded stubbornness. I take all the blame." She was tearful, and so was I. She got up, went back to the kitchen. Came out with a wad of paper towels, and we blotted our eyes. "I sure wouldn't blame you for hating me now," she said.

"Of course I don't hate you. Mom was as stubborn as you are. Two peas in a pod." I smiled, and she smiled back, weeping without restraint. Should I tell her the other secret Mom had kept from me? About Dad's suicide? Not now. Some other day. "I thought I was all alone in the world, with no family at all," I said. "But now I have you."

"Me too, sweetheart. I'm so glad you found me. I'm so happy I could burst."

In midafternoon, she drove me back to the airport, protesting all the way about the shortness of the visit. I promised again to come back for a much longer stay.

I could not get a direct flight back—I had to change planes in San Francisco. I'd been up since five o'clock in the morning; I dozed through the first flight, flitting dreams of frogs and Mom dancing with wild abandon and Evan smiling down at me from under thick lashes. I woke up with a jolt just before landing. Still sleepy, I disembarked and headed to the gate for the Monterey flight.

A bleak feeling swept over me. I was a stranger among all these throngs of other strangers. I resented the one who so cruelly resembled Evan, tall and broad shouldered, with unkempt black curls.

And then my heart began to beat hard, because it wasn't a stranger; it actually *was* Evan. And he was walking purposefully toward me.

TWENTY-EIGHT

I looked up at him in confusion. "What are you doing here?"

"Picking you up at the airport. I landed in Alta Vista a couple of hours ago and drove straight here."

"How did you know I'd be here?"

"I asked Fairfax. He told me where you'd gone and what flight you were on."

"Oh." My mind was in a jumble. "How did you get through security?"

"I bought myself a ticket," he said. "But I'm going to drive us back home."

"No," I said. "I'll take my flight."

"It's been delayed at least an hour and a half. It will probably be more. And if you won't come with me, I'll simply wait right here and get on the flight with you."

Somebody jostled me with a bag. An announcement blared, confirming the flight delay. I was still exhausted, not quite sure of anything at the moment. "Did you close your deal?" I asked.

"Yeah, I did. The funding will be in place by next week. I'll be taking over immediately as CEO of Genovation Technologies."

"And you'll be filthy rich."

A short laugh. "Not quite. Not until we go public a year or so from now. But I'll be financially back on my feet."

"And what about Liliana?"

"She will undoubtedly make partner at Saroyan. She's ecstatic."

"That's not what I mean," I said.

"I know." He looked at me intently. "I told you the truth, Jane. I didn't stay with her. There's nothing more between us than friends and colleagues. She might have wanted it to become more at some point. But it's not going to happen." His phone buzzed. My eyes darted to it. He hesitated, then shut it off. "It's off completely now, okay? I'll keep it off as long as you want."

I was still in a state of confusion. "That's a big sacrifice."

He smiled. "Yeah, it is. Look, do you want to drive back with me or spend God knows how many hours waiting around in this God-fucking airport?" I still hesitated. "I'm asking you to come with me, Jane. With all my heart."

Something in me told me to say no. Screamed at me to say no.

But the way he was gazing at me, with that kind of intensity that made me feel I was the only person who mattered in the entire world to him and always would be, shattered my resistance. With a smile, he grasped my hand, and the sensation of his broad palm closing around mine sent that familiar electric thrill through my body. "Let's go home," he said.

We made our way out of the terminal, to the valet stand outside. An attendant brought up the Tesla. We got in, and Evan navigated a labyrinthine tangle of service roads and highways until we broke south onto Highway 1. We drove in silence for some time. My thoughts continued to be in turmoil. I couldn't read his.

The highway veered west and now ran parallel to the coast, the ocean all rolling indigo waves, the sea air moist and fresh. "Let's not go back right away," Evan said. "Let's stay the night somewhere around here. Alone together."

Nothing seemed real. "What are you saying? That you want us to go back to the way we were before?"

"No. Not like before. No more sneaking around. When we get home, we'll let everybody know. I'll announce it over the intercom if you want. You'll move into my room." He paused a moment, then said, "When you walked away from me the other night, at that damned party, I was furious. I wanted to kill something. It took me a long time to cool down and realize it was me. I was a damned idiot for not running after you."

"What stopped you?"

"Hotheaded pride."

"I haven't heard from you in over a week."

"I know. Things were difficult. I had business to attend to. The pressure was insane—I was working around the clock, hardly catching a few hours' sleep. I couldn't let myself think about anything else."

"So business came first," I said coldly.

"Sometimes it has to," he said. "Not just for myself—a lot of people were counting on me to make this happen."

I wasn't ready for this. I needed some time to think. "I think we should just go back."

"Maybe you're right. The sooner we can break the news to Sophia, the better."

He began speaking of plans. Plans for the business. Plans for us. "I'll have to hire a lot of people immediately. Both for my office and Thorn Bluffs. I'll want your input, particularly for the estate. And I'll soon be able to get the tenants out of my house in San Francisco, so we'll live mostly up there for the next few years. There are great schools in SF—Sophia can have her choice. She'll live with us, of course." He talked about the travel we would do, the exotic places all over the world. About the good the money could do. A foundation—I could be involved as much as I wished.

I let these effusions wash over me. It wasn't real. I felt it strongly—that none of it was real. I was sleepwalking in the dark, and soon I'd have to open my eyes.

We had reached the outskirts of Monterey. I said, "We have to swing by the airport. I left the Land Cruiser there."

"Hector can pick it up tomorrow. And anyway, I'm buying you a new car. Pick out anything you want—it will belong to you."

"I don't need you to buy me a new car. If I stay, I'll get something for myself."

He glanced at me with amusement. "You're going to have to learn to accept things from me, Jane. Sometimes expensive things. We can't have totally different lifestyles."

"I'll keep driving the Land Cruiser for now," I said. "And living in the cottage."

He gave a snort. "We'll see about that."

We began cruising past the familiar landmarks of Big Sur. The farm stand: GARLIC CHERRIES LIVE BAIT. The wild boar crossing sign, mother and baby. Evan steered between the two white boulders and drove up to the gate. "What the hell?"

The gate was partially open. The locks were sheared off.

He pulled out his phone and turned it back on. It instantly came alive, backed-up texts flooding in. "Christ!"

"What is it?"

"The police are searching the house." He shot the Tesla forward and began speeding around bends and switchbacks. I took out my phone, which was still on airplane mode. I toggled it back, but there was now no cell reception.

We jounced over fallen branches and holes in the asphalt. The compound came into view. The motor court was filled with vehicles. Dark SUVs, patrol cars. Two police motorcycles. Evan slammed to a stop, and we both leaped out and raced to the house.

A patrolwoman appeared at the door. "Are you Mr. Rochester?"

"Yes. What the hell's going on here?"

"We've got a warrant to search the house, sir." She handed him a document. "I need you both to come in and wait in the living room."

"Where's my daughter?"

"She's in the living room with the other members of your household. Please proceed there immediately."

He snatched the warrant. "I need to read this first."

"You can read it in there, sir."

Grabbing my hand, he pushed past the officer, and we walked quickly to the Great Room, alarm rising steadily in the pit of my stomach. Sophia and Otis were huddled together on one of the long couches. Sophia was crying, and Otis's face was ashen. Hector and Annunciata sat rigid as stone in chairs near the hearth. A paunchy cop stood on guard near the doorway.

Otis shot a scared glance at Evan. "They wouldn't let me call you or anybody. They said we had to wait in here until they told us different."

"Where are the dogs?"

"They've got them shut in the office. They're going to search that next."

"Dad?" Sophia sprang up. "What's happening?"

He opened his arms, and she threw herself into them, and he cradled her. "I don't know yet, baby. But don't worry, okay?" She continued sobbing, and he rocked her in his arms. "Hey, hey, it's okay, it's all okay. It'll be fine. I promise." He gently handed her over to me. "I need to read this warrant, so go sit with Jane, okay?"

I put an arm around her shoulders. "Come on, let's go back to the couch." I guided her to it, and she sat down despondently, drew her legs against her chest and hugged them tight, tears wriggling down her face.

I settled between her and Otis. "Those two detectives are here," he said under his breath. "The same ones. I think they found her. Or her bones or something."

Sophia shot him a terrified look. "You mean Beatrice?"

I made a face at Otis: *Shut up.* "We don't know anything yet, sweetie. Let's wait and see."

I glanced at Evan. He was reading the warrant, frowning in a savage way. He finished it, took out his phone.

"I need you not to call anyone, sir," the cop said loudly.

"I'm calling my attorney." His voice was hard, dangerous.

The cop took a step. Hesitated. "Okay, attorney."

Evan punched in a number and retreated to a back corner. He talked for several minutes. Jammed the phone in his pocket. I shot him a questioning look, and he motioned to me to join him.

"Malik Anderson is already on his way. The DA's office had informed him of the search. He's bringing Isaac Dendry, the top criminal lawyer in the firm. Dendry represented me in December when the police were crawling all over me."

"What are the grounds for the warrant?"

"It's not clear yet. But Dendry's not too worried. He thinks it's all grandstanding. He says he'll get it cleared up pretty quickly."

I let out a breath of relief. "When will they be here?"

"They're about thirty-five minutes away. Don't answer any questions until they get here. Make sure Sophia and Otis understand that too. I need to talk to Hector a few minutes."

I returned to the couch. "Malik Anderson is on his way with another lawyer," I said. "They'll be here soon. But it's very important that we don't answer any questions until they arrive."

"Nobody's asked us anything," Otis said.

"So what's going to happen?" Sophia said.

"I don't know yet, Sophia."

"I'm really scared."

"I know. We all are a little. But we should try not to be. Your dad says the lawyers aren't too worried."

We fell into fidgeting silence. I heard Evan speaking low to Hector and Annunciata—Miskito with a lot of Spanglish thrown in for his benefit, the words lapping back to me like waves on a lakeshore. Several cops walked in and out, walkie-talkies scratching.

Otis nudged me. "That's them. The detectives."

A man and a woman in plain clothes were walking with official briskness into the room. The woman stocky, Filipino, brown hair clipped back at the nape. Her partner white, red complexioned, slightly stooped.

I stood up, but they walked past me in a grim manner and continued toward Evan. He got up and turned to them.

I registered the flash of something metallic.

I felt suddenly like there were wasps, dozens of them, buzzing around my head. I couldn't move; I couldn't even blink; they were buzzing too loudly and maliciously.

Evan was holding his hands out in front of him. The flash of metal became handcuffs. And words rang out, displacing the evil wasps.

Words I realized that, somewhere in the back of my mind, I had always expected to hear:

"Evander Edward Rochester, you are under arrest for the murder of Beatie June McAdams Rochester."

BEATRICE

The sky is full of colors, but black cats of clouds are creeping under the colors, and the sea is very dark. Far out in the water, I can see the Praying Hands.

I am at the little gate in the fence posts at the edge of the bluff. I am shaking and afraid, but I open the gate, and I start to go down the wooden steps. It is very difficult in my high-heeled shoes.

The waves are loud, they boom and crash. It's like music, like the music I walk to on the catwalk, my famous Beatrice McAdams cheetah walk. I'm walking for Miuccia Prada. For Donatella Versace.

I walk to the pounding music all the way down the stairs.

At the bottom, there's a ramp made of rocks. It's so hard to walk down—I slip and stumble, but I never fall on the catwalk, not even when my feet are bloodied up in the highest-heeled shoes.

It's getting darker now, the black cats curl up everywhere in the sky. I step off the ramp made of rocks and onto a strange catwalk made of sand. My heels sink way into the sand. I take them off. There are big rocks on this catwalk, and I step around them and I keep walking.

I feel a shock of something cold.

It's water. Very cold water. It slaps my ankles.

Finish the plan, Beatrice.

I don't know the plan.

A freezing wave licks higher at my ankles.

Ricky's voice is in my mind. *What are you, brain dead, BJ? Here's what you do. You get the rich guy to take you out in his boat. You make him steer it into a strong rip current, and you jump in.*

I think of when Ricky pushed me into the riptide. It wanted to gobble me up, and I was so very frightened.

You can swim it, BJ. You win every one of your heats. You blow all the other bitches out of the water. You can swim the riptide and survive. And afterward you say he tried to kill you. There's the evidence you planted to prove it. It overrides any prenup. He gets put away, and you get his money.

"I'm too frightened, Ricky," I say now. "It's too strong. I can't do it."

I hear the dogs barking high above me. I look up. My jailer's German shepherd dogs. Their job is to keep me prisoner.

And high up on the deck, I see my jailer. Standing dark against the colors in the sky.

He's your husband, Beatie June. The very young one's voice now whispers in my mind. *He'll come to rescue you. Like he did in the chapel on the island of Barbados.*

Mary hisses. *He hates you. He's going to replace you.*

I hear him shout my name, but it's from very far away.

He loves you, Beatie June. He'll come for you like he did in the chapel. Liar cunt liar bitch liar liar! He wants you dead.

The waves slash at my dress, my legs. So much colder than Fernandina Harbor. I can't swim the rip current.

Make him pay, Beatrice. Make him pay.

I keep looking up at him against all the heaven colors.

And I know suddenly he's coming to save me. I feel so very happy.

The ice tongues of water lick at me, the skirt of my dress drags wet and heavy, but I feel so very, very happy.

I stand in the licking waves and wait for him to rescue me.

TWENTY-NINE

Everything following Evan's arrest blurred into a kaleidoscope of shifting images.

The gleam of metal handcuffs snapping over his wrists.

Sophia shrieking with hysterics, trying to run to her father, restrained by a female uniform. Otis clutching my sleeve, manically chattering.

A fresh phalanx of uniformed cops marching into the Great Room.

Malik Anderson suddenly there, looking and sounding so calm I had the urge to throw myself into his arms, like Sophia had with her father.

"Did they find Beatrice's body?" Otis asked him.

"Not that I know of. All they're telling us is they've discovered evidence suggesting a violent act took place here. I don't have a great many facts yet."

"Where's the other lawyer?" I said. "Mr. Dendry?"

"He's gone directly to the precinct to be with Evan. I can assure you he's one of the best criminal defense lawyers in the country."

"So my dad's a criminal?" Sophia wailed.

"He's been arrested, dear, but that doesn't automatically make him a criminal. Many great and honest people have been arrested. But he does need a lawyer to get him through the process."

"Will you be staying here with us?" I asked.

"No, I'm going to join Isaac and Evan now. But I have an attorney from our associate office in Monterey on her way here. Her name's Carrie Horvath, she's also excellent. The important thing is that none of you are to talk to anybody or answer any questions until she gets here."

"When do I get to see my dogs?" Sophia said.

Malik gave a kindly smile. "Soon, dear."

The kaleidoscope shifted, and the Monterey lawyer, Carrie Horvath, was in the picture. Fiftyish, face also exuding calm, her suit a calming shade of gray. "You're all going to have to leave here for a few days," she told us. "Until the police have finished searching the property."

"How long will that be?" I asked.

"Two or three days, most likely."

"Where are we supposed to go?" Otis said.

"We have a house already set for you. You can pack a few things now, but then you'll have to leave immediately."

"What about the dogs?" Sophia said. "And my snake?"

Carrie narrowed her eyes. "Snake?"

"It's a pet ball python in a tank," I told her. "One of us can carry his tank."

Another turn of the kaleidoscope. I was now in the cottage, throwing things into my carryall, supervised by one of the female uniforms.

And then we were crammed into Otis's Prius since all the other cars were deemed part of the crime scene. Pilot in front beside Otis, Sophia and me in back, Hermione between us. The bulldog, Julius, crushing Sophia's lap. The shepherds had gone home with the Sandovals, and Carrie Horvath had valiantly agreed to chauffeur the python, Niall, in her Lexus. We began following her out of Thorn Bluffs.

Media trucks already gathered at the road. Reporters bellowing questions as we passed single file through the white boulders. Banging at our windows.

Otis yelling, "Scum-fuck vultures!"

A dismal howl from Hermione. Pilot yapping, delirious with excitement.

We continued to tail Carrie for about an hour to a large gated house nestled in the gently rolling hills of Carmel Valley. Six bedrooms. Luxuriously furnished. A firepit, an outdoor spa.

A place meant for young heavy-drinking revelers, bachelor and bachelorette parties. Not three forlorn refugees from a police search.

In a stunned manner, we staked out rooms. They all had Jacuzzi tubs. It seemed a stupid thing to register, but it did.

A woman from Child Protective Services materialized. She had the oversize googly eyes of a Pixar character, and I wondered vaguely if that's what had landed her the job. Sophia freaked out all over again. "I'm not a child! What's she even doing here?"

Carrie Horvath conferred at length with the woman, and she went away. "She has to contact your grandmother because she's your legal guardian," Carrie explained to Sophia. "But you can stay here at least until tomorrow."

"Stay here instead of what?"

"Safe custody. A good foster home."

"No way! And I won't go to Gram's either. Nobody can make me!" She ran to the room she'd chosen and slammed the door.

"She ought to have some say in it," I said to Carrie. "She's right, she's not a little kid."

"I agree. But in the eyes of the law, she's a minor child who has no say. We'll do what we can to let her remain with you, of course."

"When can we talk to Evan?"

"Soon, I hope. I'll keep you informed."

A Whole Foods van showed up. Groceries—fresh produce and meats, dog food, bakery goods—delivered by a rattled young man who'd had to fend off the howl of reporters who'd already sniffed us out. "We're gonna be prisoners here," Otis grumbled, unpacking the bags. "And they didn't send booze."

"There's a bar in the main room," I told him. "Fully stocked. Plus a wine fridge."

We poured ourselves stiff vodkas. Turned on the wall-size TV. The local news feed was all over the police search.

"I don't know if I can watch this," Otis said. But he didn't budge.

There were clips of Beatrice in her supermodel heyday. Then a rehash of last December. A clip of Evan, batting a mic away from his face. Helicopter footage of Thorn Bluffs, the house, the tower. Magritte Cottage peeking through the foliage.

Interviews with Carmel residents. I recognized Honey, one of the Vinyasa Semi-regulars. She described an altercation between the Rochesters on the Ventana terrace. Then an interview with a plumber who'd repaired a leaking sink at the house: "He had her shut up there, all right. I kinda felt she was a prisoner and couldn't escape."

Ella Mahmed, I was relieved to see, was not among those making statements.

Then breaking news. The face of a brunette reporter, eyes ablaze from the victory of a scoop. "I am here with Richard McAdams, the brother of Beatrice McAdams Rochester, at his apartment in Pacific Grove. He has informed me that he recently furnished the police with fresh evidence, and that is what triggered the search warrant."

Rick McAdams's face loomed on the giant screen. His head still sporting a bandage, possibly even a larger one than before.

"Fuck him," Otis muttered.

I turned up the volume.

"Yes, Ramona. I was clearing out the mailbox on one of my phone lines," Rick said. "All those messages from numbers I didn't recognize. You know the kind of stuff you get, telemarketers and scam artists. I wasn't even looking at any of it, just clicked delete, delete. But then I came to one that, by luck, I noticed was dated last December 17. The day my sister disappeared. The call was at 4:56 in the afternoon." He paused for effect. "Just about a half hour before her husband reported her alleged drowning."

"And that one you did listen to, is that correct?"

"Yes. It was as if something compelled me to."

"And tell us what you heard, Richard."

"I heard the voice of my sister, Beatrice."

"And what did she say on her message?"

"I can't reveal the specifics yet. But I can tell you she was terrified. Begging me to come help her." His voice cracked piteously. "She told me where she was going to hide from him. A secret place she had. Unfortunately, it turned out not to be secret enough to save her." The effort to relate this appeared to overwhelm him. He reached for a glass of water but didn't sip. "It was excruciating for me to listen to, Ramona. My sister's terrified voice, begging me to help when it was far too late. But it gives proof positive that she was murdered by her husband."

"How do you feel about not having listened to the message sooner?"

"I'm devastated, Ramona. But I'm just thankful I didn't automatically delete it. I think something, maybe some deep connection between us, made me listen to it. My sister and I were very, very close. It was like even after death, she was still trying to communicate with me."

"Bullshit," Otis muttered.

"So you do believe your sister is dead?" the reporter asked solemnly.

Rick's face contorted. "I do, Ramona. I have always believed that. I would have sensed it if she was alive."

A close-up on the reporter's face radiating deep commiseration. "After she disappeared in December, you were quoted as calling Evan Rochester a monster and a sociopath. And that your sister told you she feared for her safety."

"I'll let those statements stand for themselves, Ramona. I will only add there were times when I feared for my own physical safety."

"Was it Evan Rochester who caused that injury to your head?"

"I can't speak about that yet." Rick glanced into the camera, the soul of wronged earnestness. "All I can say is that I am thankful and relieved he is finally in custody."

And then the reporter was thanking him, and Rick was nodding dolefully. And back to the anchors at their news desk.

"Do you believe any of that shit?" Otis said.

I muted the sound. "I don't know. Rick had texted me last week that he had new evidence. He made a crack about how I should always listen to phone messages, and then he ghosted me. It was the last I heard from him."

"Jeez. Did you tell Evan?"

"No. I thought Rick might be bluffing. Trying to get a rise out of Evan. It seemed like something he would do. But I was going to tell Evan after the benefit."

"Jesus." Otis was white as a sheet. He refilled his glass. His hand was shaking.

I looked at him anxiously. "You okay?"

"He's guilty, isn't he? Evan?"

"We still don't know. We don't know what the evidence is."

"They've got proof now. You heard McAdams. They must have found her remains in that hiding place he talked about. And I'm going to be in real trouble, because I knew he did it."

I felt myself go cold. "What do you mean, O.?"

"I knew he was going to kill her. I mean, not *know* know, but I really thought he was going to. And then he did."

"Why were you so sure?"

He took a deep slug of vodka. "The night before the drowning? Beatrice tried to burn the house down."

"In the library room?" I asked.

"You heard?"

"The piano finish is all mucked up. Like the sprinklers had once gone off in there."

"Yeah. She set a book on fire. One of her art books, it was on the piano. I heard the alarm go off, and I ran for a fire extinguisher, but by the time I got there, the sprinklers had already put it out. Then I went to the Great Room, and Evan had Beatrice by the wrists, and Jesus . . ."

His hand holding the glass was shaking hard. I took it from him and put it down. "Go on. Tell me."

"It was like he'd caught some kind of savage animal. One with rabies or something. I could see in his face that he hated her. I mean, like he just wanted to strangle her dead." He shuddered. "He might have if I hadn't come in. So then I helped him get her up to her room. She was hysterical. Screaming and, like, 'Don't lock me up in the shed' and 'Cobwebs' and crazy shit like that. He locked her in her room anyway and put Mickey at the door to keep guard. And Minnie at the doors to her outside terrace."

"So it's true. He did keep her locked up all the time."

"No, not like that. But I never saw her do anything that crazy before. She was usually drugged out, and Annunciata kept close watch over her." He ran a hand through his hair, making it stick up even spikier. "And then the next morning, Evan tells me to make a reservation at Sierra Mar. They're going out to dinner, for their anniversary. Like nothing the night before even happened. Like she wasn't freaking insane."

On the muted TV, another aerial shot of Thorn Bluffs. I spotted that eerie little cove beneath the tower promontory. Where I'd once seen that gliding white shape through the fog. I felt very cold.

"If I get subpoenaed, I'll have to tell them all this, right?" Otis said.

"You'll have to tell them the whole truth this time."

"So I could be an accessory to murder? I could go to jail?"

"You're jumping to conclusions. We all need to calm down."

"You'll get subpoenaed too. You'll have to tell them that you've been having sex with him."

I said slowly, "I'll have to tell the whole truth too. We're going to need to get lawyers."

He gave a sardonic laugh. "Malik costs twelve hundred an hour. Dendry's probably more. Horvath probably bills around five or six hundred."

"We'll figure it out," I said. "We always do, right? We've got each other's backs."

I reached for his hand.

He squeezed mine back wanly. "Yeah, I guess."

We remained on edge for the rest of the night. Otis, too anxious to cook, steeped himself in the outdoor spa, guzzling vodka and cramming down Sweet Chili Doritos. Sophia emerged and microwaved a frozen empanada, then went back to her room, slamming the door. With almost no appetite at all, I stayed glued to the media.

Rumors abounded of what the search had uncovered. A knife. A switchblade.

A steel Japanese sushi-grade carving knife caked with blood. Or wiped clean, except for flecks on the handle.

A severed finger, a hand. Panties with bodily fluids.

A dismembered torso.

There was a repeating clip of Isaac Dendry ducking into an SUV. Iron-gray hair, patrician face. Perfectly cast for the role of crack defense attorney.

My phone flooded with messages and calls. Media. Friends. People I hadn't heard from in years. Wade and Keiko. "We've been worried out of our minds," Keiko said, and Wade put in, "Get your ass back here now, kiddo! I'm not joking."

"I can't," I said. "I'll probably be called for questioning. And if I go back to New York, everybody will be curious and all over me. I couldn't stand that right now."

"So someplace else, then," Keiko said. "Any place that's safe."

"I'm safe enough. And I've got a friend in Carmel I can stay with in a pinch. Or I could go back to my aunt's and stay with her for a while."

"What aunt?" said Wade.

Of course—they didn't even know. I told them briefly about finding my aunt Joanne. "I could rent a car and be there in under seven hours."

They made me promise I'd do that as soon as the lawyers told me it was okay to leave the state. I said if it seemed necessary, I definitely would, and it mollified them enough.

Malik Anderson swung by the following morning. He gathered us on the backyard terrace overlooking the rolling hills.

"First of all, good news. The evidence is serious but still entirely circumstantial. Isaac is pretty certain he can get the charges reduced from murder to battery. That means Evan will be able to post bond."

"So he'll be coming home?" I said.

"Yes, but not until Monday, because they don't do arraignments on weekends. And he'll probably have to wear a monitoring device."

"So *circumstantial* means there's no corpse?" Otis said.

"They haven't found a body, no. A knife with DNA on it. Hair and ripped clothing with blood evidence. It's all been sent to an FBI lab for more extensive testing."

"Where did they find it?" I asked. "By the tower?"

"No, somewhere near the main house. In some underground stairwell."

The caved-in spiral staircase behind my cottage.

"I'll know more soon," Malik continued. "You've probably heard on the news that Beatrice left a phone message for her brother just before she drowned."

"Yeah," Otis sneered.

"Isaac has listened to the message. He says it is damaging. But there's a mitigating factor."

"What does that even *mean*?" Sophia demanded.

"It means it might not be as bad as it seems," I told her.

"Yes, that's right, dear," Malik said. "Beatrice was very likely off her meds. Evan found pills hidden in her shoes about a month ago. He had an attorney not in his employ be with him as a witness. And Evan reported it to her psychiatrist as well as to me immediately. Without her medication, she would have been subject to paranoid hallucinations. Voices. Impulses to harm others or herself."

"So it's true, then," Otis said eagerly. "She did commit suicide."

"It's at least a case for reasonable doubt."

"And we won't have to testify."

"You'll be questioned." Malik took a decorous sip of his Solé water. "There could be some fairly hard questions. Otis, they know you delivered a painting to a warehouse in San Jose the day Beatrice disappeared. A Modigliani worth some millions of dollars."

Otis paled again. "So what? It was his painting, wasn't it?"

"Not entirely. It was part of the joint assets of Evan and Beatrice's estate. He used it as collateral for a large loan but didn't obtain her consent. He copied her signature on the loan agreement. Moreover, the painting wasn't authentic. It was a forgery."

A cold shock ran through me.

"Shit," Otis said. "I knew something wasn't on the level. I'm screwed. I'm going to be arrested."

"It's more likely they'll use that to make you testify against him. And, Jane, you too."

"Just because she hooked up with him?" Sophia said.

If Malik was surprised to hear this, he gave no indication. "It's something else. Jane, Richard McAdams claims Evan violently attacked him. Threatened him not to report it. He says you helped with a cover-up.

There's some footage from an emergency room camera that backs up his statement."

"What do you mean?" Sophia demanded. She looked at me, stricken.

"A man broke into Thorn Bluffs one night," I told her. "It was Beatrice's brother. He fell and cracked his head. He requested that your dad call me. Your dad did, and I took the man to the ER."

Otis stared at me.

Malik said, "We'll deal with all that later. We'll prep all of you thoroughly for questioning."

"So you'll tell us what to say?" Sophia asked.

"Not exactly. We don't want any of you to lie. We'll just help you avoid making things worse for yourself or your father." He glanced at the Rolex on his wrist. "The other good news is you can all return to Thorn Bluffs tomorrow."

"Me too?" Sophia said. "I don't have to go to Gram's?"

"No, I'm sorry, dear. Social services won't let you stay with your father. You'll have to leave before he returns."

"But it's not fair! I don't want to go. I refuse to."

"I'm afraid there's nothing more we can do about it." Malik stood up. Smiled reassuringly. "I'll leave you all now in Carrie Horvath's capable hands."

I got up too. "I can't . . ." I glanced at Otis. "*We* can't afford this kind of representation."

"That's all been taken care of. For Mr. and Mrs. Sandoval as well."

"You mean Evan's paying?" Otis said.

"Yes."

"He's already broke," Otis muttered. "Jesus."

"When can we go see him?" I asked.

"He doesn't want anyone to visit. He'll be able to call you very soon."

It was almost evening when he did. A bad connection made worse by the racket behind him. "Are you doing okay?" I asked. A stupid question. But there was so much to say, to ask him, I hardly knew where to begin.

"I'll survive." He sounded exhausted. "What about you? That house okay?"

"It's far more than we need."

"Sophia holding up?"

"To an extent. She's upset and confused and furious about getting shipped off to her grandmother's."

"There's no way around that." He spoke closer to the phone. "You don't believe any of this, do you?"

I paused. "Malik told us about the Modigliani. That you forged Beatrice's signature to allow you to borrow against it."

"Yes, I'm guilty of that."

"And the painting was a fake."

"Yes. I had commissioned a copy." An authoritarian voice rasped behind him. "I'm out of time. I'll explain everything. Tell Sophia I'll call her as soon as I can. And, Jane . . ."

"Yes?"

"Wait for me. Please." He hung up.

I went to hunt up Otis, found him staring at a rerun of *Crazy Ex-Girlfriend*. He grunted apathetically at the news of the call.

"Where's Sophia?" I asked.

He shrugged. "Haven't seen her in a while."

"Did she eat at all today?"

"She's a big girl. If she wants something, she can get it." He took off his glasses and wiped them on his Metallica T-shirt—vintage, rare, his most prized possession. He was in a serious state.

I went to Sophia's room—the leave-me-alone cubbyhole she had claimed for herself behind the laundry room. I tapped. No answer. I knocked again, called out her name, and when she still didn't answer, I opened the door.

She lay sprawled in the dark on the bed. "Go away."

I turned on a light. *Shit.* A collection of liqueur bottles on the bed stand. Kahlúa. Chartreuse. A water glass half-filled with what looked like Frangelico. Also a bottle of pills. "What's that?" I went to pick up the bottle.

She grabbed it first. Shook out a handful and stuffed them in her mouth. Gulped from the glass to wash them down.

I pounded her back hard, and pills sprayed from her mouth. "Fuck!" she yelled and began to shake out more.

I tried to snatch the bottle. We struggled a moment. She was stronger, but I was determined, and I yanked it away from her, knocking over the glass. It spilled onto the bed. Hazelnut-smelling liqueur oozed over the coverlet.

"Fuck you!" she screamed.

I checked the bottle. Bayer aspirin. *Thank God.* "How many did you take?"

She glared at me defiantly. Her mascara, at least two days old, dribbled down her face like the tracks of glitter-blue tears. Smeared purple lip gloss made her look punched in the mouth.

"How many, Sophia?" I demanded sharply.

"Some."

"How much is some?"

"I don't know. I don't give a shit. Go away."

I did a quick assessment of the bottle's contents. Mostly full. She couldn't have swallowed very many. "How many were you planning to take?"

"All of it. I was going to take the whole bottle. 'Cause I wish I was dead. Nobody cares about me, and nobody wants me, and my life is shit, and I hate everything, and I really and truly wish I was dead!"

I started to sit down beside her.

"Don't sit on Niall!"

I leaped up. From under the sticky coverlet, the little python twisted away. He slithered under a pillow, and then I sat down. "Sophia, listen to me," I said. "I understand how you feel. I know you miss your mom very much."

"No, I don't. She's a skanky bitch, and I *hate* her."

I flinched. "Don't ever say that. You don't mean it."

"I *do* mean it! She didn't give a shit about me. She *had* to go off to Africa, and if she wouldn't have gone, she wouldn't have died of stupid *peanuts*. But she went anyway. And after she died, her skanky toothbrush was still there, still in her crappy old *Incredibles* mug, and her crappy slippers next to her bed, and her shitty bicycle was still in the hall. They were all still *there*, and she's a stupid cunty bitch, and I hate her—I hate her fucking guts!"

"You don't mean any of that," I said fiercely. "You know that she didn't in a million years think she'd die. She never would have gone if she'd thought she wouldn't be coming back to you."

She rubbed at one eye, muddling the last smudges of mascara. "I don't give a shit. I hate her."

"Sophia, listen to me."

"I won't. Go away." She set her face at the wall.

It took all my control not to scream at her. "You can admire that wall all you want," I said. "But I'm not going away, and you're going to listen. You know that my mother died too. Just last year."

"I don't care."

"She got lung cancer even though she never smoked one day in her life. It was totally shitty unfair. And all the time she was dying, I was incredibly fucking angry. I thought it was about something else. I'd been in love with a guy, and while my mom was dying, he dumped me. And the worst thing was, it was for my closest friend."

She gave a snort.

"I know I was an idiot for not seeing it happen. He was an asshole—they both were. I was insanely mad at them. It took me a while to realize it wasn't really about them. Some of it, but not most of it. The one I was really furious at was Mom." I paused a second. "I blamed her for dying even though I knew it wasn't her fault. She didn't want to die and leave me. But she did, and I was left totally alone, with no family at all."

A shrug.

"And after she died, I drank a lot too. I used to work in a club, you know, and I still had friends who did, and they'd comp me drinks. I'd get totally shit faced. But it didn't help, it just made me feel worse. And then I lost my job, and I felt . . . well, one shitty thing after another, right?" I made a dismissive sound. "I went around feeling like the entire world was dark and cloudy. Until I came here."

She said something muffled.

"What?"

She turned to me. "It's cloudy *here*. With the fog."

I let out a quick laugh. "Yeah, it is, but I meant how I felt inside."

"I *know* what you mean. I'm not six."

"No, you're not. But what I'm *trying* to say is I felt what you do now—that everything's dark and the darkness is going to last forever. But I came here, and things changed. I started to feel good again. I felt like I was part of a new family. Does that make any sense?"

She was silent a moment. "It's easier for you."

"Why? Because I'm older?"

"No," she said. "Because you're pretty and I'm not."

I looked at her, thunderstruck. "What makes you think you're not pretty?"

"Because I'm not. I'm a dog. I've got zits and big ears, and my nose is funny and so are my boobs."

"That's not true, Sophia. You *are* pretty—I thought so the first time I met you, and you get prettier all the time."

"Nobody thinks that," she said.

"Who is nobody? Did somebody say something?"

Another shrug. One shouldered.

"Was it Peyton? Or her brother? What's his name—Alcott?"

She hesitated. "He didn't *say* anything."

"Then what?" I said. "Did he do something?"

"He didn't rape me, if that's what you mean."

"Just tell me, okay? Please."

She shook her head. "Nothing. Forget it."

"Have you been sexting him?"

She hesitated again. "Sometimes."

Shit. "Okay. Both top and bottom?"

"I kept my thong on. For frontal."

"Okay," I repeated softly. "And did he say something to you about your selfies?"

"They all did. Him and all his friends."

"He shared your texts?"

She ducked her head. "There's this game? It's called kiss, marry, or kill?"

"Yeah, I know it."

"Except . . ." Her voice got very small. "It's also called fuck, marry, or kill?"

"Yeah, I know that too. Did they do that with your selfies?"

"I guess. And I didn't get any marries or fucks. They all rated me kill. Except for one of them, Keller, who changed his rating to fuck but only with a bag over my head."

I felt fury rise in me. *Rotten little shits.* "How did you find out?"

"Peyton told me. *She* got all fucks, except for this one boy, Jake Goldberg, who said marry 'cause he's, like, this superhot dude who knows he could *get* her to marry him if he wanted. I mean, like, if they were older."

Goddamn nasty little creeps. I paused. She was thirteen. Her mom was dead. Her father had just been arrested. But I knew that at thirteen

341

even all that could momentarily pale compared to superhot boys mocking her naked body.

"Listen, sweetie," I said. "They're just stupid little boys who are trying to make themselves seem more manly than they really are. The truth is they're scared of you."

"They're not scared of me," she said.

"Yeah, they are. You bring out emotions they're afraid of. Real emotions. They're afraid of letting that show."

"Bullshit."

"It's not. They're nasty, insecure creeps. If your dad ever found out, he'd kill them."

"Like, literally?" she said snidely. "Like he killed Beatrice."

I felt a shock. "You don't know that, Sophia."

"They arrested him for it. They have to know he did it."

"Nothing has been proved. He could be found innocent."

"You're not saying he didn't, though. And if he never gets out of jail, what's going to happen to me? Gram's old, and she could drop dead any minute."

"She's not that old."

"*Your* mom wasn't that old. And my mom wasn't old at all." Her voice went up an octave. "You don't know anything. You don't know any fucking thing at all!"

"I know one fucking thing for sure," I snapped at her. "I'm never going to leave you."

She glanced at me, startled.

"Even if we're not living in the same place, you'll always be able to talk to me anytime you want. And if you ever really need me, I'll be there in a flash, no matter what."

Her face remained stubbornly set for a moment. But then it crumpled, suddenly and completely, and she looked so young and bereft and vulnerable that it tore me apart. I gathered her up and hugged her.

"You'll never be alone as long as I'm alive," I told her. "And I don't plan to drop dead for a long, long time to come." She let out a giggle.

She looked up at me. "You're not going to tell anybody, are you? About what I just told you?"

"Never. I promise. Come on, let's get something to eat. I'm starving, and you must be too. And let's get rid of these bottles. I never liked liqueurs very much."

"They're disgusting," she said.

THIRTY

Carrie Horvath relayed the all clear for us to return to Thorn Bluffs the next day. Only a few straggling reporters remained at the entrance to the private drive. The house was in shambles. Annunciata and Hector had arrived several hours before and were working briskly to restore order.

Sophia would be leaving for Minneapolis in the morning. Otis was taking her to SFO, and her grandmother Harriet would meet her on the other end. I'd hoped to go with them to see her off, but Delta would only issue one accompanying adult gate pass, so I'd say goodbye to her here.

Otis and I helped her pack. She wanted to take everything she owned. Then nothing at all. She settled on filling one suitcase and her knapsack but insisted she was bringing Niall. "A snake on a plane?" Otis said. "I don't think so." He promised to take care of him. "Not gonna turn him into a watchband."

He cooked a version of *le* gloop for dinner. "It's not the same," Sophia said.

We were all listless and went to bed early. My cottage had also been ransacked by the police. I made a stab at tidying up.

I couldn't sleep. I tossed and turned and switched the light on and off, trying to read, unable to concentrate. I drew open the drapes and stared out at the dark cove. No ghostly shimmer of white anywhere.

No unearthly shriek. I would have welcomed either one. Anything to keep me company.

Otis and Sophia left just after nine o'clock the next morning. I stood waving until Otis's old Prius was out of sight. It felt strangely like an ordinary Monday. Annunciata's voice from a window directing one of her part-time helpers in Spanish. Voices resonating from the grounds, a buzz saw going. Dogs barking at squirrels, and squirrels scolding them back.

Only the loud chop of a news helicopter circling above told differently.

Carrie Horvath called at three thirty. "Evan was arraigned an hour ago on a charge of aggravated battery. Bail was set at three hundred thousand, and it's been paid. They're fitting him with an ankle monitor."

"So he'll be back soon?"

"In a few hours. Isaac Dendry will be bringing him."

I hung up in a state of agitation. Did I even want to see him? He had confessed to two major lies—forging Beatrice's signature and borrowing against a painting that he knew was a fake. There was enough evidence of a violent act to trigger a search warrant.

No, I didn't want to see him. I couldn't.

A key turned in the lock on the front door. Annunciata with her cart. For the first time, not cleaning my cottage in stealth. I tried out a smile. She returned an expression that was halfway to a smile.

I set to work alongside her. The police had pulled out everything from drawers and cabinets and my closet and strewed it around. It took us over an hour to put it all away. When we were done, Annunciata replaced the burned-out votive candle with a fresh one. She lit it. Put the lighter back in a compartment of her cart next to an open can of soda.

Dr. Brown's Black Cherry. Diet.

"Annunciata?" I shouted.

She pointed to her ear. A thin wire snaked from it. She was wearing her hearing aids.

I lowered my voice. "Did you ever bring a glass of Dr. Brown's soda to the tower?"

"Jes," she said.

"Was it for Beatrice? The señora?"

A nod. "Jes."

"I mean, after she drowned?" I said. "Did you see her in the tower?"

"Outdoor. In the bushes."

I felt a quick thrill. "So she's alive? You saw her still alive?"

"*Fantasma*," she said. "She is ghost."

Just a ghost. Annunciata heard spirit voices in her hearing aids. She saw ghosts in the woods. "Why did you bring her *fantasma* a Dr. Brown's?"

"So it stay there and not come here." Her tone declared that this was self-evident.

She turned and pulled her cart back outside, her braids—tied today with orange yarn—switching at the small of her back.

❧

It was almost seven o'clock. How long, I wondered, until Evan was back? I did not want to see him. At the same time, I was desperate to.

I needed activity, or I'd go out of my mind. There was no fog; the evening was clear and still bright. I put on running shoes and headed out to the private drive, running as hard as I could, stumbling on roots and redwood bark, until, finally winded, I sank onto a large rock by the side of the road to rest.

A dark-gray SUV swept by.

I felt a tremor go through me. I remained sitting on the rock another fifteen or twenty minutes. The SUV drove by again in the opposite direction.

I got up and walked back to the cottage. I showered and changed into a fresh shirt and white jeans. And then I stepped out onto the terrace. The dipping sun painted the sky a palette of rose, azure, orange-gold, and it gave the huge jagged rock—Mary Magdalene's Praying Hands—the sheen and color of beaten copper. I remained standing there as the sky faded to duller shades. Mauve. Pewter gray. Black clouds began to lengthen on the horizon.

A shadowed figure appeared on the bluff.

My stomach tightened.

He walked to the edge of the bluff, the ankle monitor making him limp a little. Like he had limped after the spill from the Harley. The night I had startled him by coming out of the fog. Another lifetime ago.

Two silhouettes—magical beasts—came slipping up to him. He paced with an uneven step for several minutes. Then turned back to the house, the dogs at his heels, and he disappeared from my sight.

The light had faded completely now. The sea was a black terrain crossed with crazed white crests that raced every which way until flinging themselves suicidally at the bluffs. I listened to the roar and thunder.

I thought of the force of that icy current. My terror as it pulled me irresistibly with it.

I went back inside and shut the drapes. I filled a glass of water and drank it down. My text tone sounded. I glanced at the phone nervously. Looked at the text.

I'm in the Great Room. Will you come?

My heart began to pound. For some moments, I didn't reply. Then I texted: Yes.

I lingered another few minutes. Collecting my agitated thoughts. Then I went up to the main house and entered through the service porch, my arrival announced by a clarion of three yelping dogs. They accompanied me in a pack as I headed to the Great Room.

Music drifted from it, just like it had on that first night. But now it was mysterious low-pitched pipes with no discernable melody.

Just like on that first night, I paused at the entrance. I recalled how I'd pictured him: staring moodily into a smoldering hearth. How wrong I'd been.

And he wasn't now. He was at the bar cart, teasing a cork from a bottle of champagne. Minnie and Mickey crouched nearby, held rapt by his every move. He looked as vagabond as he had that first night. Unshaven. Black curls tangled. Raggedy white tee over black jeans. The way I'd always loved him best.

I said, "I called for madder music and stronger wine."

He turned. Smiled. "You can have stronger wine if you want, but I think you'll find this does the trick. As for madder music—this is Inca spirit music, or at least a modern version of it, and it's about the only thing preventing *me* from going mad right now." He popped the cork—that festive sound—and filled only one of his thick goblets. He handed it to me.

"Aren't you having any?" I said.

"I'm in jail, remember? No booze allowed. One sip and this thing I'm shackled with will start to shriek. Or so they tell me."

"Can I see it?"

"If you want." He sat on an ottoman and rolled up the cuff of his jeans.

I set down my glass and knelt to examine the monitor. A chunky digital device with a thick black strap. "It looks heavy."

"About ten pounds. It's kind of SM looking, don't you think? Which is appropriate, since I am in bondage."

I ran two fingers across the black metal device. His skin at the edges of it looked raw. "Does it hurt like a son of a bitch?"

He smiled again. "Not quite, no. It chafes a little."

I stood up. "How far does it allow you to go?"

"A hundred feet beyond the compound. Any farther and it makes a racket and also notifies the authorities." He rolled the jeans leg back down over the monitor. "I've got to plug myself in for two hours a day to recharge it. Like a fucking iPhone."

"I'm sorry," I said.

He gave a dismissive grunt. "Would you please drink that wine? It's a '98 Krug, and it should be pretty good."

I took a sip. I couldn't taste a thing.

He got up and flipped open a humidor on the coffee table. Selected a cigar. "Would you mind?"

"You've never asked me before if I would mind."

"I'm asking now."

"No," I said. "I don't mind."

He clipped the end, lit it, drew on it. Exhaled a puff of aromatic smoke. And then all his jauntiness suddenly vanished. "I'm ruined, Jane," he said. "I've lost everything. I'm flat-out broke. It turns out defending yourself for murder is very expensive."

"It's no longer a murder charge," I said.

"Not for now. The FBI lab is doing state-of-the-art DNA tests. If they confirm blood from both Beatrice and me, the DA will definitely refile for murder. Some form of second degree, I assume. Still bad enough."

"Is finding that . . ." I drew a breath. "That kind of evidence a possibility?"

"Yeah," he said. "It is."

I swallowed, without tasting, more of the Krug. "You've just closed an enormous deal. Shouldn't it be enough to pay the lawyers and still have a lot left over?"

"It's not just the legal costs. I've got millions in loans coming due very soon. And there'll be civil suits." A sardonic smile. "Richard McAdams has already filed a sixty-million-dollar suit against me. I've done a side deal with Dillon Saroyan to sell him most of my shares in Genovation. At a fraction of what they'll be worth eventually. But even that won't cover it all." He gazed grimly at me. "Even if by some miracle I'm not thrown into prison for the rest of my days, I'm completely ruined."

I was silent.

"Jane," he said. "You promised to stick by me even if I lost everything. Did you mean that?"

I raised my face to him. "I meant if you lost all your money."

"I will tell you again. I didn't kill Beatrice, nor did I ever physically harm her. I swear on my life, on my entire soul."

"You were sometimes cruel to her. People saw you."

"Cruel?" He drew on the cigar. Exhaled. "There were times when she got violently out of control, and I had to be forceful. She needed to be restrained before she could hurt herself or anybody else. Maybe it could have been interpreted as cruel. Maybe it was. But I didn't want to have her committed. I didn't know what else to do."

"You forged her name. To borrow on a forged painting."

"Yeah. I did. She had destroyed the real one."

"The one in the tower."

"Yes. Look, faking her signature was just a temporary measure. Until I got the deal closed. It just bought me a little time, that was all."

"It was fraud."

"Yeah. But the creditor is a private party. He won't press charges if I pay him back with inflated interest. Which I intend to do."

"It was still a crime. A lie. And you've lied about other things to a lot of other people." It was hard to keep my voice steady. "To your wife. To people you did business with." I took a shaky breath. "And to me."

"Yeah," he said.

"Those things I said to you at the benefit—they were all true, weren't they? You've been having an affair with Liliana Greco. And it's been going on for quite some time. Even while Beatrice was still alive."

"Just once when Beatrice was alive," he said. "Lily and I only took up again after she had drowned. In January, I moved up to the city for the winter, and we started working even more closely together on this deal." He looked defiant a moment. "Can you blame me? My wife had been insane. Sometimes viciously so. And here was a beautiful, intelligent woman who was very sane and eager to have me. And capable of being an enormous help to me with my business." He shook his head. "It was a stupid risk. We both knew it. It added to the excitement."

"But that first time you slept with her, it was here, wasn't it?" I said. "After you first met her at the Bitcoin conference and she came to see the Modigliani."

"Yes."

"And Beatrice found out about it."

He turned away. Took an agitated puff on the cigar. "I'm not sure. She might have seen me with Liliana in the cottage. I thought we'd be safe there. That no one ever went down there."

I felt an irrational sense of betrayal. *My cottage. Where he and I had made love so many times.*

"I didn't know Beatrice was hiding her cocaine in that stairwell," he continued. "She might have seen us when she was going for it. Hector found her wandering out on the service road, screaming. He brought her back to the Ocean Room."

I drew a deep breath. "And something happened there. With Beatrice and Liliana."

"Yeah." He looked anguished. "Lily and I had come back to the house. I got a call I needed to take, and Lily took the opportunity to explore. I heard her scream. I ran downstairs." He turned his face away again. "Beatrice had Liliana in her grip. She'd become something . . .

not human. A ghoul. She'd sunk her teeth into Lily's neck, and Lily had started to faint."

The story I'd already worked out. The nearly scrubbed-out bloodstain on the floor. The ugly scar.

The story I hadn't wanted to believe.

Evan looked back at me. "I pulled her off Lily, but then she turned on me and tried to rip my throat open with her teeth and nails. And her teeth, Christ . . ." He gave a violent shudder. "They were covered in blood."

I felt a shudder as well.

"She broke away from me and ran up to her room and locked the door. Annunciata had a key. We went in. She was slashing the Modigliani with a pair of nail scissors. It was like watching a murderer at work. And I'd already arranged to borrow ten million dollars against it. I tried to get the scissors out of her hand, and she stabbed me with them and bolted out of the bedroom. I chased her. A mistake. She threw herself down the stairs." He gave another grim smile. "You know what happened after that."

"You called EMS. And then got her into the treatment center."

"Yes. The Oaks."

The dogs stirred at something outside, and I glanced reflexively at the doors. Almost expecting to see her there. That furious ghostly figure.

"Last fall," he continued, "I began to work with Liliana on putting together this deal. I knew she was still attracted to me, and I was to her. Beatrice suspected it. It was uncanny the way she could pick up on things. And then, the night before she drowned . . ." He paused.

"What happened?" I whispered.

"She heard me on the phone with Lily. We were talking intimately. Beatrice set a book on fire in the library. I ran to deal with it, and when I came back, she had the phone to her ear. Liliana's voice. I took it away, hung up. I tried to convince her it was a hallucination. Just another one of her voices."

I looked at him with horror. "That was cruel."

"Yeah. I suppose it was."

"And you locked her in her bedroom. With the dogs on guard."

"I had to. She was in a totally wild state. And shortly afterward, I got her to take a clozapine. The next day, she seemed stabilized, so I tried to show her affection. Take her out to dinner for our anniversary. We never got there."

I was silent a moment. "Are you in love with Liliana?" I said.

"No," he said quickly. "I never was. I knew that if I failed, she'd drop me in an instant."

I was trembling. "At the benefit . . . did you sleep with her after I left?"

"No. But I had intended to."

A knife went through my heart. "Why didn't you?"

"I realized I was in love with somebody else."

I looked away. Not trusting him.

"I realized it clearly when you walked away from me out on the terrace. I made an excuse to Lily afterward not to go back to her hotel with her. I said that we needed to stay completely focused on the closing. She's not a fool. She knew. But she didn't want to make any waves."

I was silent. I couldn't trust anything he said.

He gazed at the black expanse outside the doors. "She set me up, Jane. Beatrice. She planned this all. She set it all up perfectly."

"What do you mean?"

"She planted that evidence. Made that call to her brother pretending she was in danger. And then she drowned herself, knowing I'd be charged with it. The perfect revenge."

I shook my head. "I don't believe she was capable of that."

"She was. She was extremely clever, and her psychosis made her devious. She and her brother used to cook up schemes to commit crimes and get away with them. She used to tell me about them. Plans to steal jewelry or boats. Or murder some rich person for their money.

She knew how to set these things up." He picked up the cigar, took a draw. Then crushed it out. "I've committed some terrible sins, I admit that. I have serious flaws. But I never purposefully harmed my wife. I would have saved her if I could."

The elusive melody of the piping music rose and fell. Putting me into an almost hypnotic state. I couldn't speak.

He came closer to me. "I've told you the absolute truth now," he said. "Please don't leave me. I'm begging you."

I lifted my face to him. It told him everything he needed to know.

"You are going to leave me, aren't you?" he said.

I felt wrenching anguish. Like I was ripping away every single thing I'd ever yearned for. "I have to," I said. "I can't be with someone I can't trust."

"I will never lie again, not to you. I swear with my entire soul. Please, just stay until all this is decided. I could get a favorable verdict. There's always that chance. And then I'll ask you to stay with me forever."

I felt such utter misery. I couldn't stand the bleakness of life without him. But he'd lied not just to me. To Beatrice as well. He'd cheated in his business dealings. And one way or another, he had driven Beatrice to commit suicide.

And even if I could forgive that . . . if I could live with the knowledge of it all . . . I still had one terrible doubt.

Did he really try to save her?

Or had he seized an opportunity to be free? Held her under the water until all life was gone from her body? Or caused her death through some other means?

"I can't stay," I whispered.

"Then, please, just for tonight. I won't touch you. I just want to have you with me one last time. Your body next to mine. To feel you breathing beside me."

Tears welled up in my eyes. "No. I can't. I'm sorry."

He turned sharply away. Struggled to collect himself. When he turned back, it was with a semblance of a smile. "Then let me ask you an even smaller favor. Have dinner with me tonight. Here, now. Let me make you dinner."

I gave a startled laugh. "Do you know how to cook?"

"I'm no Otis Fairfax, but I can fry a pretty decent steak." With sudden exuberance, he grabbed the Krug bottle and extended his other hand to me. "Please, my darling Jane. Will you be my guest for dinner tonight?"

I knew that I shouldn't, but I relented. I took his hand. Felt the spark of it closing around mine.

I looked up at him, almost beseechingly. I couldn't help it. I still loved him desperately.

I let him draw me close, and I melted into him.

Just for one last time.

THIRTY-ONE

He didn't cook dinner. Instead, he swept me up in his arms and carried me upstairs to his bed, and we made urgent love. And then long and lingering love. And then we padded downstairs and raided the fridge and ate cold leftovers.

And then we went back to his bed.

I woke up early while he was still asleep and, without disturbing him, slipped from under the comforter. I dressed quickly and returned to my cottage.

By rote, I went through my usual morning routine. Freezing/scalding shower. Coffee brewed in the dinged-up Krups. Cranberry-bread toast and vanilla yogurt eaten outside on the crumbly brick steps. Every motion familiar yet this time final. For the last time.

Evan called soon afterward. "You left me without saying goodbye."

"I haven't gone very far."

"Far enough."

We both paused. Too full of emotion to speak.

"Malik is coming soon," he said. "We'll be holed up together in the office all morning. Then he'll accompany me to his associate firm in Monterey. Isaac Dendry is meeting us there."

"I thought you weren't allowed to leave the compound."

"My shackle lets me leave to keep appointments with my lawyers."

"Oh," I said.

He paused another moment. "The DNA results could come in as early as today."

"Oh," I repeated stupidly. "And then what?"

"It depends on the results. If they go against me, a new charge will be filed. I have a deal this time that there'll be no circus of an arrest. I'll get to surrender at the precinct."

"Maybe the results will be good."

He was silent. Then said, "I'll always love you," and hung up.

A bleak wave swept through me. Would I ever see him again? The thought that I might not felt like death.

My text tone sounded. Sophia. A selfie with her grandmother and her uncle Tommy. I smiled. They looked like sensible, kind people.

A little later, a text from Otis. Still here in Berkeley. Got interview for sous-chef job in gastropub. Vomiting emoji. Back around 4:00.

I began to pack up some of my things. Moving without thinking. I opened the glass doors. The fresh sea breeze washed me and stirred the dense foliage below. I thought of that presence I'd sometimes sensed out there. The shimmer of white in the old mirror, that ghostly apparition outside the doors.

I glanced at Annunciata's beaten silver medal suspended from the pine branch.

Keeping me safe from spirits.

Annunciata believed in ghosts. In Beatrice's ghost. She'd seen it—a *fantasma*—in the woods behind Malloy's tower. She had left a glass of Dr. Brown's for it.

It occurred to me suddenly: she must have also seen it that night she got locked out of the house. Wandering here, behind my cottage. It was why she'd hung the medallion on the tree.

Annunciata believed in ghosts, but I didn't.

I was certain now I had seen the living, breathing Beatrice Rochester. But how could she still be alive? Out in that wild. All this time. It seemed impossible.

But maybe it wasn't all the time. Evan was in San Francisco until almost May. Beatrice could have sheltered in the main house. Raided the pantry. Stolen things from Sophia's room.

Okay. But after Evan had returned, where could she have gone? The tower, most likely.

I began rummaging through the hodgepodge on my table—notebooks, pages with scribbled exercises, my Fitbit that had died a month ago. I found the old architectural rendering of Thorn Bluffs I'd rescued from the half-demolished tower. I cleared a space and unfolded it, the edges crumbling like brown snow.

I scrutinized the tower. Looking for something I might have missed before. But nothing. No hidden spaces. Just the spiral staircase to the floor never built.

And if she had been hiding anywhere in there, Hector and his men would have found evidence of it when they cleared it out.

And Annunciata had seen her ghost outside. In the woods.

I flashed on when I had gone to the tower the second time—the rock that had cracked the windshield of the Land Cruiser, that mysterious shriek as I drove away.

Both coming from the woods on the far side of the tower.

I examined that area in the rendering. It was almost completely obscured by mildew. I went over it inch by inch. And then my pulse quickened. There was something. At least, I thought I could make something out under those black splotches.

A symbol like the symbol drawn behind my cottage. A spiral inside a circle that looked like a hex sign in Pennsylvania Dutch country.

So Jasper Malloy must have planned to build a second stairwell going down to that other isolated little cove. A second escape hatch.

What if he actually had built it and nobody knew?

And what if I could actually find it? And if I did, what was it I might find?

Something that might establish Evan's innocence? Or the opposite, something hideous that would prove his guilt.

My stomach clenched.

Nonsense. It would probably be nothing at all. Yet I felt compelled to go try to find it even if it resulted in the worst. And to do so immediately before my willpower failed.

I'd have to walk—the keys to all Thorn Bluffs vehicles had been impounded by the police. But in broad daylight, it wouldn't be that difficult. No great risk of wandering off the road into the sea.

I snapped a couple of photos of the hex-sign part of the plans. I hurriedly pulled on a long-sleeve shirt. Tied a cotton sweater at my waist. Put on my Mets baseball cap, blue with an orange NY logo, to protect my face from the strengthening sun. Before I could change my mind, I set out on the washed-out asphalt road.

The sky was a cloudless blue. The surf pounded high—thousands of tons of water all the way from China. I didn't want to think about anything. I just needed to keep going.

Footsteps scampered up behind me. Pilot.

My spirit animal. I was insanely glad to see him.

The heat slowed me, and it took nearly forty minutes to reach the tower. Or actually the piles of rubble that remained of it. I headed around to the dense foliage on the far side of the site and stopped at the perimeter. I drew my phone from my pocket and enlarged the photo I'd taken. I tried to assess where the symbol—that hex sign—was located in relation to where I now stood.

About a hundred feet diagonally into the underbrush.

I stared out at it. A treacherous forest of thorns and brambles. How could anyone get through it? *A fire path,* I thought. Like the one behind my cottage. Evan said they ran all through the property.

I began to pace slowly along the edge of the clearing, searching the ground through a tangle of juniper and brambles and prehistoric-looking ferns. Pilot suddenly barked. Then he went scrambling back down the road, chasing a butterfly or a rabbit or maybe just the shadow of a passing hawk.

"Pilot!" I yelled, but he was gone.

Some spirit animal. Loneliness overwhelmed me. Evan's last words to me echoed in my mind: *I will always love you.* It had seemed so final.

An acknowledgment we might never see each other again.

Don't think. Just keep going.

The sun had become blisteringly hot. I wiped my sweating face with my Mets cap. Continued walking the edge of the woods. After several more minutes, I untied my sweater and hung it from a bush. I kept going, brushing back bushes and ferns, examining the ground as best I could.

Yes! There it was—an eroded piece of asphalt barely visible beneath the foliage. The start of a fire path snaking farther into the brush.

I edged carefully through the wild growth, following the worn gray chunks, taking particular care to avoid briars. The shade from the few pine and redwood trees was minimal. The sun continued its merciless glare. Sweat dribbled down my forehead, and I blotted it again with my cap.

Something crackled in the nearby bushes. I stopped. Listened hard.

Just the rustle of a small breeze.

I continued on. And then stopped, hardly believing my eyes. There was a glint several feet ahead—the sun picking up something metal. I made my way a little closer, getting prickled by thorns. Then my heart began to beat fast. There it was—a hatch, the same size and shape as the one behind the cottage. I continued up to it.

It was coated with dried fronds and leaves. It hadn't been opened for some time. A week, a month—I couldn't tell. I crouched down, brushed off the debris.

My heart was racing wildly now. A dozen crazed scenarios ran through my head. Beatrice, alive, a prisoner, shackled to the bottom rung. Or her body at the bottom. Half-decayed. Scraps of a blue cocktail gown still clinging to rotting flesh.

Stop it! Probably just a caved-in cylinder. Like the first one I'd found.

I grasped the rusted ring. To my surprise, the hatch lifted without much effort. I pulled it all the way open, then knelt at the rim and—fearfully—looked down.

A metal spiral staircase encased in a corroded metal cylinder—and not caved in. I could smell sea breezes from the bottom, and the roar of the ocean tunneled up.

A wave of vertigo suddenly overtook me, and I sank back on my heels. It passed, and I knelt again and gazed back down the cylinder.

It couldn't be more than twenty feet to the bottom. I grasped the staircase rail and shook it experimentally. It wobbled but held up, and the handrail remained attached to the cylinder.

I turned backward and extended a leg down, feeling for the top rung with my foot. I lowered myself down onto it, grasping the flimsy handrail. I kept climbing down, one tightly winding step after another. The cylinder rattled. Swayed. It reeked of dank brine, and I felt another small wave of vertigo. I kept my eyes on the glow of light at the bottom and focused on counting the steps. *Twenty-seven, twenty-eight . . .* around and around in tight circles, *fifty-three, fifty-four . . .* until finally, *finally*, I reached the floor.

There was a rudimentary door with just a hole in the cylinder where a handle used to be. I pushed, and it swung open. I stepped out onto a flat ledge above a fairly steep slope of broken rocks.

I was standing above that eerie little cove below the tower promontory.

Where I'd seen the firefly blink on and blink off.

And that whitish figure gliding in its light.

Waves exploded onto the rocks that jutted out from the narrow beach. Spouts of foam boiled up between the rocks and saturated the air with spray, followed by a dragon-like hiss as each wave sucked itself back into the sea in a sluice of pebbles and sand and broken shells.

I gazed out at the water. Those tumultuous currents, furious white tongues racing this way and that. I surveyed the beach again. So desolate. Barely a narrow strip of wet sand. There seemed nothing alive here, except green-black mussels scabbing the rocks and scraggles of ice plant and desiccated grass clinging to the edge of the bluff. Not even a water bird wheeled in the sky above. When the tide rose even a little higher, there would not even be that tiny crescent of beach.

No one could survive for very long in this desolation.

No one except a ghost.

And then I noticed something. The grass and dirt at the edge of the sand directly beneath the slope was slightly tamped down. Or at least I thought it was.

Could it be a trail of some sort? But a trail to where?

There was nowhere to go.

I edged sideways down the broken rocks, testing each step with my sneaker, slipping a few times, narrowly catching myself. I stepped onto that sort of trail in the sand. It appeared to continue the length of the cove. I began to follow where it seemed to lead.

The wind slapped my face. I held my Mets hat down to keep it from being blown away. My clothes were already saturated with salt spray. *This is crazy,* I told myself. *A trail to nowhere.*

In about forty feet, it just stopped dead against the huge boulder that sealed off the end of the cove. Not a trail—just an effect caused by wind and water erosion.

A gust of wind suddenly snatched off my cap. I grabbed at it but too late—it was already sailing up onto the top of the massive boulder. It perched there a moment, then took off again, like a bright-blue bird flying above the rock.

And as I watched it go, I noticed something else.

An opening between the bluff and where the boulder began jutting out to sea. I continued on to the rock face. Looked up at the opening. It formed a crevice approximately body wide. Just slightly higher than an arm's reach over my head.

I felt a quick thrill. Maybe the trail—if it even was a trail—continued into the crevice?

Edging up sideways, I climbed the rubble slope beside it to a point where I could look directly inside the crevice. It leveled out into a sort of passageway. One I could fit into.

Clumsily, I half shimmied, half hoisted myself into the passageway. It was about ten feet wide and just high enough for me to stand up in. I could see daylight pouring from the end of it, not far away.

I began to step cautiously down the passageway, toward the sea light. Pausing each time a wave slammed thunderously against the rock, flooding my nose with the scent of brine and kelp.

Was the surf rising or ebbing? *Rising,* I thought, though I couldn't really tell. But I couldn't chance staying here too long.

I took five, then six steps farther, and then the passageway sloped slightly upward. In another few steps, it opened to my right onto a large natural chamber. There was a ragged hole on top that let in a strong shaft of sun. Most of the floor was eaten away, a straight drop to the roiling sea below.

I saw a wide, flattish ledge in the back, and in the blinding sheen of the sunlight, it appeared to be mounded with humps and layers of rock and sand. I edged into the chamber and stepped carefully around the open pit of the floor onto the ledge.

I gasped.

The mounds were not made of rock and sand. They were heaps of filthy rags and clothes, of blankets and towels and ripped-apart sheets. I could see bottles, both broken and intact. Jars and torn-open boxes. Mussel shells. Chicken and steak bones gnawed clean. On top of one mound, a very large piece of driftwood was draped with a filthy blanket, forming a rudimentary shelter.

She had been here. For at least some of the time.

But no longer. I saw no fresh food. The bottles and cans were empty. There was nothing to drink.

She couldn't have survived here without even water for very long.

I drew my phone from my pocket to take photos. A text pinged in a random bit of cellular connection: I jumped, and the phone flew from my hand into the yawning hole to the sea.

And then I jumped again at a sound behind me.

It had come from the murkiest depths of the chamber. A sound like a sigh.

But not a human sigh. Like the sound a corpse made when air escaped from it.

It made every hair on my arms and neck stand up.

And then a voice. Like the voice of nothing alive. Almost inaudible over the thunder of the surf.

"Why are you here?" the voice seemed to say.

And trembling, almost unable to breathe, I turned to confront my actual ghost.

BEATRICE

My lips are made of sand now, and my teeth have turned to sea pearls. I think sometimes one drops out of my mouth, like a candy dropping out of a jar. Like a Lemonhead. Ricky's favorite candy.

My hair hurts me. It's growing backward into my head, and I grab at it and pull it out to stop it from growing into my mind.

My eyes are on fire. Everything is dark and red. It's like cinders in my eyes.

But through the red fire cinders, I can see the girl.

How did she get here? How did she get into the chapel?

"Why are you here?" I say to her.

She is looking at my hand.

I am holding something in it. A piece of glass to cut with.

I lift it higher at the girl. She backs away from me.

Kill her. The voices all whisper together in my mind. *Kill her, kill the girl. Make her pay.*

I step toward her. I point my piece of glass.

She's not the one, Mary Magdalene whispers harsh in my head.

"Lilies," I say.

Through all the red cinders in my eyes, I see the girl looking scared. I hear her voice say something.

"I'm not Lily, Beatrice," her voice says to me. "My name is Jane."

It's the other one, Mary tells me. *It's not Lilies.*

I can't see. It's all red fire.

I move one step, two steps closer until I can see her through the burning cinders in my eyes. Her hair is brown like cinders no longer burning. Like soft ashes.

"Why is she here in the chapel?" I ask Mary.

"I'm here to find you, Beatrice," the girl's voice says. "Everybody's been looking for you. Evan has been looking for you."

The voices whisper together. *It's a plot. A trick, it's a plot. Kill her. Kill the girl.*

I slash her hand with my piece of glass.

The cinder-hair girl lets out a cry. I slash her again, on the forehead, and I see her blood through the red in my eyes.

She crumples down on top of my precious things.

Kill her, kill the girl.

The girl with cinder hair speaks again. "Beatie June," she says.

I stop, and I look at her through red fire. She knows my name.

I don't understand.

Ricky's voice comes up in my mind. *What are you, brain dead, BJ?*

I feel my scream come up from the bottom of my lungs. But it hurts too much, my lungs are on fire, the scream can't get through.

"Beatie June," the girl says. "Mary Magdalene sent me to find you."

The girl puts her hands together in prayer. There is red blood on her hands. On the fingers of her hands that are pointing up.

"Mary wants me to help you, Beatie June."

A plot, it's a plot. Kill the girl.

"Shut the fuck up!" Mary says to the voices. But Mary's words come out from where my lips used to be. The cinder-hair girl makes a gasp.

There are flies crawling in the fire cinders that fill my eyes. They squirm and wiggle and eat at my eyes. I let go of the piece of glass, and I swipe at the flies. But sticks have replaced my fingers, sharp twigs scratch my eyes and hurt them more.

The girl gets up to her feet. Slowly, slowly. "Your eyes are inflamed, Beatie June. Let me help you feel better."

Flies. I can't say that to her. All my words have been erased.

She creeps one step, two steps up to me. I can see her through my red fire, the cinders in my eyes. The cinders of her hair.

"Let me wipe your eyes, Beatie June." She takes off the shirt she is wearing. She lifts it to my eyes. It's soft. I feel it soft against my eyes. "Tell me how you got here, Beatie June."

"Mary sent waves." The words seep out of my mouth.

He was coming to get rid of you, Beatrice, Mary hisses at me. *You saw him. I sent waves to bring you to me.*

I remember now. I was waiting for my jailer. He was coming to rescue me.

But the ice waves pulled me into the sea, and my dress wrapped tight around me, and my hair became seaweed. But this time I did what Ricky told me. I let the riptide take me, and when it stopped trying so hard to gobble me up, I broke with all my strength to the side. I ripped off my dress, and I swam freestyle, my strongest stroke, my arms and legs pumped harder and stronger than ever before. Words come from my mouth. "I swam the riptide. I blew all the other bitches in my heat out of the water. Mary carried me here to the chapel."

"What are you saying, Beatie June?" The cinder-hair girl brushes the cinders from my eyes. "I can't understand you."

I want to say more words. But they won't come out of my mouth, all the voices are erasing them.

"You need help right away, Beatie June. Let me take you out of here before the tide gets too high."

I hear Mary laughing. *She can't get out. The chapel door is closed.*

Water is slapping up from the hole in the chapel floor. The girl turns and sees it come slapping up. "We've got to go now," she says. "Please, take my hand."

The water is coming higher than ever before. I step away from her and go to the very back of the chapel. I sit down on top of my precious things. I watch her through the red and swirling cinders in my eyes.

"The chapel door is closed." My words come out again. "We cannot leave here. We have to stay."

The girl turns, and she sees it too. The door is closed.

She has to stay here forever with me.

THIRTY-TWO

"The chapel door is closed." I felt a surge of fear. What did she mean by that?

I turned. The passageway was flooded. The tide had risen high and was still rising. I forced myself not to panic. I needed to keep my wits about me.

A wave slammed furiously, and a spout shot up through the opening in the chamber, drenching me with freezing water. I moved farther back on the ledge. I sat down on one of the mounds of clothes and objects, keeping a distance from Beatrice.

But also keeping her in my sight. She was keeping me in hers. She stood against the far wall, tall, wild looking but somehow magnificent in her wildness. She was still strong. Her reddened eyes seemed to glow with some unearthly knowledge. Something beyond human understanding.

I thought of the voices in her mind.

What are they telling her?

She had slashed my forehead and my hand, and both cuts were oozing blood. She could decide at any minute to attack me again. I rummaged in the garbage around me for something to defend myself with.

I grasped something long, metallic. A fire starter. *The firefly blinking at the bottom of the cove.* This one no longer made a spark.

I kept searching until I found a small broken bottle. I set it down close beside me.

The gash on my temple had begun to hurt. I had taken off my shirt to wipe Beatrice's eyes. Now I wrapped the arms tight around my forehead to staunch the blood. A picture flashed in my mind: Rick McAdams, our drive to the ER, clutching the bloody towel to his head. It wasn't Evan who had attacked him that night. It had to have been Beatrice.

Wandering in the grounds. Using a fire starter for a flashlight.

My thoughts began spinning. Evan had not murdered Beatrice. He was innocent. Maybe she had tried to swim to the Praying Hands, but the current swept her here.

Or no. Maybe he had tried to kill her. Assumed she could not survive the currents. Thought he was free of her once and for all.

I was in pain. Probably more frightened than I realized. I just needed to concentrate on surviving right now.

I rummaged through the mounds again. A dirty blue blanket shaped like a mermaid's tail. Sophia's missing snuggly. Crocheted by her mom.

Other things that were probably Sophia's—a sweat sock, a bikini bra. A black T-shirt of Evan's. I was right—Beatrice had taken refuge in the house when they were all up in San Francisco. Appropriated all these things and brought them here, to the cave she had already found.

I found something else—an old iron key, like the one to my cottage. *The one Otis said he had left for me but was no longer there.* I felt a shudder. She could have gotten in at any time.

I couldn't think about any of that now. Waves clashed constantly against the rock at my back. Each one sending another freezing spray up from the floor crevice.

A rush of water from the passageway foamed up and over the ledge. I had another flash of alarm. How high would it rise?

I scuttled as far back on the ledge as I could. Beatrice was no longer standing. She sat huddled against the rock wall. Speaking to herself. Her lips seemed scarcely to move, as if the words were coming from some entity living inside her.

After a while, I began to understand some of what she was saying.

"My jailer took me to the dungeon. The green umbrella trees.

"A plot. I won't be tricked.

"The island of Barbados. He moved like a cat, all the girls atwitter. And he brought me to the chapel, and we walked underneath the sea.

"He rescued me."

A ray of sun shined suddenly on her from the opening above, drenching her with a golden light. And for one instant, I saw her the way I imagined she used to be. The golden girl on a runway. The very young Beatie June, a face like an angel.

The sunbeam faded, and she was that wild figure again, lips moving compulsively.

"The girl named Lilies came down from the picture frame.

"She was going to replace me."

She began to cough. It seemed to tremble all the bones of her body. She was not well, despite her imposing figure. I suddenly felt an overwhelming sense of pity. I moved just a little closer to her.

Her eyes raged instantly.

She was not sane, I reminded myself. She had sunk her teeth like a vampire's fangs into another woman's skin. She had just ripped open my skin with a shard of glass.

And like any cornered wild creature, she could gather a sudden and enormous strength to attack.

I kept very still again.

"The chapel under the sea and the saints hanging upside down.

"And Ricky sent me snow white, and he pushed me off the powerboat."

A thunderous surge outside, and water foamed furiously in from the passageway, reaching higher up the ledge, within inches of where we were sitting. I shrank as far back as I could.

Beatrice stopped speaking. She suddenly slumped into herself as if her bones were collapsing.

She could be dying. The thought filled me with indescribable horror. I had to help her. I moved closer to her again.

"Beatie June." I repeated her name softly. "Beatie June."

She coughed again, racking her body.

I dug through the mounds for something to cover her with. My arm was burning from the cut on it, but I kept digging through until I found a tattered Oxford shirt and a blanket that had once been plaid. I laid them over her. I sat down close to her, ready to move quickly if she threatened me.

She made no move. Kept mumbling to herself.

The waves pounded ever stronger on the rock outside; more water spilled in from the passageway. Freezing water. It flowed around us, sometimes drenching us. Despite my being so cold, my throat was parched.

Broken bottles. Empty cans of Dr. Brown's.

How long had it been since she'd had anything to drink? And after the tower had been demolished nearly a month ago, she'd had nothing but this rudimentary shelter to protect her from chill winds and water and fog.

Her voice was getting thinner, weaker.

"Jailer puts poison.

"Plotting.

"Witches."

And then she stopped speaking. She sat silently. Her breath came in and out. Each breath like a sigh.

I lost track of time. The light from the opening above deepened to the color of old gold, the rays slanting onto the opposite wall. And then, finally, water ceased to flood in, and I felt limp with relief. The tide was ebbing. The pounding and roar outside were lessening.

I pulled myself to my feet. I was shivering violently. I untied my shirt from my head and put it on. "We've got to leave, Beatie June," I said.

Two red embers fixed on me.

I extended my hand. "Come with me, Beatie June."

She remained sitting. Red eyes still on me.

"Okay." I moved slowly away from her. "I'm going to go get help. But I'll be back for you. I promise."

She watched me. She didn't move.

I stepped off the ledge, and I began to wade through water into the soaked passageway. I glanced back. Beatrice still watched me.

I continued down the passage. Some water still sluiced into the gap, but not dangerously much, and I sloshed through it, my drenched clothes feeling heavy as lead. I eased myself down from the opening of the crevice, onto the slope of broken rocks.

The beach was completely gone now. The wind blew fresh. I breathed deeply. I felt like I was awakening from a terrible dream.

Dreamlike, a sea lion barked in the distance.

No, not a sea lion. A dog.

One of the German shepherds.

I looked up and saw Minnie standing on top of the bluff. Barking down at me.

And now I heard Evan's voice shouting my name. Not from on top of the bluff, from somewhere down here on the cove. I screamed with all my strength. "I'm here!"

I started scrambling over the slope toward his voice and slipped onto my hands and knees, wet rocks sliding out from under me. But I could see him agilely heading toward me, Mickey at his side.

Tears of joy flooded my eyes.

In moments, he had reached me and gathered me into his arms. I was shaking uncontrollably. He gripped me close.

"You scared the living hell out of me. Hector found your sweater in the brush up there, and you had disappeared. Where have you been?"

"In that rock." I could hardly speak. "There's a passage—she's in there—she's still alive and in there, and she's sick and could be dying."

He looked down at me. "Christ, you're bleeding. Let's get you back."

"No! We've got to go back in there. Beatrice—she's there, Evan, she's in a cave. She's still alive, but we've got to help her immediately!"

He stared at me, not comprehending.

There was the sound of a distant voice on a bullhorn.

"What's that?" I said.

"Police. I had Hector cut off my shackle. It was making too much noise."

"They'll arrest you again."

"So what? You disappeared, I was going crazy. I'll carry you back—you're in no condition to walk."

"No, I'm fine!" I insisted. "Listen to me."

Mickey began barking wildly and running toward the boulder, and from the bluff above us, Minnie began barking as well. I looked up and saw Otis standing beside Minnie. He had his phone in his hand, but he wasn't looking at it; he was staring in shock at the boulder.

I heard Evan say, "Holy God!" I turned and looked up.

Beatrice was standing on the top of the rock. Her figure dark against the reddening sky. The layers of clothes on her body flapped in the wind like strange wings. The snakes of her matted hair writhing from her head.

Evan screamed, "Beatrice!"

She looked down at him. She took a step toward the edge.

"Don't move, Beat! I'm coming to get you!" He took a darting step toward the rock.

From the depths of her failing lungs, Beatrice summoned a shriek. That unearthly shriek that had reverberated up from this cove months ago and filled me with such horror.

And then I heard myself scream as she took another, deliberate, step off the top of the boulder. And I continued to scream as I watched her plummet into the lethal waters below.

"Beatrice!" Evan yelled again. He turned and began to race down the rock slope to the water.

"No!" I called out. "You can't save her. She's gone. You'll be killed."

He kept going, already up to his ankles in the white churn. He kicked off his shoes. A large swell rolled in over the floes of shore rocks, and he dived into it and disappeared.

My heart stopped.

I could see Beatrice bobbing in the swirling eddies at the bottom of the boulder. I was aware of the sounds of crashing and ebbing surf and barking dogs. The distant honk of the bullhorn.

I felt wild relief as Evan's head emerged above the water. It disappeared again in another swell. I began to frantically scramble my way down the slope, but someone was holding me back.

Hector. "You stay here," he ordered.

I broke out of his grasp and half ran, half tumbled to the shoreline, and a swell churned up and knocked me over. I panicked, feeling it suck me into its ebb, but Hector was with me again; he reached out, and I grabbed his arms, and he yanked me back above the waterline. "You cannot help," he shouted.

Annunciata now appeared beside us, and Minnie as well. Hector continued back down to the waterline. Another surge, and my heart jumped, because this time it carried Evan with it. And in the crook of one arm, he was dragging Beatrice behind him.

The wave slammed them both against the outcroppings. Hector managed to grab hold of Beatrice and relieve her from Evan's grip. He lifted her up and over the rocks, and then handed her to Annunciata to carry up the rock slope.

Evan started dragging himself out of the surf. And now nothing could stop me—I skidded my way back down to help him, reaching for him with both hands. He grasped me with one of his. His other hand flapped mangled and useless beside him. One leg was twisted unnaturally behind him.

Hector took hold of Evan's other arm. With our help, he managed to pull himself above the waterline and high up enough on the slope to escape the highest waves. He collapsed there, gasping. His face was bloodied and bruised. His left leg twisted in that horrible manner.

I knelt on the rocks beside him.

"Is she alive?" he asked me.

I looked over to where Annunciata had laid Beatrice and was hovering over her. "I don't know."

"Go look. Tell me. I need to know—did I save her? Is she still alive?"

I edged my way over to Beatrice. I crouched down beside her. The sunset cast a fiery light, and its glow seemed to concentrate upon her in a way that was transcendent. Her long, matted tresses streamed over her broad shoulders, and her face was drained of all savagery. The bones in that face, though battered and broken, were still somehow beautiful. She might have been a sleeping sea goddess, her powers momentarily at rest but still in her full possession.

I gently wiped the muddy sand and kelp from her lips. I drew my fingers over them, hoping against all hope for even the whisper of a breath. I glanced up at Annunciata, whose tears were flowing freely down her cheeks.

I let out a shuddering sob. I turned back to Evan.

"No," I said to him. "You couldn't save her. She's not alive. Your wife is dead."

THIRTY-THREE

I sometimes dream I'm back in the sea cave.

They are nightmares. I'm all alone in the cave. Water floods in, swirling high, higher. There's no escape. I'm helpless to even move. The water will soon engulf me; it will sweep me far out to sea, and I'll be lost and gone forever.

But sometimes the dream shifts, and I'm no longer alone. There's someone beside me, some presence I can sense. I know without looking that it's Beatrice. The shaft of light is pouring down on her, and she's that golden girl, forever prowling a catwalk. I feel a radiant happiness.

That was the version of the dream I had last night. It's still resonating with me this morning. The morning of my wedding day.

I came down an hour ago to the Ocean Room, and I've been sitting on the white chaise that had been Beatrice's in the last year of her life. Looking out at her view of the cove. The jagged rock shaped like praying hands. The one she called Mary. It's been nearly two years now since she died, but the dream has made it all vivid again.

I did not go back to New York after her death. I chose to stay here at Thorn Bluffs with Evan, helping him through a long and painful recovery. Despite three operations, his surgeon couldn't save his entire left leg. They amputated at the knee and fit him with a prosthetic calf and foot. ("Me and Hermione, we're now a pair," he joked.) The doctor also amputated the middle and index fingers of his left hand. I sometimes suspect he enjoys the kind of raffish pirate look it gives him. But there was a lot of nerve damage. He can't manipulate that hand anymore. Both his plane and the Harley needed complicated modifications before he could operate them again.

He was not tried for murder. Or even attempted murder.

Otis had captured Beatrice's suicidal leap on video as well as Evan's heroic attempt to save her. It turned public sympathy abruptly to Evan's side—particularly after his severe injuries became known. The DA decided the evidence on even lesser counts was too circumstantial and did not refile charges.

Rick McAdams tried to stir up a case that Evan had kept Beatrice a captive in that cave. His handsome puppety face appeared in close-up on every news show that would have him. He pulled out his familiar hit parade of accusations. "Monster! Sociopath!" But he couldn't make anything stick. Nor has he won any of the civil lawsuits he's filed against Evan. I doubt if he'll stop trying.

Evan did have to sell a lot of assets to pay his many creditors. The Victorian house in San Francisco is gone. A property he owned in Barbados. The smaller of his two planes, the Beechcraft, sold last year. He was forced to resign from the Genovation Tech board. Ethical breaches. Borrowing against a counterfeit painting. And forging Beatrice's signature to do it.

"Fair enough," he acknowledged to me. "I did these things with my eyes wide open. I've got no one to blame but myself. I accept the consequences."

We won't be filthy rich. Not by a long shot. But we'll have enough, certainly by my standards. Dillon Saroyan has hired Evan to consult for Genovation Tech. Other biotech companies are beginning to as well. And Evan has not lost his beloved Thorn Bluffs. His Los Gatos offices have shrunk to a small suite, though, so he still works mostly out of the guesthouse.

I hear Sophia clattering downstairs. I look up as she bursts into the Ocean Room. "Oh my God, Jane! You're not even starting to get ready?"

"I've been collecting my thoughts. I don't have that much to do."

"You're the bride—you've got tons to do. I picked your bouquet, mostly white flowers—I've got the stems soaking in water. I got more flowers to wind through your hair and mine too. But that's got to be at the last minute. They're wildflowers, so they don't stay fresh that long."

"I'll be up in a moment. I'll call you after I've washed my hair. And you look amazing."

She gave the skirt of her dress—ballerina length, palest pink, befitting a bridesmaid—a little swish. Her way of acknowledging the compliment. She has bloomed in the last couple of years. Even she can see now that she is more than even just pretty.

And she's right: I should be concentrating on nothing right now except my dress and flowers and what to do with my flyaway hair, because the ceremony will be outdoors and there's bound to be a breeze.

But I continue to linger down here a little while longer.

When Evan had recuperated enough to no longer need my full attention, I found a job through Ella Mahmed's extensive network of friends as a volunteer teacher's assistant at a Monterey magnet school. It's a middle school. That age when kids are—as Otis once said—in "that stage." Acting out. It's where I feel I can make the most difference to them. In the fall, I'll be starting work on a graduate degree in education at Santa Cruz.

I didn't accept Wade's offer of a writing gig when his series got a green light at FX. "Are you positive you don't want this job?" he said.

"Yes, I am. I loved tutoring Sophia. I think I've got a real talent for teaching."

"You've got a brilliant talent for writing TV," he said. "And you loved working on *Carlotta*, didn't you?"

"Yeah. It was lots of fun. And so was working with you. But while I was tutoring, I felt something more. The satisfaction of helping her through a very troubled time in her life. It was more than just having fun. Or even loving a job. It gave me a feeling of satisfaction that went beyond all that. I can't really explain it."

"I think you just did. And I can't argue with it."

Keiko did argue. She still had suspicions about Evan. She had conceded that he had not murdered any wives, but she didn't trust him and didn't think I should either. "I've seen it happen before with these high-flying gambler types. They get caught cutting corners, and they pay a price. They claim they've learned their lesson. But sooner or later they can't keep away from the action. And maybe bending the rules a little. You need to keep your eyes open, Janie."

"My eyes are wide open," I've assured her.

Have I assured myself?

All three O'Connors arrived for the wedding yesterday. Wade's series aired last year on FX. It was a medium hit and has been renewed for a second season, and I couldn't be more thrilled for him. Benny starts first grade in the fall. I continue to spoil him by sending him robots and other completely awesome stuff. As unofficial godmother, I claim that right.

"Hey, yo, Jane!" Otis's voice sounds on the intercom.

I pick up the phone. "Hey."

"My guys just arrived. We're gonna start in on hors d'oeuvres as soon as they get organized. Folks are already starting to gather outside."

Already? I glance outside. My heart leaps as, for one second, I see Mom wandering toward the point of the promontory.

It's Aunt Jo, of course. She's wearing the same sort of gathered-skirted dress that Mom often wore. To her thrill, Evan flew up to Medford in the Mooney yesterday to pick her up. She has no reservations about him at all. He has charmed her completely.

"Okay, great," I tell Otis. "Are the bartenders here?"

"They will be any minute. I'm tempted to do it myself. Like old times, right?"

"Right." I laugh.

He's staying in his old room for the weekend, but he doesn't live at Thorn Bluffs anymore. He's managing the food court on Genovation Tech's new campus. Not quite his dream job of head chef. But getting closer.

And now I really do have to start getting ready. I get up from the chaise. It will just be a simple ceremony. Sophia my only attendant. Hector the best man. Otis was a little out of joint at not being in the wedding party. "I can be father of the bride and give you away," he had offered.

"Nobody's giving me away," I said. "I'm not a pet or a painting."

"Okay, so how about I be brother of the bride and walk you down the aisle. We are family, right?"

I had laughed. "Right. And yeah, I'd love to have you walk me down the aisle."

Though there won't really be an aisle. Just a few steps down the promontory. A very simple ceremony. Sophia had lobbied hard for me to wear a dress with a long white train she could carry. "No way!" I had said emphatically. But I did allow her a lot of authority in choosing something else. She had picked out an elegant ivory silk sheath with a significant plunge in the neckline. Because, you know, I can totally rock cleavage.

There will be only about a dozen other guests. Ella Mahmed had offered to give us the reconstructed Grayson Perry vase as a wedding present. My horrified face made her laugh. "Joking. I've already sent you something else. Not even from my gallery." It arrived yesterday—an antique Korean bowl with an exquisitely delicate celadon glaze. The Grayson Perry remains behind glass at Mystic Clay.

At the top of the stairs now, I pause and take a quick glance at the door to Beatrice's former suite. It's been fully renovated, and Sophia, who attends school in Carmel, occupies it now. I hear Pilot bark, and he comes scampering out of the room. He's got a fluffy white bow on his ruff. I wonder how long it will remain white and not covered in dirt and pine needles. Not through the ceremony, I'm sure.

I turn into the other bedroom—the suite that had been Evan's and that now we share. I hear him in his dressing room. He emerges. The prosthesis on his leg is state of the art. You'd have to be looking for it to even notice his slight limp. He's wearing a gorgeous navy suit. A tie with a soft floral pattern.

"You didn't have to put on a tie," I said.

"It's my wedding day," he said. "Of course I do."

"Then you can take it off for the reception."

He smiles. "I will."

I flash on another time he had removed his tie. A black bow tie. And another woman teasing him about it, pulling the points of his collar together. I push the memory away.

"You look gorgeous," I say. "But we're not supposed to see each other before the ceremony."

"I was never here." He leans and brushes my lips with his. Then disappears from the bedroom.

I have not put all my ghosts to rest, I reflect. They still haunt me.

The ghost of my father. I see him setting up twin cribs in a room decorated with baby jungle animals. Turning the wheel of a car hard on an icy highway at night.

Mom on a community theater stage, a radiant Juliet with a thick Jersey accent. Bringing down the house with her performance. And then going home to dance wildly, passionately, alone.

And Beatrice, of course.

Evan buried her in a little cemetery tucked amid grapevines in the Carmel Valley. He had white roses planted around the grave. Annunciata, who visits the grave frequently, makes sure they are kept blooming. And she leaves candles.

I go there once in a while. I sit down quietly beside her gravestone. I picture her as she was in the sea cave. That wild, mad creature, dangerous but also magnificent. I try to piece together exactly what happened the day she walked into the sea, both from her rambling, mumbled words in the cave as well as from what Evan has told me.

I can never be absolutely certain of what happened.

I'll always be haunted by his lies.

But he didn't hesitate to risk his life to save her. I know he was shaken and sorrowed by her death.

And I believe he loves me with all his heart, just as I love him.

I imagine we'll live happily ever after.

I've imagined it vividly.

ACKNOWLEDGMENTS

Huge thanks first of all to my agent, Nancy Yost, who had the unflagging wisdom to steer this book where it needed to go.

I'm truly grateful to Susan Wald, constant, perspicacious, and supportive reader. Thanks also to early readers Becky Aikman, Sarah Haufrect, and John Blumenthal.

I'm also very grateful to my superb editors, Liz Pearsons and Charlotte Herscher.

And profound thanks to Charlotte Brontë, who was the inspiration for this book and whose genius needs no introduction.

ABOUT THE AUTHOR

Lindsay Marcott is the author of *The Producer's Daughter* and six previous novels written as Lindsay Maracotta. Her books have been translated into eleven languages and adapted for cable. She also wrote for the Emmy-nominated HBO series *The Hitchhiker* and coproduced a number of films, including Hallmark's *The Hollywood Moms Mystery* and the feature *Breaking at the Edge*. She lives on the coast of California.